WARS™

CLOAK OF
DECEPTION

D0273078

CLOAK OF
DECEPTION

JAMES LUCENO

arrow books

Published in the United Kingdom in 2002 by Arrow Books

9 10

Copyright © LucasFilm Ltd & ™ 2001

James Luceno has asserted his right under the Copyright, Designs
and Patents Act, 1988 to be identified as the author of this work

First published in the United Kingdom in 2001 by Century
The Random House Group Limited
20 Vauxhall Bridge Road, London, SW1V 2SA

Random House Australia (Pty) Limited
20 Alfred Street, Milsons Point, Sydney
New South Wales 2061, Australia

Random House New Zealand Limited
18 Poland Road, Glenfield,
Auckland 10, New Zealand

Random House (Pty) Limited
Endulini, 5a Jubilee Road, Parktown 2193, South Africa

The Random House Group Limited Reg. No. 954009

www.starwars.com
www.starwarskids.com
www.randomhouse.co.uk

A CIP catalogue record for this book
is available from the British Library

ISBN 978 0 09 943997 4

Penguin Random House is committed to a sustainable future for
our business, our readers and our planet. This book is made from
Forest Stewardship Council® certified paper.

Printed and bound in Great Britain by Clays Ltd, St Ives plc

For Karen-Ann,
one of the few people I know who has made
a true difference in the world—most assuredly
in mine

A LONG TIME AGO IN A GALAXY
FAR, FAR AWAY. . . .

AFTER A THOUSAND GENERATIONS OF PEACE, THE
GALACTIC REPUBLIC IS CRUMBLING. ON CORUSCANT,
AT THE CENTER OF CIVILIZED SPACE, GREED AND
CORRUPTION RIDDLE THE SENATE, BEYOND EVEN
THE ABILITIES OF SUPREME CHANCELLOR VALORUM
TO REMEDY. AND IN THE OUTLYING SYSTEMS, THE
TRADE FEDERATION DOMINATES THE HYPERLANES
WITH ITS GARGANTUAN VESSELS.

BUT NOW EVEN THE TRADE FEDERATION FINDS
ITSELF ASSAILED FROM ALL QUARTERS, PREYED

UPON BY PIRATES AND RAIDERS, AND VICTIMIZED BY TERRORISTS, WHO DEMAND AN END TO THE FEDERATION'S TYRANNICAL PRACTICES.

IT IS A TIME THAT TESTS THE METTLE OF ALL THOSE WHO STRIVE TO HOLD THE REPUBLIC TOGETHER——NONE MORE THAN THE JEDI KNIGHTS, WHO HAVE LONG BEEN THE REPUBLIC'S BEST HOPE FOR PRESERVING PEACE AND JUSTICE . . . .

DORVALLA

Luxuriating in the unfailing light of countless stars, the Trade Federation freighter *Revenue* lazed at the edge of Dorvalla's veil of alabaster clouds.

Indistinguishable from its myriad brethren, the freighter resembled a saucer, whose center had been pared away to create two massive hangar arms and a stalked center-sphere that housed the great ship's hyperdrive reactors. Forward, the curving arms fell short of each other, as if in a failed attempt to close the circle. But, in fact, the gap was there by design, with each arm terminating in colossal docking claws and gaping hangar portals.

Like some gluttonous beast, a Trade Federation vessel didn't so much load as gobble cargo, and for close to three standard days, the *Revenue* had been feeding at Dorvalla.

The outlying planet's principal commodity was lommite ore, a major component in the production of transparisteel viewports and starfighter canopies. Ungainly transports ferried the strip-mined ore into high orbit, where the payloads were transferred to a fleet of self-propelled barges, tenders, and cargo pods, many of them as large as shuttles, and all bearing the Spherical Flame sigil of the Trade Federation.

By the hundreds the unpiloted crafts streamed between the Dorvallan transports and the ring-shaped freighter, lured to the breach in the curving arms by powerful tractor beams. There the docking claws nudged the crafts through the magnetic containment fields that sealed the rectangular maws of the hangars.

Safeguarding the herd from attacks by pirates or other raiders flew patrols of bullet-nosed, quad-thruster starfighters, wanting shields but armed with rapid-fire laser cannons. The droids that piloted the ships answered to a central control computer located in the freighter's centersphere.

At the aft curve of the centersphere stood a command and control tower. The ship's bridge occupied the summit, where a robed figure paced nervously before an array of inwardly inclined viewports. The interrupted view encompassed the distal ends of the hangar arms and the seemingly ceaseless flow of pods, their dorsal surfaces aglow with sunlight. Beyond the arms and the rust-brown pods spun translucent-white Dorvalla.

"Status," the robed figure hissed.

The *Revenue*'s Neimoidian navigator responded from a thronelike chair set below the burnished floor of the bridge walkway.

"The last of the cargo pods is being taken aboard, Commander Dofine." Neimoidian speech, while lilting, favored first syllables and elongated words.

"Very well, then," Dofine replied. "Recall the starfighters."

The navigator swiveled in his chair to face the walkway. "So soon, Commander?"

Dofine ceased his relentless pacing to cast a dubious look at his shipmate. Months in deep space had so honed Dofine's natural distrust that he was no longer certain of the navigator's intent. Was the navigator questioning his command in the hope of gaining status, or was there some good reason to delay recalling the starfighters? The distinction troubled Dofine, since he risked losing face by airing his suspicions and being proven wrong. He decided to gamble that the question had been prompted by concern and contained no hidden challenges.

"I want those fighters recalled. The sooner we leave Dorvalla, the better."

The navigator nodded. "As you will, Commander."

Captain of the *Revenue*'s skeleton crew of living beings, Dofine had a pair of front-facing red oval eyes, a prominent muzzle, and a fish-lipped slash of mouth. Veins and arteries pulsed visibly beneath the surface of puckered and mottled pale-green skin. Small for his species—the runt of his hive, some said behind his back—his thin frame was draped in blue robes and a tufted, shoulder-padded mantle more appropriate for a cleric than a ship's commander. A tall cone of black fabric, even his headpiece suggested wealth and high office.

The navigator was similarly attired in robes and headpiece, though his floor-length mantle was solid black and of a simpler design. He communicated with the devices that encircled the shell-like pilot's chair by means of data readout goggles that cupped his eyes and a disk-shaped comlink that hid his mouth.

The *Revenue*'s communications technician was a jowled and limpid-eyed Sullustan. The officer who interfaced with the central control computer was a Gran—three-eyed, with a hircine face. Beaked and green-complexioned, the ship's assistant bursar was an Ishi Tib.

Dofine hated having to suffer aliens aboard his bridge,

but he was compelled to do so as an accommodation to the lesser shipping concerns that had allied with the Trade Federation; small companies like Viraxo Shipping, and powerful shipbuilders like TaggeCo and Hoersch-Kessel.

Humaniform droids saw to all other tasks on the bridge.

Dofine had resumed his pacing when the Sullustan spoke.

"Commander, Dorvalla Mining reports that the payment they received is short one hundred thousand Republic credits."

Dofine waved his long-fingered hand in dismissal. "Tell her to recheck her figures."

The Sullustan relayed Dofine's words and waited for a reply. "She claims that you said the same thing the last time we were here."

Dofine exhaled theatrically and gestured to a large circular screen at the rear of the bridge. "Display her."

The magnified image of a red-haired, freckle-faced human woman was resolving on the screen by the time Dofine reached it.

"*I* am not aware of any missing credits," he said without preamble.

The woman's blue eyes flashed. "Don't lie to me, Dofine. First it was twenty thousand, then fifty, now one hundred. How much will we have to forfeit the next time the Trade Federation graces Dorvalla with a visit?"

Dofine glanced knowingly at the Ishi Tib, who returned a faint grin. "Your world is far removed from normal space lanes," he said calmly toward the screen. "As far from the Rimma Trade Route as from the Corellian Trade Spine. Your situation, therefore, demands additional expenditures. Of course, if you are displeased, you could always do business with some other concern."

The woman snorted a rueful laugh. "Other concern? The Trade Federation has put everyone else under."

Dofine spread his large hands. "Then what is a hundred thousand credits, more or less?"

"Extortion is what it is."

The sour expression Dofine adopted came naturally to his slack features. "I suggest you file a complaint with the Trade Commission on Coruscant."

The woman fumed; her nostrils flared and her cheeks reddened. "You haven't heard the last of this, Dofine."

Dofine's mouth approximated a smile. "Ah, once again, you are mistaken." Abruptly, he ended the transmission, then swung back to face his fellow Neimoidian. "Inform me when the loading process is concluded."

Deep in the hangar arms, droids supervised the disposition of the cargo pods from traffic stations located high above the deck. Humpbacked craft with bulbous noses that gave them an animated appearance, the pods entered through the hangars' magcon orifices on repulsorlift power and were routed according to contents and destination, as designated by codes stenciled on the hulls. Each hangar arm was divided into three zones, partitioned by sliding bulkhead doors, twenty stories high. Normally, zone three, closest to the centersphere, was filled first. But pods containing goods bound for destinations other than Coruscant or other Core worlds were directed to berthing bays in zones one or two, regardless of when they were brought aboard.

Scattered throughout the hangars were security automata toting modified BlasTech combat rifles, some with dispersal tips. Where the worker droids might be hollow-bodied asps, limber-necked PKs, boxy GNKs, or flat-footed binary loadlifters, the security droids appeared to have been inspired by the skeletal structure of any number of the galaxy's bipedal life-forms.

Lacking both the rounded head and alloy musculature of its near cousin, the protocol droid, the security droid had a narrow, half-cylindrical head that tapered forward to a speech processor and, at the opposite end, curved down over a stiff, backwardly canted neck. What distinguished the droid, however, was its signal boost backpack and the retractable antennae that sprouted from it.

The majority of the droids that comprised the *Revenue*'s security force were simply appendages of the freighter's central control computer, but a few had been equipped with a small measure of intelligence. The foreheads and chest plastrons of these lanky commanders were emblazoned with yellow markings similar to military unit flashes, though less for the sake of other droids than for the flesh and bloods to whom the commanders ultimately answered.

OLR-4 was one such commander.

Blaster rifle gripped in both hands and angled across his chest, the droid stood in zone two of the ship's starboard hangar arm, halfway between the bulkheads that defined the immense space. OLR-4 was aware of the activity around him—the current of cargo pods moving toward zone three, the noise of other pods settling to the deck, the incessant whirrs and clicks of machines in motion—but only in a vague way. Rather, OLR-4 had been tasked by the central control computer to watch for anything out of the ordinary—for any event that fell outside performance parameters defined by the computer itself.

The resounding thud that accompanied the roosting of a nearby cargo pod was, given the size of the craft, well within those parameters. So, too, were the sounds emanating from inside the pod, which could be ascribed to a shifting of whatever cargo the pod contained. But the same couldn't be said for the hissing of pressure relief valves or the metallic clanks and stridencies that prefaced the slow rise of the pod's uncommonly large, circular forward hatch.

OLR-4's long head pivoted and his oblique optical sensors fixed on the pod. Magnified and sharpened, the captured image was transmitted to the central control computer, which instantly compared it to a catalog of similar images.

Discrepancies were noted.

Even as OLR-4's photoreceptors were scrutinizing the rising hatch, additional security droids were already hurrying to assume positions on all sides of the suspect pod. OLR-4 planted his bootlike feet in a combat stance and leveled his blaster rifle.

The open hatch should have revealed the interior of the pod, but instead it exposed what seemed to be yet another hatch, sealed shut. OLR-4 did succeed in identifying the composition of the inner hatch, but the droid's puny processor was not up to the task of making sense of what it was seeing. That was the province of the central control computer, which was quick to solve the puzzle— though not quick enough.

Before OLR-4 could move, the inner hatch had telescoped from the pod with enough force to launch two security droids and three worker droids halfway across the hangar. Immediately, OLR-4 and three others opened fire on the battering ram and the cargo pod itself, but the blaster bolts were deflected and sent ricocheting through the hold.

A pair of droids leapt onto the wide-bodied pod, hoping to attack the striking device from behind, but their efforts were in vain. Blaster bolts found them first, quartering one, and all but obliterating the other. It was only then that OLR-4 realized, in his limited capacity, that there were unfriendlies *behind* the battering ram. And judging by the precision of the bolts, the intruders were flesh and bloods.

With cargo pods gliding overhead and a hundred labor droids continuing to tend to their tasks, oblivious to the firefight occurring in their midst, OLR-4 rushed to one side, firing steadily and intent on gaining a better vantage on the intruders. Bolts sought him as he moved, sizzling past his head and shoulders, and streaking between his pumping legs.

In front of him two security droids lost their heads to well-placed shots. A third droid remained intact, but dropped to the deck nevertheless, hopelessly dazzled by untamed, coruscating electrical charges.

OLR-4's internal monitors told him that his blaster was overheating and close to depletion. Though obviously aware of the droid's predicament, the central control computer did not countermand its orders; so OLR-4 kept firing while he attempted to angle behind the battering ram.

Off to his right another droid was blasted from the top of the pod, its torso sent twirling in clumsy circles as it flew off into the hangar, only to collide with a settling cargo pod. A droid with a missing leg hopped as it shot, until its sound leg was blown out from under it, and it fell, skidding across the deck, sparks flying from its vocoder chin.

OLR-4 shifted left and right, dodging blaster bolts. He had almost reached the pod when a bolt caught him in the left shoulder, spinning him through a complete circle. He staggered, but somehow managed to remain upright, until a second bolt struck him in the opposite shoulder. Spun through another circle, he landed on his back, with his legs wedged beneath the pod. Looking up, he had a glimpse of the armed force that had infiltrated the freighter: a dozen or so bipedal flesh and bloods, sheathed in mimetic suits and black body armor, their faces hidden behind rebreather masks, whose oxygen recyclers resembled fangs.

OLR-4's photoreceptors focused on a human with long black hair that fell in thick coils to his broad shoulders. The servomotors of the droid's right hand tightened on the blaster's trigger bar, but the fatigued and overheated weapon's only response was a mournful whirr, as it powered down and shut off.

"Uh-oh," OLR-4 said.

Glimpsing him, the long-haired human swung and fired.

OLR-4's heat sensors redlined and his overloaded systems wailed. Circuits melting, he relayed a final image to the central control computer, then winked out of existence.

The reassuring hum of machines on the *Revenue*'s bridge was interrupted by a grating tone from the scanner array. Gliding across the command walkway, Daultay Dofine queried the droid stationed at the scanner.

"Long-range monitors report a cluster of small ships advancing all speed on our position," the droid answered in a metallic monotone.

"What? What did you say?"

The Sullustan elaborated. "Authenticators identify the ships as CloakShapes and one *Tempest*-class gunship."

Dofine's jaw dropped. "An attack?"

"Commander," the droid intoned, "the ships are continuing to advance."

Dofine gestured wildly to the outsize display screen. "I want to see them!" He had started for the screen when another worrisome tone sounded, this time from the station of the systems officer, which was also set below the walkway.

"The central control computer is reporting a disturbance in zone two of the starboard hangar arm."

Dofine gaped at the Gran. "What sort of disturbance?"

"The droids are firing on one of the cargo pods."

"Those brainless machines! If they ruin any of the cargo—"

"Commander, starfighters are onscreen," the Sullustan reported.

"It could be nothing more than a glitch," the Gran went on.

Dofine's blinking red orbs darted from one alien to the other in mounting concern.

"Starfighters changing vector. Breaking into two elements." The Sullustan turned to Dofine. "Flying the imprint of the Nebula Front."

"The Nebula Front!" Dofine rushed to the display screen, then raised his long, fat forefinger to indicate the jet-black gunship. "That ship—"

"The *Hawk-Bat*," the Sullustan said in a rush. "The ship of Captain Cohl."

"Impossible!" Dofine snapped. "Cohl was reported to be at Malastare only yesterday."

Jowls quivering slightly, the Sullustan regarded the screen. "But that is his ship. And where the *Hawk-Bat* ventures, Cohl is not far behind!"

"Starfighters are forming up for attack," the droid updated.

Dofine turned to the navigator. "Enable defense systems!"

"Central control computer reports continued blasterfire in the starboard hangar. Eight security droids destroyed."

"Destroyed?"

"Defense system has the Nebula Front starfighters in target lock. Deflector shields are raised—"

"Starfighters firing!"

Intense light exploded behind the rectangular viewports and shook the bridge hard enough to rattle a droid off its feet.

"Turbolasers responding!"

Dofine swung to the viewports in time to see hyphens of pulsed, red light streak from the freighter's equatorially mounted batteries.

"Where is our closest reinforcement?"

"One star system distant," the navigator said. "The *Acquisitor*. More heavily armed than the *Revenue*."

"Send a distress call!"

"Is that wise, Commander?"

Dofine understood the implication. Rescue was always a belittling event. But Dofine was certain that he could offset the humiliation by protecting the *Revenue*'s cargo.

"Just do as I say," he told the navigator.

"Starfighter elements are forming up for a second run," the Sullustan updated.

"Where are the starfighters? Why aren't they moving in to engage?"

"You recalled them, Commander," the navigator reminded.

Dofine gestured wildly. "Well, relaunch them, relaunch them!"

"Central control computer requests permission to isolate zone two of starboard hangar."

"Seal it!" Dofine sputtered. "Seal it now!"

The masked group that had infiltrated the *Revenue* were a diverse lot—as varied as the starfighters that were flying support—humans and nonhumans, male and female, stocky and slender. Protected by camouflage suits and matte-black armorply, and sporting gripsole deckboots and combat goggles, they emerged from behind the battering ram that had afforded them an element of surprise, firing state-of-the-art assault rifles and shoulder-slung field disruptors.

The handful of security droids that were still standing collapsed to the deck, limbs splayed or hopelessly entwined.

The human OLR-4 had nearly gotten the drop on strode fearlessly to the center of the yawning hangar, checked a readout on his wrist comm, and tugged the rebreather and goggles from his face.

The firefight had left a vagrant tang in the air, the smell of ozone and scorched alloy.

"Atmosphere is enabled," he told the rest of his band. "But oxygen levels are equivalent to what you'd find at four thousand meters. Off your masks, but keep them handy—especially you t'bac addicts."

With some muffled laughter, the team complied.

Beneath the apparatus, the human's dark-complexioned face was still a mask: thickly bearded with coarse black hair, and rashed from temple to temple with small diamond-shaped tattoos. His violet eyes surveyed the damage with obvious dispassion.

There wasn't a security droid in sight, but the deck was littered with their remains. Labor droids of several varieties continued to route a few pods to berthing spaces.

A human member of the team kicked aside the severed arm of a security droid. "These things could be dangerous if they ever learn to think straight."

"Shoot straight," the bearded man amended.

"Tell that to Rasper, Captain Cohl," another said— Boiny, a Rodian. "It was a droid that sent Rasper on his way." A green-skinned and round-eyed male, Boiny had a tapered snout and a crest of pliant yellow spines.

"A lucky droid, a luckier shot," a Rodian female remarked.

"That doesn't mean we treat this like an exercise," Cohl warned, eyeing everyone. "The central control computer will be deploying backup units soon enough, and we've got a kilometer to go before we hit the centersphere."

The infiltrators glanced down the curved hangar toward a bulkhead that loomed in the distance. High overhead were massive box girders and I-beams, cranes, maintenance gantries, and hoists, a puzzle of atmosphere and vectoring ducts.

A human female—the only among them—whistled softly. "Stars' end, you could hide an invasion force in here."

As dark-complexioned as Cohl, she had short brown

hair and an elegantly angular face. Even the mimetic suit could not camouflage her shapeliness.

"That would mean spending some of the profits, Rella," a male human said. "And the Neimoidians don't do that unless they can spend it on new robes."

Boiny loosed a high-pitched laugh. "You grow up a half-starved Neimoidian grub, that's what happens."

Cohl raised his bearded chin to two of his band. "Stay with the pod. We'll make contact when we have the bridge." He swung to the others. "Team one, take the outer rim corridor. The rest of you are with me."

The *Revenue* shuddered slightly. Muted explosions could be heard in the distance.

Cohl cocked an ear. "That'll be our ships."

Sirens began to blare throughout the hangar. The labor droids stopped in their tracks, as a basso rumble gathered underfoot.

Rella gazed at the far-off bulkhead. "They're sealing off the hangar."

Cohl waved a gesture to the first team. "Move out. We'll rendezvous at the starboard turbolifts. Set your suits to pulse—that ought to confuse the droids—and use the concussion grenades sparingly. And remember to monitor your oxygen levels."

He took a few steps, then stopped. "One more thing: You get blasted by a droid, bacta rehabilitation comes out of your pay."

Daultay Dofine stood rigidly on the bridge's walkway, watching in arrant horror as the Nebula Front showed his ship no mercy.

The motley starfighters fell on the *Revenue* in full force, picking away at the freighter's fat arms and triple-thrustered hindquarters like ravenous birds of prey. Many of the unshielded droid ships were annihilated as soon as they emerged from the vessel's protective force field.

Emboldened by their effortless mastery, the enemy craft violated the embrace the hangar arms threw about the centersphere by strafing the command tower at close quarter. Ion cannon fire from the gunship sent waves of aggravation through the *Revenue*'s deflector shield. Violent light washed against the bridge viewports.

It was all Dofine could do to keep himself rooted on the walkway, as he cursed the terrorists under his breath.

In return for having been awarded what amounted to exclusive rights to trade in the outlying star systems, the Trade Federation had pledged to the Galactic Senate on Coruscant that it would content itself with remaining a mercantile power, and refrain from becoming a naval power through the accumulation of war machines. However, the further the giant ships traveled from the Core, the more often they fell victim to attacks by pirates, privateers, and terrorist groups like the Nebula Front, whose broad membership had grievances not only with the Trade Federation, but also with distant Coruscant itself.

As a result, the senate had granted permission for the freighters to be equipped with weapons of defense, to safeguard them in the unpoliced systems strewn between the major trade routes and hyperlanes. But that had only forced the raiders to upgrade their armaments and, in turn, prepared the way for periodic strengthenings of Trade Federation defenses.

Skirmishes in the Mid and Outer Rims—throughout the so-called free trade zones—had since become commonplace. But Coruscant was a long way off, even by light-speed, and it was not always easy to ascertain who was at fault and who had fired first. By the time matters reached the courts, it often came down to the word of one party against the word of another, without resolution.

Things might have gone differently for the Trade Federation but for the Neimoidians, who were as penurious as they were avaricious. When it had come to fortifying the giant ships, they had sought out the most cut-rate suppliers, and they had insisted that protecting the cargo was their paramount concern.

Against all sound judgment, it was the Neimoidians who had dictated the placement of quad laser batteries around the outer wall of the hangar arms. While the equatorial arrangement was adequate for repelling lateral attacks, it proved completely ineffective for countering attacks launched from above or below, where nearly all the freighters' crucial systems were located: tractor beam and deflector shield generators, hyperdrive reactors, and the central control computer.

Thus the Trade Federation had been forced to invest in bigger and better shield generators, thicker armor plating, and, ultimately, in squadrons of starfighters. But starfighter allotments were subject to senate sanction, and freighters like the *Revenue* frequently found themselves defenseless against fighter craft piloted by seasoned raiders.

Well aware of these shortcomings, Daultay Dofine saw the ship and its cargo of precious lommite rapidly slipping from his grasp.

"Shields holding at fifty percent," the Gran reported from across the bridge, "but we are imperiled. A few more strikes and we'll be disabled."

"Where is the *Acquisitor*?" Dofine whined. "It should have arrived by now!"

A volley from the Nebula Front's gunship—Captain Cohl's personal gunship—rocked the bridge. As Dofine had learned in previous engagements, sheer size was no guarantee of protection, much less victory, and the freighter's three-kilometer diameter only made it a target that couldn't be missed.

"Shields marginal at forty percent."

"Quad lasers one through six are not responding," the Sullustan added. "The starfighters are concentrating fire on the deflector shield generator and drive reactors."

Dofine firmed his fleshy lips in anger. "Instruct the central control computer to activate all droids, all ship defenses, and prepare to repel boarders," he brayed. "Over my dead body will Captain Cohl set foot on this bridge."

In the starboard hangar arm, Cohl's team had barely made it through the bulkhead door when every device in zone three conspired to prevent them from getting one meter closer to the acceleration compensator shaft that connected the centersphere to its embracing arms.

Overhead cranes threw grappling claws at them; towering derricks toppled in their path; binary loadlifters dogged them like mechanical nightmares; and oxygen levels plummeted. Even worker droids joined the fray, brandishing fusioncutters and power calibrators as if they were flame projectors and vibroblades.

"Central control's turned the entire ship against us," Cohl yelled.

Rella squeezed off bolts at a posse of hydrospanner-wielding PK droids. "What did you expect, Cohl—the royal welcome?"

Cohl gestured Boiny, Rella, and the rest of his team toward the final bulkhead that stood between them and the centersphere turbolifts. Sirens shrieked and howled in the thin air. Crisscrossing and ricocheting blaster bolts created a pyrotechnic display worthy of a Republic Day parade on Coruscant.

Cohl fired on the run, losing count of how many

droids he had dropped and how many blaster gas cartridges his weapon had expended. Two of his band were pinned down by droid fire, but there was little he or anyone else could do to help them. With luck they would get to the rendezvous point, even if they had to drag themselves there.

Pursued by three binary loadlifters, the team raced through the final bulkhead door and fought their way to the closest bank of turbolifts.

The hatch that accessed the transfer tubes was locked down.

"Boiny!" Cohl shouted.

The Rodian holstered his blaster and hurried forward, eyeing the hatch up and down, then moved to the control panel set into the wall. Preparing to slice the code, he rubbed his palms together and cracked his long, suction-tip-equipped fingers. Before he could lay a hand on the panel keys, Cohl slapped him in the back of the head.

"What is this, amateur night?" Cohl asked with a menacing scowl. "Blow the thing."

Dofine was pacing the walkway when the bridge hatch blew inward, loosing a brief storm of paralyzing heat that tumbled him to the deck.

Cohl's band of six hurried in behind a roiling cloud of smoke, their mimetic suits allowing them to blend even with the burnished bulkheads of the bridge. Quickly and efficiently, they disarmed the Gran and shot restraining bolts onto the chest plastrons of the droids.

Cohl waved one of his men toward the communications station.

"Contact the *Hawk-Bat*. Tell them we've secured the bridge. Have the starfighters deploy for defense, and stand by to cover our exfiltration."

He waved another of his cohorts toward the Gran's

duty station. "Order the central control computer to stand down. Have it open all bulkheads in the hangar arms."

The human nodded and dropped down below the walkway.

Cohl tapped a code into his wrist comlink and raised it to his mouth. "Base team, we have the bridge. Move the pod into zone three and set it down as close as possible to the inner wall hangar portal. We'll be there soon enough."

Cohl zeroed the comlink. His eyes roamed over the faces of his five living captives, settling finally on Dofine. Then he drew his blaster.

Spreading his arms wide in a gesture of surrender, Dofine took two backward steps as Cohl approached.

"You would shoot an unarmed individual, Captain Cohl?"

Cohl pressed the barrel of the weapon to Dofine's ribcage. "I'd shoot an unarmed Neimoidian—and I'd sleep better for it."

He glared at Dofine for a long moment, then holstered the blaster and turned to the Rodian member of his band. "Boiny, get to work. And be quick about it."

Cohl swung back to Dofine.

"Where's the rest of your crew, Commander?"

Dofine swallowed and found his voice. "Returning by shuttle from Dorvalla."

Cohl nodded. "Good, that'll simplify things."

Repeatedly poking Dofine in the chest with his forefinger, Cohl moved him backwards along the walkway until they reached the navigator's chair. A final poke sent Dofine off the walkway and into the seat.

Cohl jumped down to face him. "We need to discuss your cargo, Commander."

"The cargo?" Dofine stammered. "Lommite—destined for Sluis Van."

"To the depths with the ore," Cohl snarled. "I'm talking about the aurodium."

Dofine tried to keep his red eyes from bulging. His nictitating membranes spasmed, and he blinked half a dozen times. "Aurodium?"

Cohl leaned toward him. "You're carrying two billion in aurodium ingots."

Dofine stiffened under Cohl's gaze. "You—you must be mistaken, Captain. The *Revenue* is carrying ore."

Cohl raised himself to his considerable height. "I'll say it once more. You're carrying aurodium ingots—bribes proffered by Outer Rim worlds to ensure the continued blessing of the Trade Federation."

Dofine sneered, in spite of himself. "So it is currency you seek. I had always heard that the notorious Captain Cohl was an idealist. Now I see that he is a simple thief."

Cohl almost grinned. "We can't all be licensed thieves like you and the rest of your bunch."

"The Trade Federation does not deal in violence and death, Captain."

Cohl grabbed two fistfuls of Dofine's rich raiment and yanked him halfway out of the chair. "Not yet you don't." He pushed Dofine back into the seat. "But we'll save that for another day. What matters now is the aurodium."

"And should I refuse to submit?"

Without taking his eyes from Dofine, Cohl pointed to his Rodian comrade. "Boiny, there, is affixing a thermal detonator to the *Revenue*'s fuel-driver control system. As I understand it, the device will trigger an explosion large enough to destroy your ship in . . . Boiny?"

"Sixty minutes, Captain," Boiny shouted, holding aloft a metallic sphere the size of a stinkmelon.

Cohl pulled an object from the thigh pouch pocket of his mimetic suit and slapped it against the back of Dofine's left hand. Dofine saw that it was a timer, already counting down from sixty minutes. He raised his eyes to Cohl's steadfast gaze.

"About the ingots," Cohl said.

Dofine nodded. "Yes, all right—if you promise to spare the ship."

Cohl laughed shortly. "The *Revenue* is history. But you have my word I'll spare your life if you do as you're told."

Again, Dofine nodded. "That way I'll at least live to see you executed."

Cohl shrugged. "You never know, Commander." He straightened and grinned at Rella. "What did I tell you? Easy as—"

"Captain," Cohl's man at the communications station cut him off. "Vessel emerging from hyperspace. Authenticators paint her as the TradeFed freighter *Acquisitor*."

Rella made a plosive sound. "You were saying, Cohl?"

The look Cohl directed at Dofine was one of genuine surprise. "Maybe you're not as thick-skulled as you look." He leapt up onto the walkway and turned to the viewport array. Rella joined him.

"The scenario has changed," Cohl announced to everyone. "The *Acquisitor* will launch starfighters as soon as it's within range. Order the *Hawk-Bat* to take the fight to the freighter."

Dofine allowed a smile of satisfaction. "Perhaps you will have to forgo your treasure, after all, Captain Cohl."

Cohl shot him a withering glance. "I'm not leaving without it, Commander—and neither are you." He reached for Dofine's left wrist to regard the countdown timer. "Fifty-five minutes."

"Cohl," Rella said leadingly.

He looked at her askance. "Without the aurodium, we don't get paid, sweetheart."

She took her lower lip between her perfect teeth. "Yes, but we have to be alive to spend it."

He shook his head. "Death's not in the cards—at least not in this hand."

Close to the bridge, a Nebula Front starfighter, chased down by packets of lethal energy, vanished in a nimbus of white-hot gas and debris.

"Fire from the *Acquisitor*," one of the mercenaries reported.

Sudden disquiet tugged at Rella's features.

Cohl ignored the look she sent him. Plucking Dofine from the command chair and standing him on the walkway, Cohl shoved him toward the bridge's ruined hatch.

"Double time, Commander. Our departure window has just narrowed."

In the chaotic gloom of the starboard hangar arm, a final pod moving on repulsorlift toward a zone three docking bay didn't draw much attention. Somewhat turnip shaped, it was larger than most of the pods that had been routed into zone three, though not as large as the one the Nebula Front had infiltrated, and nowhere near the size of some of the ore barges. More, the pod gave no hint that, like the terrorists' craft, it carried a living cargo.

Strapped into back-to-back seats were two human males who, in dress, were the polar opposite of Daultay Dofine. Their light-colored tunics and trousers were loose fitting and unadorned, their knee-high boots were made of nerf hide, and they affected neither headpieces nor jewelry.

Their modest garments only made their obvious guile all the more mysterious.

The fraudulent cargo pod lacked viewports of any sort, but vidcams concealed in the hull transmitted assorted views of the hangar to display screens inside the craft.

On observing the disorder Cohl's band had left in its

wake, the young man in the forward seat remarked in a nasal voice, "Captain Cohl has left us an easy trail to follow, Master."

"He has indeed, Padawan. But the trail you take into the forest may not be the one you wish to follow when leaving. Stretch out with your feelings, Obi-Wan."

Fairly squeezed into the aft seat, the older man was also the larger of the pair. His broad face was fully bearded, and his thick mane of graying hair was pulled back from a gently sloping, noble brow. His eyes were a sharp blue, and the bridge of his strong nose was flattened, as if it had been broken beyond the repair of bacta treatments.

His name was Qui-Gon Jinn.

His counterpart at the controls of the pod, Obi-Wan Kenobi, had a youthful, clean-shaven face, a cleft chin, and a high, straight forehead. His brown hair was cropped short, save for a short tail at the rear of his head, and a single, thin plait that fell behind his ear to his right shoulder, a sign of his Padawan rank. Peculiar to the order to which Qui-Gon and Obi-Wan belonged, the word meant apprentice or protégé.

That order was known as the Jedi Knights.

"Master, do you see any sign of their craft?" Obi-Wan asked over his shoulder.

Qui-Gon turned in his seat to indicate an open pod at the lower left of Obi-Wan's heads-up display screen.

"That one. They must be planning to launch from the inner rim hangar portal. Set us down nearby, with our hatch facing away from their pod. But be mindful not to draw attention. Cohl is sure to have posted sentries."

"Would you like to assume the piloting, Master?" Obi-Wan asked peevishly.

Qui-Gon smiled to himself. "Only if you're tiring, Padawan."

Obi-Wan compressed his lips. "I'm anything but tired, Master." He regarded the display screen for a moment. "I've found us a good place."

As if under the guidance of droids in the hangar traffic stations, the pod settled on its quartet of disk-shaped landing gear. The two Jedi fell silent while they watched the vidcam feeds. After a long moment, a pair of human males emerged from Cohl's pod, oxygen masks covering their faces and disruptor rifles cradled in their arms.

"You were right, Master," Obi-Wan said softly. "Cohl is becoming predictable."

"We can hope, Obi-Wan."

One of the sentries circled the pod, then returned to the open hatch, where the other was waiting.

"Now's our chance," Qui-Gon said. "You know—"

"I know what to do, Master. But I still don't understand your reasoning. We could surprise Cohl here and now."

"It's more important that we discover the location of the Nebula Front's base, Padawan. There'll be time then to put an end to Captain Cohl's exploits."

Qui-Gon inserted a small breathing device into his mouth and flipped a switch that opened the circular front hatch. A cacophony of skirling sirens greeted them. The two Jedi climbed out into the red glow of emergency lighting that suffused the hold.

No object was more symbolic of the Jedi Knights than the polished alloy cylinders Qui-Gon and Obi-Wan wore on the hide belts that cinched their tunics. With the belts' abundance of utility pouches, the thirty-centimeter-long cylinders might have been tools of a sort—and, indeed, the Jedi viewed them as such—but, in fact, they were weapons of light, actual and figurative, and had been employed by the Jedi for thousands of generations in their self-appointed mandate to serve the Galactic Republic as the stewards of peace and justice.

The crystal-focused lightsaber, however, was not the true source of a Jedi's power, for that sprang from the omnipresent energy field that permeated all life and bound the galaxy together, an energy field the Jedi knew as the Force.

Tens of thousands of years the order had devoted to the study and contemplation of the Force, and as by-products of that devotion had come powers beyond the ken of ordinary folks: the power to move objects at will, to cloud the thoughts of lesser minds, to peer forward in time. But most of all, the ability to live in symbiotic accord with all life, and thus be allied to the Force itself.

Moving with preternatural silence and swiftness, Qui-Gon advanced on Cohl's pod, the lightsaber gripped in his right hand, concealing himself at every opportunity behind other pods. With all the noise in the hangar, he knew that it wasn't going to be easy to distract the two guards. But he had to buy Obi-Wan at least a few moments.

Sprawled atop the curving nose of one of the pods was what remained of a battle droid's upper torso and elongated head. Glancing at Cohl's sentries, Qui-Gon thumbed the activator button above the lightsaber's ridged handgrip.

A rod of brilliant green energy hissed from the sword's alloy hilt, thrumming as it came in contact with the thin air. With a single one-handed swipe of his lightsaber, Qui-Gon cleaved the droid's head from its thin neck. At the same time, he extended his left hand, palm outward, and with a blast of Force power sent the severed head hurtling across the hangar, where it struck the deck with a strident clank, not five meters from where the terrorists stood.

The pair swung to the sound, with weapons raised.

And in that instant, Obi-Wan disappeared in a blur, headed for Cohl's pod.

Midlevel in the freighter's centersphere, Cohl, Rella, Boiny, and the rest of Cohl's band gazed wide-eyed and open-mouthed at the cache of aurodium ingots, which had been removed from the *Revenue*'s security cabin and piled—lovingly—atop a repulsorsled. Hypnotic in their beauty, the ingots glowed with a constantly shifting inner light that summoned all colors of the rainbow.

Even Dofine and his four bridge officers could scarcely tear their eyes away.

"Take my breath and call me wheezy," Boiny said. "Now I've seen it all."

Cohl snapped out of his reverie and turned to Dofine, whose thin wrists were secured in shiny stun cuffs.

"You have our gratitude, Commander. Most Neimoidians wouldn't have been so obliging."

Dofine glowered. "You go too far, Captain."

Cohl's broad shoulders heaved in dismissal. "Tell that to the members of the Trade Federation Directorate."

He nodded to Rella to get the sled under way, then took Boiny by the shoulders and steered him toward an inset control panel.

"Patch into the central control computer and tell it to run a diagnostic on the fuel-drivers. When the computer locates the thermal detonator, it should order an abandon ship."

Boiny nodded in comprehension.

"Be sure to convince it to jettison all the cargo pods and barges," Cohl added.

Dofine's eyes widened in revelation. "So, the lommite is important, after all."

Cohl turned to him. "You're confusing me with someone who cares one way or another what goes on between the Trade Federation and the Nebula Front."

Dofine was confused. "Then why are you saving the cargo?"

"Saving it?" Cohl put his hands on his hips and laughed heartily. "I'm merely providing the *Acquisitor* with a target-rich environment, Commander."

With the same extraordinary nimbleness that had guided him to the terrorists' pod, Obi-Wan returned to the Jedi craft.

"Everything is in place, Master," he said, just loudly enough to be heard over the wailing sirens.

Qui-Gon motioned him toward the hatch. But Obi-Wan hadn't even raised a foot when all the pods in the hangar began to levitate and wheel toward one hangar portal or another.

"What's happening?"

Qui-Gon looked around in mild perplexity. "They're jettisoning the cargo."

"Hardly the act of terrorists, Master."

Qui-Gon's brow furrowed in thought. "The central control computer wouldn't allow this unless the freighter was in serious jeopardy."

"Perhaps it is, Master."

Qui-Gon agreed. "Either way, Padawan, we're better off inside our craft. Unless Cohl has failed in his mission, he should be arriving at any moment."

Barely keeping pace with the ingot-heaped repulsorsled, Cohl's band jogged down the broad avenue of the starboard hangar toward the rendezvous point. The *Revenue*'s bridge crew struggled to keep up, despite being equipped with rebreather masks and even when

prodded in the back by the emitter nozzles of the terrorists' blasters. To all sides of them hovered cargo pods and
tenders, moving toward inner and outer wall hangar
portals.

Even Cohl was out of breath by the time everyone
reached zone three and the waiting pod. Only one member of the first team—a blond-furred Bothan—had made
it back, but Cohl refused to concern himself just then
with the fate of the rest. Every member chosen for the
operation had been apprised of the risks.

"Get the aurodium stowed," he shouted to Boiny
through the rebreather's communicator. "Rella, do a head
count and get everyone aboard."

Daultay Dofine glanced worriedly at the countdown
timer still affixed to the back of his hand. "What is to become of us?" he yelled.

A human member of Cohl's band motioned broadly
toward a large, nearby pod that had yet to lift off. "I suggest you unload that one and cram yourselves inside."

Dofine blinked back panic. "We'll die in there."

The human laughed scornfully. "That's the idea."

Dofine looked at Cohl. "Your word . . ."

Cohl twisted his head to one side to read the display
on the countdown timer, then cut his eyes to Dofine.

"If you hurry, you'll make it to the escape pods in
time."

Obi-Wan waited for the terrorists' pod to rise from the hangar deck before activating the repulsorlift engines. In addition to the huge portals at the ends of the hangar arms, magnetic containment portals along the inner curve of the arms had opened up in each zone. Scores of cargo pods and barges had begun to converge on these smaller egresses, but bottlenecks were forming quickly, despite the supervisory efforts of the central control computer.

Obi-Wan understood that if they were too late in reaching the portal, he and Qui-Gon would be forced to resort to some other means of abandoning ship. But the young Jedi was nothing if not methodical. He spent a long moment studying the flow of traffic and anticipating where jams were likely to occur before deciding on a course.

That course took them straight up into the hangar's lofty reaches of hoists and cranes, before descending acutely for the zone three portal. Grazing three pods on the way down, Obi-Wan neatly avoided a collision with a barge that was fast becoming lodged in the opening.

Cohl had exited the hangar arm minutes earlier, but the tracker Obi-Wan had affixed assured that the Jedi would be able to single Cohl's pod out from the now stampeding herd.

"We have them, Master," he told Qui-Gon, who was studying the rear display screens. "They're heading straight for the centersphere. I'm not certain if they intend to climb over it or dive beneath it, but they are accelerating."

"Stay with them, Obi-Wan. But keep a fixed distance. We don't want to reveal ourselves just yet."

With the bone-white centersphere looming and the broad sweep of the immense arms to either side, the inner district of the annular freighter was a sight to behold—especially with crafts of all size and shape pouring from the holds. But the erratic motion of those same pods and barges left Obi-Wan little time to appreciate the view. He divided his attention between the flashing bezel that was Cohl's pod on the heads-up display, and the console screens, which showed exterior views to either side.

With most of the pods streaming toward the lower portion of the centersphere, even slight encounters were causing chain reactions within the bunch. Many pods were already spinning out of control, and a few were on collision courses for the hangar arms.

It all began to remind Obi-Wan of some of the exercises he had endured during his youth in the Jedi Temple on Coruscant, where the goal of a student was to remain unswervingly attentive to a single task, while as many as five teachers did all they could to distract.

"Watch our stern, Padawan," Qui-Gon warned.

A pod had emerged from below them, catching them aft on its ascent. In danger of being tipped end over end, Obi-Wan applied power to the nose attitude jets and managed just in time to stabilize their craft. But the brush had knocked them off course, and suddenly they were closing on the thick structural stalk that wedded the immense centersphere to the hangar arms.

Obi-Wan glanced at the heads-up display, but found no pulsing bezel.

"Master, I've lost them."

"Focus on where you want to go, Obi-Wan," Qui-Gon said in a calm voice. "Forget the display screen, and let the Force guide you."

Obi-Wan closed his eyes for a moment, then, following his instincts, adjusted their course. Glancing at the display, he saw Cohl's pod ahead of them, off to starboard.

"I see them, Master. They're angling for the top of the centersphere."

"Captain Cohl was never one to remain long in the herd."

Obi-Wan fired the pod's attitude jets to adjust course and soon saw the reassuring blinking of the bezel.

The centersphere filled the display screens linked to the pod's nose vidcams, revealing level after level of what Obi-Wan knew had once been conference rooms and living spaces for the ship's crew, before the Trade Federation had turned to droid labor. They were almost to the crown of the centersphere when a lone starfighter streaked across one of the display screens, dual laser cannons loosing bursts at some unseen target.

"A Nebula Front CloakShape," Qui-Gon said in mild surprise.

A sturdy, low-profile starfighter with downsloping wings, CloakShapes had been designed for atmospheric combat. But the terrorist group had retrofitted this one with rear-mounted maneuvering fins and a strap-on hyperdrive.

"But what are they firing at?" Obi-Wan asked. "Cohl's pilots must have destroyed the *Revenue*'s starfighters by now."

"I suspect we'll know soon enough, Padawan. In the meantime, stay focused on the matter at hand."

Obi-Wan bristled slightly at the mild reprimand, but it was deserved. He had a habit of looking forward, as opposed to staying in the moment, as Qui-Gon preferred—of attending to what the Jedi called the living Force.

Well above the bald crown of the centersphere and the boxy scanners that topped the freighter's command tower, Cohl's pod was gathering speed and, with bold maneuvers, was emerging from the cloud of pods within which it had hidden. In danger of falling too far behind, Obi-Wan called on the drives for added power.

By the time they were coming around the top curve of the centersphere, Obi-Wan had greatly reduced the distance between the two pods. He was preparing to follow Cohl into space when another starfighter—a modified Z-95 Headhunter—flashed into view on the display screens and exploded.

"The battle continues," Qui-Gon said.

Emerged from the embrace of the arms, the two Jedi saw the source of the return fire. Floating like a ring above Dorvalla's nightside was a second freighter, engulfed in blossoms of fire sown by the Nebula Front ships.

"Trade Federation reinforcements," Obi-Wan said.

"That freighter could complicate matters," Qui-Gon mused.

"But surely we have Cohl this time."

"Cohl is a sly one, Obi-Wan. He would have anticipated

this. He doesn't make a move without a contingency plan."

"But, Master, without his support ships—"

"Expect nothing," Qui-Gon interrupted. "Simply stay your course."

Inside the equally cramped quarters of the terrorists' pod, Cohl's band of eight carried out their preassigned tasks.

"Outer and inner hatches sealed, Captain," Boiny reported from his wedge of space at the curved instrument console. "All systems nominal."

"Prepare to convert from repulsorlift to fusial propulsion," Cohl said, snugging his seat harness.

"Preparing to convert," Rella relayed.

"Comm is enabled," another said. "Switching to priority frequency."

"Clear space, Captain. Passing the thousand-meter mark from the centersphere."

"Easy does it," Cohl said, aware of a certain tension in the recirculating air. "We'll maintain a low profile until ten thousand meters. Then we go for broke."

Rella cast him an approving glance. "Plan precisely; perform faultlessly—"

"And avoid detection—before, during, and after," Boiny completed.

"Set course for one-one-seven, freighter's bow," Cohl told them. "Accelerate to point five. Fusial thrust on standby."

He reclined his chair and switched on the starboard display. The *Hawk-Bat* and the support ships had managed to hold the *Acquisitor* at bay. But the Trade-Fed's starfighters were all over the arena, harried by Nebula Front pilots and confounded by the torrents of cargo gushing from the *Revenue*'s hangar bays. Still, it was just a matter of rendezvousing with the *Hawk-Bat* and putting a couple of parsecs between the gunship and the *Acquisitor*.

Rella leaned toward him to whisper. "Cohl, if we survive this, I forgive you for saying yes to this operation to begin with."

Cohl had his mouth open to respond when Boiny said, "Captain, something peculiar. Could be a fluke, but we've got one cargo pod hanging dead on our six."

"Show me," Cohl said, cutting his violet eyes to the screen.

"Smack in the center. The one with the pointed snout."

Cohl fell silent for a moment, then said, "Alter our course to one-one-nine."

Rella set herself to the task.

Boiny squeaked a nervous laugh. "The pod's changing course to one-one-nine."

"Some kind of gravity drag?" one of the others asked—a human named Jalan.

"Gravity drag?" Rella said in obvious derision. "What in the moons of Bodgen is gravity drag?"

"It's what keeps Jalan from thinking straight," Boiny muttered.

"Fasten it, the bunch of you," Cohl said, stroking his bearded jaw in thought. "Can we scan that pod?"

"We can try."

Cohl forced a breath and folded his arms across his chest. "Let's play this safe. Steer us back into the thick of things."

"Master, they're scanning us," Obi-Wan said. "They're altering course, as well."

"They're planning to hide in that cluster of cargo pods," Qui-Gon said, mostly to himself. "It's time we give them something else to worry about, Obi-Wan.

Activate the thermal detonator as soon as they're a bit farther from the freighter."

Cohl gripped the armrests of his narrow seat as the terrorists' pod took a buffeting from its neighbors in the throng that was pouring into the space between the two Trade Federation freighters.

"We can't take much more of this," Boiny warned, his sucker-fingered hands gripped on the instrument console.

"Cohl," Rella said harshly. "Unless we get out now, we're going to end up in the middle of a starfighter engagement."

Cohl kept his eyes glued to the overhead display screen. "What's the pod doing?"

"Matching our every maneuver."

One of the humans cursed under his breath. "What's in that thing?"

"Or who?" another put in.

"Something's not right," Cohl said, shaking his head. "I smell a womp rat."

Boiny glanced at him. "Never met one that could pilot a pod like that, Captain."

Cohl slapped the armrests in a gesture of finality. "No more wasting time. Engage the primary fusials."

"Now you're talking," Rella remarked, carrying out the command.

Without warning, Boiny all but shot from his seat, gesticulating madly at one of the console sensors and tripping over his own words.

"Boiny!" Cohl shouted, as if to break whatever spell the Rodian was under. "Out with it!"

Boiny swung about, his black orbs radiating incredulity. "Captain, we've got a thermal detonator affixed to the pod's drive core!"

Cohl stared at him in similar disbelief. "How long to detonation?"

"Five minutes and counting!"

With its sterile surfaces, sunken control stations, and circular plasma screens that shone like aquariums, the bridge of the *Acquisitor* was identical to that of her sister ship, save that it held a full complement of bridge officers, and all eight were Neimoidians.

Commander Nap Lagard gazed out the forward viewports at the distant *Revenue*. At this remove, the bulbous-nosed pods and barges flooding from her cargo holds were mere specks glinting in the sunlight, but magnified views had revealed hundreds of burst pods—the result of collisions and of starfighter laser bolts—their payloads of lommite surrendered to space. A heartrending sight to behold; but Lagard had already decided that he would retrieve as much of the cargo as possible—assuming that the terrorists could be chased off.

The stamp of the Nebula Front was all over the crippled *Revenue*, in the form of blistered durasteel, erose penetrations in the hull, pieces of twisted superstructure. Recently strengthened and overlapping deflector shields had prevented the terrorists from inflicting similar damage on the *Acquisitor*. More, the *Acquisitor* carried twice the usual number of droid-piloted craft.

No sooner had the freighter decanted from hyperspace than the Nebula Front ships had flown against her. In concert with the freighters' quad lasers, the starfighters had succeeded in warding off the attack and forcing the terrorists back toward the *Revenue*, where the conflict was still raging. Countless droid ships had disappeared in globular explosions, but the Nebula Front had not been spared casualties, having lost two CloakShapes and one Z-95 Headhunter.

Only the *Hawk-Bat*—the light-freighter-size gunship of the mercenary known as Captain Cohl—had been a continuing menace to the *Acquisitor*, trying the fortitude of the freighter's new shields with disabling runs.

Just now, however, even the *Hawk-Bat* was in retreat, streaking off in the direction of Dorvalla's polar ice cap, the blue vortices of the gunship's thrusters visible from the *Acquisitor*'s bridge.

"It seems we have driven them off," one of Lagard's subalterns remarked in the Neimoidian tongue.

Lagard grunted noncommittally.

"Captain Cohl must have issued the abandon-ship order," the subaltern continued. "The Nebula Front would rather see our lommite lost to space than allow it to reach our customers on Sluis Van."

Lagard grunted again. "They may think they have struck a blow against the Trade Federation. But they will think again when Dorvalla is forced to make restitution to us."

The subaltern nodded. "The courts will stand with us."

Lagard turned briefly from the view. "Yes. But these acts of terrorism cannot be allowed to continue."

"Commander," the communications officer intruded.

"We are receiving a coded transmission from Commander Dofine."

"From the *Revenue*?"

"From an escape pod, Commander."

"Put the message through the annunciators, and ready the tractor beam to retrieve the escape pod."

The bridge's speakers crackled to life. "*Acquisitor,* this is Commander Daultay Dofine."

Lagard hastened to the center of the walkway. "Dofine, this is Commander Lagard. We will have you safely on board as quickly as possible."

"Lagard, listen closely," Dofine said. "Contact Viceroy Gunray. It is urgent that I speak with him immediately."

"Viceroy Gunray? What is so urgent?"

"That is for the viceroy alone to hear," Dofine hissed.

Realizing that he had suffered a loss of face, Lagard stung back. "And what of Captain Cohl, Commander Dofine? Is he in possession of your ship?"

Dofine's brief silence assured Lagard that the barb had found its mark.

"Captain Cohl fled the ship in a facsimile cargo pod."

Lagard turned to the viewports. "Can you identify it?"

"Identify it?" Dofine asked sharply. "It was a pod like all the others."

"And the *Revenue*?"

"The *Revenue* is about to blow to pieces!"

In the terrorists' pod, Boiny studied the instrument console in dismay. "Thirty seconds to detonation."

"Cohl!" Rella yelled when he failed to respond. "Do something!"

Cohl glanced at her, tight-lipped. "All right, jettison the husk."

To a one, the terrorists settled back in relief, while

Boiny tapped a flurry of commands into the console keypad.

"Charges activated," the Rodian reported. "Separation in ten seconds."

Cohl sniffed. "Times like this, you wish you could see the faces of your adversaries."

Qui-Gon and Obi-Wan watched Cohl's pod on their separate screens. Abruptly, a series of small explosions ringed the humpbacked craft along its equator, and it split into two parts, revealing an oblate shuttle concealed inside.

The shuttle's fusial thrust engines ignited, and the craft rocketed away from the pieces of its discarded husk. Then the lower half exploded.

"That would be our thermal detonator," Qui-Gon said. "And the tracking device?"

"Affixed to the hull of the shuttle and still functioning, Master," Obi-Wan reported, gazing at the flashing bezel. "Again, you have anticipated Captain Cohl."

"Not without help, Padawan. You know what to do."

Obi-Wan smiled as he reached for the controls. "I only wish I could see Cohl's face."

Cohl's mouth fell open as he watched the pursuing pod burst apart along a midline seam. Inside was a wingless Corellian Lancet, painted a telltale crimson from pointed nose to sleek-finned tail.

"It's flying Coruscant colors!" Boiny said in astonishment. "Judicial Department."

"Matching us maneuver for maneuver," Rella reported as she wove the terrorist's shuttle through a swarm of cargo pods and clusters of loosed lommite ore.

"*Gaining* on us," Boiny updated.

Rella refused to accept it. "Since when do judicials pilot like that?"

"Who else could be piloting?" one of the humans asked. "It sure isn't Neimoidians."

Cohl locked eyes with Rella.

"Jedi?" they said in unison.

Cohl considered it, then shook his head. "What would the Jedi be doing out here? This isn't Republic space. Besides, no one—and I mean no one—knew about this operation."

Boiny and the rest were quick to agree. "The captain's right. No one knew about this operation."

But the uncertainty in the Rodian's voice was glaring, and Cohl was suddenly aware that everyone was watching him.

"No one, Cohl?" Rella said leadingly.

He frowned at her. "Outside the Nebula Front, anyway."

"Maybe the Force told them," Boiny mumbled.

Rella studied the displays. "We might still make the *Hawk-Bat*."

Cohl leaned toward the shuttle's wraparound viewport. "Where is she?"

"Holding at the rendezvous point above Dorvalla's pole." When, after a long moment, Cohl still hadn't responded, she added, "I'll just keep flying in circles while you make your mind up about what to do."

Cohl looked at Boiny. "Run a surface scan of the shuttle hull."

"Surface scan?" the Rodian asked dubiously.

"Now," Cohl said sharply.

Boiny bent over the console, then straightened in his seat. "We're hosting a locator!"

Cohl's eyes narrowed. "They're hoping to track us."

"Correction, Cohl," Rella said. "They are tracking us."

Cohl ignored the remark and glanced at Boiny again. "How much time before the *Revenue* blows?"

"Seven minutes."

"Can you calculate the shape of the freighter's explosion?"

Boiny and Rella swapped troubled glances. "To a certain extent," the Rodian said in a tentative voice.

"Do it. Then give me your best estimate of the blast radius and the extent of the debris cloud."

Boiny swallowed hard. "Even my best estimate is going to be plus or minus a couple of hundred kilometers, Captain."

Cohl mulled it over in silence, then glanced at Rella. "Come about—hard."

She stared at him. "It's confirmed: You've lost your mind."

"You heard me," Cohl snapped. "It's back to the freighter for us."

Just inside the magcon portal of the *Acquisitor*'s portside hangar arm, Daultay Dofine crawled indecorously from the barrel-shaped escape pod the freighter's powerful tractor beam had retrieved.

The navigator and the rest followed him out.

Commander Lagard was on hand to meet them.

"It is an honor to rescue so celebrated a person," Lagard said.

Dofine adjusted the fit of his robes and straightened his command miter. "Yes, I'm sure it is," he replied. "Did you do as I asked and contact Viceroy Gunray?"

Lagard indicated the Neimoidian mechno-chair that had probably conveyed him from the bridge. "The viceroy is eager to hear what you have to report. As am I, Commander."

Dofine pushed past Lagard to get to the chair, which

immediately began to move off in the direction of the centersphere—no doubt at Lagard's remote behest.

A product of Affodies Crafthouse of Pure Neimoidia, the curious and prohibitively costly device had two sickle-shaped rear legs that terminated in single-claw feet, and a pair of double-clawed articulated guidance limbs. The laser-etched designs that covered its metallic surface were modeled after the shell ornamentation of Neimoidia's sovereign beetle. Gyroscopically balanced, the high-backed chair was more status symbol than practical mode of transport, but Dofine had grasped that the chair had not been provided for his benefit.

Where one would have sat was a circular hologram plate, from which projected the miniature holopresence of Viceroy Nute Gunray himself, leader of the Neimoidian Inner Circle and a member of the seven-person Trade Federation Directorate. Impediments of interstellar origin dazed the feed with diagonal lines of noise.

"Viceroy," Dofine said, bowing in obeisance before he hurried to catch up with the slowly scuttling chair.

Gunray had a jutting lower jaw, and his thick lower lip was uncompanioned. A deep fissure separated his bulging forehead into two lateral lobes. His skin was kept a healthy gray-blue by means of frequent massages and meals of the finest fungus. Red and orange robes of exquisite hand fell from his narrow shoulders, along with a round-collared brown surplice that reached his knees. Around his neck hung a pectoral of elongated teardrops of electrum, and a black tiara—triple-crested, with a pair of dangling tails—sat atop his regal head.

"What is so urgent, Commander Dofine?" Gunray asked.

"Viceroy, it is my sad duty to report that the *Revenue* has been seized by members of the Nebula Front. The cargo of lommite ore floats in space, and, even as we speak, an explosive device counts down the moments to the ship's destruction."

Realizing that he had forgotten to peel the timer from the back of his hand, Dofine retracted his hand into the loose sleeve of his robe.

"So Captain Cohl strikes again," Gunray said.

"Yes, Viceroy. But I bring news of an even more distressing nature." Dofine glanced around him, in the hope that Lagard was out of earshot, but, of course, he wasn't. "The cache of aurodium ingots," he said at last. "Cohl somehow knew about it. I had no recourse but to turn it over to him."

Expecting rebuke or worse, Dofine hung his head in shame as he trailed the mechno-chair. But the viceroy surprised him.

"The lives of you and your crew were at stake."

"Just so, Excellency."

"Then stand tall, Commander Dofine," Gunray said. "For what has happened today may well prove a boon for the Trade Federation, and a blessing for all Neimoidians."

"A boon, Viceroy?"

Gunray nodded. "I order you to assume command of the *Acquisitor*. Recall the starfighters and withdraw the freighter from combat."

"Cohl is headed back to the freighter," Obi-Wan said from the controls of the Judicial Department starfighter. "Could he have tricked the freighter into abandoning its cargo, even though it wasn't in jeopardy?"

"I doubt it," Qui-Gon said. He pressed his face close to the Lancet's transparisteel canopy. "All of Cohl's support ships—even the corvette—are distancing themselves from the *Revenue*."

"It's true, Master. Even the *Acquisitor* is under way."

"Then we're safe in concluding that the freighter is

marked for destruction. And yet, Captain Cohl is speeding toward it."

"As we are, Master," Obi-Wan thought to point out.

"What could Cohl have in mind?" Qui-Gon asked himself aloud. "He's not a man to undertake desperate acts, Obi-Wan, let alone suicidal ones."

"The shuttle isn't decelerating or changing course. Cohl is shooting straight for the starboard hangar arm."

"Just where we started."

Obi-Wan's brow began to furrow in concern. "Master, we're getting awfully close. If the freighter is truly marked for destruction . . ."

"I realize that, Padawan. Perhaps Captain Cohl is merely testing us."

Obi-Wan waited a long moment before he allowed concern to show in his voice. "Master?"

Qui-Gon watched the shuttle angle down toward the center of the circle that was the *Revenue*. Stretching out with his feelings, he did not like what he found.

"Abort the pursuit, Obi-Wan," he said suddenly. "Quickly!"

Obi-Wan fed full power to the Lancet's drives and pulled the yoke sharply toward him. At full boost, the ship climbed in a long loop away from the freighter.

Suddenly, the *Revenue* exploded. In the Lancet's cockpit, it was as if someone had draped a bright white curtain over the canopy. The small craft received a punch in the tail that sent it rocking forward, riding the crest of the detonation wave. Great hunks of molten durasteel streaked like comets to all sides. The Lancet shook to the breaking point, systems shorting out with showers of sparks, and displays showing nothing but noise before they darkened.

Glancing over his shoulder, Obi-Wan watched the *Revenue* burst into sections, the massive hangar arms making brief, fist-first contact, then rolling off to opposite sides, as two loosed crescents. The centersphere and bridge tower spun away from the destroyed acceleration compensator stalk and what was left of the ship's trio of gaping exhaust ports.

Some distance away the *Acquisitor* was moving for the safety of Dorvalla's dark side. Cohl's corvette and two of the support starfighters streaked away from the planet and made the jump to hyperspace.

"Dorvalla is either about to gain a moonlet or fall victim to a devastating meteor," Obi-Wan said when he could.

"I fear the latter," Qui-Gon said. "Contact Coruscant. Inform the Reconciliation Council that Dorvalla needs immediate emergency relief."

"I'll try, Master." Obi-Wan began to flip switches on the console, hoping that at least some of the communications systems had survived the electronic storm that had accompanied the explosion.

"Is there any sign of Cohl's shuttle?"

Obi-Wan glanced at the display screen. "No signal from the tracking device."

Qui-Gon didn't reply.

"Master, I know Cohl hated the Trade Federation. But could he have cared so little about his own life?"

Qui-Gon took a long moment to respond. "What are the sixth and seventh Rules of Engagement, Padawan?"

Obi-Wan tried to recall them. "The sixth is, Understand the dark and light in all things."

"That is the fifth rule."

Obi-Wan thought again. "Exercise caution, even in trivial matters."

"That is the eighth."

"Learn to see accurately."

"Yes," Qui-Gon said, "that is the sixth. And the seventh?"

Obi-Wan shook his head. "I'm sorry, Master. I cannot recall it."

"Open your eyes to what is not evident."

Obi-Wan considered it. "Then this isn't the end of it."

"Hardly, young Padawan. I sense instead a menacing beginning."

CORUSCANT

The four walls of Finis Valorum's office, at the summit of the governmental district's stateliest if not most statuesque edifice, were made of transparisteel, paneled by structural members into a continuous band of regular and inverted triangles.

The city-planet that was Coruscant—"Scintillant Orb," "Jewel of the Core," choked heart of the Galactic Republic—spread to all sides in a welter of lustrous domes, knife-edged spires, and terraced superstructures that climbed to the sky. The taller buildings resembled outsize rocketships that had never left their launch pads, or the wind-eroded lava tors of long-dead volcanoes. Some of the domes were flattened hemispheres perched on cylindrical bases, while others had the look of shallow, hand-thrown ceramic bowls with finialed lids.

Striations of magnetically guided sky traffic moved swiftly above the cityscape—streams of transports, air buses, taxis, and limousines, coursing between the tall spires and over the measureless chasms like schools of exotic fish. Instead of feeding, however, they were the feeders, distributing the galaxy's wealth among the greedy trillion to whom Coruscant was home.

As often as Valorum had beheld the view—which was to say, nearly every day of his now seven years as Supreme Chancellor of the Republic—he had yet to grow indifferent to the spectacle of Coruscant. As worlds went, it was neither large nor especially rugged, but history had transformed it into a uniquely vertical place, a vertical experience more common to ocean than atmospheric life.

Valorum's principal office was located in the lower level of the Galactic Senate dome, but he was generally so swamped by requests and business there that he reserved this lofty perch for meetings of a more private nature.

Pale hands clasped at his back, he stood at the bank of transparisteel windows that faced the dawn, though daybreak was hours behind him. He wore a magenta tunic that was high collared and double-breasted, with matching trousers and a wide cummerbund. Southern light, polarized by the transparisteel panels, flooded the room. But Valorum's sole guest had taken a seat well out of the light's reach.

"I fear, Supreme Chancellor, that we face a monumental challenge," Senator Palpatine was saying from the shadows. "Frayed at its far-flung borders and hollowed at its very heart by corruption, the Republic is in grave danger of unraveling. Order is needed, directives that will restore balance. Even the most desperate remedies should not be overlooked."

Although such opinions had become the common sentiment, Palpatine's words pierced Valorum like a sword. The fact that he knew them to be true made them all the more difficult to hear. He turned his back to the view and returned to his desk, where he sat heavily into his padded chair.

Aging with distinction, Valorum had a receding cap of shorn silver hair, pouches under piercing blue eyes, and dark, bushy brows. His stern features and deep voice belied a compassionate spirit and questing intellect. But as the latest in the line of a political dynasty that stretched back thousands of years—a dynasty many thought weakened by its uncommon longevity—he had never been fully successful at overcoming an innate patrician aloofness.

"Where have we gone wrong?" he asked in a firm but sad voice. "How did we manage to miss the portents along the way?"

Palpatine showed him an understanding look. "The fault is not in ourselves, Supreme Chancellor. The fault lies in the outlying star systems, and the civil strife iniquity has engendered there." His voice was carefully modulated, occasionally world-weary, seemingly immune to anger or alarm. "This most recent situation at Dorvalla, for example."

Valorum nodded soberly. "The Judicial Department has requested that I meet with them later today, so they can brief me on the latest developments."

"Perhaps I could save you the trouble, Supreme Chancellor. As least in terms of what I've been hearing in the senate."

"Rumor or facts?"

"A bit of both, I suspect. The senate is filled with delegates who interpret matters as they will, regardless of facts." Palpatine paused, as if to gather his thoughts.

Prominent in a kind if somewhat doughy face were his heavy-lidded, watery blue eyes and rudder of a nose. Red hair that had lost its youth he wore in the provincial style of the outlying systems: combed back from his high forehead but left thick and long behind his low-set ears. In dress, too, he demonstrated singular allegiance to his home system, favoring embroidered tunics with V-shaped double collars and outmoded cloaks of quilted fabric.

A sectorial senator representing the outlying world of Naboo, along with thirty-six other inhabited planets, Palpatine had earned a reputation for integrity and frankness that had set him high in the hearts of many of his senatorial peers. As he had made clear to Valorum in numerous meetings, both public and private, he was more interested in doing whatever needed to be done than in blind obedience to the rules and regulations that had made the senate such a tangle of procedures.

"As the Judicial Department is certain to tell you," he began at last, "the mercenaries who assaulted and destroyed the Trade Federation vessel *Revenue* were in the employ of the Nebula Front terrorist group. It seems likely that they gained access to the freighter with the complicity of dockworkers at Dorvalla. How the Nebula Front learned that the freighter was carrying a fortune in aurodium ingots has yet to be established. But clearly the Nebula Front planned to use the aurodium to finance additional acts of terrorism directed against the Trade Federation, and perhaps against Republic colonies in the Outer Rim."

"Planned?" Valorum said.

"All indications are that Captain Cohl and his team of assassins perished in the explosion that destroyed the *Revenue*. But the incident has had wide-ranging repercussions, nevertheless."

"I'm well aware of some of those," Valorum said, with a note of disgust. "As a result of continuing raids and harassment, the Trade Federation plans to demand Republic intervention, or, failing that, senate approval to further augment their droid contingent."

Palpatine made his lips a thin line and nodded. "I must

confess, Supreme Chancellor, that my first instinct was to refuse their requests out of hand. The Trade Federation is already too powerful—in wealth and in military might. However, I've since reassessed my position."

Valorum regarded him with interest. "I'd appreciate hearing your thoughts."

"Well, to begin with, the Trade Federation is made up of entrepreneurs, not warriors. The Neimoidians, especially, are cowards in any theater other than commerce. So granting them permission to enlarge their droid defenses—slightly, at any rate—doesn't concern me unduly. More important, there may be some advantage to doing so."

Valorum interlocked his fingers and leaned forward. "What possible advantage?"

Palpatine took a breath. "In exchange for honoring their requests for intervention and additional defenses, the senate would be in a position to demand that all trade in the outlying systems would henceforth be subject to Republic taxation."

Valorum sat back in his chair, clearly disappointed. "We've been through all this before, Senator. You and I both know that a majority of the senate has no interest in what happens in the outer systems, much less in the free trade zones. But they do care about what happens to the Trade Federation."

"Yes, because the shimmersilk pockets of many a senatorial robe are being lined with graft from the Neimoidians."

Valorum snorted. "Self-indulgence is the order of the day."

"Undeniably so, Supreme Chancellor," Palpatine said tolerantly. "But that, in itself, is no reason to allow the practice to continue."

"Of course not," Valorum said. "For both my terms of office I have sought to end the corruption that plagues the senate, and to unravel the knot of policies and procedures that thwart us. We enact legislation, only to find that we cannot implement it. The committees proliferate like viruses, without leadership. No fewer than twenty committees are needed just to determine the decor of the senate corridors.

"The Trade Federation has prospered by taking advantage of the very bureaucracy we've created. Grievances brought against the Federation languish in the courts, while commissions belabor each and every aspect. It's little wonder that Dorvalla and many of the worlds along the Rimma Trade Route support terrorist groups like the Nebula Front.

"But taxation isn't likely to solve anything. In fact, such a move could prompt the Trade Federation to abandon the outlying systems entirely, in favor of more lucrative markets closer to the Core."

"Thus depriving Coruscant and its neighbors of important outer system resources and luxury goods," Palpatine interjected, seemingly by rote. "Certainly the Neimoidians will see taxation as a betrayal, if for no other reason than the Trade Federation blazed many of the hyperspace routes that link the Core to the outlying systems. Regardless, this could be the opportunity many of us have waited for—the chance to exercise senate control over those very trade routes."

Valorum mulled it over briefly. "It could be political suicide."

"Oh, I'm well aware of that, Supreme Chancellor. Proponents of taxation would suffer merciless attacks from the Commerce Guild, the Techno Union, and the rest of the shipping conglomerates awarded franchises to operate in the free trade zones. But it is the appropriate measure."

Valorum shook his head slowly, then got to his feet and moved to the windows. "Nothing would cheer me more than getting the upper hand on the Trade Federation."

"Then now is the time to act," Palpatine said.

Valorum kept his gaze fixed on the distant towers. "I could count on your support?"

Palpatine rose and joined him at the view.

"Let me be frank about that. My position as representative of an outlying sector places me in an awkward situation. Make no mistake about it, Supreme Chancellor, I stand with you in advocating central control and taxation. But Naboo and other outlying systems will undoubtedly be forced to assume the burden of taxation by paying more for Trade Federation services." He paused briefly. "I would be compelled to act with utmost circumspection."

Valorum merely nodded.

"That much said," Palpatine was quick to add, "rest assured that I would do all in my power to rally senate support for taxation."

Valorum turned slightly in Palpatine's direction and smiled lightly. "As always, I'm grateful for your counsel, Senator. Particularly now, what with troubles erupting in your home system."

Palpatine sighed with purpose. "Sadly, King Veruna finds himself enmeshed in a scandal. While he and I have never seen eye to eye with regard to expanding Naboo's influence in the Republic, I am concerned for him, for his predicament has not only cast a pall over Naboo, but also over many neighboring worlds."

Valorum clasped his hands behind his back and paced to the center of the spacious room. When he swung to face Palpatine, his expression made clear that his thoughts had returned to issues of wider concern.

"Is it conceivable that the Trade Federation would accept taxation in exchange for a loosening of the defense restraints we have placed them under?"

Palpatine steepled his long fingers and brought them to his chin. "Merchandise—of whatever nature—is precious to the Neimoidians. The continuing assaults on their vessels by pirates and terrorists have made them desperate. They will rail against taxation, but in the end they will tolerate it. Our only other option would be to take direct action against the groups that are harassing them, and I know that you're opposed to doing that."

Valorum confirmed it with a determined nod. "The Republic hasn't had a standing military in generations, and I certainly won't be the person to reinstate one. Coruscant must remain a place where groups can come together to find peaceful solutions to conflicts."

He took a breath. "A better course would be to allow the Trade Federation adequate protection to defend itself against acts of terrorism. After all, the Judicial Department can't very well suggest the Jedi dedicate themselves to solving the Neimoidians' problems."

"No," Palpatine said. "The judicials and the Jedi Knights have more important matters to attend to than keeping the space lanes safe for commerce."

"At least some constants remain," Valorum mused. "Just think where we might be without the Jedi."

"I can only imagine."

Valorum advanced a few steps and laid his hands on Palpatine's shoulders. "You're a good friend, Senator."

Palpatine returned the gesture. "My interests are the interests of the Republic, Supreme Chancellor."

Sheathed from pole to pole in duracrete, plasteel, and a thousand other impervious materials, Coruscant seemed invulnerable to the vagaries of time or assaults by any would-be agents of entropy.

It was said that a person could live out his entire life on Coruscant without once leaving the building he called home. And that even if someone devoted his life to exploring as much of Coruscant as possible, he would scarcely be able to take in a few square kilometers; that he would be better off trying to visit all the far-flung worlds of the Republic. The planet's original surface was so long forgotten and so seldom visited that it had become an underworld of mythic dimension, whose denizens actually boasted of the fact that their subterranean realm hadn't seen the sun in twenty-five thousand standard years.

Closer to the sky, however, where the air was continually scrubbed and giant mirrors lit the floor of shallower canyons, wealth and privilege ruled. Here, kilometers above the murky depths, resided those who fashioned their own rarified atmospheres; who moved about by private skylimo, and watched the diffuse sun set blazing red around the curve of the planet; and who ventured below the two-kilometer level only to conduct transactions of a sinister sort, or to visit the statuary-studded squares that fronted those landmark structures whose sublime architecture hadn't been razed, buried, or walled in by mediocrity.

One such landmark was the Jedi Temple.

A kilometer-high truncated pyramid crowned by five elegant towers, it soared above its surroundings, purposefully isolated from the babble of Coruscant's overlapping electromagnetic fields, and holding forth against the blight of modernization. Below it stretched a plain of rooftops, skybridges, and aerial thoroughfares that had conspired to create a mosaic of sumptuous geometries—colossal spirals and concentricities, crosses and triangles, quilts and diamonds—great mandalas aimed at the stars, or perhaps the temporal complements of the constellations to be found there.

At once, though, there was something comforting and forbidding about the Temple. For while it was a constant reminder of an older, less complicated world, the Temple was also somewhat austere and unapproachable, off-limits to tourists or any whose desire to visit was inspired by mere curiosity.

The design of the Temple was said to be symbolic of the Padawan's path to enlightenment—to unity with the Force, through fealty to the Jedi Codes. But the design artfully concealed a secondary and more practical purpose, in that the quincunx of towers—four oriented to the cardinal directions, with a taller one rising from the center—were whiskered with antennae and transmitters that kept the Jedi abreast of circumstances and crises throughout the galaxy they served.

Thus had contemplation and social responsibility been given equal voice.

Nowhere in the Temple was that wedding of purposes more evident than in the elevated chamber of the Reconciliation Council. Like the High Council Chamber, at the summit of an adjacent tower, the room was circular, with an arched ceiling and tall windows all around. But, less formal, it lacked the ring of seats occupied only by the twelve members of the High Council, who presided over matters of momentous concern.

Qui-Gon Jinn had been back on Coruscant for three standard days before the Reconciliation Council had asked him to appear before it. During that time, he had done little more than meditate, peruse ancient texts, pace the Temple's dimly lighted hallways, or engage in lightsaber training sessions with other Jedi Knights and Padawans.

Through acquaintances employed in the Galactic Senate, he had been apprised of the Trade Federation's requests for Republic intervention in repressing acts of terrorism, and for permission to augment their droid defenses, in the face of continuing harassment. Although those requests were nothing new, Qui-Gon had been surprised to learn of the Trade Federation's claim that Captain Cohl, in addition to destroying the *Revenue*, had made off with a secret cache of aurodium ingots, rumored to be worth billions of credits.

The revelation was much on his mind as he went before the members of the Reconciliation Council, unaware that they, too, were interested in discussing the incident at Dorvalla.

Many held the opinion that Qui-Gon would have been seated on the council, if not for his penchant for bending the rules and following his own instincts—even when those instincts conflicted with the combined wisdom of the council members. This had not endeared him to his loftier peers. In fact, rather than treat him like a peer, they viewed his unwillingness to amend his ways and accept a seat on the council as a further sign of his incorrigibility.

The Reconciliation Council was made up of five members—though rarely the same five—and today there were only four on hand: Jedi Masters Plo Koon, Oppo Rancisis, Adi Gallia, and Yoda.

Qui-Gon fielded their questions from the center of the room, where he would have been permitted to sit but had elected to stand.

"How knew you, Qui-Gon, of Captain Cohl's designs on the *Revenue*, eh?" Yoda asked as he paced the polished-stone floor, supported by his gimer stick cane.

"I have a contact in the Nebula Front," Qui-Gon replied.

Yoda stopped moving to regard him. "A contact, you say?"

"A Bith," Qui-Gon said. "He made contact with me on Malastare, and later apprised me of Cohl's plan to attack the *Revenue* at Dorvalla. On Dorvalla, I was able to learn that Cohl had altered a cargo pod to suit his ends. Obi-Wan and I did the same."

Yoda shook his head back and forth in seeming astonishment. "News, this is. One of Qui-Gon's many surprises."

An ancient and diminutive alien—a patriarch, of sorts—Yoda had an almost human face, with large knowing eyes, a small nose, and a thin-lipped mouth. But most similarities to the human species ended there, for he was green from hairless crown to triple-digited feet, and his ears were large and pointed, extending from the sides of his wizened head like small wings.

A senior member of the High Council, he was something of a trickster, who preferred to teach by means of thought-puzzles and conundrums, rather than by lecture and recitation.

Yoda and Qui-Gon had a long-standing relationship, but Yoda was one of those who sometimes took issue with Qui-Gon's focus on the living Force over the unifying Force. As Qui-Gon explained it, he was simply built that way. Even in lightsaber training, he rarely entered into a match with a strategy in mind. Instead he allowed himself to improvise, and to alter his technique according to the demands of the moment—even when the longer view might have helped him.

"Qui-Gon," Adi Gallia said, "we were given to understand that the Nebula Front had hired Captain Cohl. What was your contact's purpose in sabotaging an operation the Nebula Front itself had sanctioned?"

She was a young and handsome human woman from Corellia, with exotic eyes, a long slender neck, and full lips. Tall and dark-complexioned, she wore a tight-fitting skullcap, from which dangled eight tails, resembling seed pods.

Qui-Gon turned to her. "The operation was not sanctioned. That's why my Padawan and I were there."

Yoda lifted his gimer stick to point at Qui-Gon. "Explain this, you must."

Qui-Gon folded his thick arms across his chest. "The Nebula Front speaks for many worlds in the Mid and Outer Rims, which contest the prohibitive practices and strong-arm tactics of the Trade Federation. Some of those worlds were originally colonized by species who fled the civilized repression of the Core. Fiercely independent, they want no part of the Republic. And yet, in order to trade, they are forced to do business with consortiums like the Federation. Worlds that have attempted to ship with other enterprises have found themselves cut off from trade entirely."

"The Nebula Front may have laudable goals, but their methods are ruthless," Oppo Rancisis commented, breaking a brief silence.

A scion of royalty from Thisspias, he had red-rimmed eyes and a tiny mouth in a large head that was otherwise covered entirely by dense white hair—piled high at the crown, and extending from his hidden chin in a long beard.

"Go on, Qui-Gon," Plo Koon told him from beneath the mask he was forced to wear in oxygen-rich environments. Like Rancisis, Koon had a keen mind for military strategy.

Qui-Gon tipped his head in a bow of acknowledgment. "Without trying to justify the actions of the Nebula Front, I will say that they tried to reason with the Trade Federation before turning to acts of terrorism. Where they might have financed their operations by smuggling spice for the Hutts, they refused to deal with any species that condoned slavery. Even when they finally did turn to violence, they restricted their actions to interfering with Trade Federation shipments or delaying their vessels whenever possible."

"Destroying a freighter is certainly one way to delay it," Rancisis said.

Qui-Gon glanced at him. "Cohl's actions were something new."

"Then what drove the Nebula Front to escalate the violence?" Gallia asked.

Qui-Gon sensed that she was asking as much for the sake of the council as for Supreme Chancellor Valorum, with whom she had close ties. "My contact claims that the Nebula Front has grown a radical wing, and it is those militants who contracted with Captain Cohl. The Bith and many others were opposed to employing mercenaries, but the militants have assumed command of the organization."

Yoda rubbed his chin in thought. "After the aurodium ingots, were they not?"

Qui-Gon shook his head. "Frankly, Master, I'm not sure if I accept the Federation's claim."

"You have reason to doubt it?" Koon asked.

"It's a question of method. The Trade Federation concedes a preoccupation with safeguarding their cargos. Why, then, would they entrust a shipment of aurodium to a poorly defended freighter like the *Revenue*, when the more heavily armed *Acquisitor* was only a star system away?"

"A point, he has," Yoda said.

"I consider the reason obvious," Rancisis disagreed. "The Trade Federation falsely assumed that no one would suspect the *Revenue* of harboring such wealth."

"The question is of little consequence," Gallia said. "The use of mercenaries like Cohl signals the beginning of a coordinated campaign to counter the Trade Federation's droid defenses by force, and ultimately to overthrow Trade Federation influence in the outlying systems."

"Fortunately, Captain Cohl is no longer a concern," Plo Koon remarked.

Yoda adopted a wide-eyed look. "Concern Qui-Gon, Cohl does."

Qui-Gon felt the council's close scrutiny. "I don't believe that he perished with the freighter," he said at last.

"You were there, were you not?" Rancisis asked.

"Saw it with his own eyes, he did," Yoda said, with a twinkle in his eye.

Qui-Gon compressed his lips. "Cohl planned for every eventuality. He wouldn't have piloted his craft into an explosion just to evade pursuit."

"Then why didn't you capture him as you hoped to do?" Rancisis asked.

Qui-Gon planted his hands on his hips, thumbs pointed behind him. "As Master Gallia has said, Cohl is only the beginning. My Padawan and I attached a tracking device to Cohl's ship, in the hope of tracking it to the Nebula Front's current base, which could be on one of the Rimma worlds that support the terrorists. After the explosion, the tracker failed to return a signal."

Gallia stared at him for a moment. "You searched for Cohl, Qui-Gon?"

"Obi-Wan and I found no signs of his shuttle. For all we know, he rode the leading edge of the explosion right down Dorvalla's gravity well."

"You have informed the Judicial Department of your suspicions?" Rancisis asked.

"Some of Cohl's better-known haunts are under surveillance," Gallia answered for Qui-Gon.

Koon left his chair to stand alongside Qui-Gon. "Captain Cohl may be the best of his ilk, but there are many more like him, just as heartless, just as rapacious. The Nebula Front militants will have no trouble finding eager replacements."

Rancisis nodded gravely. "This is something we need to watch closely."

Yoda crossed the room, shaking his head back and forth. "Avoid a conflict with the Nebula Front, we must. Speak for many, they do. Compromise us, they will."

"I agree," Rancisis said. "We can't afford to take sides."

"But we have to take sides," Qui-Gon blurted. "I'm not an ally of the Trade Federation. But acts of terrorism by the Nebula Front won't be limited to freighters. Innocent beings will be endangered."

Everyone fell silent, except for Yoda.

"A true Knight, Qui-Gon is," he said, with a note of gentle rebuke. "Forever on his own quest."

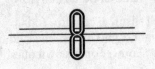

A small, humid world disdained by an aging sun, Neimoidia was a place to be avoided—even by Neimoidians. Instead of profiting from its relative proximity to self-reliant Corellia and industrialized Kuat, Neimoidia had actually suffered for its placement, having been passed over, time and again, by the fraternity of Core worlds. That heritage of being shunned had informed Neimoidian society.

Scorn had imparted to the species a conviction that progress came to only those who proved themselves not merely capable but predatory. Reaching the top of the food chain required that the bodies of the weak be used as stepping-stones. Once the summit was attained, it was held by seizing whatever resources were available and preventing others from grabbing them.

Those tenets were frequently offered as explanation as to how and why the Neimoidians had risen so rapidly to the fore of the Trade Federation, whose signature was callousness.

Neimoidia's most able typically left home at an early

age, opting for lives of itinerant trading aboard the vessels of the Trade Federation fleet. As a result, Neimoidia was scarcely populated by the weakest of the species, who tended to the planet's vast insect hives, fungus farms, and beetle hatcheries.

Viceroy Nute Gunray shared with his fellow self-exiles a peculiar distaste for his homeworld. But circumstance had demanded that he meet with the members of his Inner Circle in a location that guaranteed protection from the prying eyes of Coruscant. And in that sense, Neimoidia provided the best possible sanctuary.

The problem inherent in returning home was that one couldn't escape recalling—on some level of cellular memory—the seven formative years Neimoidians spent as puny, pale, wriggling grubs, in competition with every other grub for survival and the chance to mature into red-eyed, noseless, fish-lipped, and decidedly distrustful adults.

Adults, like Gunray, at any rate, who swathed their bodies in the finest raiment credits could buy, and who rarely, if ever, looked back.

The viceroy gave himself over to momentary reflection on such matters while the mechno-chair carried him to the meeting place, through cavernous halls of finely cut stone that mimicked the early hives, and past row after row of protocol droids standing at attention on both sides.

His ultimate destination was a dark, dank grotto, the antithesis of the gleaming bridges of Trade Federation freighters. On display were several examples of exotic flora left to fend for themselves in capturing what moisture they could from the stuffy air. The arching walls were graced with the twin emblems of piety and power: the Spherical Flame and the garhai—the armored fish that symbolized obedience and dedication to enlightened leadership.

Gunray's key advisers were waiting: Deputy Viceroy Hath Monchar and legal counsel Rune Haako. Each affected a black headpiece appropriate to his status. Monchar's was a triple-crested crown, similar to but smaller than the one Gunray wore; Haako's was an elaborate cowl, with two horns in front, and a tall, rounded back.

The two advisers made deferential gestures to Gunray as the mechno-chair eased him onto his feet.

"Welcome, Viceroy," Haako said, approaching him stooped and limping, his left arm crooked by his side. "We hope you have not come in vain." Hollow-cheeked and somewhat spidery, he had a deeply lined face, bags under his eyes, and puckered flesh on his chin and thin neck.

Gunray made a harsh gesture of dismissal. "He said he would come. That is enough for me."

"For you," Monchar muttered.

Gunray glared at his deputy. "Events transpired just as he promised they would. Cohl's mercenaries attacked, and the *Revenue* was destroyed."

"And this is a reason to rejoice?" Haako asked, his prominent voice box bobbing. "This plan of yours has cost the Trade Federation a class-I freighter and billions in aurodium."

Gunray's nictitating membranes betrayed his seeming self-possession. He blinked repeatedly, then quickly regained his composure.

"One ship and a treasure box. If our benefactor really is who he claims to be, such losses are meaningless."

Haako raised a palsied hand. "And *if* he is, he is a thing to fear, not to delight. And how can we be certain, in any case? What proof does he offer, Viceroy? He contacts you out of the ether, only by hologram. He can claim to be anyone."

Gunray worked his jutting jaw. "Who would be brain-dead enough to make such a claim without being able to support it?"

He brought forth a portable holoprojector and set it down on a table.

When the Dark Lord of the Sith had first contacted him, months earlier, he seemed to know everything about Nute Gunray and his rise to personal power. How Gunray had testified to the Trade Federation Directorate against Pulsar Supertanker—at the time a participatory company within the conglomerate—accusing Pulsar of "malicious disregard for profit" and "charitable donations lacking discernible reward."

Indeed, it appeared to have been that testimony and similar declarations of avidity that had first attracted the notice of Darth Sidious.

Even so, Gunray had remained as skeptical then as his advisers were now, despite demonstrations by Darth Sidious of his wide-ranging influence and sway. Secretly, Sidious had arranged for several key resource worlds to join the Trade Federation as signatory members, abdicating their representation in the Galactic Senate in exchange for lucrative trade opportunities, and, where possible, protection from smuggling concerns and pirates. And at each turn Sidious had made the procurements appear the doing of Gunray, thus helping to consolidate Gunray's increasing authority and assuring his appointment to the directorate.

As to whether Sidious's influence truly owed to Sith powers, Gunray could not say, nor did he care to know, based on what little he knew of the Sith—an ancient, perhaps legendary order of black mages, absent from the galaxy for the past thousand years.

Some referred to the Sith as the dark side of the Jedi; others claimed that it was the Jedi who had ended the reign of the Sith, in a war that had pitted dark and light against each other. Still others said the Sith, greedy for power, killed one another. But Gunray knew nothing of the truth of these things, and he hoped to keep it that way.

He stared pointedly at the holoprojector; the appointed moment was close at hand.

Gunray hadn't finished the thought when the head and shoulders of a cloaked apparition rose from the device, the cowl of his dark garment pulled down over his eyes, revealing a deeply furrowed chin and a jowly, aged face. An elaborate broach closed the cloak at the neck.

When the figure spoke, his voice was a prolonged rasp.

"I see, Viceroy, that you have assembled your underlings, as I asked," Darth Sidious began.

Gunray knew that the word *underlings* wasn't going to find favor among Monchar and Haako. Though there was little he could do about that, he thought it best at least to attempt to rectify matters.

"My advisors, Lord Sidious."

Sidious's face betrayed nothing. "Of course—your advisors." He paused for a moment, as if probing the incalculable distance that separated them. "I perceive an atmosphere of misgiving, Viceroy. Has the aftermath of our plan failed to please you?"

"No, not at all, Lord Sidious," Gunray stammered. "It's only that the loss of the freighter and the aurodium ingots is a matter of concern to some." He glanced with purpose at his two counselors.

"The others lack your grasp of the larger purpose, Viceroy," Sidious said with a note of disdain. "Perhaps we need to reacquaint them with our intent to stir sympathy for the Trade Federation in the senate. That is why we informed the Nebula Front militants of the shipment of aurodium. The loss of the ingots will further our cause. Soon you will have the politicians and bureaucrats eating out of your hands, and then the Trade Federation will at last have the droid army it needs. Baktoid, Haor Chall Engineering, and the Colicoids are waiting to fill your orders."

Gunray began to fidget. "Army, Lord Sidious?"

"The riches of the Outer Rim await those with the courage to grab them."

Gunray gulped. "But, Lord Sidious, perhaps the time isn't right to take such actions—"

"Not right? It is your *destiny*. With a droid army to support you, who would dare question Neimoidia's authority to rule the space lanes?"

"We would welcome the ability to defend ourselves against pirates and agitators," Rune Haako risked saying. "But we don't wish to break the terms of our trade treaty with the Republic. Not when the price of a droid army is taxation of the free trade zones."

"So you've heard about Chancellor Valorum's intentions," Sidious said.

"Only that he is likely to give his full weight to the proposal," Gunray said.

Sidious nodded. "Rest assured, Viceroy, Supreme Chancellor Valorum is our strongest ally in the senate."

"Lord Sidious has some influence in the senate?" Haako asked carefully.

But Sidious was too clever to take the bait.

"You will come to learn that there are many that do my bidding," he said. "They understand, as you will understand, that they serve themselves best by serving me."

Haako and Monchar traded quick looks.

"The ruling members of the Trade Federation Directorate are not likely to sanction spending hard-earned profits on droids," Monchar said. "As it is, they consider us Neimoidians to be unnecessarily suspicious."

"I am well aware of the opinions of your partners," Sidious rasped. "Be advised that foolish friends are no better than enemies."

"Nevertheless, they will oppose this arrangement."

"Then we will just have to find some way to convince them."

"He doesn't mean to sound unappreciative, Lord Sidious," Gunray apologized. "It's simply that . . . It's simply that we don't really know who you are, and what you are capable of providing. You could be a powerful Jedi, hoping to entrap us."

"A *Jedi*," Sidious said. "Now you do mock me. But you will see that I am a forgiving master. As to your concerns about my identity—my *heritage*, let us say—my actions will speak for me."

The Neimoidians exchanged perplexed looks. "What about the Jedi?" Haako asked. "They won't simply stand by."

"The Jedi will do only what the senate bids them to do," Sidious said. "You are woefully mistaken if you believe they would jeopardize their lofty real estate on Coruscant to challenge the Trade Federation without Senate approval."

Gunray glanced meaningfully at his advisors before replying. "We place ourselves in your hands, Lord Sidious."

Sidious almost smiled. "I thought you might see things my way, Viceroy. I know that you will not fail me in the future."

The apparition vanished as abruptly as it arrived, leaving the three Neimoidians to ponder the nature of the shadowy alliance they had just entered into.

Night was a stranger to Coruscant. The sun set as ever, but so ambient was the light from the cityscape's forest of skyscraping towers that true darkness was a thing that prowled only the deepest canyons, or was summoned with purpose by those residents who could afford blackout transparisteel. From space, the planet's dark side sparkled like a finely wrought ornament strung with bioluminescent life-forms, such as might be displayed in an heirloom cabinet or a museum devoted to folk art.

The stars never appeared in the sky, except to those who resided in the tallest buildings. But stars of a different sort turned up nightly at Coruscant's celebrated entertainment complexes—singers, performers, artists, and politicians. As a rule more faddish than the rest, the latter group had taken lately to attending the opera, following the lead of Supreme Chancellor Valorum, whose renowned family had been patrons of the arts for as long as anyone could remember.

In a galaxy boasting millions of species and a thousand times as many worlds, cultural arts were never in short supply. At any given moment a performance was debuting somewhere on Coruscant. But few companies or troupes of any sort had the privilege of performing at the Coruscant Opera.

The building was a marvel of pre-Republic baroque, all frosting and embellishment, with an old-fashioned orchestra pit, tiered seating, and private balconies in the time-honored design. As a nod to Coruscant's citizens, there was even a warren of lower-level galleries where common folks could view the performance via real-time hologram and pretend to be hobnobbing with celebrities seated overhead.

The opera of the moment was *The Brief Reign of Future Wraiths*, a production that had originated on Corellia, but was being performed by a company of Bith, who had been touring the opera world to world for the past twenty standard years.

A bipedal species with large rounded craniums, lidless black eyes, receding noses, and baggy epidermal folds beneath their jaws, Bith were native to the outlying world of Clak'dor VII, and were known to perceive sounds as humans perceived colors.

Considering that it was Finis Valorum's parents who had underwritten *Brief Reign* to begin with, it was only fitting that the supreme chancellor be on hand for the opera's long-awaited return to Coruscant. The mere fact that he would be attending had driven up the price of tickets and made them as difficult to procure as Adegan crystals. As a result, the building was more packed with luminaries than it had been in a long while.

As was customary, Valorum delayed his arrival, so as to ensure that he would be last to be seated. Restless for a glance at him, the audience came to its feet in prolonged applause as he stepped onto the elaborate balcony that had been reserved for Valorum family members for well over five hundred years.

Eschewing his usual surround of blue-caped and helmeted Senate Guards, Valorum was accompanied only by his administrative aide, Sei Taria—in matching burgundy septsilk—a petite young woman half his age, with oblique eyes and skin the color of burrmillet grain.

In true Coruscant manner, rumors began circulating even before Valorum took his seat. But the Supreme Chancellor was inured to innuendo, not merely as an effect of his aristocratic upbringing, but also because of the fact that nearly every sectorial senator—marital status notwithstanding—had made it their practice to appear in public with attractive young consorts.

Valorum waved graciously and inclined his head in a show of benign sufferance. Then, before sitting down, he directed a second bow to a private balcony directly across the amphitheater.

The dozen or so prosperous-looking patrons in the balcony Valorum singled out returned the bow, and remained standing until Sei Taria was also seated—no small feat for the owner of the box, Senator Orn Free Taa, who had grown so corpulent during his tenure on Coruscant that his bulk filled the space of what had once been three separate seats.

Cerulean, with pouty red lips and eyelids, Taa had a huge oval face and a double chin the size of a bantha's feed bag. He was a Twi'lek of Rutian descent; his lekku head-tails, engorged with fat, hung like sated snakes to his massive chest. His gaudy robe was the size of a tent. Prominently on display was his Lethan Twi'lek consort, nubile and high-cheekboned, her red body draped in bolts of pure shimmersilk.

A member of the Appropriations Committee, Taa was

a vocal opponent of Valorum, since his spice-producing homeworld of Ryloth had, time and again, been denied favored-world status.

Taa's guests in the box included Senators Toonbuck Toora, Passel Argente, Edcel Bar Gane, and Palpatine, along with two of Palpatine's personal aides, Kinman Doriana and Sate Pestage.

"Do you know why Valorum loves to attend the opera?" Taa asked in Basic, out of the corner of his huge mouth. "Because it's the only place on Coruscant where an entire audience will applaud him."

"And he does little more here than he does in the senate," Toora said. "He merely observes the protocols and feigns interest."

Fabulously wealthy, she was a hairy biped with a wide mouth, a triple-bearded chin, and beady eyes and a pug nose squeezed onto the bony ridge that capped her squat head.

"Valorum is toothless," Passel Argente chimed in. A sallow-complexioned humanoid affiliated with the Corporate Alliance, he wore a black turban and bib that revealed only his face and the swirling horn that emerged from the crown of his head. "At a time when we need vigor, direction, unity, Valorum insists on taking the tried-and-true route. The route guaranteed not to upset the status quo."

"Much to our enjoyment," Toora murmured.

"But a confidential bow," Taa said, as he was maneuvering into the chair that had been specially made to conform to his girth. "To what could we possibly owe the honor?"

Toora gestured in dismissal. "This nonsense about the Trade Federation's requests. Valorum needs all the support he can muster if he's to succeed in convincing us to enact taxation of the free trade zones."

"Then it is even more curious that he should acknowledge us," Taa remarked. He motioned broadly to other balconies. "There, all but in Valorum's lap, sit Senators Antilles, Horox Ryyder, Tendau Bendon . . . Any of them, more than worthy of a bow."

Taa raised his fat hand in a wave when the group in the box realized that they were being observed.

"Then the gesture must have been solely for Senator Palpatine," Toora remarked meaningfully. "From what I hear, our delegate from Naboo has the Supreme Chancellor's ear."

Taa turned to Palpatine. "Is that so, Senator?"

Palpatine smiled lightly. "Not in the manner you imagine, I can assure you. The Supreme Chancellor met with me to solicit my opinion as to how taxation might be received by the outlying systems. We spoke of little else. In any event, Valorum scarcely needs my support to see the proposal through. He is not as ineffectual as many seem to think."

"Nonsense," Taa said. "It will come down to partisanship—a contest between the factions of Bail Antilles, and those who allow Ainlee Teem to speak for them. As ever, the Core worlds will stand with Valorum; the near colonies, against."

"He's going to polarize the senate further," Edcel Bar Gane opined in a sibilant voice. Representing the world of Roona, Bar Gane had a bulbous head and eyes that narrowed and slanted upward at their outer corners.

Toora absorbed the remark without comment. Once more, she eyed Palpatine. "I'm curious, Senator. Just what did you tell Valorum, with regard to the impact of taxation on the outer systems?"

"Activate the balcony's noise cancellation feature, and I might be inclined to tell you," Palpatine said.

"Oh, do it, Taa," Toora enthused. "I so love intrigue."

Taa flipped a switch on the balcony railing, activating a containment field that effectively sealed the box from audio surveillance. But Palpatine didn't speak until Sate Pestage—a trim human with pointed features and thinning black hair—had double-checked that the field was indeed functioning.

Pestage's actions impressed Argente. "Is everyone on Naboo as careful as you are, Senator?"

Palpatine shrugged. "Consider it a personal flaw."

Argente nodded soberly. "I'll remember that."

"So tell us," Toora said, "is the Supreme Chancellor embarking on a dangerous course by taking on the Trade Federation?"

"The danger is that he sees only half the picture," Palpatine began. "Though he would be the first to deny it, Valorum is essentially a bureaucrat at heart, just as his ancestors were. He favors rules and procedure over direct action. He lacks judgment. The Valorum dynasty was largely responsible for granting the Trade Federation free rein decades ago. How do you think they accumulated their vast holdings? Certainly not by favoring the outer systems. But by making gainful deals with the InterGalactic Bank Clan and corporations like TaggeCo. That this latest crisis should revolve around the Nebula Front is especially ironic, since Valorum's father had an opportunity to eradicate the group, and he failed, chastising them rather than disbanding them."

"You surprise me, Senator," Toora said. "In a good way, I think. Do go on."

Palpatine crossed his legs and sat tall in his chair. "The Supreme Chancellor fails to grasp that the future of the Republic very much depends on what occurs in the Mid and Outer Rims. As corrupt as Coruscant has become, the real corrosion—the sort that can eventually eat away at the center—always begins on the edges. It progresses from the outside in.

"Unless Valorum does something to stay the tide, Coruscant itself will someday be a slave to those systems, unable to enact any legislation without their consent. Unless we placate them now, we'll be forced to bring them under central authority at some later date. They are the key to the survival of the Republic."

Taa huffed. "Unless I misread you, you're saying that the Trade Federation is our link with those systems—Coruscant's ambassador, if you will—and that therefore we can't afford to alienate the Neimoidians and the rest."

"You are misreading me," Palpatine said firmly. "The Trade Federation needs to be brought under control. Valorum is correct to push for taxation, because the Trade Federation already has too much influence in the outlying sectors. Desperate to conduct trade with the Core, hundreds of outer systems have joined the Federation as signatory members, yielding their rights to individual representation in the senate. At the moment, the Neimoidians and their partners lack enough votes to block taxation. But in a year, in two years, they could have adequate backing to overrule the senate at every opportunity."

"Then you'll stand with Valorum," Toora said. "You'll support taxation."

"Not yet," Palpatine said carefully. "He views taxation as a means of punishing the Trade Federation and, at the same time, of enriching Coruscant—an approach that will alienate not only the Trade Federation members, but also the outlying systems. Before I cast Naboo's support with one side or the other, I want to see how the votes stack up. Just now, those who hold the middle ground stand to reap the most. Those who see all sides clearly will be in the best position to guide the Republic through this critical transition. If Valorum has sufficient support without the backing of my sector, so much the better. But I won't flinch in my obligation to do what is ultimately best for the general good."

"Spoken like a future party whip," Taa said, with a guffaw.

"Indeed," Argente said, in all seriousness.

Toora appraised Palpatine openly. "A few more questions, if you wouldn't mind."

Palpatine gestured toward the stage. "While I'd be glad to discuss these matters at greater length, the performance is about to begin."

Outfitted in lackluster tunics and soft boots, the Jedi students stood in two opposing lines, two dozen lightsabers ignited in brilliant cast, raised in twice as many hands.

At a word from the lightsaber Master, the twelve students comprising one line took three backward steps in unison and set themselves in defensive postures—feet planted wide and lightsabers held straight out from their midsections.

Custom-built by each student, to suit hands of varying size and dexterousness, no two of the lightsabers were alike, though they did share some features in common: charging ports, blade projection plates, actuators, diatium power cells, and the rare and remarkable Adegan crystals that gave birth to the blade itself. There were few known materials in the galaxy that a lightsaber could not cut. Fully powered, and in the right hands, a lightsaber could cleave duracrete or burn its way slowly though a starship's durasteel blast doors.

At the next word from the Master, the second line set themselves in attack stances, giving their shoulders a quarter turn, lowering their center of gravity by bending slightly at the knees, and raising their lightsabers in two-fisted grips, as if to swat a pitched ball.

At the instructor's final word, the second line advanced in earnest. The students in the first line set their lightsabers to defend and, with choreographed precision, retreated purposefully as they allowed their opponents to hammer repeatedly at their elevated blades. When the defenders had been driven halfway across the room, the lightsaber Master called the exercise to a halt and had the groups reverse positions.

Now it was those who had defended who attacked, the blades of light thrumming and grating riotously against one another, auras merging, filling the air of the training room with blinding flashes of illumination.

Qui-Gon and Obi-Wan watched from an observation gallery set slightly above the room's padded floor, deep within the pyramid that was the Jedi Temple's towering base. The exercise had been going on all morning, but only a few of the students showed signs of fatigue.

"I can remember this like yesterday," Obi-Wan said.

Qui-Gon quirked a smile. "It's a good deal of yesterdays for me, Padawan."

Though separated by more than a score of years, they had both passed their youths in the Temple, as was the case with all Jedi, whether students, Padawans, Jedi Knights, or Masters. The Force revealed itself in infancy, and most potential Jedi were residents of the Temple by the age of six months, either discovered on Coruscant or distant worlds by full-fledged Jedi, or delivered to the Temple by family members. Tests were frequently used to establish the relative vitality of the Force residing in candidates, but those tests didn't necessarily forecast where a candidate might end up; whether he or she, human or alien, might take up the lightsaber in defense of peace and justice, or pass a lifetime of service in the Agricultural Corps, helping to feed the galaxy's poor or deprived.

"As often as I trained, I always worried that I lacked the temperament to become a Padawan, let alone a Jedi Knight," Obi-Wan added. "I fought harder than anyone to mask my self-doubt."

Qui-Gon glanced at him askance, his arms folded. "If you had fought a bit harder, Padawan, you surely would have remained in the Agricultural Corps. It was when you stopped trying so hard that you found your path."

"I couldn't keep my mind in the moment."

"And you still can't."

Twelve years earlier, Obi-Wan had been assigned to the Agricultural Corps on the planet Bandomeer, and it was there that he had formed a connection with Qui-Gon, whose previous Padawan had fallen to the dark side of the Force and left the Jedi Order. But despite the bond he and Qui-Gon had formed, there were times when he wondered if he had the makings of a Jedi Knight.

"How do I know that the Agricultural Corps wasn't my intended path, Master? Perhaps our meeting on Bandomeer was a fork in the path I shouldn't have taken."

Qui-Gon finally turned to him. "There are many paths to take, Obi-Wan. Not all of us are fortunate enough to find the one with heart, the path the Force has set before us. What do you find when you search your feelings about the choices you have made?"

"I feel that I've found the right path, Master."

"I agree." Qui-Gon clapped Obi-Wan on the shoulders, then smiled as he turned to regard the students. "Even so, I think you would have made a good field hand."

The students were kneeling in two rows, legs tucked underneath, with feet crossed behind them. The room was still, save for the sound of the lightsaber Master's bare feet adhering to the floor mat as he sauntered between the two rows, appraising each of his students.

A Twi'lek, with slender head-tails and a heavily muscled upper body, his name was Anoon Bondara, a duelist of unparalleled skill. Qui-Gon engaged him in matches at every opportunity. For a match with Bondara, no matter how brief, was more instructive than twenty contests against lesser opponents.

The lightsaber Master stopped in front of a female human student named Darsha Assant, who happened also to be his Padawan. Bondara squatted down on his haunches to regard her at eye level.

"What were you thinking when you attacked?"

"What was I thinking, Master?"

"What was in your thoughts? What was your intent?"

"Merely to be as forceful as possible, Master."

"You wanted to win."

"Not to win, Master. I wanted to strike impeccably."

Bondara made a face. "Rid yourself of thinking. Don't expect to win; don't expect to lose. Expect nothing."

Obi-Wan glanced at Qui-Gon. "Now where have I heard that before?"

Qui-Gon shushed him, without taking his eyes from Bondara, who was in motion once more.

"The lightsaber is not a weapon with which to vanquish foes or rivals," Bondara said. "With it, you destroy your own greed, anger, and folly. The forger and wielder of a lightsaber must live in such a manner as to represent the annihilation of anything that impedes the path of justice and peace." He stopped and glanced at everyone. "Do you understand?"

"Yes, Master," They replied in one voice.

Bondara clapped his hands together loudly. "No, you don't. You must learn to hold the lightsaber by loosening your grip on it. You must learn to advance rhythmically so that you will learn to produce formless rhythms. Do you understand?"

"Yes, Master," they replied.

"No, you don't." He scowled and sat down at the end of the rows. "I will tell you a story.

"A human, wrongly accused of a crime, was being transported by repulsorlift vehicle across the desert wastes of a remote world, to a prison, located even deeper in the wastes. Without warning, the vehicle experienced a malfunction directly over a pit that was, in fact, the huge and ravenous mouth of a creature that inhabited the wastes.

"The sudden malfunction catapulted the human's escorts down into the mucus-coated maw of the creature. The human was also thrown from his perch. But at the last instant he was able to grab on to the vehicle's landing strut. Not with hands, however—for they were shackled in stun cuffs behind him—but with his teeth.

"Shortly a caravan of travelers happened by. Lost and hungry, the travelers inquired to know the whereabouts of the closest settlement, so they might replenish their meager stores.

"The human found himself in a quandary. By failing to respond, he understood that he might be sentencing the lost travelers to certain death in the sand wastes. But merely by opening his mouth and uttering a word, he would be sentencing himself to certain death in the digestive tract of the sand creature."

Bondara paused. "Under such circumstances, what must the human do?"

The students knew in advance that they were not likely to hear the answer from Anoon Bondara.

Getting to his feet, the lightsaber Master added, "I will hear your responses tomorrow."

The students bowed at the waist and kept their foreheads to the mat until Bondara had left the room. Then they rose, eager to compare opinions of the training session, though not a one spoke of possible solutions to the instructor's thought-puzzle.

Qui-Gon tapped Obi-Wan on the shoulder. "Come, Padawan, there's someone I wish to speak with."

Obi-Wan trailed him down the steps and onto the soft floor. There, several Jedi Masters were conferring with their Padawans. Obi-Wan knew some of the Masters slightly, but the person Qui-Gon steered them toward was not someone he had ever met.

She was perhaps one of the most exotic women Obi-Wan had ever seen. Her eyes were oblique and widely spaced, with large blue irises that seemed to favor her upper lids. Her nose was broad and flat, and her skin was the color of fruitwood.

"Obi-Wan, I want you to meet Master Luminara Unduli."

"Master Jinn," the woman said, taken by surprise, and inclining her head in a bow of respect.

Qui-Gon returned the gesture. "Luminara, this is Obi-Wan Kenobi, my Padawan."

She bowed her head to Obi-Wan, as well. Her face was triangular in shape, and the lower portion was tattooed in small diamond shapes that formed a vertical stripe from her lush, blue-black lower lip to the tip of her round chin. The backs of her hands also bore tattoos, atop each knuckle joint.

Qui-Gon's expression became serious. "Luminara, Obi-Wan and I have had a recent encounter with someone who bears markings similar to yours."

"Arwen Cohl," Luminara said before Qui-Gon could go on. She smiled faintly. "Had I grown up on my homeworld and not in the Temple, I'm certain I would have heard tales of Arwen Cohl throughout my youth."

She met Qui-Gon's curious gaze. "He was a freedom

fighter, a hero to our people during a war fought with a neighboring world. He was a great warrior, and he made many sacrifices. But soon after our people won their freedom, he was accused of being a conspirator by the very people on whose side he had fought. That was their way of assuring that Cohl would not be elevated to the position of authority our people wished him to assume. He spent many years in prison, subjected to cruel punishments and harsh conditions, and those further hardened a man who already had been hardened by war.

"When he left those conditions—when he escaped that awful place, with the help of some of his former confederates—he avenged himself on those who did him wrong, and he swore that he would have nothing more to do with the world that he had fought so hard to liberate.

"He became a mercenary, boasting openly that he would never make the mistakes he had once made. That he now understood the nature of the cosmos, and would always be one step ahead of those who would seek to bring him down, capture him, or in any way thwart him."

Qui-Gon inhaled through his nose. "Did he bear any special grudge against the Trade Federation?"

Luminara shook her head. "No more than anyone else in my home system. The Trade Federation brought us into the Republic, though they did so at the expense of my world's resources.

"In the beginning, Arwen Cohl would hire himself out only to those whose cause he felt was justified. But over time—no doubt because of the blood he shed—he became nothing more than a pirate and a contract killer. He was said never to have betrayed a friend or an ally."

She paused for a moment, then added, "It is regrettable that history will remember the criminal Cohl rather than the exemplary Cohl. I was sad to hear that he had perished at Dorvalla."

When Qui-Gon didn't respond, Luminara asked, "Did he not?"

Qui-Gon appeared preoccupied. "For now, I'll grant that he vanished at Dorvalla."

Luminara nodded uncertainly. "Whether Cohl is dead or alive, the matter is in the hands of the Judicial Department, is it not?"

Again, Qui-Gon took a moment to respond. "All that is certain is that Cohl's destiny is in hands other than mine."

Carbon scored and blistered by the explosion that had sundered the freighter, an arc of the *Revenue*'s starboard hangar arm hung over Dorvalla's wan polar cap. Just outside the reach of the planet's shadow, the great curve of durasteel appeared to have been there forever. Perpetual sunlight poured in through the main hangar portal—where the arm's hand might have been— illuminating a shambles of cargo pods and barges.

Affixed like a barnacle to the inner hull, however, sat a lone battered shuttle. Inside the shuttle, and even the worse for wear, sat her crew of eight.

"I'm still waiting for that pardon you promised," Cohl said to Rella.

She shot him a look. "If and when you get us out of this, and not a moment before."

They were each in their chairs, as were the others, some of them asleep, heads pillowed on folded arms or hung backwards with mouths ajar. Lighting was faint, the air was frigid, and the scrubbed and rescrubbed oxygen had a distinctly metallic taste.

The much-abused refresher was rank.

They had been inside the arm for almost four standard days, subsisting on food pellets and relieving the boredom by putting on EVA suits and venturing out into the hangar. Where the shuttle had artificial gravity, moving about in the arm was like exploring a deep-sea wreck. Many of the cargo pods had massed along the outer wall of the arm, but clouds of lommite and tangles of droids drifted about like flotsam and jetsam. Boiny had even discovered the body of one of the Twi'leks who hadn't made it back to the rendezvous point, burned almost beyond recognition by blasterfire.

They hadn't planned on remaining in the hangar arm after the explosion. But once it had been determined that the arm was just outside the tug of Dorvalla's gravity, Cohl had decided that the hangar would be the best place to bide their time. The *Hawk-Bat* and the Nebula Front support ships had fled, and even the *Acquisitor* had disappeared—a fact that Cohl found curious, since it was unlike the Neimoidians to leave cargo behind, jettisoned or otherwise.

Another option would have been to race for Dorvalla's surface, to what had been their base before the boarding operation. But Cohl suspected that the base had been discovered and would probably be under surveillance. When Rella and some of the others had suggested striking out instead for nearby Dorvalla IV, it was Cohl who reminded them that salvage and relief ships would be on their way to Dorvalla, and a lone shuttle, crawling through space, would certainly attract unwanted attention.

In fact, salvage crews had arrived within local hours of the explosion. Since then, Dorvalla Mining had been employing their ferries to gather up what cargo pods they could, though much of the lommite had plunged into the atmosphere, as if bent on returning home. The detached centersphere and the other hangar arm had been hauled off, in advance of Dorvalla's bringing them down. Soon the salvagers would turn their efforts to the starboard arm.

For Cohl, the long days were no more than tedious; nothing like the years of confinement he had endured after being imprisoned on false conspiracy charges by people he had fought beside and had counted as friends. Because the rest of the shuttle's crew trusted him implicitly, they, too, suffered the monotony without complaint. Most of them were stoic by nature and no strangers to privation, in any case. Anyone who wasn't wouldn't have been selected for the operation.

Only Rella was inclined to speak her mind. But she and Cohl had an understanding.

"Anything on the comm?" Cohl asked Boiny.

"Not a peep, Captain."

Rella snorted. "Who are you expecting to hear from, Cohl? The *Hawk-Bat* is long gone."

Cohl looked past her to the Rodian. "What's the status of the systems?"

"Nominal."

Rella growled impatiently. "You know, I can last in here as long as any of you, but this litany is driving me space happy." She mimicked Cohl's voice, "Systems status," then Boiny's, "Nominal." She gave her head a shake. "Can't you at least come up with other ways of saying it?"

"Here's something that will cheer you up, Rella," Jalan said irritably. "The arm's orbit is deteriorating."

She forced her eyes wide open. "If you mean we're actually in danger of falling from the sky, you're right: I'm thrilled!"

Jalan looked at Cohl. "No imminent danger, Captain. But we should probably begin to think about leaving."

Cohl nodded. "You're right. It's time we bid good-bye to this place. Served us well, though."

Rella raised her eyes to the low ceiling. "Thank the stars."

"Where are we off to, Captain?" Boiny asked.

"Downside."

"Captain, I hope you're not thinking of riding this thing down to Dorvalla," Jalan said. "The salvage crews will—"

Cohl shook his head negatively. "We're returning to base under our own power."

The crew members traded uneasy looks.

"Begging your pardon, Captain," Jalan said, "but didn't you say the base was probably being watched?"

"I'm sure it is being watched."

Rella stared at him for a moment. "Are you scrambled, Cohl? We've been monitoring Judicial Department ships for the past four days, not to mention Dorvalla Space Corps corvettes. If you wanted to be caught, why did you make us sit through—" She gestured broadly. "—this?"

The others muttered in agreement.

"Even if we make it to the base in one piece," Rella went on, "what happens then? Without a spaceworthy ship, we'll be stranded."

"Maybe Dorvalla IV's worth a shot, after all, Captain," Jalan interjected. "If we manage to make it . . . I mean, with the Nebula Front likely thinking that we're dead, and all that aurodium right here with us . . ."

Rella cast Cohl a sly glance. "Are you listening?"

Cohl firmed his lips. "And when the Nebula Front learns that we survived? You don't think they'll move planets to hunt us down?"

"Might not matter, Captain," Boiny said guardedly. "That much aurodium could buy all of us new lives in the Corporate Sector or somewhere."

Cohl's gaze darkened. "That's not going to happen. We took this job on, and we'll see it through. Then we collect our pay." He swung angrily to Rella. "Begin your preflight. The rest of you, prepare for launch."

The small ship burned its way through sunlit Dorvalla's nebulous envelope, red nose aglow and losing pieces of itself to the thin air. The crew cinched their harnesses tighter and focused silently on their separate tasks, even as items broke loose from the consoles and began to carom around the cramped cabinspace like deadly missiles.

Rella aimed the trembling shuttle for a broad valley in the equatorial region, defined by two steep escarpments. There, where ancient seas had once ruled and plate tectonics had wreaked havoc with the terrain, the land was blanketed by thick forest, with trees and ferns primeval in scale. Massive, sheer-faced tors, crowned with rampant vegetation, rose like islands from the forest floor. Blinding white in the sunlight, the tors were the birthplace of waterfalls that plunged thousands of meters to turbulent turquoise pools.

But for all the wildness, it wasn't a wilderness. Dorvalla Mining had carved wide roads to the bases of most of the larger cliffs, and two circular landing fields, expansive enough to accommodate ferries, had been hollowed out of the forest. The tors were gouged and honeycombed with mines, and a thick layer of lommite dust blanketed much of the vegetation. Likewise the product of outsize machines, deep craters filled with polluted runoff water reflected the sun and sky like fogged mirrors.

It was from here, with an assist from several disenfranchised employees of Dorvalla Mining, that Cohl had finalized his plans for boarding the *Revenue*. But not all of Dorvalla expressed a loathing for the Trade Federation, much less a tolerance for mercenaries; certainly not those who saw the Trade Federation as Dorvalla's salvation, as the planet's only link to the Core Worlds.

The shuttle was leveling out of its bone-rattling ride down the well when a blunt-nosed ship tore past to port, intent on making its presence known.

"Who was that?" Rella asked, reflexively ducking as the sonic boom of the ship's passing overtook the shuttle.

"Dorvalla Space Corps," Boiny reported, his black orbs fixed on the authenticators. "Coming about for another pass."

Cohl swiveled his chair to the viewport to watch the ship's lightning-fast approach. It was a fixed-wing picket ship, single-piloted but packing dual laser cannons.

"Incoming transmission, Captain," Boiny said. "They're ordering us to set down."

"Did they ask us to identify ourselves?"

"Negative. They just want us on the ground."

Cohl frowned. "Then they already know who we are."

"That Judicial Department Lancet," Rella said, turning to Cohl. "Whoever was piloting it probably registered our drive signature."

The picket ship screamed overhead, closer this time.

"Another pass like that and they're going to knock us to the ground, Captain," Jalan warned.

"Stay on course for the base," Cohl ordered.

The picket barrel-rolled through a tight loop and came back at them once more, this time firing a burst from its forward laser cannons. Red hyphens streaked across the shuttle's rounded nose.

"They mean business, Captain!" Boiny said.

Cohl swung to Rella. "Keep an eye out for a place to crash."

She gaped at him. "You mean land, don't you?"

"As I said," Cohl emphasized. "Until then, all speed. Get us as close to the base as you can."

She gritted her teeth. "There had better be an aurodium ring at the end of this thrill ride, Cohl."

"The picket's firing."

"Evasive," Cohl said.

"No good, Captain. We can't outmaneuver it!"

The picket's lasers stitched a ragged line across the shuttle's tail, flipping it through a complete rotation. What had been a steady roar from the engines became a distressed whine. Flames licked their way through the aft bulkhead, and the cabin began to fill with thick, coiling smoke.

"We're dirtbound!" Rella shouted.

Cohl clamped his right hand on her shoulder. "Hold her steady! Fire repulsors and brace for impact."

Trailing black smoke as it swept past one of the tors, the shuttle clipped the top of the forest canopy, pruning huge branches from the tallest trees. Rella managed to keep them horizontal for a moment more, then they began to nosedive. The ship slammed into a massive tree and slued to starboard, spinning like a disk as it buzz-sawed through the upper reaches of the canopy.

Birds flew screeching from the crowns, as wood splintered to all sides. Seat restraints snapped, and two of the crew were flung like dolls into the starboard bulkhead. Rolled over on its back, the shuttle rocketed toward the forest floor. The viewports cracked, spiderwebbed, then blew into the cabin.

Contact with the ground was even harsher than any of them had anticipated. The starboard stabilizer plowed into the leaf-littered soil at an acute angle, causing the ship to flip like a tossed coin. Seats tore loose from the deck, and instrumentation ripped away from the bulkheads. The roll seemed to go on forever, punctuated by the deafening clamor of collisions. The hull caved in, and conduits burst, loosing noxious fluids and gases.

All at once it was over.

New sounds filled the air: the pinging of cooling metal, the hiss of punctured pipes, the boisterous calls of frightened birds, the tattoo of falling limbs, fruits, and whatever else, striking the hull. Coughs, whimpers, moans . . .

Gravity told Cohl that they were still upside down. He unclipped his harness and allowed himself to drop to the ceiling of the shuttle. Rella and Boiny were already there, bruised and bleeding, but regaining consciousness even as Cohl went to them. He put an arm under Rella's shoulders and took a quick look around.

The rest of the crew were surely dead, or dying. Satisfied that Rella would be all right, Cohl sprang the portside hatch. Moisture-saturated heat rushed in on everyone, but blessed oxygen, as well. Cohl bellied outside and immediately consulted his comlink's compass display. Unaccustomed to standard gravity, he felt twice his weight. Every motion was laborious.

"Did Jalan make it?" Rella asked weakly.

The human answered for himself. "Barely."

Cohl squirmed back inside. Jalan was hopelessly wedged beneath the console. He placed a hand on Jalan's shoulder. "We can't take you with us," he said quietly.

Jalan nodded. "Then let me take a few of them with me, Captain."

Rella crawled over to Jalan. "You don't have to do this," she started to say.

"I'm most-wanted in three systems," he cut her off. "If they find me alive, they're only going to make me wish I was dead anyway."

Boiny looked at Cohl, who nodded.

"Give him the destruct code. Rella, separate the ingots into four equal allotments. Put two allotments in my pack, one in yours, and one in Boiny's." He glanced back at Boiny. "Weapons and aurodium only. No need for food or water, because if we don't make it to the base, Dorvalla Penal will be providing all of that for us. If that isn't inspiration enough for you, I don't know what to tell you."

Moments later the three of them exited the ship.

Cohl shouldered his weighty pack, took a final compass reading, and set off toward a nearby tor at a resolute clip. Rella and Boiny kept up as best they could, climbing steadily under thick canopy for the first quarter hour while the picket ship made pass after pass in search of some sign of them. From the high ground, at the base of the lommite cliff, they could see the picket ship hovering over the treetops.

Rella grimaced. "He found the shuttle."

"Unlucky for him," Cohl said.

No sooner had the words left Cohl's mouth than an explosion ripped from the forest floor, catching the picket ship unawares. The pilot managed to evade the roiling fireball, but the damage had already been done. Engines slagged, the fighter listed to port and dropped like a stone.

A second picket ship roared overhead, just as the first was exploding. A third followed, angling directly for the base of the tor where Cohl and the others were concealed.

The picket poured fire at the tor, blowing boulder-size chunks of lommite from the cliff face. Cohl watched the ship complete its turn and set itself on course for a second run. As it approached, a deeper, more dangerous sound rolled through the humid air. Without warning, crimson energy lanced from the underbelly of the clouds, clipping the picket's wings in midflight. Unable to maneuver, the fighter flew nose first into the cliff face and came apart.

"That's another one we won't have to worry about," Cohl said, loud enough to be heard over the roar in the sky.

Rella raised her head in time to see a large ship tear overhead.

"The *Hawk-Bat*!" She glanced at Cohl in surprise. "You *knew*. You knew she would be down here."

He shook his head. "The contingency plan called for her to be here. But I didn't know for sure."

She almost smiled. "You may get that pardon yet."

"Save it for when we're safely aboard."

The three of them scampered to their feet and began a hurried descent of a scree field skirting the cliff face. Not far away, her weapons blazing, the *Hawk-Bat* was setting down at the center of a muddy and befouled catch basin.

Thousands of sentient species had a home on Coruscant, though it might be only a kilometer-high block of nondescript building. And nearly all those species had a voice there, though it might be only that of a representative long corrupted by the diverse pleasures Coruscant offered.

Those manifold voices had their say in the Galactic Senate, which sprouted like a squat mushroom from the heart of Coruscant's governmental district. Surrounded by lesser domes and buttressed buildings whose summits disappeared into the busy sky, the senate was fronted by an expansive pedestrian plaza. The plaza itself lorded over a sprawl of spired skyscrapers and was studded with impressionistic statues thirty meters high, dedicated to the Core World founders. Angular and humaniform in design, the long-limbed and genderless sculptures stood on tall duracrete bases and held slender ceremonial staffs.

The iconic motif was continued inside the senate, where

many of the public corridors that encircled the rotunda featured statues of similar spindly design.

Proceeding briskly along one of those corridors, Senator Palpatine marveled at the fact that the senate had yet to commission and display sculptures of nonhumanoid configuration. Where some delegates were willing to dismiss the lack of nonhuman representation as a simple oversight, others viewed it as an outright slight. To still others, the decor was a matter of small concern, either way. But with nonhumanoid species dominant in the Mid and Outer Rims, and their delegations fast overwhelming the senate—to the secret dismay of many a Core World human delegate—changes were certainly in order.

With its multilevel walkways, corridors, and vertical and horizontal turbolifts, the hemispherical building was as labyrinthine as the inner workings of the senate itself. Courtesy of Supreme Chancellor Valorum's announcement of a special session, the corridors were even more jammed than usual, but Palpatine was heartened to find that the delegates could still be motivated to set aside their personal affairs for matters of broader import.

Flanked by his two aides, Doriana and Pestage, he smiled pleasantly as he threaded his way toward the rotunda, easing past the blue-robed Senate Guard stationed at the doorway and stepping down into Naboo's balcony platform in the vast amphitheater.

One of 1,024 identical balconies that lined the inner wall of the dome, the platform was circular and spacious enough to accommodate half a dozen or more humans. Each balcony was actually the apex of a wedge-shaped slice of the building—stretching from the rotunda clear to the outer rim of the hemisphere—in which the separate delegations were quartered, and where most of the senate's mundane affairs and illicit business were transacted.

Adjusting the fall of his elaborate cloak, Palpatine stepped to the podiumlike console at the front lip of the platform. Given Naboo's elevated position in the rotunda, the view to the floor was vertiginous.

The amphitheater was purposely sealed off from natural light, as well as from Coruscant's dubious atmosphere, to minimize the effects of nightfall on the delegates; that is, to encourage everyone to remain focused on the matters at hand, despite the possibility that the sessions might continue late into the evening. But more and more citizens had come to view the rotunda's unnatural circumstances as symbolic of the senate's insularity—its separation from reality. The senate was thought to exist apart, debating issues of minor or occult concern, save for those that touched directly on the illegal enrichment of its membership.

Nevertheless, Palpatine sensed renewed intensity in the recycled air. Gossip had alerted everyone to the topics Valorum planned to discuss, but many were eager to hear for themselves and hungry to respond.

In an effort to take a measure of senatorial opinion regarding taxation of the outlying trade routes, Palpatine had spent the past few days meeting with as many senators as possible. Gently, he had attempted to persuade the undecided into backing Valorum, so that the Supreme Chancellor might carry the day without the support of Naboo and its neighboring worlds. At the same time, Palpatine had devised alternative plans, sufficient for dealing with a host of eventualities.

His own sense of urgency took him by surprise; the buzz in the rotunda was that infectious. But just as he had done at the opera, Valorum delayed his arrival. By the time the Supreme Chancellor finally showed himself, the atmosphere was agitated.

Valorum's perch was a thirty-meter-tall dais that rose

from the center of the floor like the stalk of a flower. Conveyed to the bud of the flower by turbolift, Valorum stood alone, with the senate's sergeant-at-arms, parlimentarian, journal clerk, and official reporter seated below him in a round dish that cradled the bud. Echoing the predominant color scheme of the amphitheater, he wore a lavender brocade cloak, with voluminous sleeves and matching cummerbund.

It occurred to Palpatine as he applauded that the Supreme Chancellor's lofty position made him as much a center of attention as target of opportunity.

When the clapping and the occasional verbal accolades had gone on long enough, Valorum held up his hands in a gesture that begged silence. His first words brought a faint smile to Palpatine's lips.

"Delegates of the Galactic Senate, we find ourselves beset by a confluence of sobering challenges. Frayed at its far-flung borders by internecine skirmishes and hollowed at its very heart by corruption, the Republic is in grave danger of unraveling. Recent events in the Mid and Outer Rim demand that we stem the rising tide of strife by restoring order and balance. So dire is our plight, that even extreme measures should not be dismissed out of hand."

Valorum paused briefly to allow his words to sink in.

"The free trade zones were originally created to foster exchange between the Core Worlds and the outlying systems of the Mid and Outer Rims. At the time, it was thought that free and open trade would prove a benefit to all concerned. But those zones have since become a haven not only for smugglers and pirates, but also for shipping and trading cartels that have availed themselves of the liberties we ensured, by setting themselves up as entities of political and military leverage."

Murmurs of concurrence and discord stirred the already impassioned air.

"The Trade Federation comes before us with a request that we do something to safeguard commerce in the outlying sectors. They are within their rights to request this, and we are obliged by our covenant to respond. But in a very real sense it is the questionable practices of the Trade Federation that have made it a target for thieves and terrorists."

Valorum raised his voice to be heard over hundreds of separate conversations, in as many tongues.

"In the same way, we must accept some of the blame for this, since it was this body that granted the Trade Federation such latitude, and it is this body that has chosen to turn a deaf ear time and again to what transpires in the outlying systems. This practice cannot be allowed to continue. The Trade Federation has become a bloated creature, ingesting lesser concerns and refusing to do business with worlds that seek to ship with its few remaining competitors. It would not be overstatement to say that these trade zones are no longer free.

"And yet the Trade Federation comes before us to solicit our help in putting an end to the disorder it has fashioned.

"The Federation asks for protection—as if this body can blithely deploy a military force against the pirates and terrorists who prey on the Federation's freighters. As if this body could provide starfighters and Dreadnaughts and, in so doing, turn the free trade zones into contested space—a battleground.

"There is, however, a solution to all this. If the Trade Federation wants *us* to ensure that the outlying systems be made safe for commerce—a task that will require action from this body, as well as from the many systems that lie within the free trade zones—then those planetary systems must be brought into the Republic as member worlds. Those worlds that the Trade Federation currently represents in the senate must abjure their affiliation with the Federation and bring their individual voices to this hall, to be heard as autonomous systems once more."

Valorum allowed the grumbling to go on for several moments before he gestured again for silence.

"We urge that the worlds of the free trade zones move quickly and decisively. Terrorist groups like the Nebula Front are merely the tip of a more deep-seated discontent. By working in accordance, the volunteer militaries and space corps of the affected systems can quell local insurrections before they swell to widespread revolution.

"The direct consequence of this will be the abolition of the free trade zones. The trade routes to those outlying systems that join the Republic would henceforth be subject to the same taxation that applies to routes in the Core, the Colonies, and the Inner Rim. I urge you to consider that such action is long overdue. For free trade is no longer that when all trade is controlled by one cartel."

Clamorous cheers and boos punctuated the air, but reaction was not as mixed as Palpatine had feared it might be. Still, he was disappointed. Valorum had made a case for taxation without addressing any of the consequences or the possible compromises that might be made.

Before such a motion could be enacted as legislation, special interest groups—on the payroll of the Trade Federation or similar concerns—would register their protests. Then the motion would move to committee, where it would be further weakened. After that, it would be burdened with ancillary legislation, aimed at appeasing the special interest groups and lobbyists. Finally, it would be endlessly debated, in the hope of continued deferral.

But there were ways to cut through the bureaucratic tangle. Exasperated, Palpatine glanced around the amphitheater, wondering who would make the first move—figuratively and literally.

It was the Neimoidians who acted, loosing their balcony from the inner wall and directing it to the center of the rotunda. Detached, the platforms resembled sleeker versions of the repulsorlift air taxis that filled Coruscant's skies. Word had it that some of the platforms moved more rapidly than others—even on autopilot—which was crucial, since delegates frequently raced to be recognized by the Supreme Chancellor.

"We recognize Delegate Lott Dod," Valorum said, "representing the Trade Federation."

Lott Dod wore rich robes and a tall, black miter. A saucer-shaped hovercam with a single antenna rushed in to broadcast his flat-faced likeness to the screens built into the display consoles of the balconies.

"We submit that the senate does not have the right or the authority to enact taxation of the outlying trade zones. This is nothing more than a ploy to break up our consortium.

"It was the Trade Federation who opened the hyperlanes to the outlying systems, who risked the lives of its space-faring captains to bring formerly primitive worlds into the Republic, and new resources into the Core.

"Now we learn that we are expected to defend ourselves against the mercenaries and pirates who masquerade as freedom fighters, merely to enrich themselves at our expense. We come before you asking for aid, and instead become the victim of an indirect attack."

From delegations representing the Commerce Guild and the Techno Union came loud shouts of encouragement.

"If the senate does not wish to intercede with the

Nebula Front—or, indeed, if it is incapable of doing so,"
Dod continued, "then it must at least grant us what we
need to defend ourselves. As it is, we are defenseless in
the face of far superior fighters."

Where some cheered and some booed, Valorum merely
nodded. "Commissions can be appointed to determine if
additional defense capabilities are warranted at this time,"
he said sternly.

Another balcony dropped from the curved wall.

"We recognize Ainlee Teem, delegate of Malastare,"
Valorum said.

A Gran, Teem had a trio of eyestalks that were thick
and closely set.

"Since the Trade Federation is willing to defend itself,
at its own expense, there is no justification for taxing the
trade routes." Teem's voice was deep and abrasive. "We
have precedent in the Corporate Alliance. Otherwise, it
appears that the Republic is interested in nothing more
than skimming profits from those who endangered themselves to blaze the hyperspace routes now used by one
and all."

Half the amphitheater applauded. But even in the
midst of it, a third platform was floating to the center.

"We recognize Bail Antilles of Alderaan."

"Supreme Chancellor," the human said with great emotion, "under no circumstances should the senate allow the
Trade Federation to augment its droid defenses. If the
Nebula Front has succeeded in making certain sectors dangerous, then the Federation should avoid those
trouble spots until such time as the involved sectors find
a way to counter terrorism. By sanctioning increases to
the Trade Federation's defenses, we imperil the balance
of power throughout the Outer Rim."

"And what becomes of the worlds in those contested

sectors?" Senator Orn Free Taa of Ryloth asked, his blue head-tails draped over the bodice of an exorbitant cloak. "How do we trade with the Core? With whom do we ship?"

Rejoinders flew fast and furious from all sides of the chamber—from the Wookiee delegation, the Sullustans, the Bimms, and Bothans. Valorum attempted to quote the rules, but many of the senators had had enough of the rules, and shouted him down.

"The Trade Federation will seek to offset the taxes by charging more for their services," the Bothan delegate argued. "The outlying systems will, in turn, be forced to assume the burden of taxation."

Palpatine saw what was coming and quickly dispatched black-cloaked Sate Pestage to deliver a hand-written note to the sergeant-at-arms, who relayed the note to the Supreme Chancellor. Valorum received the message a moment after the Bothan delegate had demanded to know how the credits garnered from taxation would be allocated.

Lifting his eyes from the note, Valorum glanced at the Naboo balcony before responding. "I propose that a percentage of the revenues garnered through taxation be allocated for relief and development of the outlying systems."

Cheers roared from most of the upper-tier balconies, and many of the senators in the platforms there came to their feet to applaud. Closer to the floor, encouragement came from Wookiee Senator Yarua, Tendau Bendon of Ithor, and Horox Ryyder, who represented thousands of worlds in the Raioballo sector.

Palpatine made a mental note of the naysayers, including Toonbuck Toora, Po Nudo, Wat Tambor, and other delegates. Then he detached the platform and dropped for the center of the rotunda, chased by two hovercams.

"We recognize the senator from the sovereign system of Naboo," Valorum said.

"Supreme Chancellor," Palpatine said, "may I suggest that, while many important points have been made, these issues are far from resolved, and should perhaps be explored in greater depth in a different forum, after everyone has had an opportunity to reflect on what has been said."

Valorum appeared confused for a moment. "What sort of forum, Senator Palpatine?"

"Before the motion goes to committee, I propose that a summit be held, where delegates from the Trade Federation and its signatory members can meet openly to offer their solutions to these . . . 'sobering challenges,' as you say."

The same senators who had cheered Valorum, now applauded Palpatine.

Uncertainty and perhaps vague misgiving drained some of the color from Valorum's face. "Do you have some specific location in mind, Senator?" he asked.

Palpatine considered it. "May I suggest . . . Eriadu?"

A platform joined Palpatine's at the center of the rotunda. The delegation's dark-complexioned human members wore loose-fitting garments and cloth turbans.

"Supreme Chancellor," their spokesman said, "Eriadu would be honored to host such a summit."

Senator Toora seconded the motion and moved to enact a moratorium on the taxation proposal.

Valorum had no choice but to comply.

"I will confer with all relevant parties and set a date for the summit," he said when the furor had abated. "With regard to taxation of the outlying trade routes, there will be a moratorium on the voting process until the summit concludes and all viewpoints have been expressed. Furthermore, as a sign of the senate's commitment to foster peace and stability, I shall attend the summit personally."

Many in the rotunda rose and applauded.

Valorum's gaze found Palpatine and lingered on him for a moment. Palpatine smiled and nodded conspiratorially.

Sporting jagged wounds it hadn't had when it had first appeared over Dorvalla, or later, when it had settled down to retrieve Cohl and what was left of his team, the *Hawk-Bat* floated in space, gravitationally anchored to a buff-colored world of arid mountain ranges and ice-blue seas. Five CloakShape starfighters surrounded her, with a sixth nuzzled up to the gunship's starboard airlock. Far beyond the ships spread a band of space mines, made to resemble asteroids.

On the *Hawk-Bat*'s side of the airlock, Cohl waited vigilantly for his visitors to board. His bare arms were lacerated from the razor ferns he had been forced to forge through on Dorvalla, and his dark face, with its eye mask of diamond-shaped tattoos, was bruised black and blue beneath his beard. Adding severity to features many thought ferocious to begin with, his coiled hair framed his countenance like the hood of a serpent.

The airlock's indicator light flashed.

"Do you want me to disappear?" Rella asked from behind him.

She was in even worse shape than Cohl. Her left eye was concealed by a bacta patch and her left forearm wore a plascast. Boiny remained in a bacta tank.

Cohl shook his head without taking his gaze from the airlock. "Stick around. Keep your blaster handy."

Rella drew the weapon from the holster on her right hip and checked the charge.

The airlock hissed opened, and a slim human and a reptilian humanoid stepped into the corridor, dressed alike in caftans, coarsely woven trousers, and knee-high boots. The latter had tough, corrugated skin, iridescent in sunlight, and hands the size of scoopball mitts. His flat face had multiple nostrils, and four small horns protruded from his forehead. From his left hand dangled a sizable carrycase.

"Welcome to Asmeru, Captain Cohl," the human said in Basic. "It's good to see you alive and comparatively well."

Cohl nodded curtly in greeting. "Havac."

Havac motioned to his hulking partner. "You remember Cindar."

Cohl nodded again. Neither he nor the *Hawk-Bat*'s scanners saw signs of concealed weapons on the pair.

"Rella," he said, motioning to her by way of introduction.

Havac smiled and extended his hand to her in a courtly gesture. "How could I forget?"

"Let's go forward, where we can talk," Cohl said.

He appraised his guests as they walked. Havac wasn't the human's real name, but rather his combat name. A former holo-documentarian, Havac had been an alien-rights activist during the Stark Hyperspace Conflict and had spent the past several years chronicling the various abuses of the Trade Federation. In fact, he had no stomach for violence, but he was sharp and had a talent for treachery.

He and Cindar weren't characteristic of the thousands of human and nonhuman members of the Nebula Front. But they were standard issue in the organization's burgeoning militant wing. Now headquartered on the arid planet below, the Front had recruited from worlds up and down the Rimma Trade Route, from Sullust to Sluis Van, but only the Ancient Houses that ruled the Senex sector had granted them a base of operations.

"Where's the rest of your crew, Captain?" Havac asked over his shoulder.

The question hit Cohl like a just-remembered nightmare. It was the same question he had asked the commander of the *Revenue* days earlier, when Cohl's team had numbered twelve.

"You might say that a lot of them never left Dorvalla space," he said finally.

It took Havac a moment to grasp Cohl's meaning, then he frowned in sympathy. "I'm sorry to hear that, Captain. We thought we'd lost you, as well."

Cohl shook his head. "Not a chance."

"Half the Rim is talking about what happened at Dorvalla. We really weren't expecting you to obliterate the *Revenue*."

"I don't like to waste time—especially when I'm dealing with Neimoidians," Cohl said. "They'd sooner sacrifice themselves than their cargo. Fortunately, the *Revenue*'s commander was more cowardly than most of them. As for destroying the freighter, you can consider that a gift."

The four of them entered the main forward cabin and seated themselves around a circular table. Cindar placed the carrycase at the center of the table.

"I have to hand it to you, Captain," Havac said, "you've

got the Trade Federation running scared. They've even so-licited help from Coruscant."

Cohl shrugged. "No harm in trying."

Havac leaned forward with a certain eagerness. "You have the aurodium?"

Cohl glanced at Rella, who unclipped a remote from her belt and keyed a short code. A small repulsorsled bearing a lockbox lifted off the deck nearby and floated toward the table. Rella entered another code and the lid of the box opened, its contents of ingots spilling rainbow light into the cabin.

Havac's and Cindar's eyes widened.

"I can't tell you what this will mean to us," Havac said.

But a hint of suspicion had crept into his partner's gaze. "It's all here?" Cindar asked.

Cohl's neutral look became a glare. "What are you asking me?"

The humanoid shrugged. "Just wondering if any of it happened to get misplaced along the way."

Abruptly, Cohl reached across the table, grabbing Cindar by the front of his caftan and yanking him forward. "That treasure is bloodied. Good people died bringing it to you." He pushed Cindar back into his seat. "You'd better put it to good use."

"Stop this, please," Havac said.

Cohl glowered. "You don't like violence—except on your orders, is that it?"

Havac studied his hands, then lifted his eyes. "Rest assured that the aurodium will be put to good use, Captain."

Cindar smoothed the front of his garment, but was otherwise unruffled by Cohl's fury. He slid the carrycase forward. Cohl removed it from the tabletop and set it down on the deck.

Cindar watched him for a moment, then said, "Aren't you going to ask if it's all there?"

Cohl stared at him. "Let me put it this way. For every credit it's short, I'll take a kilo of meat from you."

"So, I'd be a fool," Cindar said with a grin.

Cohl nodded. "You'd be a fool."

Rella handed the remote to Havac, and Cindar closed the lid on the lockbox.

"Where's the aurodium going?" Cohl asked mildly.

Havac looked surprised. "Captain, did I ask what you're planning to do with your payment?"

Cohl smiled. "Fair enough."

Following the exchange, Rella turned to Cohl. "I'm sure he plans to donate it to his favorite charity."

Havac laughed. "You're not far off the mark."

"Here's another bonus for you, Havac," Cohl said. "We had some unexpected trouble at Dorvalla. Someone infiltrated the *Revenue* using the same technique we used. They hid a ship inside a cargo pod, just like we did. They tracked us when we left the freighter and came close to ruining what I thought was a secure plan. Their ship turned out to be a Judicial Department Lancet."

Havac and Cindar traded surprised looks. "Judicials?" Havac said. "At Dorvalla, of all places?"

Cohl watched them carefully. "Actually, I think they were Jedi."

Havac's incredulity increased. "Why do you think that?"

"Call it a hunch. The point is, no one was supposed to know about that operation."

Havac sat back in his seat, perplexed. "Now it's my turn to wonder, Captain. What are you asking me?"

"Who else in the Nebula Front knew about the operation?"

Cindar snorted in derision. "Think it through, Cohl. Why would any of us sabotage our own campaign?"

"That's what I'm asking," Cohl said. "It could be that

not everyone down below agrees with your methods—your hiring us, for example. Someone could have been trying to sabotage *you*, not me."

Havac nodded. "Thank you, Captain. I'll bear that in mind." He paused briefly, then said, "What's next for you two?"

"We thought we'd retire from mayhem," Rella said, taking hold of Cohl's left hand at the same time. "Maybe take up moisture farming."

Havac grinned. "I can see that. The two of you on Tatooine or somewhere, living among banthas and dewbacks. It's just your style."

"Why the curiosity?" Cohl said.

Havac's grin straightened. "We may have something big in the works. Something perfectly suited to your talents." He glanced at Rella, then back at Cohl. "It would pay enough to guarantee your retirement."

Rella shot Cohl a warning look. "Don't listen to him, Cohl. Let someone else hire out to the Nebula Front." She cut her eyes to Havac. "Besides, we plan to retire in high style."

"You want to retire rich?" Cindar said. "Buy a Neimoidian for what he's worth, then sell him for what he thinks he's worth."

"The job I have in mind would allow you to retire in high style," Havac baited.

"Cohl," Rella said, "are you going to tell these guys to take a hike back to their own ship, or do I have to do it?"

Cohl let go of her hand and tugged at his beard. "It can't hurt to hear them out."

"Yes, it can, Cohl, yes, it can."

He looked at her, then laughed shortly. "Rella's right," he told Havac. "We're not interested."

Havac heaved his shoulders and stood up, extending

his hand to Cohl. "Come and see us if you have a change of heart."

Much closer to the Core, the *Acquisitor* had returned home. Sullen Neimoidia rotated slowly beneath the ring-shaped freighter. As was the case in the far-off Senex system, meetings of a sinister sort were under way; discussions centered around weapons and strategy, destruction and death. But the ships that had brought the *Acquisitor's* guests had had no need to sidle up to airlocks. Not when the hangar arms themselves were commodious enough to conceal an invasion army.

In zone two of the port arm, balanced atop his claw-footed mechno-chair, sat Viceroy Nute Gunray, in rich burgundy robes and triple-crested tiara. Off to Gunray's right stood legal counsel Rune Haako and Deputy Viceroy Hath Monchar; and to Gunray's left, the *Acquisitor's* new commander, smallish Daultay Dofine, fresh from the debacle at Dorvalla and still bewildered by his unexpected promotion.

In the center of the hangar floor hunkered a double-winged behemoth, which bore a vague resemblance to Neimoidia's gauzy-winged needle fliers. Ponderously exiting the wide-open jaws of the behemoth's foot ramp rode thickly armored, russet-colored vehicles that might have been modeled on charging banthas—backs humped in anger, huffing clouds of hot exhaust, laser cannons extended like tusks. And behind those came droid-operated repulsorlift tanks, with shovel-shaped prows and top-mounted gun turrets.

Prototype war machines, the gargantuan landing craft, the monstrous multitroop transports, and the sleekly styled tanks had been designed and built by Haor Chall Engineering and Baktoid Armor, whose alien representatives were standing in full view of Gunray and beaming with pride.

To Haor Chall, especially, design perfection amounted to a religious edict.

"Behold, Viceroy," Haor Chall's insectoid representative said, gesturing with all four arms to the closest transport, whose circular deployment hatch, hinged at the top, was just swinging open.

Gunray watched in amazement as a rack telescoped from the hatch and dozens of battle droids *unfolded* themselves before his eyes.

"And this, Viceroy," Baktoid's winged representative added.

Gunray's red eyes moved back to the landing craft in time to see a dozen airhooks soar toward the upper reaches of the hangar arm. Blade-thin vehicles with twin footrests and top-mounted blasters, all were piloted by droids, whose backward leaning postures made them appear to be hanging on to the slender handlebars for dear life.

Gunray was speechless.

While he had never seen their like, in each of the prototypes he recognized elements of the very machines the Trade Federation had employed for centuries in transporting natural resources and other commodities. In the fuselage of the double-winged landing craft, for example, he recognized the Federation's narrow ore barge. But Haor Chall had set the fuselage on a pedestal and capped it with two enormous wings, presumably kept from sagging by powerful tensor fields.

Despite the animistic look Baktoid had imparted to the troop transports, Gunray recognized the Trade Federation's own repulsorlift cargo pod, built on an even more gargantuan scale. As for the folding battle droids and the Single Trooper Aerial Platforms, they were simply variations of Baktoid's security droids, and Longspur and Alloi's Bespin airhooks.

But one thing was clear: everything he was being shown

spoke less to spaceborne defense than to groundside deployment. The realization was more than Gunray could absorb; more than he wished to absorb.

"As you have probably observed, Viceroy," Haor Chall's representative was saying, "the Trade Federation already has most of the raw materials needed to create your army." He motioned to the representative from Baktoid. "In partnership with Baktoid, we can convert your security and worker droids to battle models, and your barges and cargo pods to landing craft."

"More units, less money," the Baktoid representative added.

"Best of all, since the components of the landing crafts can be stored in various places—wings, fuselages, and pedestals—they can be assembled at a moment's notice. You could place one landing craft in each of a hundred freighters, or a hundred landing craft in but one of your freighters—for singularly thorny circumstances. Either way, none who come aboard to inspect your freighters will comprehend what they are seeing. As our mutual friend says, you will have an army without giving the appearance of having an army."

"Mutual friend," Rune Haako muttered, just loudly enough for Gunray to hear. "When Darth Sidious says do this, it is performed."

"We enjoy dealing with Neimoidians," Baktoid's representative stepped forward to say, "because of the enthusiasm and awe you demonstrate for our creations. Therefore, we have other weapons in mind for you: starfighters that will no longer have to rely on droid pilots, but will themselves answer to a central control computer.

"You may even wish to contact the Colicoids of Colla IV, who are rumored to have developed a combat droid capable of *rolling* to its destinations." The alien gestured broadly to the immense hangar. "Perfect for covering the vast distances inside your freighters, and defending against boarding parties."

Gunray heard Dofine swallow audibly, but, once more, it was Haako who spoke.

"This is madness," he said, lowering his voice and limping closer to the mechno-chair. "Are we merchants, or are we would-be conquerors?"

"You heard Darth Sidious," Gunray hissed. "These weapons will ensure that we *remain* merchants. They are our guarantee that groups like the Nebula Front or mercenaries like Captain Cohl will never again risk going against us. Ask Commander Dofine. He'll tell you."

"Darth Sidious keeps us in servile fearfulness," Haako said, blinking repeatedly.

"What can we do, otherwise? Instead of honoring our request for additional defenses, the senate threatens us with taxation. We need to take matters into our own hands if we are to protect our cargos. Or would you have us continue to lose ships to terrorists, in addition to losing profits to taxation?"

"But the other members of the directorate—?"

"For the time being, they are to not to know anything of this. We will apprise them of these things gradually."

"And only if necessary."

"Yes," Gunray said. "Only if necessary."

With its countless dark canyons, precipitous ledges, hidden recesses, and jutting parapets—its surfeit of places to hide in plain sight—Coruscant invited corruption. Its very geography inspired secrecy.

Palpatine had been on Coruscant for several years, and he felt that he knew the place better than many life-long residents did. He knew it the way a jungle cat knew its territory. He had an instinctual understanding of its shifting moods, and an instinctual feel for its power spots and dangerous zones. It was almost as if he could *see* the coiling blackness that inhabited the senate, and the refulgent light that poured from the spires of the Jedi Temple.

It was a wonderful place to be for someone who had long been a scholar, a historian, a lover of art, and a collector of rare objects; someone with a passion for exploring life's manifold heights and depths.

Frequently he would shrug off his elaborate cloak and take up the simple dress of a trader or a recluse. He would throw a hood over his head and wander the lightless abysses, the dark paths and neglected plazas, the tunnels and alleyways, the seedy underworld. Anonymous, he would make trips to the equator, the poles, and other remote places. Beneath his ambitions—for himself, for Naboo, for the Republic at large—he had always been unassuming, and that apparent lack of guile allowed him to pass without being recognized; to all but disappear in a crowd, as only a person of solitude might—as one who had kept his own company for so many years.

And yet, others sought him out. Perhaps for the very reason that he revealed so little about himself. Initially he assumed that others found his reclusiveness intriguing, as if he led a secret life. But he quickly learned that what they really wanted to do was talk about themselves; to solicit not his counsel but his ear, trusting that he would guard the secrets of their lives as closely as he guarded his own.

That had been the case with Valorum, who had forged a relationship with Palpatine at the start of the Supreme Chancellor's second four-year term of office.

What Palpatine lacked in charisma, he made up for in candor, and it was that directness that had led to his widespread appeal in the senate. Here was Palpatine, with his ready smile; above corruption, above deception or duplicity, a kind of confessor, willing to hear the most banal confessions or the basest of misdeeds without passing judgment—aloud, at any rate. For in his heart he judged the universe on his own terms, with a clear sense of right and wrong.

He looked to no other guide than himself.

Among the delegates who represented the worlds of the outlying systems, his reputation was particularly exalted, primarily because tiny Naboo was one of those worlds, all by itself at the edge of the Mid Rim, with Malastare— home to Gran and Dugs—its only neighbor of significance.

Like many of its neighbors, Naboo was ruled by an elected monarch—and an unenlightened one, at that—but it was a peaceful world, unspoiled, rich in classic elements, and inhabited not only by humans, but also by a mostly aquatic indigenous species known as Gungans.

When most of his peers had left public service at the accepted age of twenty, Palpatine had elected to remain a politician, and his tenure on Coruscant had provided him with singular insight into the afflictions that vexed the outlying star systems.

It was while befriending a group of Bith delegates that he first learned of the Nebula Front, and later, it was a Bith who introduced him to some of the members who commanded the organization. By rights Palpatine should have had nothing to do with terrorists, but the founding members of the Nebula Front were neither fanatics nor anarchists. Many of their grievances with the Trade Federation, and Coruscant, were legitimate. More important, wherever the Federation was involved, it was difficult to remain impartial.

Had Palpatine been one of the many senators receiving Trade Federation kickbacks, it would have been easy to look the other way, or to turn a deaf ear—as Valorum had put it. But as the representative of a world that depended on the Trade Federation for food and other imports, as Naboo did, it was impossible to dismiss what he had heard and seen.

Eventually, the Bith had introduced him to the Front's newest leader, Havac.

For previous meetings with Havac, Palpatine had selected out-of-the-way places in Coruscant's lawless lower levels. But the current crisis in the senate had necessitated that they exercise a greater measure of secrecy, so Palpatine had chosen a humans-only club in Coruscant's midlevel—a place where patricians could gather for t'bac, brandy, games of dejarik, and quiet reading—and where there were actually fewer prying eyes than lower down. He had taken the added precaution of informing Havac of the location at the last possible moment. As tactically minded as Havac was, he lacked the expertise to catch Palpatine with his guard lowered.

"Valorum is audacious," Havac said angrily, as soon as they were seated at a table in the club's hardwood-paneled dining room. "He has the gall to announce a summit in the Outer Rim—on Eriadu, no less—without asking the Nebula Front to participate."

"Unlike the Trade Federation," Palpatine said, "the Nebula Front does not enjoy representation in the senate."

"Yes, but the Front has many friends on Eriadu, Senator."

"Then all the better for you, I should think."

Havac had come alone, as had Palpatine, though both Sate Pestage and Kinman Doriana were seated nearby. Palpatine had accepted from the start that "Havac" was an alias, and Pestage had subsequently confirmed the fact. Pestage had also learned that Havac was native to Eriadu, where his impassioned holo-documentaries had established him to a few as an enemy of the Trade Federation, a proponent of nonhuman rights, a malcontent and idealist. He wanted desperately to change the galaxy, but his visual tirades against injustice had largely gone unnoticed.

He was a relative newcomer to the Nebula Front, but the Front's militant faction had recruited him to serve a special agenda. Exasperated by Senate indifference and the Trade Federation's continued violation of the trade agreements, the militants had decided to up the stakes from mere interference in Federation business to terrorism. Havac and the Front's new radicals were determined to hit the Trade Federation where the Neimoidians and the rest would feel it the most—in their distended purses.

Palpatine had encouraged Havac, without actually advocating violence. Rather, he had maintained that the surest way to effect lasting change was to work through the senate.

"We're fed up with Valorum," Havac was saying. "He treads docilely when and wherever the Trade Federation is concerned. His threat to tax the trade routes is pure rhetoric. It's time that someone convince him that the Nebula Front can be a more dangerous foe than the Trade Federation."

Palpatine made an offhand gesture, as if in dismissal. "It's true that the Supreme Chancellor has little understanding of the Nebula Front's objectives, but he is not your primary obstacle."

Havac held Palpatine's heavy-lidded gaze. "We need a stronger chancellor. Someone who wasn't born into wealth."

Palpatine gestured again. "Look elsewhere for your enemies. Look to the members of the Trade Federation Directorate."

Havac mulled it over for a moment. "Perhaps you're right. Perhaps we do need to look elsewhere." He grinned faintly and lowered his voice to add, "We have made a powerful new ally, who has suggested several courses of action."

"Indeed?"

"It was he who provided the data we needed to destroy a Trade Federation freighter at Dorvalla."

"The Federation has thousands of freighters," Palpatine said. "If you expect to be victorious by destroying their ships, you're deluding yourselves. You must get to the principals. Just as I have been doing in the senate."

"Do we have *any* friends there?"

"A meager few. Whereas the Trade Federation has the support of many important delegates—Toonbuck Toora, Tessek, Passel Argente . . . They are enriched for their loyalty."

Havac shook his head in outrage. "It's pathetic that the Front needs to *buy* senatorial support, in the same deplorable fashion that it is compelled to employ mercenaries."

"There is no other way," Palpatine said, with a purposeful sigh. "The courts are useless and biased. But corruption has its advantages when you can simply purchase the votes of unscrupulous delegates instead of having to convince them of the virtues of your position."

Havac rested his elbows on the table and leaned forward. "We have the funds you asked for."

Palpatine's eyebrows went up. "Already?"

"Our benefactor told us that the *Revenue*—"

"It's best if I don't know how you received them," Palpatine interrupted.

Havac nodded in comprehension. "One possible problem. It's in the form of aurodium ingots."

"Aurodium?" Palpatine sat back in his chair, steepling his fingers. "Yes, that could present a problem. I can't very well distribute ingots to those senators we hope to . . . impress."

"Too easy to trace," Havac said.

"Precisely. We'll have to have the aurodium converted to Republic dataries, even though that will require some time." Palpatine fell silent for a moment, then said, "May I suggest that one of my aides help you set up a special account with a bank on an outlying world that won't ask questions about the origin of the ingots. Once the aurodium is safely deposited there, you'll be able to transfer funds through the InterGalactic Bank, and draw against the account in the form of Republic credits."

Havac clearly liked the idea. "I know you'll put the funds to the best possible use."

"I'll do all within my power."

Havac smiled in admiration. "You are the voice of the outer systems, Senator."

"I am not a voice of the outer systems, Havac," Palpatine rejoined. "If you insist on awarding me an honorific, then consider me the voice of the Republic. You need to remember this, because if you begin to think in terms of inner systems against outer systems, star sectors against rims, there can be no unity. Instead of equality for all, we will end up with anarchy and secession."

Standing just outside of the Jedi Temple's east-facing gate, Qui-Gon gave thought to where he should wander. The day was warm and cloudless, except to the north, where microclimatic storms were swirling about the summits of some of Coruscant's taller buildings, and Qui-Gon had nothing to do.

He set out walking into the sun, memories of his youth surfacing, as if images glimpsed in the riffling of a deck of sabacc cards. As ever, he saw himself inside the Temple, meditating, studying, training, making friends and losing some. He recalled a day he had stolen into one of the spires and had had his first real look at Coruscant's fantastic cityscape, and how from that moment forward he had yearned to explore the city-planet from bottom to top. A quest that would remain a dream until well into his teen years and, in fact, had yet to be completely fulfilled.

On those rare occasions when students were permitted to leave the Temple, they moved about like groups of tourists, and always in the company of chaperons of one sort or another. Visits to the Galactic Senate, the Courts Building, the Municipal Authorities Building . . . But in those early explorations Qui-Gon saw enough to understand that Coruscant was not the fabled land he had first imagined it to be. The planet's climate was more or less regulated, its original topography had long ago been leveled or buried, and what nature there was existed indoors, where it could be tended to and controlled.

Because it resided in all life, the Force was in some sense concentrated on Coruscant. But one felt the Force differently there than on worlds in their natural state, where the interconnectedness of all life created subtle shifts and rhythms. If on many worlds the Force was a gentle murmur, on Coruscant it was a howl—a white noise of sentience.

Qui-Gon had nothing in mind beyond walking. The huge holomap in the High Council spire indicated hundreds of distant trouble spots and emergencies, but the Reconciliation Council hadn't gotten around to assigning him and Obi-Wan to any of them. He wondered if Yoda and some of the others were angry about his seeming obsession with Captain Cohl.

To Qui-Gon's thinking, the council members were too willing to dismiss Cohl as nothing more than a symptom of trying times, when he was much more than that. But, then, the Council had a tendency to dwell on repercussions, on future events, rather than the present. Yoda, especially, was fond of saying that the future was always in motion, and yet he and Mace Windu sometimes acted as if that wasn't the case at all.

Did they know of some great event looming on the horizon? Qui-Gon wondered. And would he fail to recognize that event, even were he to trip over it? He supposed he should at least remain open to the possibility that the High Council Masters knew something he didn't.

The one thing he accepted as beyond dispute was that the Force was even more mysterious than any of the Jedi perceived it to be.

He hadn't gone half a kilometer when Adi Gallia fell into step beside him, catching him by surprise.

"In search of something purposeful, Qui-Gon, or just hoping you'll bump into something worthy of your attention?"

He smiled at her. "I have—you."

She laughed, then scolded him with a look.

Adi's fingernails were polished, and the same blue cosmetic that rimmed her dark blue eyes traced the ligaments on the backs of her hands. She had been a permanent member of the High Council for over a decade, and a Jedi Master for much longer than that. Her parents were Corellian diplomats, but, like Qui-Gon, she had been raised in the Temple. Adi had always been enthralled by Coruscant, and knew the planet about as well as anyone. Over the years, she had forged a close friendship with Supreme Chancellor Valorum, along with several Core World delegates.

"Where is your young apprentice?" she asked as they sauntered.

"Sharpening his wits."

"So you actually give him an occasional respite from your resolute tutelage," she teased.

"It's a mutual thing," Qui-Gon said.

She laughed again, then grew serious. "I have news that's bound to interest you. It seems that you might have been right about Cohl's surviving the explosion of that Trade Federation freighter."

Qui-Gon came to a dead stop in the center of the sky bridge they were crossing. Droids and pedestrians ambled past him to both sides.

"Has Cohl been seen?"

Adi leaned on the bridge railing and gazed back toward the Temple. "Dorvalla Space Corps pursued a shuttle that matched the description and drive signature you and Obi-Wan furnished. The shuttle crashed and exploded onworld, apparently not far from where Cohl had established a temporary base."

Qui-Gon nodded. "I know the area."

"There wasn't much left to investigate at the crash site, but the remains of three humans found in the wreckage were identified as associates of Cohl. But here's the interesting part: The shuttle was clearly attempting to rendezvous with Cohl's personal ship."

"The *Hawk-Bat*."

"It set down close to the crash site, then proceeded to blast its way off Dorvalla, taking out a number of Dorvalla's picket ships on the way."

"Cohl made it to the ship," Qui-Gon said.

"You're that certain?"

"I am."

Adi nodded. "One of the picket ship pilots reported that two or three of Cohl's band might have made it alive to the *Hawk-Bat*."

"Has there been any sign of the ship since?"

"It jumped to hyperspace as soon as it left Dorvalla behind. But surveillance has been doubled at all of Cohl's known retreats. Assuming he did survive, he'll be spotted and, with luck, captured."

"Adi, is there a chance that Obi-Wan and I could—"

"Cohl is no longer our concern," she cut him off. "Supreme Chancellor Valorum is attempting to encourage the systems along the Rimma Trade Route to assume responsibility for curtailing acts of terrorism in their separate sectors. Intervention on our part would likely be viewed as indirect support of the Trade Federation."

Qui-Gon frowned. "That's shortsighted. Most of the

worlds along the Rimma support the Nebula Front to one degree or another. Recruits, funding, intelligence . . . The Rimma worlds supply these and more."

Adi regarded him for a long moment. "Qui-Gon, suppose I could arrange for you to meet with Chancellor Valorum, so you could apprise him of these matters personally?"

Qui-Gon nodded. "All right."

"Then it's settled. I'm on my way to meet with him now, and there's no time like the present."

"I couldn't have put it better."

In his chambers beneath the senate rotunda, Valorum reclined in his chair, exhaling wearily as he stretched his arms over his head. Finished with the morning's business, he now had to face those delegates who hadn't been able to secure appointments and were undoubtedly lingering outside his office, anxious for a moment of his time.

"What's on the agenda for this afternoon?" he asked Sei Taria as she came through the office's tall, ornate door.

The young human woman glanced at her wrist comm screen. "You have a meeting with Adi Gallia, then a follow-up meeting with Bail Antilles and Horox Ryyder. After that, you are meeting with the representatives of the Corporate Alliance and the trade delegation from Ord Mantell. Then—"

"Enough," Valorum said, holding up his hands and shutting his eyes. He gestured to the door and the corridors beyond. "How bad are things out there?"

"As crowded as I've ever seen it, sir," she said. "But I'm afraid that that's not the half of it."

Valorum stood up and reached for his cloak. "Tell me the rest."

"The plaza is swarming with demonstrators. Some are calling for the breakup of the Trade Federation, others are denouncing your stand on taxation. Security recommends that we leave by way of the rooftop platforms."

"No," Valorum said firmly. "This was to be expected, and now is hardly the time for me to avoid my critics."

Sei smiled approvingly. "I told security you would say that. They said that if you insisted on exiting through the plaza, they would be tripling the guard."

"Very well." Valorum squared his shoulders. "Are you ready?"

Sei went to the door. "After you, sir."

No sooner did Valorum enter the anteroom than two tall Senate Guards stepped in to flank him. They wore long dark-blue robes and gloves, and double-crested helmet cowls that left visible only the eyes and mouth. Over their right shoulders, the guards carried long, cumbersome rifles that were more ceremonial than practical. By the time Valorum had passed into the front offices, more guards had fallen in before and behind him. Short of the public corridors another pair joined the group, and yet two more the moment Valorum emerged in the corridor.

Wide as it was, the walkway was crammed with beings, who had been forced to stand shoulder to shoulder along both walls behind hastily erected barricades.

The guards in front of Valorum closed ranks in a wedge formation, thrusting through a forest of outstretched arms. Still, some hands managed to get through, bearing messages meant for the deep pockets of Valorum's cloaks but more often than not ending up trampled underfoot on the polished stone floor.

The corridor was loud with voices, as well, most of them entreating Valorum to attend to one urgent matter or another.

"Supreme Chancellor, about the terms of the peace negotiation . . ."

"Supreme Chancellor, regarding the recent devaluation of the Bothan credit . . ."

"Supreme Chancellor, your promise to respond to accusations of corruption leveled against Senator Maxim . . ."

Valorum recognized some of the voices and many of the faces. Crushed against the left wall he noticed the delegate from New Bornalex. Behind him, Senator Grebleips and his trio of large-eyed, puddle-footed delegates from Brodo Asogi. Off to the right, straining to reach to the front of the crowd in time for Valorum's passing, stood Malastare delegate Aks Moe.

As they neared the exit to the plaza, the voices in the corridor were overwhelmed by the chants and bellows of crowds of demonstrators massed along the Avenue of the Core Founders, with its towering statues and sunken sitting areas.

The Senate Guards pressed closer still, all but lifting Valorum off his feet and spiriting him outside the building on their shoulders.

The chief of the guard detail swung to Valorum. "Sir, we'll be proceeding directly to the north hover platform. Your personal shuttle is already waiting. There will be no stopping along the way to respond to reporters or protestors. In the event of any untoward activity, you will submit to our custody and do as we say. Any questions, sir?"

"No questions," Valorum said by rote. "But let's at least attempt to appear cordial, Captain."

"You didn't mention you were inviting me to a political rally," Qui-Gon said, as he and Adi Gallia arrived at the expansive plaza that fronted the senate.

"I didn't know," Adi said, plainly astonished by the sight.

Mixed-species crowds extended from the pedestaled

building itself, clear to the terminus of the Avenue of the Core Founders. The balconies there overlooked a sprawl of spired buildings, their close-set summits rising below the plaza.

"Where are you supposed to meet him?" Qui-Gon said loudly enough to be heard over the periodic chants and general clamor.

"Outside the north entrance," she answered, close to his ear.

Tall enough to see over the heads of many in the crowd, Qui-Gon gazed toward the senate dome. "There'll be no getting to him—not if I know the Senate Guard."

"Let's try, anyway," Adi said. "Otherwise, we'll go to his private office in the Presidential Tower."

Qui-Gon took Adi's hand and began to edge into the crowd. This far from the building, there was no telling the pro-Valorum from the anti-Valorum protestors.

Qui-Gon stretched out with his feelings.

Beneath the current of anger and dissent, something else was in the air. Coruscant's usual howl was charged with menace. He sensed danger—not the vague sort that might emanate from any gathering of this nature, but specific and targeted. He closed his eyes momentarily and allowed the Force to guide him.

His opened eyes found a Bith, standing at the leading edge of one gathering. The Force bade Qui-Gon look to his left, to two Rodians, lurking near the tall base of one of the statues. Closer to the senate's north exit stood two Twi'leks and a Bothan.

Qui-Gon raised his gaze to the ceaseless traffic flow above the plaza's north end. A green air taxi caught his eye. Disk-shaped and open-topped, with a semicircle of stabilizers below, it was no different from most of the other taxis that filled Coruscant's sky. But the fact that it was riding outside the defined corridor of the autonavigation lane told Qui-Gon that the pilot—another Rodian—knew the skylanes well enough to have been granted a free-travel permit.

Not far below the taxi, just at the rim of the plaza, hovered an eight-lobed repulsorlift platform, atop which sat Chancellor Valorum's personal shuttle.

Qui-Gon swung to Adi. "I sense a disturbance in the Force."

She nodded. "I feel it, Qui-Gon."

He glanced up at the air taxi, then cut his eyes to the Rodians positioned near the statue base. "The Supreme Chancellor is in danger. We need to hurry."

Unclipping their lightsabers from their belts, they began to thread their way through the crowd, their brown cloaks billowing behind them. They reached the north exit in time to see a phalanx of guards surge into the plaza. Behind them came Valorum and his young aide, at the center of six other guards, who were steering the couple toward the docking platform.

Qui-Gon looked up. The air taxi reversed direction and began to hover above the plaza. At the same instant, the two Twi'leks began to hasten toward Valorum, their hands buried in the sleeves of their loose robes.

The chanting rose to a crescendo.

Suddenly, blaster bolts streaked from the crowd, catching two of the most forward guards and dropping them to the paving stones. Screams erupted and the crowd panicked, rushing every which way to avoid danger.

Qui-Gon ignited his lightsaber and moved toward the Twi'leks. Weapons drawn, they fired, only to see the bolts deflected by the brilliant green blade of Qui-Gon's lightsaber. Additional bolts darted from the Rodians' blasters, but Qui-Gon moved quickly and managed to deflect those. He twirled, raising his weapon to parry fire, careful to divert the bolts above the heads of the scattering demonstrators.

The Force told him that Adi, her azure blade ignited, had angled for Valorum, who was effectively pinned to the plaza by his guards.

A muffled explosion sounded nearby, launching clouds of astringent white smoke and further terrifying the fleeing demonstrators.

Qui-Gon understood at once that the detonation was only a distraction. The real danger came from the opposite side of the plaza, where two more assassins were racing forward, armed with small hand blasters. As another guard fell, one of the assassins fired into the gap that had been opened in Valorum's protective cordon. Adi turned two of the energy darts, but a third got through.

Valorum grimaced in pain and toppled sideways.

A Senate Guard advanced, his long rifle blazing, felling both assassins.

Qui-Gon heard the air taxi begin a rapid descent, its rounded form trailing a trio of hauling cables. A Twi'lek and the two Rodians fought their way to a clear area in the plaza and grabbed hold of the cables.

Qui-Gon prized a liquid-cable launcher from a pouch on his belt and fired it as he ran. The hook bit deep into the underside of the taxi, and the monofilament cable began to unspool. Qui-Gon hooked onto the cable, thumbed the winding mechanism, and rode it skyward, his lightsaber extended in his right hand.

Coming alongside the two Rodians, he severed their cables with his blade, sending them plummeting back to the plaza. The Twi'lek, however, was still above him, and Qui-Gon realized that he would never reach him in time. The air taxi was already banking for the northern lip of the plaza, clearly hoping to shake Qui-Gon loose into one of the chasms below.

Level with the tallest of the Core Founder statues, Qui-Gon let go and dropped, landing on the shoulders of the statue, then leaping to the pedestal base, and finally to the plaza.

Backing away and firing steadily, one of the Rodians ran into the arms of two Senate Guards, who threw him harshly to the paving stones. A broken leg kept the other Rodian rooted to the spot where he had fallen.

Qui-Gon spun on his boot heels and hurried for Valorum. Formed up into an unbreachable perimeter, the remaining guards stood with their feet planted and their rifles pointed straight out. Adi saw Qui-Gon approaching and told the guards to make room for him.

The right side of Valorum's cloak showed a large blood stain.

"We have to get him to the medcenter," Adi said in a rush.

Qui-Gon put his right hand under Valorum's left arm and eased him to his feet. Adi supported him from the other side. With their lightsabers still ignited, they began to move the Supreme Chancellor back into the senate building, while the guards covered their retreat.

It was theorized—by those who devoted themselves to such things—that one could fall from the roof of the senate dome and land directly in the medcenter at which the delegates enjoyed exclusive privilege, assuming, of course, that the winds that blew through Coruscant's chasms were just right, and that one managed to miss being struck by passing vehicles during the plunge through the traffic lanes.

A safer and more certain method for arriving intact at the Galactic Senate Medcenter was to ride a turbolift from the rotunda, or be delivered there by skycar, as Senator Palpatine had chosen to do.

The medcenter occupied the top five stories of an ordinary building that rose precipitously to Coruscant's midlevel. Its numerous entrances were coded, by color and other means, to individual species, many of whom required specific atmospheres and gravities, as was also the case with many of the senate rotunda balconies.

Sate Pestage piloted the skycar to an unoccupied lobe of a docking platform anchored to the entrance coded for humans and near-humans, by far the most adorned of all the rectangular admitting areas.

"Waste no time," Palpatine said from the backseat, "but be discreet."

Pestage nodded. "Consider it done."

Palpatine stepped from the rear of the circular skycar, gave a smart tug to the front of his embroidered cloak, and disappeared through the entrance. In the lobby he encountered Senator Orn Free Taa.

"I heard that you were here," Palpatine said.

The corpulent Twi'lek gave his massive head a presumably mournful shake. "A tragic event. Truly terrible."

Palpatine raised an eyebrow.

"All right," Taa huffed. "The truth is that Valorum has been blocking my requests for reduced tariffs for the exportation of ryll from Ryloth. If I can ease that by visiting him in the medcenter, so be it."

"We do what we must," Palpatine said mildly.

Taa studied him for a moment. "And I take it that your visit is prompted by genuine concern?"

"The supreme chancellor is the voice of the Republic, is he not?"

"For the moment," Taa said nastily.

With Senate Guard sentries posted throughout the admitting area, Palpatine was made to show his identification no fewer than six times before being ushered into a waiting room reserved for Valorum's visitors. There, he exchanged greetings with Alderaan's delegate to the senate, Bail Antilles—a tall, handsome man with dark hair—and with the equally distinguished senator from Corellia, Com Fordox.

"You've heard who's to blame for what happened?" Fordox asked as Palpatine sat down on the couch opposite him.

"Only that the Nebula Front appears to have been involved."

"We have confirmed evidence of their involvement," Antilles said.

Fordox's features reflected anger and confusion. "This is beyond comprehension."

"An act that cannot go unpunished," Antilles agreed.

Commiserating with them, Palpatine firmed his lips and shook his head. "A terrible sign of the times," he said.

Most of the infirmities that landed delegates in the med-center were usually the result of overindulgence in food or drink, or injuries sustained on the scoopball courts, in air taxi accidents, or as the outcome of the occasional honor duel. Rarely were delegates admitted because of illnesses, and even more rarely as a consequence of an assassination attempt.

Palpatine held himself accountable.

He should have seen what was coming during the meeting with Havac. More than once the young militant had stressed that Valorum needed to appreciate just how dangerous the Nebula Front was. But Palpatine hadn't thought Havac desperate enough to resort to assassination.

The fact that Havac was also a fool made him especially dangerous. Did he actually believe that things would go better for the Nebula Front with someone other than Valorum leading the senate? Didn't he realize that Valorum was the Front's best hope for restraining the Trade Federation, through taxation and other means? By attempting to kill Valorum, Havac had not only reinforced the Federation's assertion that the Nebula Front was a public menace, he had also given added weight to the Neimoidians' demand for additional defensive weapons.

Havac would need to be reminded just who his enemies were.

Unless, of course, there was more to Havac than met the eye, Palpatine told himself. Was Havac's pleasant but nondescript countenance masking a cunning intellect?

Palpatine deliberated while Fordox and Antilles had their visit with Valorum. He was still mulling it over when Sei Taria entered the waiting room some time later.

Palpatine rose and nodded. "How good to see you, Sei. Are you all right?"

She mustered a warm smile. "I'm fine now, Senator. But it was terrible."

Palpatine adopted a grave look. "We will do all we can to protect the Supreme Chancellor."

"I know you will."

"How is he?"

She glanced at the door. "Eager to see you."

Armed guards flanked the door to Valorum's room—a windowless corral of monitoring devices, overseen by a bipedal medical droid equipped with servogrip pincers and a rebreatherlike vocabulator.

Valorum looked pale and grim, but he was sitting up in bed, his right arm, from wrist to shoulder, encased in a soft tube filled with bacta. A transparent, gelatinous fluid produced by an insectoid alien species, bacta had the ability to promote rapid cell rejuvenation and healing, usually without scarring. Palpatine often felt that the wondrous substance was as key to the survival of the Republic as were the Jedi.

"Supreme Chancellor," he said, approaching the bed, "I came as soon as I heard."

Valorum made a gesture of dismissal with his left hand. "You shouldn't have bothered. They're releasing me later today." He motioned Palpatine to a chair. "Do you know what the guards did when they brought me in here? They cleared every patient from the emergency room, then emptied this entire floor, with scarcely a concern for the condition of the patients."

"The security was warranted," Palpatine said. "Knowing you would be brought here if they failed, the assassins could have stationed a second team in the admitting area."

"Perhaps," Valorum granted. "But I doubt the actions of my protectors earned me any new allies." He frowned. "Worse, I have to suffer the transparent concern of delegates like Orn Free Taa."

"Even Senator Taa understands that the Republic needs you," Palpatine said.

"Nonsense. There are many who are qualified to fill my position. Bail Antilles, Ainlee Teem . . . even you, Senator."

Palpatine feigned a startled expression. "Hardly, Supreme Chancellor."

Valorum grinned. "I couldn't help but note how the delegates responded to you during the special session."

"The Outer Rim is desperate for voices. I'm merely one of many."

Valorum shook his head. "It's more than that." He paused briefly. "In any event, I want to thank you for the message your aide delivered to the podium. But why didn't you inform me in advance of your plan to propose a summit meeting?"

Palpatine spread his graceful hands. "It was a spur-of-the-moment decision. Something had to be done before the taxation proposal went to committee, where it may have been crushed out of hand."

"A brilliant stroke." Valorum fell silent for a long moment. "The Judicial Department has advised me that my attackers are members of the Nebula Front."

"I've also heard."

Valorum forced an exhale. "Now I see what the Trade Federation is up against."

Palpatine said nothing.

"But what was the Nebula Front's motive in attacking me? I'm doing what I can to find a peaceful solution to all this."

"Your efforts are obviously not enough for them," Palpatine said.

"Are they so convinced that Antilles or Teem would act differently?"

Palpatine formed his response carefully. "Senator Antilles thinks only of the Core Worlds. Doubtless he would advocate a policy of nonintervention. As for Senator Teem, he would probably bestow whatever the Trade Federation requests in the way of advanced weaponry or additional franchises."

Valorum thought about it. "Perhaps I was wrong in ruling that the Nebula Front shouldn't be allowed to participate in the Eriadu summit. I feared giving the impression that the Republic would be recognizing them as a political entity. Furthermore, I couldn't envision them sitting down at the same table with the Neimoidians." Confusion clouded his eyes. "But what could they hope to gain by having me killed?"

Palpatine recalled Havac ranting about not being invited to the summit. *We need a stronger Supreme Chancellor,* Havac had said.

"I've been asking myself the same question," Palpatine replied. "But you were right not to solicit their participation. They are dangerous—and deluded."

Valorum nodded. "We can't risk having them interfere at Eriadu. Too much is at stake. The outlying systems must be encouraged to speak for themselves, without fear of reprimand by the Trade Federation or reprisals by the Nebula Front."

Palpatine steepled his fingers in reflection, summoning memories of the recent meeting with Havac, hearing again his every word . . .

"Perhaps it is time to ask the Jedi for help," he said at last.

Valorum regarded him for a long moment. "Yes, perhaps the Jedi would be willing to intervene." He brightened somewhat. "Two of them helped thwart my would-be assassins."

"Indeed?"

"The senate will have to sanction Jedi involvement. Would you consider introducing the motion?"

Palpatine smiled with his eyes. "I would consider it a great honor, Supreme Chancellor."

Leaving the hospital docking platform behind, Sate Pestage accelerated into a midlevel traffic lane, then, at each vertical exchange, began to ascend toward the upper-tier thoroughfares, until he had entered a rarefied zone of limousines and private skycars. Here, one seldom encountered a taxi, much less a delivery craft, because those who resided in the heights owned their own vehicles, and goods were delivered to the lower stories of the buildings and moved skyward by turbolift.

Pestage kept climbing until he was in the uppermost lane. In that part of Coruscant, the lane was restricted to skycars the mobile traffic scanners could verify as enjoying diplomatic privilege, which Senator Palpatine's vehicle did.

He piloted the car to the attached platform of a luxurious, kilometer-high skyscraper and docked. From the car's luggage compartment, he retrieved two expensive-looking bags. The larger was a square handheld piece; the other was a sphere about the size of a sweetmelon, which fit snugly into a specially designed shoulder bag.

Pestage carried both into the building's upper-tier

lobby, where he was scanned head to toe before being allowed to enter the turbolift that accessed the penthouse. Once again, his employer's credentials opened many a door that would otherwise have been locked to him. Few residents were about, and none gave him a second look, trusting implicitly that anyone who had managed to get into the building had every right to be there.

He rode the turbolift to the penthouse, which was owned by one of Palpatine's peers in the senate, but was presently unoccupied, as the senator had, only the previous day, embarked on a visit to her homeworld.

In the penthouse alcove, Pestage carried the bags to the entry and tapped a code into a touchpad mounted on the wall. When the scanner asked for retinal corroboration, he entered a second code, which essentially commanded the scanner to cut short its usual security routine and simply open the suite.

The bypass code did the job, and the door pocketed itself into the wall.

Soft lighting came up as Pestage moved into the elegant front room. Furniture and artwork attesting to the senator's refined taste were everywhere in evidence. Pestage went directly to the terrace doors and stepped outside.

Traffic hummed below the tiled enclosure, and the lights of still-higher buildings shone down on him. The air was ten degrees cooler than at midlevel, and nowhere near as grimy. From the chest-high wall at the edge of the terrace, Pestage could see clear to the Jedi Temple in one direction and the Galactic Senate in the other.

But those weren't the views that interested him; only the view directly across the cityscape canyon, into a mostly darkened penthouse of similar size.

Pestage set the two pieces of luggage on the floor and opened them. The square one contained a computer, with a built-in display and keypad. The second was a surveillance droid, black and round, with three antennae projecting from its metallic pate and sides. Standing the computer on end, Pestage positioned the droid alongside it.

The two devices conversed for a long moment, in a dialogue of beeps and warbles. Then the surveillance droid levitated of its own accord and began to float out into the canyon.

Pestage repositioned the computer so that he could monitor the flight of the surveillance droid while he entered commands on the keyboard.

By then the black sphere had crossed the abyss and was hovering just outside one of the penthouse's lighted rooms, and relaying color images back to the computer's display screen. The small screen showed five Twi'lek females, lounging together on comfortable furniture. One of the females was Senator Orn Free Taa's red-skinned Lethan consort. The others may have been lesser consorts, or simply friends of the Lethan, indulging in drink and gossip while the fat-faced senator was off visiting Valorum at the medcenter.

Pestage was pleased. The females were so absorbed in debauched merriment that they were unlikely to interfere with his business.

He instructed the surveillance droid to move to an unlighted window, three rooms away, and go to infrared mode. A moment later the screen displayed a close-up of Taa's computer terminal, which, while it was capable of interfacing with distant systems, could not be accessed remotely.

Pestage did rapid input at the keyboard.

Pressing close to the window, the droid activated a laser and burned a small hole in the sound-silencing and blasterproof pane—just large enough to accommodate the computer interface arm that telescoped from its spherical body. At the end of the arm's extensible rod was a magnetic lock, which the droid inserted into the access port of Taa's system.

The computer booted up and asked for a passcode, which Pestage provided. A novice operative might have thought to ask Senator Palpatine how he had secured the passcode. But part of what made Pestage a true professional was knowing when not to ask questions.

Taa's computer welcomed him inside.

Now it was simply a matter of slicing into the relevant files and planting the bits of coded information Pestage had been given. Even so, the infiltration was hardly routine. First of all, the data had to be untraceable, and it had to be implanted in such a way that the computer would be convinced that it had, in fact, discovered the data. Then the computer had to be instructed to reveal the data—to flag it—only in response to specific requests from Taa.

Most important, Taa himself would have to be persuaded that he had uncovered data of such resounding import that he was compelled to shout it from the rooftops.

At the center of the Jedi Temple's High Council spire was an enormous holographic representation of the galaxy, which highlighted trouble spots and locations of Jedi activity. The spherical projection changed in accordance with signals received by a multifeed assembly located in the tower's summit chamber, while a collimating disk located beneath the projection focused the signal beams and sustained them through power fluctuations.

Qui-Gon and Obi-Wan stood on the circular walkway that surrounded the holomap, waiting to be called before the members of the High Council. Several other Jedi were about, studying the map or headed for one of the three exterior contemplation balconies that overlooked the vast plain of cityscape below the Temple. It was from the dawn-facing balcony that Qui-Gon had had his first real look at Coruscant.

"This is the first time I've ever seen Coruscant singled out," Obi-Wan remarked as he gazed up at the sphere, his elbows resting on the walkway railing.

Qui-Gon glanced at the flashing spheroid that was Coruscant, then allowed his eyes to roam midway to the holomap's perimeter, where a second spheroid was aglow.

Dorvalla.

"Coruscant should remain illuminated at all times," he started to say, when yet another spheroid, at even greater remove than Dorvalla, began to flash.

"Eriadu," Obi-Wan said, reading the graphic attached to it. He looked questioningly at Qui-Gon.

"The site of the upcoming trade summit."

"Whose idea was that, Master?" Obi-Wan asked.

"Senator Palpatine," a baritone human voice said from behind them.

They turned to find Jorus C'baoth watching them. An elder human Jedi Master, C'baoth had a chiseled face, white hair as long as Qui-Gon's, and a beard three times as long.

"Palpatine represents Naboo," C'baoth added.

"Just the world for Qui-Gon," another human Jedi said from farther along the walkway.

C'baoth nodded. "More indigenous species in one square kilometer than you normally encounter on a hundred worlds." He smiled faintly. "I could easily see Master Qui-Gon losing himself there."

Before either Qui-Gon or Obi-Wan could respond, Adi Gallia entered the holomap room. "We're ready for you, Qui-Gon," she announced.

Qui-Gon and Obi-Wan folded their arms, so that each hand disappeared into the opposite sleeve of their cloaks, and followed Gallia to the turbolift that accessed the summit chamber.

"Don't say anything, Padawan," Qui-Gon said quietly when they reached the circular chamber. "Simply listen and learn."

Obi-Wan nodded. "Yes, Master."

Arch-topped panes of transparisteel afforded unob-structed views in all directions. The ceiling was also arched, and the lustrous floor was designed as a series of concentric circles, inlaid with floral motifs.

Leaving Obi-Wan to wait by the turbolift, Qui-Gon advanced to the center of the room and stood with his hands crossed in front of him.

To the right of the turbolift sat Depa Billaba, a slender near-human female from Chalacta, who wore a mark of illumination between and slightly above her eyes. Beside her was Eeth Koth, his face a jigsaw puzzle of lines, and his hairless head studded with vestigial yellow horns of varying length. Next came the long-necked Quermian, Yarael Poof; then Adi, Oppo Rancisis, and Even Piell, a Lannik warrior whose face bore a puckered scar. To Piell's left sat Yaddle, a female of Yoda's species; Saesee Tiin, an Iktotchi, with downward-facing horns; Ki-Adi-Mundi, a strikingly tall humanoid from Cerea; Yoda, in the red chair that cupped him; and Yoda's peer, Mace Windu, a powerfully built, dark-complexioned human with a shaved skull. To Windu's left, close to the opposite side of the turbolift entrance, sat Plo Koon.

Fingers interlocked, Mace Windu leaned forward in his seat to address Qui-Gon. "We've just met with members of the Judicial Department, regarding the attempted as-sassination of Supreme Chancellor Valorum. We're trust-ing that you can shed additional light on what transpired at the Galactic Senate."

Qui-Gon nodded. "I trust that I can."

Yoda glanced at Windu, then leveled his gaze at Qui-Gon. "How came you to be at the senate, Qui-Gon? Alerted by your source in the Nebula Front, were you?"

"I'll answer that," Adi Gallia said. "I asked Qui-Gon to accompany me to the Senate, to speak personally with Supreme Chancellor Valorum."

Windu regarded her with a frown. "For what purpose?"

Adi looked briefly to Qui-Gon. "Qui-Gon has reason to believe that the Supreme Chancellor errs by relying on worlds along the Rimma Trade Route to end terrorism in those sectors."

"Is this so, Qui-Gon?" Ki-Adi-Mundi asked.

Qui-Gon nodded. "The Nebula Front receives much of its funding from those very worlds."

"Knows much about the situation, Qui-Gon does," Yoda said with false flattery. "Correct he was about Captain Cohl surviving the explosion at Dorvalla." He paused. "Behind the attempted assassination attempt, is Cohl?"

"No, Master," Qui-Gon said. "Cohl is on the run. Furthermore, I'm not persuaded that the Nebula Front actually wished to harm the Supreme Chancellor."

Yoda's expression hardened. "Shot him, they did. Traced by documentation to their secret base in the Senex sector, they were."

"Too easily, Master," Qui-Gon said, holding his ground. "The signs were far too obvious."

"Terrorists they are. Not soldiers."

Windu looked at Yoda, then at Qui-Gon. "You've obviously given thought to this. Continue."

"The assassins aimed their bolts at Supreme Chancellor Valorum's guards. I believe that the bolt that grazed him was inadvertent. The escape was also unconvincing. And since they must have known in advance that there was little chance of all of them getting away, why would they carry documentation?"

"Unlike Captain Cohl, eh, Qui-Gon?"

Qui-Gon nodded. "He would not have been so careless."

Yoda brought his right forefinger to his mouth. "Plan this he did—from afar. Seek out your Bith contact in the Nebula Front, you must."

Qui-Gon turned to him. "I'll do that, Master. Still, why would the Front target the Supreme Chancellor, when he has finally taken a stand against the Trade Federation?"

"Answer your own question," Windu said.

Qui-Gon took a breath and gave his head a quick shake. "I'm not certain, Masters. But I fear that the Nebula Front has something even more treacherous in mind."

Hyphens of angry light streaking past her to all sides, the *Hawk-Bat* fled the surface of a green planet, graced by two small, close-set, and heavily cratered moons. Her ardent pursuers were a trio of slender-bodied vessels, Coruscant red from stem to stern, with blunt bows, a trio of large, drum-shaped sublight thrusters, and multiple pairs of turbolaser batteries.

In the gunship's cramped bridge, Boiny studied the console's authenticator displays. "Corellian space cruisers, Captain! Gaining fast! Estimated time before they overtake us is—"

"I don't want to know," Cohl said from the captain's chair, as an explosion pitched the ship roughly to port. "Blasted Judicial Department! Don't they have better things to do?"

"Apparently not, Captain," Boiny rejoined.

Cohl swiveled away from the forward viewports to regard Rella, who had the controls. "How soon before we can make the jump to lightspeed?"

She shot him an angry look. "The navicomputer is holding out on us."

Cohl glanced at Boiny. "Persuade it."

The Rodian staggered across the cockpit and slammed his hand against the navicomputer.

"That'll do it," Rella said, relieved.

Another bolt rocked the ship.

"Route power to the rear deflectors," Cohl ordered.

"I'm on it, Captain," Boiny said, as he strapped back into his chair.

Rella turned slightly to Cohl. "You know, not everyone thrives on close calls."

He laughed theatrically. "This from someone who claims that an escape isn't worthwhile unless it's narrow?"

"That was the old me. The new me has different ideas about what's fun and what isn't."

"Then you'd better stow the new you until we hit clear space."

Stung in the tail, the *Hawk-Bat* shuddered as she rolled to one side.

"Where are those jump coordinates?" Cohl snapped.

"Coming up now," Rella assured him. "It's time we put this sector behind us, Cohl. Every one of our hideouts is under surveillance."

"And just where are we supposed to go?"

"I don't care if we go live with the Hutts. I just know it's gotten too hot for us here."

Cohl grimaced. "Don't tell me you'd work for those bloated worms."

"Who said anything about working?"

"What about our retiring in high style?"

"Right about now, I'll settle for retiring, plain and simple."

Cohl shook his head. "That's not the way I planned it. Besides, I don't like the idea of getting chased out of my own hunting ground."

"Even when it's clear you've become the prey?"

Cohl watched Rella for a long moment. "You're serious, aren't you? You're thinking of quitting this tour."

She bit her lip and nodded. "Unless you decide to come to your senses, Cohl. We're too old for this. I want to make good on some of the promises we made ourselves, before it's too late."

He thought about it, then laughed. "You won't walk. You know you'd miss me and come looking for me."

Rella showed him a sad look. "You're still thinking of the old me, Cohl."

He glanced at Boiny. "Am I right or wrong about her looking for me?"

The Rodian ducked his crested head. "Don't get me in the middle of this. I'm only good at following orders."

Cohl shook his head at Rella. "Our first fight."

"Wrong, Cohl. Our last." She reached for the throttle. "Making the jump to hyperspace."

With laser bolts still nipping at her, the *Hawk-Bat* surged forward. The stars elongated, and the gunship blinked from view.

In the greeting room of his office in the Galactic Senate, Valorum slipped into his veda cloth robe and regarded his image in an elaborately framed mirror. His right arm was almost healed, and instead of the cumbersome tube, a soft case was in place, concealed within the ample sleeve of his overcloak.

A pair of Senate Guards flanked the door, facing into the room, but Valorum ignored them as he prepared for the imminent arrival of Jedi Masters Mace Windu and Yoda.

The Valorum dynasty had long hoped that one of its offspring might be strong in the Force, but, by all accounts, it appeared that the Force just wasn't in Valorum blood. That regrettable absence, however, hadn't stopped Finis Valorum from revering the Jedi. As an entitled youth on Coruscant and on other Core worlds, he had passed countless hours with the family chronicles, devouring accounts of his ancestors' dealings with the order—often with Jedi Knights and Masters of legendary status. The tales had only firmed a belief developed early on that, even if he couldn't be a Jedi, he could at least model his life after them, behaving as if the Force were his ally, and devoting himself to upholding peace and justice at all times.

But the Republic Valorum had inherited had afforded him few opportunities to foster peace or justice. Weakened by greed and corruption, the senate had become a tool for widening the rift between rich and poor, and bolstering the ambitions of the privileged and influential. Try as he might to remain faithful to his ideals, Valorum had found himself foiled by delegates fattened on bribes or enslaved to self-interest. Why serve the common good when it was more profitable to serve the Commerce Guild, the Techno Union, the Corporate Alliance, or the Trade Federation?

Whether for personal reasons or in exchange for trade favors for their home systems, more than half the senate's delegates answered to the powerful corporations, which, in return, asked only that certain motions be quashed, or others be supported. Time and again Valorum was made to appear weak by being overruled, and that perceived weakness had made those who should have known better to consider him to be ineffectual.

Ineptitude, of course, was the unexpressed goal of the corruptors themselves. Where a weak leader would have been replaced, and a strong one counterproductive, one who had simply given up the fight was seen as the best of all possible solutions.

The rueful middle ground had been Valorum's domain for too many years, until recently, when senators like Bail Antilles, Horox Ryyder, Palpatine, and a few others had begun to rally round, pledging their support to help end corruption—or, at the very least, to keep it in check. Many thought that the current crisis involving the Trade Federation would be a testing ground for what lay ahead. Valorum hoped only that he could spend the final years of his term in office doing right by everyone, in true service to peace and justice.

That was why the Nebula Front had to be contained.

Normally the Jedi were not asked to intervene in trade disputes, but the attempt on Valorum's life had had less to do with trade than with preserving law and order. Because the Jedi answered to the Supreme Chancellor and the Judicial Department, their assistance could now be solicited, and in that sense, the assassination attempt had been a blessing in disguise.

Valorum could not recall an instance where they had refused to serve, in any case. On occasion, though, dealing with them had made Valorum feel as if he were contracting with a power even greater than that enjoyed by the various trade consortiums or the Republic.

Ten thousand strong, their collective strength was such that they could rule the Republic if they so wished—if their dedication to peace was any less demonstrably earnest. Although the Republic government funded the order, at times there seemed to exist an added price for their support—a sense that they might one day come to Valorum and demand that the favors they had rendered be returned tenfold. Although Valorum couldn't imagine what they might ask for that either he or the Republic could provide. While the Jedi operated in the world, they were at once outside it, living within the Force, as if it were a separate reality.

It sometimes seemed to Valorum that the Jedi behaved as if the Force ruled the ordinary world, and that the role of the Jedi was to behave in such a way that a balance between good and evil, light and dark, was forever preserved—lest the scales tip one way or the other, opening a portal for the dark to come streaming in, or for allowing the light to blind everyone to some greater truth.

Two thousand years earlier, the Jedi had faced a

menacing threat to continuing peace, in the form of the Sith Lords and their armies of dark-side apprentices. Founded by a fallen Jedi, the Sith believed that power disavowed was power squandered. In place of justice for all, they sought single-minded authority. Agitation and conflict were thought to be more crucial to transformation than was gradual understanding.

Fortunately, dark power was not easily harnessed, and over the course of a thousand years, the Sith had ultimately destroyed themselves.

Valorum heard the guards snap to attention as the greeting room opened and Sei Taria entered, followed by the two Jedi Masters. Dignified in his hooded robe, linen-white tunic, and knee-high brown boots, Mace Windu seemed to fill the room. But it was the slight and enigmatic Yoda, in well-seasoned and less-tailored robes, who took up the most space.

"Masters Windu and Yoda," Valorum said warmly. "Thank you for coming."

Yoda regarded him for a moment, then smiled lightly. "Restored, you are."

Valorum touched his right forearm beneath the cloak. "Nearly. If the assassin had been a better shot . . ."

Windu and Yoda traded meaningful looks.

"How may the Jedi be of service, Supreme Chancellor?" Windu asked.

Valorum motioned to chairs in the sitting area. "Won't you be seated?"

Windu sat tall and straight, with his feet flat on the floor. Yoda considered sitting, then paced to the center of the room, tapping the floor with his cane.

"Think better in motion, I do."

Valorum dismissed Sei Taria and the two guards and sat down opposite Windu, where he could watch Yoda, as well.

"I trust you've heard that the assassins have been identified as members of the Nebula Front." Valorum waited for Windu's nod before continuing. "The few that managed to escape were traced to Asmeru, a world on the edge of the Senex sector."

Leaning toward the table that separated him from Windu, Valorum activated a holoprojector. In a cone of translucent blue light, a star map took shape. Valorum indicated a cluster of star systems.

"The Senex is an autonomous sector, ruled by a line of fiercely self-reliant royal houses. The Republic respects the independence of the Senex worlds, and has no interest in meddling in the affairs of those worlds—given especially my recent request that worlds along the nearby Rimma Trade Route unite to curtail terrorism in their sector of space. However, when affairs there reach across the stars to affect Coruscant, we cannot stand idly by."

Valorum switched off the holoprojector.

"I have communicated with the rulers of Houses Vandron and Elegin, who hold sway over Asmeru and other systems in that part of the Senex sector. They deny granting the Nebula Front safe haven. Rather, they contend that the terrorists seized Asmeru from a scant indigenous population, and have been using the planet as a base of operations for raids against ships plying the Rimma Trade Route and Corellian Trade Spine. Wishing to avoid becoming targets of the Nebula Front, Houses Vandron and Elegin have essentially ignored activities on Asmeru."

"Until now," Windu interjected.

Valorum nodded. "They have agreed to help us in our effort to contain the Nebula Front on Asmeru until the Eriadu trade summit concludes."

Yoda frowned. "Breeders of slaves, they are. No better than those who make up the Nebula Front."

Valorum acknowledged it with a fatigued sigh. "It's

true. Slavery is what has prevented the Senex sector from trading openly with the Republic. The possibility of trade is what prompts their willingness to help us."

Windu's eyebrows beetled. "What help are the Senex Houses offering?"

"Logistical support. Owing to a nearby gravitic sink, as well as to space mines sown by the Nebula Front, Asmeru is not easily approached. House Vandron has offered to guide us in."

Windu considered it. "You wish us to accompany the Judicial Department cruisers."

"Yes," Valorum said flatly. "Should you consent, I will petition the senate for authorization. But allow me to explain. This operation is not designed to be a show of force, nor an attempt at retaliation for what happened here. I propose to dispatch two cruisers, carrying thirty judicials, along with as many Jedi as you see fit to include.

"For all we know, those responsible for the attempt on my life could be members of a radical faction. The rest may know nothing of the assassination plot. Nevertheless, I don't want them disrupting the Eriadu summit. I also wish to learn what they hoped to accomplish by assassinating me. If their actions sprang from not being included in the trade summit, then I want them to know that I am willing to meet with them, as soon as they agree to desist in attacking Trade Federation vessels. If they are unwilling to enact a truce, the Trade Federation will likely be given consent to increase their already substantial arsenal of weapons."

Windu glanced at Yoda before replying. "And if our attempt to communicate these things to those in charge is rebuffed?"

Valorum frowned. "Then I would ask that the Jedi see to it that no one involved with the Nebula Front leaves Asmeru. They are to be contained there until further notice."

Windu stroked his smooth chin. "You could be sending your judicials into a trap."

"We have to take that risk," Valorum said sternly, then softened his voice to add, "We should at least attempt to negotiate before deciding on desperate measures." He looked from Windu to Yoda, and back again.

Yoda stopped moving to gaze unsympathetically at Valorum. "Want to see this conflict resolved, we do."

Windu interlocked his fingers and leaned forward in his chair. "The Trade Federation should not be granted additional weaponry. Defensive or otherwise, weapons are not the way to settle this. Such actions will lead only to further escalation."

"I agree," Valorum said sadly. "And I wish it was that simple. But the Trade Federation is deeply entrenched in Republic politics."

"At war with yourself, you are," Yoda remarked. "Caught up in your own conflict."

Chagrined by the remark, Valorum shook his head from side to side. "These matters require great delicacy, and deals of a sort I am loathe to make."

Windu firmed his lips. "We will consider what help we could lend at Asmeru."

Valorum was disappointed "Thank you, Master Windu. I would also request that you consider providing security at the Eriadu summit. No one, I fear, is safe."

Windu nodded, stood up, and walked to the door. Yoda turned to Valorum before leaving.

"Confer we will, and inform you of our decision."

Docking rings linked by a rigid cofferdam, the *Hawk-Bat* and a modified CloakShape orbited drab Asmeru in deeply shadowed concert.

"To be honest, I didn't expect you to come back,"

Havac was telling Captain Cohl in the forward compartment of the gunship.

Cohl sniffed. "To be honest, I didn't expect to come back."

Havac's partner, Cindar, made a show of glancing around the compartment. "Where's your first mate, Captain?"

"She walked," Cohl said.

Havac regarded him for a moment. "And you didn't walk with her? Why not?"

"My business," Cohl snapped.

Cindar couldn't suppress a smug grin. "You came back because you couldn't resist the credits, and she could."

Cohl gave his head a smart shake. "It's not the credits that brought me back. It's the life." He laughed bitterly. "How does someone like me retire? What do I know about farming?" He slapped the blaster on his hip. "This is what I know. This is how I am."

Havac swapped satisfied looks with Cindar. "Then we're even more pleased to have you back aboard, Captain."

Cohl planted his elbows on the table. "Then make it worth the trip."

Havac nodded. "Maybe you haven't heard, but Supreme Chancellor Valorum intends to press for taxation of the free trade zones. If the proposal meets with Senate approval, the Trade Federation stands to see a lot of its profits end up on Coruscant. All well and good, if the Neimoidians would agree to take it on the chin, but they won't. They'll try to offset the taxes by raising the costs for shipping with them. Without anyone else to ship with, the outlying systems will have no choice but to pay whatever the Federation demands. Worlds that refuse to play by the new rules will be overlooked, and their markets will collapse."

"Competition will get cutthroat," Cindar added. "Especially hard for worlds desperate to do trade with the Core. There'll be credits galore for anyone willing to take advantage of the situation."

Cohl gazed at the two of them and smirked. "What's all that got to do with me? I couldn't care less what happens to either side."

Havac's gaze narrowed. "Disinterest is exactly what this job calls for, since our goal is to change the rules."

Cohl waited.

"We want you to assemble a team of spotters, trackers, and weapons experts," Havac said. "They have to be highly skilled, and they should share your penchant for impartiality. But I don't want to use professionals. I don't want to take the chance of their being under surveillance already, or first-choice suspects after the fact."

"You're looking for assassins," Cohl said.

"We're not asking you to be involved in the act," Cindar said. "Only the delivery. In case you need to soothe your conscience any, think of the team as a shipment of weapons."

Cohl's upper lip curled. "I'll let you know when my conscience needs soothing. Who's the target?"

"Supreme Chancellor Valorum," Havac said carefully.

"We want to strike during the trade summit on Eriadu," Cindar elaborated.

Cohl stared at them in amusement. "This is the major job you promised?"

Cindar spread his huge hands. "Your assured retirement, Captain."

Cohl shook his head and laughed. "Who put this bright idea in your head, Havac?"

Havac stiffened. "We're receiving help from a powerful outside agency, sympathetic to our cause."

"The same one who told you about the shipment of aurodium."

"The less you know, the better," Cindar warned.

Cohl laughed again. "Secret information, huh?"

Havac's forehead wrinkled in concern. "You don't think the job can be done?"

Cohl shrugged. "Anyone can be killed."

"Then why are you hesitant?"

Cohl blew out his breath in scorn. "You two must take me for a furbog trader. Just because I've been chased up and down the Rimma and all over this sector doesn't mean I don't keep an ear to the background noise. You tried to kill Valorum on Coruscant, and you fumbled the job. Now you're turning to me, which you should have done in the first place."

Cindar returned the sneer. "You weren't interested, remember? You were bent on a life of moisture farming on Tatooine."

"Besides, we didn't fumble anything," Havac said. "We thought we could scare Valorum into inviting the Nebula Front to attend the summit. He didn't bite, so now we mean to finish the job on Eriadu."

Cindar grinned malevolently. "We're going to ruin his summit in a way no one will soon forget."

Cohl scratched at his beard. "For what? So Valorum won't tax the free trade zones? How does that help the Nebula Front or the outlying systems?"

"I thought you weren't interested in politics," Havac said.

"Pure curiosity."

"All right," Havac allowed. "Without taxation, no worlds have to worry about increased costs. As for the

Trade Federation, we'll continue to deal with them in our own way."

Cohl was unconvinced. "You're going to cultivate a crop of new enemies, Havac—including the Jedi, if I know anything about anything. But I guess you're not paying me to think."

"Exactly," Cindar made clear. "Suppose you let us worry about the backlash."

"Fine with me," Cohl said. "But let's talk about Eriadu. Because of what you pulled on Coruscant, security is going to be extra tight. No matter what you were trying to do, you've already undermined yourselves."

"All the more reason to gather a highly skilled team," Havac agreed.

Cohl put his hands on the table. "I'll need a new ship. The *Hawk-Bat* is too well known."

"Done," Cindar promised. "What else?"

Cohl considered it briefly. "I don't suppose you could do anything about keeping the Jedi clear of my trajectory?"

Havac smiled. "As a matter of fact, Captain, I can practically guarantee that the Jedi are going to be busy elsewhere."

THE OUTLYING
SYSTEMS

Edging into jaded sunlight around the curve of a tiny moon, two diplomatic cruisers closed on pale-brown Asmeru. In front and to either side of the crimson Corellian ships flew a dark escort of Tikiar fighters, resembling beaked and taloned predatory birds. Lagging behind, still in the shadow of the moon, came a pair of colossal dreadnaughts with fanged bows and elegantly finned sterns, prickly with weapons and bearing the royal crest of House Vandron.

Light-years distant, etched into the star-strewn backdrop, loomed an immense spiral of light, attenuating toward a center of utter blackness.

Qui-Gon regarded the crazed sky from the cockpit of the trailing cruiser. Obi-Wan stood beside him, peering between the forward seats for a better view. The female pilot and male copilot wore the tight-fitting blue uniforms of the Judicial Department.

"Coming up on the minefield," the pilot said while her hands were busy making adjustments to the instruments.

A scattering of glinting cylinders caught Qui-Gon's eye.

"I might have mistaken them for asteroids," the co-pilot said.

Obi-Wan leaned toward him. "Things are not always what they appear to be."

Qui-Gon shot him a disapproving glance. "Remember that when we are on the surface, Padawan," he said quietly.

Obi-Wan bit back a retort and nodded. "Yes, Master."

The copilot called up a magnified view of one of the mines. "Command detonated," he said over his shoulder to Qui-Gon. "They can probably be triggered by the terrorists' sentry ships or from down below."

As Qui-Gon was considering it, a female voice issued from the cockpit annunciators.

"*Prominence,* this is *Ecliptic.* Our escort advises that we raise deflector shields and hold fast to our course. Long-range scans show three fighter craft on the far side of the minefield. We have high confidence that they are aware of us."

Qui-Gon touched Obi-Wan on the shoulder. "It's time we rejoined the others in the salon pod."

They left the cramped cockpit and walked aft down a narrow corridor that passed directly through the navigator's station, the communications station, and the crew lounge. The corridor terminated at a turbolift, which they rode to the lower deck. Then they walked forward through the salon pod's vestibule and into the roomy pod itself.

Nuzzled beneath the cruiser's abrupt bow and forward sensor array, the cone-shaped pods were interchangeable and capable of providing customized atmospheres. In emergency situations, they could be jettisoned and employed as escape vehicles. This one featured port and starboard viewports and a large circular table, with a holoprojector at its center.

"We're negotiating the minefield," Qui-Gon said.

"Indeed we are," Jedi Knight Ki-Adi-Mundi said from

the starboard viewport. He had a smooth, elongated skull and a piercing gaze. His chin sported a long tuft of gray hair; his upper lip, dangling gray mustachios that matched his thick eyebrows.

"Worried your young Padawan appears, Qui-Gon," Yaddle remarked from her seat at the table. "The minefield is it, or other concerns?"

Qui-Gon almost smiled. "That's his normal look of foreboding. When he's actually worried, you can see steam escaping his ears."

"Yes," Yaddle said. "Watch him train I did. Saw the steam."

"I'm not worried, Masters," Obi-Wan said good-naturedly. "I'm only thinking forward." He waited for Qui-Gon to offer some piece of wisdom regarding the living Force, but for once his Master kept silent.

"Right you are to think forward, Padawan," Yaddle told him. "Deal lightly with matters of consequence, and decisively with those of little consequence. Difficult it is to face a crisis and solve it gently, if not resolved beforehand you are, for uncertainty will impede your efforts. When comes the time, thinking forward allows you to deal lightly."

Her big eyes shifted to favor Qui-Gon. "Agree do you, Qui-Gon?"

He bowed his head. "As you say, Master."

Diagonally across the table from Yaddle, Saesee Tiin glanced up and smiled, as if reading Qui-Gon's thoughts. Next to him, and as small in stature as Yaddle, sat Vergere, a female Fosh, and the former apprentice of Thracia Cho Leem, who had left the Jedi Order several years earlier. Vergere's trim torso was covered with short feathers of varied color. Her slightly concave face was slant-eyed, wide-mouthed, delicately whiskered, and bracketed by willowy ears and twin antennae. A pair of reverse-articulated legs and splayed feet propelled her.

Alongside Vergere stood Depa Billaba, the hood of her brown cloak raised over her head.

The voice of the *Prominence*'s pilot crackled from the pod's speakers. "Master Tiin, incoming transmission from our escort."

Qui-Gon stepped closer to the table. Shortly, the image of an aristocratic human male appeared above the holoprojector.

"Esteemed members of the Jedi Order," the man began. "On behalf of Lord Crueya and Lady Theala of House Vandron, it is our honor to welcome you to the Senex sector. We apologize for the circuitous route we have been obliged to follow, and likewise for the precautions circumstances have obliged us to exercise. Tidal forces and orbital weapons make for an uncommonly hazardous mix."

He smiled thinly. "Be that as it may, we trust that you will not judge the Senex sector by what you are likely to encounter on Asmeru. The planet once supported great cities and grand palaces, but all those fell victim to sudden climatic change. The current population is comprised of Ossan slaves created on the Vandron world of Karfeddion, but banished here owing to defects of one sort or another. Bred for agricultural work, the slaves have managed to make a life for themselves, though we doubt that you will find them especially welcoming. That might have been the case with the members of the Nebula Front, as well, but for their superior weapons."

"Charming," Depa said, just loudly enough to be heard by her comrades.

"We're sorry we can't be of more assistance at this time," the human added. "Perhaps when the present crisis is resolved, the Senex Houses and the Republic can meet to discuss matters of mutual concern and benefit."

The miniature figure disappeared, leaving the seven Jedi to trade looks of misgiving.

"And not yet midway through the minefield are we," Yaddle said.

The comm chimed again.

"Communication from Asmeru downside," the pilot announced. "Nebula Front sentry ships are presenting no overt threat, but House Vandron fighters have dispersed to remove themselves from any possible action."

Through the port viewport Qui-Gon could see the sleek Tikiars peeling gracefully away from the *Prominence*. When he turned back to the table, a leathery-skinned humanoid with a barbarous twist to his mouth stood in the holoprojector's cone of blue light. His face was deeply pitted and his features were large. His skull was shaved, save for a braided topknot that fell to his shoulders. Qui-Gon thought that he was getting his first glimpse of one of Asmeru's banished slaves, until the humanoid spoke.

"Republic cruisers, identify yourselves or risk being fired on."

Saesee Tiin positioned himself for the holocam and spoke for the Jedi, his cowl lowered to reveal his tight, shiny face and downward-facing horns. "We are members of a diplomatic mission dispatched by Coruscant."

"This is not Republic space, Jedi. You have no authority here."

"We acknowledge that," Tiin replied in a calm voice. "But we have prevailed upon the rulers of this sector to guide us to Asmeru for the purpose of opening negotiations with the Nebula Front."

The humanoid showed his teeth. "The Nebula Front's grievances are with the Trade Federation, not Coruscant—

and we can settle those in our own fashion. What's more, we know full well how the Jedi 'negotiate.' "

Tiin leaned toward the holocam pickup, narrowing already narrow eyes. "Then let me provide you with a reason. Coruscant has grievances with the Nebula Front when they make an attempt on the life of a Republic dignitary."

The humanoid blinked in apparent bafflement. "Your meaning escapes me, Jedi. Whose life was threatened?"

"The life of Supreme Chancellor Valorum."

Concern tugged at the humanoid's gross features. "Your guides have misled you. As I said, we have no issue with the Republic."

"Some of the assassins were tracked to Asmeru," Tiin pressed.

"They may have been tracked here, but we know nothing of their actions."

Tiin pressed his point. "I propose that someone in a position of command come aboard and speak with us."

The humanoid scoffed. "You must be space happy."

"Then will you allow us to come to the surface and speak with you?"

"Do we have a choice in the matter?"

"No, not really."

"I thought as much," the humanoid said. "How many Jedi are you?"

"Seven."

"And how many judicials?"

"Perhaps twenty."

The humanoid turned to discuss the matter with someone out of view. "As a gesture of good faith, leave one of your cruisers in orbit, along with most of the Judicial force," he replied at last. "Two of our CloakShapes will usher the other cruiser down."

Tiin glanced at Yaddle, then Billaba, both of whom

nodded. He swung back to the holocam pickup. "We await your escort."

"Is there anyone here who feels confident about this?" Vergere asked while the cruiser was descending through the thin clouds that barely masked Asmeru's wrinkled surface. When no one responded to the delicate, feathered Jedi's question, she shook her disproportionately large head. "Just as I feared."

Qui-Gon glanced meaningfully at Obi-Wan. The two of them left the pod and retraced their steps to the cockpit. By the time they arrived, features of the landscape were coming into view: ice-capped mountain ranges; arid plateaus; steep and intricately terraced hillsides, pale-green with crops, climbing above ribbons of racing black water.

"What should we do in the event of trouble, Master?" Obi-Wan asked quietly.

Qui-Gon's gaze didn't leave the cockpit viewport. "In a rainstorm, you try to keep dry by hurrying for shelter. But you get soaked regardless."

"It's better to conclude beforehand that you're going to get wet," Obi-Wan said.

Qui-Gon nodded.

The ruins of an ancient city of quarried stone appeared on the horizon—monolithic monuments, rectangular platforms, and stepped pyramids, silhouetted against the sky, as if they were a range of hills. Directly below, enormous geometric shapes and animistic symbols had been etched into the perpetually thirsty ground. The city was bounded by walls made of cyclopean boulders, assembled in the shape of lightning bolts.

Surrounding the ruins spread a maze of primitive dwellings built of mud and sun-baked clay. Tiny figures could be glimpsed moving along dirt roadways, some of them in wheeled wagons, and others driving herds of long-haired pack animals, as large as banthas. To the north, an expansive lake dotted with rocky islands stretched across the creased terrain like a spill of liquid jet.

"There's the landing area," the pilot said.

She directed Qui-Gon's attention to a large plaza at the center of the ruins, as wide as the hangar arm of a Trade Federation freighter and twice as long. Bordered on all four sides by flat-faced pyramids, the plaza was large enough to accommodate a flotilla of cruisers.

"*Prominence*, this is *Ecliptic*," the same female voice said in haste over the cockpit speakers. "Our scanners have detected five unidentified vessels emerging from Asmeru's dark side. House Vandron's Tikiars and Dreadnaughts are leaving orbit."

Qui-Gon glanced sharply at the pilot. "It's a trap, Captain. Order the *Ecliptic* to get clear."

"*Ecliptic*," the pilot started to say, when a long burst of static issued from the cockpit speakers. Then the female voice returned, her words shot through with alarm.

"*Prominence*, they're detonating the mines! We can't maneuver! Unidentified ships closing. Four starfighters and a *Tempest*-class gunship."

Obi-Wan shot Qui-Gon a wide-eyed look. "The *Hawk-Bat*?"

"We'll know soon enough."

A prolonged screech erupted from the speakers. At the same time, the *Prominence* began to shudder violently.

"We're being pulled in," the pilot said in astonishment.

She and the copilot began to struggle with the controls. Qui-Gon pressed his face to the cool transparisteel viewport. A rectangular opening had appeared in the inclined face of one of the plaza pyramids, revealing the telltale grid of a tractor beam.

"It's a commercial array," Qui-Gon said. "Can we break away?"

"We can try," the pilot said.

"We could also end up blowing out the sublight drives," Obi-Wan thought to point out.

The copilot opened a channel to the communications station. "Send a burst transmission to Coruscant, alerting them to our situation."

Below, the flat roof of a sprawling building was parting like a curtain. The barrel of a weapon elevated into view.

"Ion cannon," the pilot said through gritted teeth.

Qui-Gon squatted down next to her. "Our visit was clearly anticipated, Captain."

Abruptly, she pivoted to the controls that enabled the salon pod ejection system. "Master, tell your comrades to exit the salon pod. There may yet be a way out of this."

Qui-Gon glanced out the viewport. One of the escort CloakShapes had altered vector to move in front of the cruiser. The landing area was directly ahead, only a few kilometers distant. "There are ways, Captain. But not the one you have in mind."

"Do as I say," she snapped.

Qui-Gon hesitated, then leaned toward the intercom pickup. "Master Tiin, evacuate the salon pod immediately."

"Why, Qui-Gon?"

"There's no time to explain. Hurry."

The pilot waited for confirmation that the pod was empty. Then she triggered the pod's separator charges. The cruiser's bow tipped up as the magnoclamps below the cockpit blew, and the pod broke away from the fuselage.

All but immune to the effects of the tractor beam because of its small size, the pod rocketed ahead of the decelerating cruiser, its self-contained jets flaring, but its course dictated by the *Prominence*'s captain.

The pilot of the CloakShape flying point couldn't have known what hit him.

Rammed forcefully in the tail by the pod, the fighter lurched forward, then veered violently to one side. The pilot tried to correct, but the repulsorlift engine had been fatally damaged, and the small craft was out of control. Belching intermittent puffs of white smoke and a stream of viscous fluids, the CloakShape tipped up onto its right stabilizer, then began a corkscrewing plummet toward the city's central plaza.

The pilot leaned forward to track the fighter, her right hand clenched. "Stay on target," she urged the fighter. "Stay on target . . ."

The CloakShape slammed nose first into the sloping face of the pyramid that housed the tractor beam, and blew to pieces. Narrowly missed, the grid held for a moment, then sparks began to gambol across the invisible perimeter of its deflector shield.

"That's all we needed!" the pilot said.

She fed full power to the tri-thrusters, and was just starting her climb when the cruiser jerked to a halt, then was released, only to be jerked motionless once more.

"You damaged it, Captain," Qui-Gon said, "but you didn't kill it."

The pilot's continued efforts to pull away succeeded only in throwing the cruiser into a dizzying horizontal spin. Still half in the grip of the dazed grid, the *Prominence* slued sharply to starboard, flying over the plaza and headed straight for the city's northernmost pyramid. Qui-Gon was certain that they were going to hit the structure head-on, but at the last moment, the cruiser surged upward. Even so, the tail struck the pyramid's upper platform, shearing off the central and starboard thrusters.

At the same instant, the ion cannon opened fire.

Energy pulsed from the weapon's reciprocating barrels, finding soft spots in the belly of the ship. Charges leapt about the deflector shield, forking like lightning, then encasing the ship in a scintillating web of blue light.

All shipboard systems failed.

Silence reigned for a split second, then sporadic power returned. The cruiser commenced a rapid, diagonal glide, held aloft by its sole remaining engine.

Lambent with late sunlight, the black lake expanded below.

"And I thought you were just being figurative about getting wet, Master," Obi-Wan said as he looked around for something to hold on to.

19

The *Prominence* skimmed the surface of the lake, then bellied into the water and began to hydroplane toward the center. The cruiser was on a collision course with one of the rocky islands, until its blunt bow dropped, and the lake robbed it of forward momentum. It came to a shuddering stop in turbulent water, then listed to its damaged side and slowly began to sink.

By then the seven Jedi and the few judicials aboard had gathered at the starboard docking ring airlock. Blowing the hatch, they eased down into the frigid water and started to swim for the nearest island, which rose in a jumble of wind- and water-smoothed boulders to a height of one hundred or so meters.

First to reach shore, Qui-Gon launched himself to dry land, landing on his feet on a narrow stretch of rocky beach. Waves generated by the cruiser's plunge crashed around his ankles. He used his hands to sluice some of the water out of his long hair and beard. Then he emptied his boots, plucked his soaked tunic away from his chest, and slipped into the cloak he had held above the waves while swimming. Unclipping his lightsaber, he activated the blade and swept it in front of him. Satisfied that the weapon hadn't been damaged, he switched it off and reclipped it to his broad leather belt.

He inhaled deeply, but didn't come close to filling his lungs with oxygen. The high-altitude air was thin; the sky, an inverted bowl of the deepest blue, was seemingly supported on the ice-white shoulders of mountain ranges that ringed the horizon. Asmeru's sun was a huge red smear on the western horizon. The temperature was falling fast, and certainly would be below freezing by sunset.

To the south, the sky was streaked with the contrails of ships rocketing down the planet's gravity well, no doubt headed for the landing area. Qui-Gon wondered briefly which one of them might be the *Hawk-Bat*.

He turned his back to the lake and let his gaze wander up over the lifeless rocks. Assembled by hand rather than nature, the island was itself a pyramid, with the ruins of ancient structures surmounting it.

To both sides of Qui-Gon, Jedi and judicials were beginning to climb from the lake, their waterlogged tunics and uniforms weighing them down. Following Qui-Gon's lead, Obi-Wan sprang from the water, landing atop one of the smaller rocks. Vergere floated in like a water fowl until she reached the stony beach, then she called on her powerful reverse-articulated legs to catapult her ashore. Saesee Tiin's big hands cut through the waves like flippers. Yaddle rode in atop Ki-Adi-Mundi's broad shoulders, her short arms wrapped around his tall head, and her topknot of golden-brown hair plastered to her green skull. Close by, Depa Billaba stepped gracefully to the beach, as if emerging from a warm bath.

Three hundred meters away, the dorsal hull of the *Prominence* was still visible above the waterline. Giant air bubbles broke the surface of the lake and popped loudly.

Everyone was a bit stunned. With a fractured arm, the cruiser's pilot was the most seriously injured. In obvious pain, she made her way over to Qui-Gon, breathless when she reached him.

"I thought we could break free," she said, by way of apology.

"Don't condemn your actions just yet," Qui-Gon replied. "Nothing happens by chance."

The pilot nodded and looked at Saesee Tiin. "Was it House Vandron that betrayed us?"

The Iktotchi folded his arms across his massive chest. "That has little bearing on our present situation." He glanced at Yaddle. "The question is, what do we do next?"

"An immediate answer, that question begs," the small Jedi replied, "as company we're about to have."

Qui-Gon followed her gaze. Several vessels were approaching from the lake's south shore.

Obi-Wan reached to unclip his lightsaber, but Qui-Gon restrained him with a look. "There's always time for that. Just now we need to assess where we stand."

Obi-Wan glanced around. "On an island, in the middle of a lake, with adversaries on the approach, Master."

"Wasn't it you who said that things are not always what they appear to be?"

Obi-Wan frowned. "I stand corrected."

Qui-Gon touched him on the shoulder and nodded his chin to the others. "There's no sense making ourselves easy targets."

Drawing on the Force, and taking the judicials with them, the Jedi vaulted and bounded up into the boulders. From higher up, they had a better vantage from which to see just what was approaching. Driven by repulsorlifts, the vessels were as gruesomely fanciful as the spaceships of House Vandron. Some had upturned animistic prows and ribcage gunwales; others had elaborately raised sterns, carved with ghastly visages. All were equipped with mounted repeating blasters.

The bestial flotilla came to a hovering halt just short of the island, weapons traversing the shore. Each vessel carried a crew of humans, Weequays, Rodians, Bith, Sullustans, and others, many of them layered in heavy garments, gloves, and headpieces that covered noses and mouths.

Standing in the bow of the lead craft, a tall human unwound the colorful scarf that masked his lower face and cupped his hands to his mouth.

"For what it's worth, Jedi, we had planned on providing you with a warmer, and certainly drier, welcome."

Saesee Tiin, Ki-Adi-Mundi, and Qui-Gon showed themselves. "The same warm welcome you provided our other cruiser?" Tiin said.

The human had the boat brought about to face Tiin. "In attempting to flee, your other cruiser struck several mines and was destroyed. We had no intentions of firing on it."

"What are your intentions here?" Ki-Adi-Mundi asked.

"First, to declare that we are dismayed that the Jedi would oppose free trade in the outlying systems, by choosing to side with the Trade Federation."

"We have taken no sides," Tiin said gruffly. "Our sole aim is to resolve this crisis before it intensifies into open warfare. That, too, is the goal of Supreme Chancellor Valorum, who is anything but your enemy is this matter."

"We had nothing to do with the assassination attempt," someone in one of the other boats shouted.

The terrorists' spokesman whirled angrily to the source of the outburst, then regained his composure. "If Valorum is not our enemy, why was the Nebula Front excluded from the Eriadu summit?"

"If you will agree to meet with the Supreme Chancellor, he will explain his reasons."

The human shook his head at Tiin. "That's not good enough. The conference will unite the Trade Federation and the Commerce Guild against us. We demand that Valorum cancel the summit."

"Is that what this is about?" Qui-Gon asked, gesturing broadly. "You intend to hold us hostage while you issue your demands?"

The human spread his gloved hands. "What are the chances of Valorum listening to us otherwise, Jedi?"

Tiin responded to it. "And should the Supreme Chancellor refuse to listen to you now?"

"Then the blood of however many of you die here will be on Valorum's hands," the man said after a long moment. He continued before any of the Jedi could respond. "All of us are aware of your abilities. We're not yet desperate enough to attempt to take you by force. We know that you can probably survive on this pile of rocks for as long as you wish, even without adequate food and water. But that is also acceptable to us. For the moment, the fact that you are stranded here is all that matters. It is our hope, however, that you will come to your senses and allow us to imprison you in a style more in keeping with that which you are accustomed."

Night passed slowly.

Warming themselves through the Force, the Jedi huddled on the stone floor of the island's ruined summit temple, with the judicials pressed in among them. Glow sticks provided light when they needed it, and food tablets provided some sustenance. But there was no water, even from the lake, because of its dangerously high salinity.

Vergere tucked her legs beneath her and sat as if

roosting. Yaddle pulled her delicate robes around her and slipped easily into a trance state. Qui-Gon, Obi-Wan, Depa Billaba, Ki-Adi-Mundi, and Saesee Tiin took turns at guard duty.

Lifeless as the island was, the Force was strong there, in the lingering presence of the ancients who had assembled it.

Through trapezoidal windows in the temple walls, dawn cast long red shadows into the room. When everyone was awake, Yaddle and Depa Billaba got right down to business.

"By now, Coruscant has learned of our predicament," Billaba said. "I'm certain that the Supreme Chancellor will not delay the Eriadu summit. But he may dispatch more judicials to Asmeru."

"A conflict that guarantees," Yaddle said. "Lost already is the *Ecliptic*, presumably with all hands. Now, additional deaths in the offing are. A better way to resolve this there is."

It was not the first time in her 476 years that the tiny Jedi had been imprisoned. According to legend, she had ascended to the rank of Master as a result of having spent more than a hundred years in an underground prison on Koba.

"The Nebula Front can't hope to gain anything by holding us here," Qui-Gon said with patent suspicion. "Surely they know that we were able to communicate with Coruscant before we crashed."

"Perhaps they don't think that way," Ki-Adi-Mundi suggested. "Perhaps strategy of that sort doesn't come into play."

Qui-Gon looked at him. "But it does. I've already seen it in action."

"Explain it to you Cohl will, when finally you confront

him," Yaddle said. "Until that time, resolve to yield or fight we must."

Vergere's willowy ears pricked up. She glanced knowingly at Qui-Gon, then cut her oblique eyes to the doorless portal that led to the temple's adjoining room. Qui-Gon listened intently for a moment, then he and Ki-Adi-Mundi stood up and moved silently to either side of the gaping opening.

Yaddle, Depa, and Vergere began to converse again, as if nothing were amiss. Suddenly, Qui-Gon and Ki-Adi-Mundi reached into the doorway, tugging into the scant sunlight a humanoid who looked as if he, or perhaps she, had risen from the ground itself. The being's thick skin was certainly impervious to wind, snow, or high-altitude solar radiation. Its four hands and bare feet were configured for digging and scooping, and its back was built for carrying loads. Eyes clearly capable of seeing in the dark were prominent in a mere suggestion of a face, lacking ears or nose, with a mouth barely suited to speech.

Held in the grip of the two Jedi, the biped began to babble nervously in an unknown tongue.

Depa got to her feet. "He speaks the traders tongue of the Senex sector Houses," she said.

Yaddle nodded. "One of their allegedly flawed bio-engineered slaves, he is."

The slave continued to speak, his gaze riveted on Depa. She listened, then smiled gently and touched his shoulder. "It seems there's an alternative we hadn't considered," she told everyone. "This one is offering to help us escape."

Qui-Gon spoke to the slave. "By what method?"

Depa translated the reply. "By taking the route he took to reach us."

The slave motioned to the adjoining room. Qui-Gon and Obi-Wan lighted two glow sticks and ducked through the doorway. In the room's rear wall, a hinged stone door, a meter thick, was ajar.

"Explored this place during the night, did you not?" Yaddle asked from behind them.

"We did, Master," Obi-Wan said.

She shook her head in rebuke. "Careless, you are."

The slave said something to Depa.

"This one says that this temple and the city are linked by underground tunnels. Some of the tunnels lead to the structures that surround the main plaza—the landing platform. Apparently, the plaza is lightly guarded, and this one believes that we could easily seize the starfighters parked there."

Yaddle's eyes narrowed somewhat. "Clearly what we are meant to do," she said. "Less certain, I am, about our chances of leaving Asmeru."

Tiin nodded decisively. "We'll defer any decision until that option is in hand."

In single file they moved through the hidden doorway into a cold and dank corridor. At the bottom of a steep flight of stairs, two more slaves, all but identical to the first, were waiting. Oily black and acrid smoke curled from the torches they carried.

The wide tunnel beyond the stairway was constructed of unmortared but precisely cut stones, some of which were perfectly curved to form vaulted supports. Shifts in the land had wrought damage to the ancients' work. Lake water dripped through formerly solid joints and puddled on the stone floor. In several places, the walls were entirely encrusted in salt.

Depa continued to converse with the slave as they began to descend beneath the shallow lake.

"When the Nebula Front first arrived on Asmeru, they

asked the slaves for shelter, and made no demands of them," she explained. "But the later arrivals—the members this one calls 'the soldiers'—forced the slaves to surrender their homes and provide food. The soldiers are as cruel as the Senex Lords, and they frequently clash with the Front's more nonviolent founders about how things should be done. Fortunately, there are few commanding soldiers onworld just now."

"Few soldiers," Qui-Gon said to Obi-Wan. "That's odd."

"How so, Master?"

"Where are they, while we are here?"

The tunnel began to angle up and the dripping ceased, indicating that they had reached the mainland. Smaller tunnels branched off in all directions, and there were visible signs that the passageways were used on a regular basis for moving about the ancient city. Crude sconces were affixed to the walls, and the edges of stones at the tunnel intersections had been polished to a gloss by the caresses of countless hands.

"We're close to the landing platform," Depa announced quietly.

The central tunnel debouched into a large rectangular cavern, with stairways leading up at the center of each wall. Depa pointed to the nearest one.

"This will take us into the northern pyramid. The starfighters are parked near the structure that houses the tractor beam generator."

"That's a good distance away," Qui-Gon said.

Depa nodded. "Most of the guards are quartered in the tractor beam pyramid. We're certain to encounter resistance."

The slave led them up the stairs and guided them through a series of small rooms to a massive portal that looked out on the plaza. Several CloakShapes could be seen, along with the *Hawk-Bat*, resting on a trio of landing pads.

In the middle distance, a few armed guards traded remarks in Basic.

Qui-Gon and Obi-Wan led everyone but the slaves out into the plaza, most of which lay in deep morning shadow. They weren't even halfway to the closest starfighter when a voice called out.

"I'm glad to see that you've decided to join us."

Seven lightsabers igniting in a rush, the Jedi formed a protective circle, with their energy blades poised for deflection. At the center of the circle, the judicials crouched with drawn blasters.

The human who had spoken to them from the hover vessel stepped out onto the balcony of a palatial structure that overlooked the plaza. Then, to all sides of the plaza, appeared Nebula Front soldiers brandishing all styles of blaster weapons. Behind the terrorists gathered a curious but wary audience of slaves.

"Again, we are betrayed," Ki-Adi-Mundi said.

Depa looked back at the pyramid doorway. Quaking with primitive fear, the three slaves were being shoved forward by two armed terrorists.

"Only by our predictability," she said.

"Master, who is our enemy here?" Obi-Wan asked quietly.

Qui-Gon shook his head. "I've been wondering that since Dorvalla, Padawan. There is more to all this than we know."

The terrorists' spokesman followed an exterior stairway down into the plaza, where he was joined by a second member—a Bith.

Obi-Wan glanced briefly at Qui-Gon. "Master, isn't that—"

"Quiet, Padawan," Qui-Gon cut him off.

The human and the Bith stopped while they were still some distance from the ominous circle the Jedi had formed.

"We have two choices here," the human began. "Of course, we could fight. Ultimately, you would certainly emerge the victors. But some of you might die in the process, and those who don't will be forced to kill all of us. Or—" He paused briefly. "—we could all lower our weapons."

Qui-Gon looked to Yaddle and Tiin, who nodded curtly and deactivated their lightsabers. At a signal from the spokesman, the terrorists began to holster their blasters. Qui-Gon and the other Jedi followed suit, dousing their lightsaber blades but keeping the hilts at ready.

"I'm delighted that we could reach an understanding," the human said in what sounded like genuine relief.

Qui-Gon's gaze roamed over the terrorists in front of him. "Where is Captain Cohl?" He asked after a moment.

The question took the human off his guard. "Ah, of course," he replied, after a moment. "You recognized his ship."

"Where is he?" Qui-Gon repeated.

The human shook his head. "I'm sorry to report that Captain Cohl is no longer with us. I believe he retired. But back to matters at hand, do we have a truce here?"

"A temporary one, at best," Tiin cautioned.

"One piece of business first," the terrorist said, then turned to the soldiers who had herded the three slaves into the plaza.

Without warning, blasters discharged and the slaves fell to the ground. Depa broke from the circle and hurried over to them, going down on one knee as she reached the slave who had guided them out of the pyramid. She touched the slave's neck, then glanced up at Yaddle and gave her head a mournful shake.

"That's what happens to traitors," the human was shouting to the slaves who had gathered round the plaza.

Qui-Gon exchanged brief looks with Yaddle and Tiin. Seven lightsabers reignited.

"We're annulling the truce," Tiin announced.

The hologram showed a diplomatic cruiser attempting to maneuver through a field of asteroidlike space mines, grazing one then another, and another, losing pieces of itself with each encounter, and in the end vanishing in a brief-lived tempest of expanding fire.

"That was the *Ecliptic*," Valorum explained to Senators Bail Antilles, Horox Ryyder, and Palpatine, in his office in the Republic Executive Building. "The images were relayed to Coruscant by the *Famulus*, one of the ships of House Vandron that led our mission into the Senex sector. All twenty judicials aboard the *Ecliptic* are presumed dead."

Valorum switched off the holoprojector and lowered himself into his soft chair.

"Has there been further word from the *Prominence*?" Antilles asked.

Valorum shook his head. "We know only that those aboard—seven Jedi and five judicials—survived the crash. By now they could be in captivity."

"Is there any evidence to suggest that House Vandron was involved in this?" Senator Ryyder asked.

He was exceptionally tall, even for an Anx, with a long, bearded head that rose like a mountain spire from his curved neck. His skin was a variegated yellow-green, and his fingers were elongated spindles. He favored bright red robes, with high round collars.

"No evidence whatever," Valorum said. "Lord Crueya maintains that the commanders of their ships were ordered beforehand to avoid engagement, no matter what occurred."

"I don't accept that for a moment," Antilles said.

Valorum blew out his breath. "I'm not certain that I do, either. Master Yoda was right about the rulers of the Senex. They are no better than the Nebula Front terrorists."

"Has the Front issued any demands?" Palpatine asked mildly.

"Not yet. But I suspect we can sense what's coming: demands that the Trade Federation be disbanded, or that the Republic guarantee reduced tariffs for the outlying systems. I will not consent to those, but, if nothing else, we should at least postpone the trade summit until this crisis is settled."

"I respectfully disagree," Palpatine said. "I'm certain that is precisely what the Nebula Front wishes us to do."

Valorum's forehead furrowed. "They could be holding the survivors hostage, Senator. And I'm responsible for having sent them into danger."

"All the more reason to stand firm." Palpatine glanced around the room. "Supreme Chancellor, if I may say so, the moment is ripe to demonstrate the far-reaching authority of the Republic, and thus ensure Senate approval of taxation of the trade routes. Moreover, with the Nebula

Front eliminated, the Trade Federation will be more inclined to accept taxation."

Valorum frowned at him. "Need I remind you that the Senex sector is not Republic space? Sending additional forces to Asmeru would constitute a violation of Senex sovereignty. The senate would never sanction such action."

Palpatine remained calm. "Again, I beg to disagree. The senate will sanction it because Republic interests are at stake." Again he glanced at Antilles and Ryyder. "Assuming for the moment that the Jedi have failed in their diplomatic mission, the Nebula Front is free to disrupt the Eriadu summit, and thus broaden the existing conflict to include not only the Trade Federation, but also the Commerce Guild and the Corporate Alliance. Supreme Chancellor, you yourself said that the summit should, under no circumstances, be jeopardized. That was your paramount reason for dispatching the Jedi to Asmeru."

"Yes," Valorum conceded, "you're right."

"And what of the Senex Houses?" Ryyder asked Palpatine.

"They will support whatever actions we take, if only on the chance that we will rescind the restrictions that have prevented them from trading directly with the Republic."

Valorum considered Palpatine's remarks, then shook his head. "Even if we are successful in securing Senate approval to proceed as you suggest, a show of force at Asmeru could provoke the Nebula Front to kill their hostages."

Palpatine smiled tolerantly. "Supreme Chancellor, the hostages are Jedi Knights."

"Even Jedi can be killed," Antilles argued.

"Then perhaps we should leave it to the Jedi High Council to decide a course of action."

Valorum stretched the baggy skin under his eyes. "I concur. I will attend to the matter personally."

The lean air of the plateau was sibilant with the hiss of laser bolts, resonant with the thrum of lightsabers, energized by detonations of artificial light.

Qui-Gon, Obi-Wan, and Ki-Adi-Mundi stood with their backs pressed to one another, deflecting a hail of blaster bolts the terrorists poured into the plaza. The blades of their lightsabers—green, blue, and purple—moved faster than the eye could follow, blazing bright as novas as they sent the bolts caroming from the ancient stone walls and ricocheting off the sloping faces of the pyramids.

Elsewhere, standing tall on her extended legs, Vergere led a fleet assault up the staircase of an adjacent structure, her gleaming emerald blade raised above her downy head. Two of the judicials followed in her long stride, discharging their weapons as they ran.

Not far away, Saesee Tiin led another pair of judicials in a charge against a half a dozen terrorists entrenched in a narrow alley between two of the pyramids, his blade a blur of cobalt as it parried bolts and sent blasters flying from outstretched hands.

Yaddle and Depa remained with the injured cruiser captain near the entrance to the northern pyramid. Pinned down by a torrent of fire from the summit of the ion cannon bunker, they swung and windmilled their lightsabers, repulsing bolts as if in some crazed sports contest.

Most of the slaves had scattered with the first bolts fired after the brutal execution of the three who had helped the Jedi. But several of the bioengineered bipeds were being used as living shields.

Qui-Gon, Obi-Wan, and Ki-Adi-Mundi began to work their way deeper into the plaza, intent on reaching the grounded CloakShape fighters, or perhaps even the gunship, before any of the terrorists could get to the crafts.

Qui-Gon advanced with determination, scarcely aware of the thrum of his blade, or the chaotic fusillade of blaster bolts. His mind turned with each and every action of his adversaries, whirling right, left, or wherever needed. He left no traces of himself in any particular place or direction, focusing only on what lay ahead, with the past smoothing out behind him like the wake of a settling boat.

He remained subtle and imperceptible, invisible in his detachment, never lingering to watch, or clinging to thoughts of what he might have done.

Wounded by deflected bolts, terrorists fell in his path, though he had yet to meet any of them head-on, and by the looks of things wouldn't. Already they were retreating fast for the fighters.

"If they launch, we'll really have our hands full," he told Obi-Wan in a moment of quiet.

Then a new sound whipped up the frigid air. Around the sharp edge of the southern pyramid came two of the repulsorlift vessels the Jedi had last seen on the lake.

Bolts from the crafts' repeating blasters lanced into the plaza, carbonizing the cut stones where they hit. In unison, Qui-Gon and Obi-Wan leapt for cover, while Ki-Adi-Mundi parried a stream of fire that nearly spun him completely around.

The vessels came about for another run, firing wildly.

Momentarily overwhelmed, the trio of Jedi were forced to fall back. Qui-Gon saw that Vergere's and Tiin's teams were also being driven back down the steps and into the plaza. First to hit level ground, Vergere directed the judicials to race for the shelter of the northern pyramid, but only one of the men made it. The other was cut down by fire from a nearby tower.

The two judicials who had fought beside Tiin were wounded. The Iktotchi carried one of them under his left arm, while he continued to divert bolts with the lightsaber clutched in his right hand. The other judicial scampered backwards, covering their retreat amid a storm of fire from the gunboats.

In a blur of motion, Qui-Gon and Obi-Wan hurried to Tiin's aid, spinning and leaping in the face of the onslaught.

The gunboats had completed their pass and were swooping in for another strafing run. At a nod from Qui-Gon, he and Obi-Wan leapt ten meters into the air with their swords raised, ripping the repulsorlift engine from the lead craft.

Sparks showered down on them as they landed and rolled for cover. Overhead, the gunboat careened out of control and struck the upper story of the palace, exploding into white-hot fragments and loosing an avalanche of stone onto the plaza.

Tiin and the judicials reached the safety of the pyramid entrance just ahead of the rockslide. Qui-Gon and Obi-Wan followed them inside, as bolts from the second gunboat's repeater blaster rained against the portal's engraved columns and monolithic lintel.

Yaddle and the others were massed in the rear of the corridor.

Flattened against the wall, Qui-Gon peered into the plaza. "We have to get to the fighters."

"If we have to, we will," Tiin said.

Obi-Wan nodded at Qui-Gon and reactivated his blade.

Lightsabers raised, they charged back into the plaza.

*   *   *

The High Council Chamber felt empty without the three Masters who had accompanied Vergere, Qui-Gon, and his Padawan to Asmeru. Now it was Yoda who stood at the center of the inlaid mosaic floor, pacing while Mace Windu and the others discussed what was to be done.

"Even without word from the *Prominence*, we can't assume that the ship was destroyed, or that any who were aboard have been killed," Windu was saying. "Everything I feel about the situation tells me that Yaddle and the others are alive."

"Alive, she is," Yoda said. "The others, too. But in grave danger, they are."

"That supports the Nebula Front's claim that they're holding a dozen hostages," Adi Gallia said. "They're demanding that the Eriadu summit be cancelled."

"Valorum must not give in to them," Oppo Rancisis cautioned.

"He isn't going to acquiesce to the demands," Windu assured everyone. "He's aware that by doing so he would only lessen the chances for ratification of the taxation proposal."

"The Nebula Front is not the important concern here," Yarael Poof said. "It is the Trade Federation that matters."

Yoda turned to the long-necked Master. "*Thought* to be less important, the Nebula Front is. But directing this, they are. Directing all of this." He paced through a circle, then stopped. "Moving us around like pieces on a holo-game board."

"Then we need to finish the game," Even Piell said with conviction.

Windu nodded. "I assured Supreme Chancellor

Valorum that there was no need for him to deliver an apology in person. We agreed to intervene in this matter. Therefore, this is as much our responsibility as it is his."

"Too little thought, we gave this," Yoda said pensively. "Unrevealed forces at work." He glanced at Windu. "Clouded, this is. Muddled by motives difficult to perceive."

Windu interlocked his hands and rested his elbows on his knees. "The senate has promised the Supreme Chancellor whatever authority he needs to deal with the crisis. But we cannot leave the decision to him."

Yoda nodded. "Focused on the trade summit, he is."

"The Judicial Department has also been given expanded authority," Windu continued. "They advocate dispatching additional forces from Eriadu, which is only a jump from Asmeru's location in the Senex sector."

"The judicials are on Eriadu to safeguard Supreme Chancellor Valorum and the delegates," Gallia said.

"The Judicial Department feels certain that they have enough personnel there to deal with both situations."

"Do we have any assurances that the Senex Houses will stay out of this?" Poof asked.

"We could offer them a deal," Piell said. "They have long wanted to trade with the Republic, but have been shunned because of continued violations of the Rights of Sentience. If we offer to arbitrate an accord between them and the Republic, I'm certain they would agree to overlook any territorial infringements that arise from the situation at Asmeru."

Yoda gazed at the floor and shook his head back and forth. "Deeper and darker and murkier this becomes." He looked up at Windu. "How many Jedi on Eriadu?"

"Twenty."

"Send ten to Asmeru with the judicials to help Master

Tiin and the others," Yoda said in a troubled voice. "Pay our debts when they come due, we will."

Windu nodded somberly.

"May the Force be with them," Gallia said for everyone.

21

Qui-Gon, Obi-Wan, Tiin, and Ki-Adi-Mundi surged from the pyramid entrance, engaging the terrorists that had driven them back. A quarter of the way across the immense plaza, the Jedi spread out in a wedge formation, their constantly moving blades fending off blaster bolts loosed from ahead and to either side. Behind the energy barrier fashioned by the lightsabers, Yaddle, Depa, Vergere, and two of the judicials raced out to divert fire from the rear.

The point of the wedge, Qui-Gon advanced steadily into the fray, whirling and crouching, his green blade sonorous as it sent bolts arching every which way. Terrorists fell wounded from the surrounding stairways, balconies, and rooftops, but none of them fled.

You will have to kill all of us, the spokesman had said.

Unexpectedly, the unrelenting blasterfire began to taper off. Qui-Gon took a moment to look around, realizing in a rush that the terrorists were suddenly directing fire toward the heavily bulwarked perimeter of the plaza.

With eerie, tremolo war cries, hundreds of slaves

charged into the plaza from the deep alleys separating the pyramids. Lacking anything in the way of shields, they brandished stone axes and knives, spears fashioned from the wooden handles of tools, and whatever other implements they had managed to sharpen or provide with an edge.

Blaster bolts felled them by the score, but still they came, resolved to overthrow the outsiders who had robbed them of what little freedom and dignity they possessed.

Qui-Gon grasped that the uprising had to have been in the works for some time. But determination alone wasn't going to win the day against blasters.

He and Obi-Wan pressed their attack, Vergere off to one side of them, leaping high into the air and returning to the ground with her lightsaber slashing. Caught between the rebelling slaves and the Jedi, the terrorists gathered in two lines, one to handle each front.

A second surprise gave Qui-Gon pause. Some of the terrorists were succumbing to blasterfire. It seemed improbable that the slaves had somehow managed to reconfigure blasters to suit their fingerless hands.

Then he saw where the fire was coming from.

Advancing in leap-frog fashion came a contingent of terrorists, led by the Bith who had been Qui-Gon's informant.

Events of the day had splintered the Nebula Front into two factions: the militants responsible for the attack on Valorum, and the moderates who had for so many years restricted themselves to nonviolent actions against the Trade Federation.

The militants clearly hadn't anticipated insurrection by their own confederates. All at once the race for the grounded CloakShape fighters became more desperate than ever.

One of the starfighters was already lifting off on repulsorlift power. Realizing what was occurring below, the pilot wheeled the craft through a half turn and opened up with the forward laser cannons. Each hyphen of raw energy decimated the opposition. Stone blasted from the encompassing structures, and lightning-bolt walls whizzed through the air like shrapnel, tearing into those who had managed to flee the fatal energy beams themselves.

Qui-Gon understood that the one starfighter could turn the tide of battle—not only against the alliance of slaves and moderates, but also against the Jedi.

Even as he was thinking it, the hovering CloakShape began to rotate toward the Jedi's side of the battle arena. The wingtip lasers had swung into view, poised to fire, when without warning the starfighter exploded. Pieces of its angled wings slammed against the face of the tractor beam grid, and its flaming fuselage spun down into the plaza.

Qui-Gon glanced up from where he had flattened himself to the ground. The landing platform was littered with white-hot wreckage, small bits of which had burned holes in his cloak.

His eyes searched the plaza for signs of the weapon that had brought down the ship, only to grasp that the devastating bolt hadn't come from any downside emplacement.

It had come from above.

A crimson and white craft streaked overhead, so close that it rattled Qui-Gon's teeth.

"Judicial Lancet," Obi-Wan said when the sound of the starfighter's passing had roared through.

White veins in the blue dome of the sky told Qui-Gon that other ships were coming down the well.

He swung back to regard Depa and the judicials, one of whom was speaking into his wrist comm. Sensing Qui-Gon's gaze on him, the judicial looked up and raised his left fist in a sign of confidence.

Qui-Gon raised his gaze to the sky. From the south, a Corellian cruiser was on the approach.

The sight of the descending fighters didn't deter the radicals from continuing their fight for the CloakShapes, however. Three more starfighters lifted out of the plaza. But rather than waste time pouring fire against the slaves, the ships rocketed off to the east, with a pair Lancets in close pursuit. A fourth CloakShape whirred noisily to life, managing, during its reeling ascent, to take out an incoming Lancet.

Off to Qui-Gon's left, the ion cannon pulsed. Dazed by a direct hit, another Lancet rolled over on its back and dived silently toward the parched ground. Shortly, an explosion boiled high into the air behind the southern pyramid.

The cannon continued to send darts of disabling fire skyward, but the alliance of slaves and moderates were already storming the emplacement. A dozen warriors fell to the charge, but the rest persevered, lobbing thermal grenades from where they hunkered behind a toppled monument.

A moment later the gun emplacement belched a column of howling fire and collapsed in on itself.

The ongoing turmoil in the plaza had prevented the cruiser from landing. While it hovered at the level of the pyramid summits, hatches opened in the underside of the ship and twenty or more figures rappeled down on monofilament cables. Half of them were armed with blasters, and the rest with glowing lightsabers.

The battle raged furiously for several more minutes. Then, hemmed in on all sides, the militants began to surrender their weapons and drop to their knees. Captives of the slaves, other groups were marched into the plaza with hands raised above their heads.

Tiin, Depa Billaba, and some of the Jedi reinforcements

started to meander through the devastation, gathering up weapons and tending to the wounded. Qui-Gon saw Yaddle standing at the entrance to the northern pyramid, shaking her head in dismay.

He and Obi-Wan set out to find the Bith. Shortly, he saw Obi-Wan waving him over to the southwest corner of the plaza.

Qui-Gon clipped his lightsaber to his belt and broke into a jog. He knew before he arrived that calamity was waiting.

The Bith was curled on his side, his long-fingered hands pressed to a blackened hole in his midsection. Qui-Gon went down on one knee beside him.

"I tried to contact you on Coruscant," the black-eyed alien began in a weak voice. "But after what happened at Dorvalla, Havac and the others suspected that there was an informant among them."

"Havac?" Qui-Gon said. "Is he the one who had the slaves executed?"

The Bith shook his large head. "He's just a lieutenant. Havac is the leader. But he's not onworld—many of the militants aren't." He paused to take a breath. "They've undone everything we tried to do. They've turned this into a war with the Trade Federation, and now the Republic."

"It's over," Qui-Gon said. "You've deposed them. Save your strength, friend."

The Bith clamped his hand on Qui-Gon's forearm. "It's not over. They have something dreadful planned."

"Where?" Obi-Wan asked. "When?"

The Bith turned partway to him. "I don't know. The plan was kept secret from most of us. But I know that it involves Captain Cohl . . ."

The Bith's words trailed off. Qui-Gon felt Obi-Wan's gaze on him. At the same time, all light fled the alien's eyes.

"He's dead, Master," Obi-Wan said.

"Jedi," someone said from behind Qui-Gon. The speaker was a Nikto humanoid, flat-faced and horned. "I don't mean to intrude, but your friend was my friend, as well."

Qui-Gon stood up. "What do you know about this plan involving the one he called Havac and Captain Cohl?"

"I know that it had something to do with Karfeddion."

"Karfeddion?" Obi-Wan repeated, while he showed the Nikto his most disapproving gaze.

"The homeworld of House Vandron," Qui-Gon said. "Deep in the Senex." He turned back to the humanoid. "Your name?"

"Cindar."

"Do you know this Havac on sight?"

"I do."

Qui-Gon considered something, then said, "Come with us."

He led the way to where Tiin, Yaddle, and some of the others were gathered in the plaza.

"There's no time to sort all this out," Tiin was saying, gesturing broadly to ruination. "The High Council and the Judicial Department have ordered us to leave the Senex sector as quickly as possible."

"We need to make one stop first," Qui-Gon interrupted. "At Karfeddion."

Tiin stared at him, awaiting an explanation.

"Cohl is executing another plan." Qui-Gon indicated Cindar. "This one is going to help us pick up Cohl's trail."

Tiin and Yaddle traded brief glances. "Cohl is no longer working for the Front," Tiin said. "We all heard as much."

"The plan has been a closely guarded secret. Someone named Havac is behind it. We must go to Karfeddion."

"Impossible, Qui-Gon," Yaddle said, shaking her head back and forth. "Leave the Senex, we must."

Qui-Gon squared his shoulders. "Then my Padawan and I will go."

Obi-Wan's jaw dropped slightly.

"Not in any of our ships, Qui-Gon," Tiin said in challenge.

Qui-Gon glanced around. "Then we'll use the *Hawk-Bat*."

"Making this personal, you are," Yaddle said. "Defying a direct order from the High Council, you'll be."

Qui-Gon didn't argue the point. "My duty is to the Force, Master."

Yaddle studied him for a long moment. "To what end, Qui-Gon? To what end?"

The holobanner glowing through the t'bac smoke in the cantina read: THE TIPSY MYNOCK WELCOMES THE KARFEDDION SKULL CRACKERS. A smashball team, the Skull Crackers were known throughout the Senex for their blatant disregard for the rules of play and for the lives of their opponents. A boisterous dozen of the local heroes were gathered in a corner of the Tipsy Mynock, raising flagons of fermented drink to one another and whomever happened by, growing more inebriated by the minute, and fairly itching to cause trouble of a major sort.

A few booths away, Cohl and Boiny sat with a hulking human who might have been a member of the Skull Crackers—had he been a few centimeters shorter and a lot less dangerous looking.

A pleasant-looking humanoid female bred on one of the Karfeddion slave farms placed a tall shot of bright-yellow liquid in front of Cohl's guest, who downed the notoriously strong drink in one swallow.

"Thanks, Captain," the human said genuinely, wiping

his mouth with the back of his hand. "It's not often I get a taste of the real article."

Cohl appraised Lope, as the man called himself, from across the table that separated them. The fact that Lope could handle himself in a brawl was beyond dispute. But the Eriadu operation would not turn on brute strength, but on a combination of skill and intelligence. Of course, situations could arise in the most carefully designed scenarios when it came down to muscle. But Cohl still wasn't convinced that Lope was suited to handle even that eventuality.

"What's your specialty?" he asked after a moment.

Lope planted his elbows on the table. "Vibroblade, stun baton, nerve pick. But I can also handle a blaster—BlasTechs, Merr-Sonns, Czerkas . . ."

"But you prefer in-close work."

Lope shrugged. "When it comes right down to it, yeah, I guess I do. Why, what's the job, Captain?"

Cohl shook his head. "I can't tell you that unless I decide to bring you aboard."

Lope nodded. "I understand. But I'd sure like to hire on with you, Captain. They don't come any better than you."

Cohl ignored the flattery. "Where have you worked?"

"Up and down the Corellian Trade Spine, mostly. I did a stint in the Stark Conflict. I'd still be in the Core, if I didn't have a price on my head for a bit of wet work I did on Sacorria."

"Are you wanted anywhere else?"

"Only there, Captain."

Cohl was mildly encouraged. Lope was typical of the outlaws that fled to the outlying systems, but he wasn't a professional.

"You have any problem working with aliens, Lope?"

Lope glanced briefly at Boiny. "Not Rodians. Why, you've got others on your crew?"

"A Gotal."

Lope stroked his stubbled jaw. "Gotal, huh? I can work with those."

A sudden commotion erupted at the entrance to the cantina, and four large and mean-looking humans shouldered their way to the bar. Cohl thought they might be members of the Skull Crackers or some rival team, until the largest among them climbed up onto the bar and fired a blaster bolt into the ceiling.

"Lope, I know you're in here somewhere," he shouted while plaster dust drifted down around him and he scanned the tables and booths. "Where are you, you double-dealing slime?"

Cohl glanced from the man at the bar to Lope. "Friend of yours?"

"Not for long," Lope said, getting to his feet and waving his arm. "Right here, Pezzle."

Pezzle squinted in Lope's direction, then jumped down from the bar and began to shove and barrel his way through the crowd, his cohorts following in his wake.

"You're a no-good cheat," he said as soon as he reached the booth. "You figured you could walk out without paying us, is that it?"

Cohl watched Lope take in everything at a glance: Pezzle's raised weapon, the position of the other three men, how far their hands were from their blasters.

"You weren't worth paying," Lope said flatly. "You only took care of one of them, and you left me to clean up after you."

Cohl and Boiny started to slide out of the booth, but Lope put his hand on Cohl's shoulder. "Don't leave, Captain. This won't take a minute. Maybe you could consider it an audition."

"All right," Cohl told him, settling back down.

Customers in the adjacent booths weren't as confident as Cohl. Climbing over seats and whatever else stood in their way, they began to scramble out of the line of fire.

Sweating profusely, Pezzle gulped and found his voice. "You'll pay now," he said, flinging spittle from his thick lips.

Cohl never saw Lope's blaster leave its holster.

He saw the blur of Lope's right hand, he heard several weapons discharge, and the next thing he knew, Pezzle and his trio were piled in a heap on the floor.

His smoking blaster still in hand, Lope regarded Cohl expectantly.

"You'll do," Cohl said, nodding his head.

Karfeddion Spaceport was a sprawl of docking bays, repair shops, and cantinas even seedier than the Tipsy Mynock. Nodding to the several members of Docking Bay 331's maintenance crew, Cohl, Boiny, and Lope closed on the battered freighter the Nebula Front had provided.

"What happened to the *Hawk-Bat*, Captain?" Lope asked as he gazed uncertainly at the ship.

"Too well known for where we're headed," Cohl said.

Cohl introduced Lope to the pair of humans who were standing at the foot of the freighter's boarding ramp.

"Captain," one of them said in a scratchy voice, "some dame is waiting for you in the forward compartment."

"Who?" Cohl said.

"She wouldn't say."

Cohl and Boiny traded looks. "Maybe it's that bounty hunter you were searching for," the Rodian suggested.

"I've got another idea," Cohl said, without elaborating.

"You don't think—"

"Who else could it be? The only thing I can't figure is how she found me."

"Maybe she attached a tracker to some part of you before she left," Boiny suggested.

They left Lope and the others to get acquainted and climbed the ramp.

"Did I tell you she would miss me?" Cohl asked over his shoulder as soon as he had stepped into the forward hold.

Rella was sitting in Cohl's chair, with her long legs crossed.

"You're right, Cohl," she said. "I couldn't stay away—but not for the reasons you think." Her outfit of tunic, trousers, capelet, and cowl was made of a silvery metallic fiber that shimmered as she moved.

"By the look of you, I'd say you've been dipping too deeply into your retirement fund, and you need the credits."

She scowled at him. "Is it safe to talk in here?"

Cohl nodded to Boiny, who enabled the cabin's security system.

"I've been hearing rumors that you're putting together a new crew," Rella said when Cohl sat down.

He shrugged. "What else could I do after you walked out on me?"

She didn't even crack a smile. "The way I hear it, you're in the market for lookouts and second-rate exterminators—like that brute you just brought in."

"Tough jobs call for tough personnel."

Rella looked him in the eye. "What have you gotten yourself into, Cohl? Be straight with me—for old times' sake."

Cohl considered it, then said, "It's an execution."

She nodded knowingly. "Who's the target?"

"Valorum—on Eriadu."

Rella seemed to shrink in the chair, as if her worst fears had been realized. "You can't do this, Cohl."

He laughed shortly. "You're welcome to watch."

"Listen to me," she started to say.

"What, you bought yourself some scruples to go along with the new outfit—the new you?"

"Scruples? Don't insult me, Cohl."

"Then what is it about Valorum?"

She shook her head. "It's not about Valorum. It's about you—your reputation. Without even trying, I found out that you'd been to Belsavis, Malastare, Clak'dor, and Yetoom. How hard do you think it's going to be for anyone else to track you? And I don't mean thugs looking to hire on with you. I'm talking about judicials or Jedi."

"I appreciate the warning, Rella, but it won't matter now. I've got everyone I need. Unless, of course, you want to sign aboard."

She held his gaze. "I do."

He blinked.

"No, I'm not kidding you, Cohl," she said.

All at once Cohl grew serious and reached for her hands. "Listen, kid, I appreciate your finding me, but this operation isn't something you want to get involved in."

She appraised him. "I don't get it. A minute ago you were acting like you had the galaxy by the tail."

"Bluster, Rella, pure and simple."

"Are you saying you wish you hadn't taken the job on?"

"Maybe I'm just feeling my age, but, yeah, I should have stepped out of the life when I could. I mean, moisture farming can't be all that difficult to learn, right? And there'll still be exciting times . . . ."

Rella smiled broadly. "Of course there'll be exciting times, Cohl. Just drop this thing. You can walk away right now."

He shook his head. "I gave my word. I have to at least see this through."

Rella studied him for a moment, then forced an exhale. "All the more reason for me to tag along. If you can't look out for yourself, then I'll have to do it for you."

A world of rugged landmasses and slender seas, slate-gray Eriadu had long sought to be the Coruscant of the Outer Rim. That goal had been furthered by dint of Eriadu's choice location in the heart of the Seswenna sector, at the intersection of the Rimma Trade Route and the Hydian Way. But where Coruscant had confined most of its factories and foundries to specific areas, industry held sway over all Eriadu, fouling air, land, and sea with unrelenting outpourings of toxic by-products. Worse, while the planet was prosperous compared to its neighbors, Eriadu's legislators remained more interested in unbridled growth than in investing in the atmosphere scrubbers, aquifer purifiers, and waste disposal systems that made Coruscant livable.

The planet's principal city was in the southern hemisphere. A thriving seaport that had grown up around the mouth of a major river, it spread almost one hundred kilometers inland, sprawling along the shores of a finger-shaped bay to the west, and creeping up and over the once thickly forested hills that rose at its back.

From the rear of the energy-shielded, repulsorlift limousine that had swept him past crowds of demonstrators at Eriadu Spaceport, Valorum surmised that the city must have been a scenic wonder, once upon a time.

Now it was a gloomy warren of tiled domes, narrow alleyways, lofty arches and towers, and open-air marketplaces, thronged with turbaned merchants, veiled women, bearded men drawing on the spouts of bubbling waterpipes, and six-legged beasts of burden, heaped with trade goods, vying for space with rusting landspeeders and aged repulsorsleds.

Valorum couldn't help thinking of Eriadu as a dusty and forlorn flip side of Theed, the capital city of Naboo.

The din of voices and vehicles was nearly enough to overwhelm the tinted, sound-cancellation windows of his limousine, though many of the city's streets had been cleared for his passing. Traffic had been diverted, and security personnel and droids were stationed at nearly every intersection. Citizens were allowed to watch from the narrow sidewalks, but anyone caught peering from an upperstory window or overhead walkway risked being shot by judicial snipers stationed on the rooftops and riding in speeders above the Coruscant delegation hovercade.

Earlier, Valorum had learned that several decoy convoys had been dispatched from the spaceport, and that the route his hovercade was following through the city had been altered at the last moment, to thwart premeditated attacks.

To the protective force of judicials, Senate Guards, and security droids, he was known in code as "The Goods." After the decision to send half the supplemental force of Jedi Knights to Asmeru, to deal with the crisis there, the security detail chiefs had demanded that Valorum submit to wearing a temporary locator implant, so that they would know where he was at all times.

It was ironic that he should find himself in the spotlight, when the whole idea behind the trade summit had been to focus attention on the Outer Rim worlds. Still, he was glad that he had had sense enough to listen to Senator Palpatine about going through with the summit as planned, despite what was occurring in the Senex sector.

An added irony was that the Valorum family had played a part in fouling Eriadu's atmosphere, as well as in cooking it, courtesy of the enormous balls of flame that spewed periodically from the factory stacks that dominated the outskirts of the city.

The family's contribution was a space vessel construction and shipping concern, based in orbit and in several downside facilities. In terms of output, the company wasn't in the same league as TaggeCo and the other giant corporations, and in terms of transport it was no match for Duro Shipping, let alone the Trade Federation. But thanks in part to the Valorum name, the company had never failed to show a profit.

Valorum's onworld relatives had offered their stately homes and mansions for use during his visit, but once again he had followed a suggestion by Senator Palpatine, that he stay at the home of the sector's lieutenant governor, who was an acquaintance of Palpatine's.

The lieutenant governor's name was Wilhuff Tarkin, and his compound was said to overlook the artificially blue waters of the bay.

Tarkin was rumored to be an ambitious man, with grandiose ideas, and, in that, his manse by the sea did not disappoint.

Equal in size to those of Valorum's wealthy cousins on Eriadu, the house was an ostentatious blend of Core Classic and Mid Rim Ornate, which declared itself with huge, domed enclosures, gilded columns, and stone floors polished to a liquid sheen. There was, however, something impersonal about the great, high-ceilinged rooms and stately colonnades. It was as if the costly furnishings and framed artwork were there merely for show, when what the owner actually preferred was the antiseptic gleam of a space-worthy freighter.

Valorum was ushered into the manse by a surround of Senate Guards. Also under escort, walked Sei Taria and a dozen members of the Coruscant delegation to the summit. Trailing them came Adi Gallia and three other Jedi, who had assented to Valorum's request that they be as unobtrusive as possible.

Once inside, the guards allowed Valorum a bit of breathing room, but that was only because every guest and every droid servant had been scanned, well in advance of his arrival. The house itself had been gone over top to bottom by the security detail, who had turned part of the estate into their tactical command and control headquarters. Snipers roosted in the trees and on the parapets, and gunships patrolled the offshore waters.

Testament to the priorities of Eriadu's leaders, Seswenna Hall, where the summit was to take place, was an even more elaborate structure. A dome of enormous dimensions, it crowned a high mount at the center of the city and rose in mosaic splendor to a height of some two hundred meters.

Valorum had expected to be feted, but he had not been prepared for so sizable a gathering. With Sei Taria at his side, he was announced to a ballroom filled with dignitaries representing worlds throughout the Mid and Outer Rims. From Sullust, Malastare, Ryloth, and Bespin they had come; few of them enamored with Valorum, but all of them eager to be heard on the matter of taxation of the free trade zones.

"Supreme Chancellor Valorum," the man who had

made it all happen said, "Eriadu is honored to receive you."

Lieutenant Governor Tarkin was a wiry man, with intense blue eyes, sunken cheeks, and an expressionless mouth. His brow was high and bony, and his taut face seemed to reveal the size and shape of every bone beneath. Already receding at the temples, his black hair was combed straight back and meticulously cut. He stood tall and straight as a military officer and projected an air of aristocratic officiousness.

Valorum recalled hearing that Tarkin, in fact, had served in the military when Eriadu was part of what had then been known as the Outland Regions.

"Did Senator Palpatine arrive with you?" Tarkin asked.

"He had some lingering business to attend to on Coruscant," Valorum replied. "But I'm certain that the Naboo delegation will arrive in time for the summit's opening remarks."

Tarkin appraised Valorum openly as they stepped down into the ballroom, the crowd parting before them.

"It's a rare occasion when anyone involved in Republic politics leaves Coruscant," Tarkin continued. "Something of a prison, isn't it? Should duty ever call for me to be confined to one place, I will at least demand that I have ample space around me." He waved his thin arms through a broad circle.

Valorum forced a smile. "The trip was short and pleasant."

"Yes, but for you to leave the Core, and to come here . . . It's nothing less than extraordinary."

"Nothing less than necessary," Valorum said.

Tarkin arched a brow as he turned slightly. "Necessary perhaps, but certainly unprecedented. And I believe it speaks strongly of your desire to do what is best and right for the outlying systems." He lowered his voice to add, "I trust you weren't distressed by the riots."

Valorum frowned. "I observed no riots. There was a crowd of protestors at the spaceport, but—"

"Ah, yes. Of course, you couldn't have seen the rioters, because your convoy was rerouted at the last instant."

Valorum wasn't sure how he was meant to respond.

"May I say how disquieted we were to learn of the recent attempt on your life, Supreme Chancellor. But then, I suppose we all have our local troubles. Ryloth has its smugglers, King Veruna of Naboo has his detractors, and Eriadu has the Trade Federation and the possibility of taxation of the trade routes."

Valorum was aware of some of the less-than-welcoming looks he was receiving from Tarkin's guests. "News of the assassination attempt doesn't appear to have granted me much sympathy in this room."

Tarkin gestured in dismissal. "Our fears regarding taxation revolve around the potential for increased corruption, as is ever the case when additional layers of bureaucracy are positioned between those with power and those without.

"But that doesn't mean we favor separatism, or encourage open rebellion. Like other worlds along the Rimma, Eriadu has many Nebula Front supporters, but I am not one of them, nor are any of those in the governor's administration. Threats of insurrection must be met with strong, centralized power. One must seize the moment, and strike."

Tarkin lightened his diatribe with a self-deprecating laugh. "Forgive the ravings of a lowly lieutenant governor, Supreme Chancellor. Moreover, I realize that it is hardly the Republic's way to answer violence with violence."

"I would have thought the same, until recently," someone nearby interjected.

Disdain and provocation mixed in the genteel, feminine voice, and the speaker was every centimeter a lady, from the train of her priceless gown to her dazzlingly jeweled tiara.

Tarkin smiled thinly as he offered his crooked arm to the heavyset woman and introduced her. "Supreme Chancellor Valorum, it is my pleasure to present Lady Theala Vandron, of the Senex sector."

Taken off his guard, a flushed Valorum nodded his head in a courtly bow. "Lady Vandron," he said without emotion.

"It may interest you to know, Supreme Chancellor, that the hostage situation on Asmeru has been, shall we say, resolved."

"Asmeru?" Tarkin said. "What's this?"

Valorum quickly regained his composure. "The Republic dispatched a peace delegation of judicials and Jedi to confront agents of the Nebula Front based there."

Tarkin looked at him askance. "Confront or contain?"

"Whichever was deemed appropriate."

Tarkin's face lit up in revelation. "So that's why several judicials and Jedi were called away from Eriadu. Well, either way, it appears that our policies are perhaps not so antithetical, after all, Supreme Chancellor."

"On the heels of an assassination attempt, the Supreme Chancellor takes direct action in non-Republic space," Lady Vandron said, looking at Tarkin. "We are obliged to commend him on his willingness to venture so far from home in such difficult times."

Valorum accepted the left-handed compliment with wellborn reserve. "Rest assured, madam, and Lieutenant Governor Tarkin, that Coruscant is in good hands."

While Valorum didn't enjoy universal support even on Coruscant, his absence was felt, especially in the governmental district, where there was a hint of mischief in the air.

The members of the Galactic Senate awarded themselves liberal leave while the trade summit was in progress. But a diligent few reported to their offices in the senate building, if only to catch up on work.

Bail Antilles was one of them.

He had spent the morning drafting a proposal that would ease the trading tension between his native Alderaan and neighboring Delaya. When he broke for lunch, he had nothing more on his mind than a tall glass of Gizer ale at his favorite restaurant near the Courts Building. But politics foiled his plan, in the form of Senator Orn Free Taa, who intercepted him in the senate's most public of corridors.

The corpulent blue Twi'lek was riding a hoversled.

"May I glide beside you for a moment, Senator Antilles?" he asked.

Antilles made a gesture of acceptance. "What is it?" he said, plainly annoyed.

"To come directly to the point, some rather interesting data has found its way to me. I thought to bring it to the attention of Senator Palpatine, but he suggested that you, as chair of the Internal Activities Committee, were the one to whom I should speak."

Antilles started to protest, then sighed in resignation. "Go ahead, Senator."

Taa's thick head-tails quivered slightly in anticipation. "As you know, I've recently been appointed to the Allocations Committee, and in that capacity I have been delving into precedents and legalities for Supreme Chancellor Valorum's proposed taxation of the free trade zones. Clearly, such taxation will have unanticipated consequences and ramifications, but we're hoping to impede corruption by imagining scenarios of what is likely to occur, should the proposal pass muster in the Senate."

"I'm certain you are," Antilles muttered.

Taa took the sarcasm in stride. "The Supreme Chancellor has stated his wish that a percentage of those revenues garnered through taxation of the trade routes—for all intents and purposes, taxation of the Trade Federation—be allocated for social and technological aid to worlds in the Mid and Outer Rim that may be adversely affected by taxation.

"This, however, presents a dilemma. If the motion is ratified and the Trade Federation is forced to surrender some of its hold on the space lanes, many smaller shipping concerns stand to profit—not only as a result of a newly fashioned competitive market, but also from those tax revenues earmarked for outer system development."

Antilles allowed his puzzlement to show. "I'm not sure I see the dilemma."

"Well, then, permit me to illustrate a specific case. The Allocations Committee database conducted a search for Outer Rim corporations poised to benefit from taxation, and cross-checked the results of the search with data on file with the Appropriations Committee, of which I am also a member. Out of the compiled list of thousands of corporations, one concern was singled out: A shipping concern based on Eriadu that has received a sudden and, may I add, substantial inflow of capital."

"That doesn't surprise me," Antilles said. "Investors with their noses to the air are doing the same thing your committee is doing, except that they're looking for financial opportunities."

"Exactly," Taa said. "Investor speculation. But in this case the dilemma arises from the fact that the concern is owned by relatives of Supreme Chancellor Valorum."

Antilles came to a halt and turned to the hovering Twi'lek.

Taa showed the palms of his big hands. "Let me make perfectly clear that I am not suggesting impropriety on the part of the Supreme Chancellor. I'm certain he is aware that anyone with privileged information about legislative proposals or construction contracts and the like is constrained by Statute 435, Substatute 1759 of the Amended Proprieties Bill, to refrain from profiting by such knowledge, by investment or other means."

Antilles narrowed his eyes. "But you are suggesting something by not suggesting it."

Taa shook his head. "I merely find it curious that the Supreme Chancellor has not brought this seeming conflict of interest to the attention of the senate. I'm confident that the dilemma will disappear once we have determined the origin of the investment and are satisfied that there is no link between those investors and Supreme Chancellor Valorum himself."

"Have you learned anything?" Antilles asked.

"That's the other peculiar thing," Taa said. "The deeper I dig for the source, the more dead ends I encounter. It's almost as if someone doesn't wish to have it known where or with whom the investment originated. My lack of success is partially explained by the fact that I lack the necessary clearance to access the relevant financial files. Access of the sort to which I refer requires someone of high standing. Someone, well, like yourself."

Antilles stared at him. "I assume that you've collected the pertinent data, Senator."

Taa restrained a smile. "As a matter of fact, I happen to have a copy with me."

He proffered a data holocron.

Antilles took it. "I'll see what I can find out."

23

The commandeered *Hawk-Bat* streaked toward Karfeddion, a mottled green semicircle filling the gunship's forward viewports. In the slung cockpit, Qui-Gon sat at the controls. Dressed in a poncho, scarf, and boots borrowed from Asmeru, he looked every part a member of the Nebula Front.

Obi-Wan stood behind the copilot's chair, shrugging out of his brown cloak.

"Put your robes there," Qui-Gon said, gesturing to the empty navigator's chair. "Along with your lightsaber."

Obi-Wan froze. "My lightsaber?"

"Once we land, we want to be sure to give the wrong impression."

Obi-Wan thought about it for a moment, then nodded uncertainly and unclipped the cylinder from his belt. Setting the lightsaber down, he eased back into the copilot's chair.

"Master, did we take the right action on Asmeru?" he asked, breaking a prolonged silence. "Could the violence have been avoided, as Master Yaddle wished?"

"What can be avoided, whose end is purposed by the Force?"

Obi-Wan fell silent for another long moment. "Is it dangerous to give too much thought to the dark side?"

"I keep my gaze fixed on the light, Padawan. But to answer your question: Thought and action are very different things."

"But how can we be certain our thoughts don't color our actions? The path we walk is at times so narrow."

Qui-Gon put the *Hawk-Bat* on autopilot and swung to face his apprentice. "Shall I tell you how Yoda explained it to me when I was even younger than you are?"

"Yes, Master."

Qui-Gon gazed out the viewport while he spoke. "On distant Generis stands an especially dark, dense, and near impenetrable growth of sallap trees. For many generations it was necessary to travel a long distance around the forest to reach the glorious deep-water lake on the far side. But then a Sith Lord thought to blaze a trail directly through the trees, in the hope of providing a quicker route to the lake.

"As you might imagine, only a few have taken both routes and lived to tell of their experiences. But all agree that while the path through that dark wood is shorter, it actually fails to arrive at the lake. Whereas the path that skirts the forest, though long and arduous, not only arrives at the shore, but is, in itself, a destination."

Without glancing at Obi-Wan, Qui-Gon asked, "On Asmeru, did you venture into that dark wood, or did you remain in the light, with the Force as your companion and ally?"

"I had no destination in mind, other than to follow where the Force led me."

"Then you have the answer."

Obi-Wan swung to face the starfield. "The Sith were before Master Yoda's time, were they not, Master?"

Qui-Gon came close to smiling. "Nothing was before Yoda's time, Padawan."

Obi-Wan turned to glance toward the gunship's forward cabin. "Master, about Cindar—"

"No, I don't trust him at all."

"Then why have we come to Karfeddion?"

"We have to begin somewhere, Obi-Wan. In time, even Cindar's lies will betray his true intentions."

"In time for us to prevent Captain Cohl from doing whatever Havac has tasked him to do?"

"That, I can't say, Padawan."

Just then, Cindar wandered forward, his gaze falling on the discarded Jedi robes and lightsabers.

"Won't you feel naked without them?"

Obi-Wan swung away from the console to face him. "We want to be certain to give the wrong impression."

"That's good planning," the Nikto said. "Especially since I'm new to Karfeddion myself, and haven't an idea where to begin looking for Cohl or Havac."

Qui-Gon glanced at him. "Don't concern yourself about that. I suspect we've already made a beginning."

With the gunship grounded in the docking bay, Qui-Gon, Obi-Wan, and Cindar descended the boarding ramp and set out to make inquiries at some of the disreputable cantinas and tapcafs that surrounded the spaceport. They weren't twenty meters from the ship when a pair of maintenance technicians intercepted them at the exit to the street.

"*Hawk-Bat*, right?" the taller of the two said to Qui-Gon.

Qui-Gon looked the man in the eye. "Who's asking?"

"No offense, Captain," the other said, showing his

grease-stained hands in a mollifying gesture. "We just wanted to tell you that you just missed him."

Obi-Wan started to say something, but thought better of it.

"We just missed him?"

"Launched a couple of hours back," the tall one replied, "with a full complement of crew in a beat-up Corellian freighter."

"Oh, that ship," Qui-Gon said.

The shorter tech adopted a conspiratorial look. "Are you three part of this Eriadu business?"

"What do you think?" Qui-Gon said rhetorically.

The two techs traded meaningful glances. "You wouldn't by chance need a couple of spare hands, would you, Captain?" the taller one asked.

Qui-Gon pretended to assess them. "I've no need for technicians. What are your other talents?"

"Same as the ones Cohl was flying with, Captain," the tall one said with increasing assurance. "Light and heavy arms, melee weapons, explosives, you name it."

"Small wars and revolutions," the other enthused.

Qui-Gon nodded. "I'll pass the word along to Captain Cohl."

The taller one nudged his partner in anticipation. "Much appreciated, Captain."

"Can you tell us what's planned?" the other asked. "Just so we know how to prepare?"

Qui-Gon shook his head firmly.

The taller man frowned. "We understand. It's only that we heard it was extermination work."

Qui-Gon said nothing in a blank-faced definite way.

"Well, you know where to find us, Captain," the short one said.

Qui-Gon let them take a few steps toward the exit before he called out. "By the way, was Havac with him?"

The question clearly puzzled them.

"Don't know the name, Captain," the shorter of the pair said. "Just Cohl, his Rodian sidekick, and the ones Cohl had hired."

The other man grinned broadly. "And the woman."

Qui-Gon raised his eyebrows. "So she was there, too."

The tall one laughed shortly. "If looks could kill, eh, Captain?"

Qui-Gon didn't so much as glance at Obi-Wan until the pair had left the docking bay. But by that time, Cindar had already made his move.

"You're one lucky fellow," the humanoid said, holding his blaster where he could cover both of them.

"Not from where I'm standing," Qui-Gon said.

"You weren't meant to hear any of that," Cindar went on. "I didn't know anything about Cohl's coming to Karfeddion."

"So this was just to keep us away from Eriadu."

Cindar sneered. "Yeah, and this is as far as it goes, Jedi. Too bad you left your lightsabers on board."

Qui-Gon folded his arms. "We had to make you feel confident about drawing your blaster and revealing yourself."

"Huh?"

Obi-Wan threw a small sound toward the ship, and Cindar whirled. When he spun back to the two Jedi, they had moved.

Spying Obi-Wan ten meters to his right, Cindar triggered a bolt, but Qui-Gon called on the Force to shove Cindar's blaster hand, and the bolt went wild. At the same instant, Obi-Wan leapt over Cindar's head, landing directly behind him.

Cindar spun on his heel, prepared to fire.

Obi-Wan swept his right leg through a forward circle, knocking the blaster from Cindar's hand. Crouching suddenly, he whirled one foot, kicking Cindar's legs out from under him.

The thickset humanoid fell hard on his side, but sprang nimbly to his feet and began to advance, throwing combinations of punches and kicks, which Obi-Wan blocked with his raised forearms and knees.

Frustrated, Cindar threw his arms around Obi-Wan in a front-facing hug, only to end up hugging himself when Obi-Wan made himself slender and dropped out of the embrace. Off-balanced, Cindar staggered forward and crashed into one of the *Hawk-Bat*'s landing struts.

Obi-Wan leapt and landed.

Cindar charged—but with hidden purpose.

Anticipating Obi-Wan's next leap, Cindar stopped short, then threw a powerful roundhouse kick. Tagged in the torso as he was landing, Obi-Wan moved with the force of the blow, cartwheeling to one side, and landing square on both feet, facing Cindar. The humanoid charged once more, catching the impact of Obi-Wan's abrupt back flip, full in the jaw.

Cindar blundered backwards into the same strut. Evading Obi-Wan's follow-up blows with bobs and twists, he squatted and made a sudden grab for Obi-Wan's right ankle. But Obi-Wan distanced himself by executing another back flip.

The momentary lapse in the fighting was all Cindar needed. From an ankle holster he drew a hold-out blaster.

The first bolt nicked Obi-Wan's right leg and sent him down on one knee. Qui-Gon appeared out of nowhere to drive him out of the path of the next bolt. Compact packets of energized light ripped through the docking bay, glancing off the walls and ceiling.

Cindar tried to track the Jedi, but they moved too quickly for him. His next blasts caromed from the underside of the *Hawk-Bat* and recoiled crazily from the floor.

Then the firing ceased.

Standing rigidly in front of Qui-Gon and Obi-Wan, Cindar's gaze was unfocused and his mouth a rictus of surprise. When he toppled facedown, they saw the burn of a blaster bolt that had ricocheted into the center of his back.

Qui-Gon went to him and checked for signs of life. "He's told us all he can."

Obi-Wan picked himself up from the floor, favoring his sound leg. "What now, Master?" he asked.

Qui-Gon nodded to the *Hawk-Bat*. "We race Captain Cohl to Eriadu."

"Karfeddion?" Yoda said in puzzlement. "Off on another quest, is he?"

Saesee Tiin glanced at Yaddle before replying. "None other than the quest that has preoccupied him for the past month."

Yoda touched his forefinger to his lips, closed his eyes, and shook his head in dismay. "Again, Captain Cohl."

Eleven of the twelve members of the Jedi Council were gathered in their high tower, with the sun disappearing around the western curve of Coruscant in an eruption of color. Adi Gallia's chair was empty.

"It's not like Qui-Gon to defy the express wishes of the Council and the Supreme Chancellor," Plo Koon said.

Yoda's eyes snapped opened and he raised his cane. "No. *Like* Qui-Gon, this is. Always forward, the Living Force. Adjust to Qui-Gon's actions, the future will." He shook his head again.

"The only real danger is if he does anything to further a rift between the Republic and the Senex sector," Oppo Rancisis said. "I fear that the events on Asmeru have already placed Supreme Chancellor Valorum in an awkward position."

"At a critical time," Even Piell added. "Vandron and the other Senex noble houses could point to Asmeru as an example of the Republic's disregard for self-governing sectors. Valorum's goal of fostering trust in the Republic among the outlying systems would be subverted."

Mace Windu had his mouth open to reply when Ki-Adi-Mundi emerged from the turbolift.

"I'm sorry to intrude, Master Windu," the Cerean said. "But we have received an urgent communication from Qui-Gon Jinn."

"What is the transmission?" Mace Windu asked.

"He and Obi-Wan are bound for Eriadu in the *Hawk-Bat*."

Yoda made his eyes wide in theatrical surprise. "*Become* Captain Cohl, Qui-Gon has!"

24

As a trading port, Eriadu was accustomed to seeing its polluted skies filled with vessels. The trade summit, however, set a new record for traffic, both below and high in orbit.

Among the thousands of ships anchored above the planet's bright side was a run-down Corellian freighter, the current object of interest of a heavily armed picket ship bearing the emblem of Eriadu Customs and Immigration. Between the picket and the freighter moved a small single-winged craft, twice the size of a standard starfighter.

Rella and Boiny watched the craft approach from one of the freighter's starboard viewports. Dressed alike in knee-high boots, bloused trousers, vests, and soft caps with short brims, they might have been veteran spacers.

"We'll play this by the numbers," Rella said. "Customs officials aren't trained to be nasty, they're born that way." She glanced at Boiny. "Want to go over any of it again?"

The Rodian shook his head. "I'll follow your lead."

They went to the starboard airlock and waited for it to cycle. Shortly, three humans in flashy uniforms came aboard, accompanied by a mean-tempered saurian quadruped fitted with an electronic collar. The beast's tongue flicked from its slash of mouth, licking the air.

Nearly as tall as Rella, the chief inspector was a slender, light-complexioned woman. Her blond hair was pulled severely back and woven into a long braid behind her head.

"Take Chack aft and work your way forward," she ordered her two companions. "Let him take his time. Tag anything that gets his attention, and we'll deal with it separately."

The two customs agents and their sniffer headed for the rear of the ship. The chief watched them go, then followed Rella and Boiny into the freighter's forward cabin.

"Your shipping manifest," she demanded, extending her right hand to Rella.

Rella prized a data card from the breast pocket of her vest and slapped it into the woman's palm. The chief inserted the card into a portable reader and studied the device's small display screen.

From aft came a sudden growling sound. The chief looked over her shoulder.

"Your sniffer must have gotten a whiff of our galley," Boiny said jocularly.

The woman's stern expression didn't waver. "I can't make sense of this," she said after a moment, motioning to the reader's display screen with the backs of her fingertips. She eyed Rella with suspicion. "What, exactly, is your cargo, Captain?"

Rella leveled a blaster at her. "Trouble."

The woman's eyes widened. Noises behind her prompted her to glance over her shoulder once more. Two robust humans and a Gotal answered her obvious surprise with pernicious grins.

"We're holding the other two aft," Lope said. "The animal's dead."

"Good work," Rella said, deftly disarming the chief.

Pressing the blaster to the woman's ribs, she steered her toward the freighter's communication suite.

"I want you to raise your ship," Rella said while they walked. "Tell whoever's in charge that you've discovered a load of contraband, and that you need the entire inspection crew over here on the quick."

The woman tried to turn out of Rella's grip, but Rella only tightened her hold and shoved her down into the chair at the control console.

"Do it," Rella warned.

The woman hesitated, then complied, resignedly.

"The entire crew?" someone on the picket ship asked in disbelief. "Is it that bad?"

"It's that bad," the chief said toward the console pickup.

Rella switched off the feed and took a step back to appraise the chief. "I'm going to need your uniform."

The woman stared at her. "My uniform?"

Rella patted her on the shoulder. "That's a good girl." She swung back to Boiny and the others. "Position yourselves at the airlock and be ready to receive company."

The mercenaries enabled their blasters and hurried off.

Not fifteen minutes later, and now wearing the chief's uniform, Rella entered the bridge of the picket ship and swept her eyes over the instruments. Boiny's charge, the chief, followed, her wrists sporting stun cuffs and the rest of her clothed in Rella's spacer garb.

Boiny motioned the woman into the copilot's chair,

then pressed his sucker-tipped forefinger to a communications bead in his right ear.

"Lope wants to know what he should do with the inspection team," he said to Rella.

She answered while continuing to study the instruments. "Tell him to secure them in the aft hold of the freighter."

She eased into the pilot's chair and adjusted it to her liking. Drab Eriadu filled the forward viewport. Rella switched on the communications array and swiveled to face the chief.

"Send a message that you're bringing a load of confiscated cargo down the well. Say that you want the cargo transferred to the customs building for immediate inspection, and to have hoversleds standing by to meet you."

The woman smirked. "That's against procedure. They won't do it."

Rella smiled. "Thanks for the warning. But they will do it this time, because the people in the customs building are on my team." She gave it a moment to register. "Glare at me all you want, chief, but you're going to do it eventually."

The woman bent toward the audio pickup, clearly hoping that Rella would be proved wrong. But after listening to the transmission, the voice on the other end replied, "We'll have the hoversleds waiting."

The chief continued to glower at Rella. "You think no one knows we boarded your ship?"

"I'm aware of that," Rella said. "But we don't need all day to accomplish what we came here to do."

She fastened the chief's seat harness in such a way that the woman could scarcely move. Then she accepted an adhesive strip from Boiny and plastered it over the chief's mouth.

"You sit tight for a while," Rella said, squatting to eye level with the woman. "We won't be long."

She and Boiny went aft to the picket's small rear compartment. Cohl and the mercenaries were already there, pressed in among a half-dozen two-meter-tall cargo tubes that had been conveyed from the freighter. All of them were wearing rebreathers and extravehicular suits, with armorply vests beneath.

"Is this necessary?" one of the humans was asking Cohl, gesturing to the upright cargo tubes.

"I suppose you'd rather blast your way through customs, is that it?"

"No, Captain," the man answered sullenly. "It's just that I don't like tight spots."

Cohl laughed ruefully. "Get used to it. It's going to be nothing but tight spots from this point on. Now, in you go."

Reluctantly the man opened the cargo tube's narrow hatch and squeezed inside. "It's like a coffin in here!"

"Then just be happy you're still alive," Cohl said, securing the door from the outside.

With similar aversion, the others began to secrete themselves.

"You, too, Cohl," Rella said.

"Wish I could be joining you, Captain," Boiny said with a smile.

Cohl scowled. "You're lucky there was a Rodian on the inspection team, or I'd have you sharing a canister with Lope." He turned to Rella. "I don't know exactly how we would have pulled this off without your help."

She narrowed her eyes at him. "Save it, Cohl. I just want to get us out of it in one piece."

He stepped into the canister. "Seriously. I don't deserve you."

"That's the first true thing you've said. But that's just who I am." She reached into the canister to fasten the collar of Cohl's space suit. "We can't have you catching a chill."

Cohl grinned at her.

She sealed the cargo tube and looked at Boiny. "Ready the ship to leave orbit."

As promised, a half-dozen hoversleds were on hand to meet the customs ship when it touched down at Eriadu's overtaxed spaceport.

Now fettered only by stun cuffs, the chief was the first to step from the picket's hatch. She took one look at the humanoid and alien operators of the hoversleds and inhaled sharply.

"Who *are* you people?" She asked in utter dismay.

"You don't really want to know that," Rella said from just behind her.

She nodded to Boiny, who placed a small styrette to the chief's neck and injected her with a measure of clear fluid. Instantly, the woman slumped back into Boiny's arms.

"Stow her in one of the empty cargo canisters," Rella said. "We'll take her with us for safekeeping."

She hopped down onto one of the hoversleds. "We have to work fast," she cautioned Havac's downside contingent of terrorists. "It won't be long before the freighter is discovered and searched."

Rella rode one of the repulsorlift flatbeds to the picket's aft hatch, which was already open. There, she leapt into the rear compartment and rapped her knuckles against the matte surface of Cohl's container.

"Not much longer," she said quietly.

When the coffinlike canisters had been loaded, the flotilla of hoversleds moved across the spaceport's duracrete apron to the customs warehouse, where more of Havac's terrorists were guarding the roll-away doors.

To all sides, ships were arriving and launching. Closer to the spaceport terminals, passengers were disembarking from the shuttles that had carried them from transports

anchored in orbit. PK and protocol droids were everywhere, as were teams of security agents, waiting to hustle
diplomats and dignitaries through immigration. Massed
along the spaceport's stun-fenced perimeter, mobs of
demonstrators were declaring their discontent, with
chanted slogans and crudely lettered signs.

The hoversleds streamed into the warehouse in single
file, the roll-away doors closing behind them. At once,
the humanoid and alien pilots began to unseal the canisters, which opened with a hiss of escaping atmosphere.

Cohl climbed from his coffin, pulled off his rebreather,
and jumped to the sawdust-covered floor, gazing around
expectantly. The place smelled of spacecraft exhaust and
hydrocarbons.

"Punctual, as ever, Captain," Havac said, as he and a
group of his cohorts emerged from behind a palisade of
stacked cargo bins. Sporting a colorful headcloth and
scarf that left only his eyes exposed, the Nebula Front
militant started for the now motionless sleds, coming to
an abrupt halt when he saw Rella.

"I thought you'd retired."

"I had a memory lapse," she told him. "But I'm about
to get over it."

Havac appraised the gathered mercenaries and turned
to Cohl. "Will they follow orders?"

"If you feed them regularly," Cohl said.

"What do we do with this one?" Lope asked, indicating the still-unconscious customs chief.

"Leave her there," Havac answered. "We'll take care
of her." He swung back to Cohl. "Captain, if you'll follow me, we can conclude your part in this."

"That suits me fine," Cohl said.

Havac glanced at Lope and the others. "The rest of
you wait here. I'll brief you when I return."

In a restricted area of the spaceport, Adi Gallia met Qui-Gon and Obi-Wan as they stepped from the sharp-nosed shuttle that had brought them downside.

"The High Council's favorite Jedi," Adi said as Qui-Gon approached, his long hair and brown cloak stirred by the wind. "I half expected you and your loyal Padawan to come bolting overhead in Captain Cohl's gunship."

"We left the *Hawk-Bat* in orbit," Qui-Gon replied without humor. "What's the situation here?"

"Master Tiin, Ki-Adi-Mundi, Vergere, and some of the others are on their way from Coruscant."

Qui-Gon planted his hands on his hips. "Did you ask security to run a check on Corellian freighters?"

Adi gave him a long-suffering look. "Do you know how many Corellian freighters are in orbit just now? Unless you can provide a registry or a drive signature of some sort, there's little anyone can do. As it is, it will take customs and security a week to search every vessel."

"What about Captain Cohl?"

Adi shook her head, the tails of her tight-fitting bonnet whipping about her handsome features. "No one fitting Cohl's description has passed through Eriadu immigration."

"Could we have arrived first, Master?" Obi-Wan asked. "The *Hawk-Bat* is about the fastest ship I've ever flown in."

Adi waited for Qui-Gon's response, which was to shake his head negatively.

"Cohl is here somewhere. I can feel him."

The three of them glanced around, reaching out with the Force.

"There is so much disturbance just now, it's difficult to focus on any one thing," Adi said after a long moment.

Determination quickened Qui-Gon's gaze. "We must prevail on the Supreme Chancellor to allow us to take the place of his Senate Guards. It's our best hope."

Havac led the way down a long corridor. Against one wall were slumped a dozen or so bound, gagged, and blindfolded customs agents, who voiced muffled exclamations of fury as Cohl, Rella, and Boiny passed. Havac continued on to a room that housed the warehouse's small power plant.

He opened the door and gestured everyone inside. Flickering overhead fixtures illuminated a clamorous generator, along with scores of unopened shipping crates. The room reeked of lubricants and liquid fuel.

Havac's demeanor changed as soon as he shut the door behind him. He unwound the cloth scarf that concealed his face and threw it to the floor.

Cohl regarded him curiously. "What's gotten you so jumpy, Havac?"

"You," Havac seethed. "You've nearly ruined everything!"

Cohl swapped brief looks with his comrades, then said, "What are you babbling about?"

Havac fought to compose himself. "The Jedi learned that you've been hiring assassins, and that you're planning something for Eriadu. Your likeness is all over the HoloNet!"

"Again, the Jedi." Cohl narrowed his gaze at Havac. "I thought you and Cindar were supposed to keep them occupied."

"We did our part. We lured the Jedi to Asmeru, and we managed to lure even more of them away from Eriadu. But you, you left a trail any amateur could follow, and now Cindar's dead because of it."

"You'll forgive me if I don't sob," Cohl said flatly.

Havac ignored the remark and began to pace the floor. "I've been forced to modify the entire plan. If it wasn't for the help of our advisor—"

"Take it easy, Havac," Cohl cut him off. "You're going to give yourself a stroke."

Havac came to a halt behind Rella and aimed his forefinger at Cohl. "I'm going to have to use the ones you delivered to fashion a diversion."

Cohl's features warped into a mask of acrimony. "I can't allow that, Havac. I didn't deliver them here to be killed. They trust me."

"Content yourself that they'll die rich, Captain. What's more, I don't care what you think you can and cannot allow. I won't have you interfering in this."

Cohl laughed shortly. "You're going to stop me?" He turned and started for the door.

"Stay where you are!"

Havac made a sudden grab for Rella's blaster. She tried to turn away, but wasn't in time. Havac threw his left forearm around her neck and pressed the blaster to the side of her head.

Cohl stopped dead in his tracks and turned slowly toward him. Boiny was about as far from Havac as he was, but neither of them risked a move.

"You haven't got the stomach for this kind of work, Havac," Cohl said in a controlled voice. "Put the blaster down and let her go."

Havac only tightened his choke hold on Rella. She clamped her hands on his forearm.

"You said it yourself, Captain: anyone can be killed. I'll do it if you try to leave. I swear, I'll do it."

Cohl glanced at Boiny before replying. "Havac, think it through. You're the brains, remember? You hired us to be the brawn."

Havac's face was red with fury and panic; he was trembling from head to foot. "You underestimate me. You always have."

"All right," Cohl said. "Maybe I have. That still doesn't mean—"

"I'm sorry it has to be this way," Havac interrupted. "But when it comes to safeguarding the interests of the Outer Rim, people like you and Rella and me are expendable. Our advisor prefers as few loose ends as possible, in any case."

The door opened and two of Havac's confederates entered the room with blasters raised.

Cohl saw the sorrow in Rella's dark, beautiful eyes. "Oh, Cohl," she said in a sad, quiet voice.

Abruptly, Havac turned his blaster and fired.

The bolt whizzed past Rella's head, hitting Cohl in the chest. A second bolt struck the wall behind Cohl and glanced off into the room. Twisting to one side, Cohl threw himself at the two men by the door, dropping both with a body block.

At the same instant, Rella bent her right leg, raising her foot into Havac's groin. He stumbled backwards, gasping for breath, but managed to hold on to the blaster. Boiny hurled himself at Rella, intent on driving her to the floor, but Havac began to fire wildly, catching Rella in the neck and Boiny in the side of the head.

Wrestling with the two men he had knocked down, Cohl heard the blaster bolts and saw Rella collapse in a heap. Sudden rage rushed to his aid in ripping a blaster from one of the men and killing him with shot to the face. The other man rolled and came to his feet in a crouch, loosing a volley of bolts at Cohl.

Cohl felt intense heat sear his thigh, abdomen, and forehead. He flew back against the wall and slid slowly to the floor, the blaster slipping from his grip.

Across the room a groan escaped Boiny, and he turned over onto his back, blood oozing from his head.

Through half-closed eyes Cohl stared at Rella. A single tear moved in fits and starts down her right cheek to her jawline. Cohl extended his right hand toward her, only to have it fall to his side, like dead weight.

"Havac," he said weakly, before his head fell to his chest.

His back pressed to the wall, a quaking Havac dropped Rella's blaster, as if he had just realized he was holding it. He gazed wide-eyed at his comrade.

"Is—is she dead?"

Keeping his blaster ready, the human went first to Rella, then to Boiny, and finally to Cohl. "Yes—and these two are well on the way. What should we do with them?"

Havac swallowed audibly. "The authorities are hunting for Captain Cohl," he stammered. "Perhaps we should let them find him."

"And the others—the ones Cohl brought?"

Havac considered it briefly. Then he retrieved the scarf he had thrown to the floor and began to wind it around his lower face.

"They know me only as Havac," he said, and moved for the door.

A uniformed detachment of Eriadu security guards escorted Qui-Gon, Obi-Wan, and Adi Gallia to the heavily guarded door of the Supreme Chancellor's temporary quarters in the majestic home of Lieutenant Governor Tarkin.

Sei Taria led them the rest of the way.

"I never got to thank you personally for your actions at the Senate," Valorum said to Qui-Gon. "If it wasn't for you and Master Gallia, I might not be standing here today."

Qui-Gon nodded in respect and acknowledgment. "The Force was with you that day, Supreme Chancellor. But we're not satisfied that the threat has been removed. There is reason to believe that the assault in the plaza was contrived to lure Republic law enforcement to the Senex sector, and thus distract us from a similar plan the Nebula Front hopes to execute on Eriadu."

Valorum beetled his thick brows. "A strike against me here would undermine what little support the Nebula Front currently enjoys in the Outer Rim."

"The Nebula Front has no more faith in the Republic than it does in the coalition of outlying worlds," Qui-Gon replied calmly but firmly. "By attacking you here, the Front may be hoping to induce the Republic to forsake any interest in the free trade zones, and lay the ground work for a separatist movement in the Outer Rim." He compressed his lips. "I know that it defies all reason, Supreme Chancellor, but the Nebula Front appears to have abandoned reason."

Valorum paced away from Qui-Gon, then whirled around. "Then it's up to me to convince the delegates of the outlying sectors to loosen the yoke the Nebula Front and Trade Federation have thrown about them."

"Supreme Chancellor," Adi interjected, "will you at least consider postponing your opening remarks until we've had a chance to uncover the Nebula Front's plan? It's possible that assassins have already managed to penetrate Eriadu security."

Valorum shook his head. "I won't hear of it. At this late stage, any change to the proceedings would be interpreted as weakness or hesitancy." He glanced at the three Jedi. "I'm sorry. I realize that you have my best interests in mind. But for the sake of the Republic, I can't allow you to interfere."

Adi bowed her head. "We will honor your wishes, Supreme Chancellor."

The three Jedi turned and exited the room.

No sooner did the door close behind them than Qui-Gon said, "We must go directly to the site of the summit and see what we can learn."

26

"**I**f the attack on Valorum didn't make him the focus of this summit, Asmeru certainly did," Senator Bor Gracus of Sluis Van was telling Palpatine as they moved in step with the slow flow of other delegates toward Eriadu Spaceport's immigration scanners.

Human or alien, almost everyone was draped in robes and capes of the finest cloth, including Palpatine and his temporary companion in the snaking line, who were dressed alike in richly adorned cloaks with roomy sleeves and high double collars.

Sate Pestage and Kinman Doriana, also dressed alike in black cloaks, followed closely behind Palpatine.

"Gossip to which I've been privy suggests many of the Core and Inner Rim delegates are whispering that the Supreme Chancellor's actions at Asmeru were a bald attempt to curry favor with the Trade Federation."

Gracus was a stout human with protruding eyes and a putty nose. His homeworld boasted a small but flourishing shipyard. As with other worlds along and in close proximity to the Rimma Trade Route, Sluis Van viewed its future import as preordained.

"Gossip is valuable only if it is accurate, Senator," Palpatine said after a moment. "Supreme Chancellor Valorum is scarcely an advocate of unfair trade policies."

"Unfair, you say? I didn't hear you stand up and cheer when Valorum made his speech championing the advantages of taxation of the free trade zones."

"That doesn't mean that I think otherwise," Palpatine said in a composed voice. "But, like you, my station compels me to echo the voice of those I represent, and, at present, Naboo remains undecided."

Gracus gave him a sidelong glance. "King Veruna is undecided, you mean to say."

"His troubles are on the rise, to be sure. Our regent is too enmeshed in scandal to give much thought to what lies ahead for Naboo. He forgets that our world relies on the Trade Federation for much of its industrial imports, in addition to some of its food. Naboo risks as much, if not more than any other outlying system in actively opposing the Trade Federation. It was only after much discussion and debate that I convinced King Veruna of the importance of my attending this summit."

"You are most judicious, Senator," Gracus said, in a way that mixed mild annoyance with admiration. "You answer my question without actually answering it. You prop Valorum, and yet you don't." When it was evident that Palpatine wasn't going to reply, Gracus added, "It is my understanding that you briefed the Supreme Chancellor on the subject of dispatching an armed force to Asmeru."

"A diplomatic delegation," Palpatine amended.

"Call it what you will, you can't change what happened there. And you can't deny that what happened there doesn't smell more of might than right."

Palpatine gestured in dismissal. "The details of the incident are sketchy at best, Senator. What's more, you are ignoring the fact that, by trying to kill the Supreme Chancellor, the Nebula Front made themselves Republic business."

"So Valorum claims," Gracus demurred.

"The delegation came under almost immediate attack, and responded accordingly," Palpatine said.

Gracus sniffed in derision. "The professed justification. Valorum used the incident to launch a preemptive strike, eliminating the Nebula Front's ability to disrupt the summit, and at the same time inveigling the Trade Federation into accepting taxation.

"And I suspect that he had other reasons, as well. Everyone anticipated the Senex Houses to protest the violation of their territory, but they have been very silent thus far. It wouldn't surprise me to learn that a deal has been struck between Valorum and House Vandron. Should House Vandron agree not to protest what happened at Asmeru, the senate—or at least Valorum—will agree to overlook House Vandron's continuing Rights of Sentience violations and lift the restrictions that have made it impossible for the Senex to trade with Republic worlds."

"Whether slavery or spice smuggling, the Core Worlds take little interest in the injustices that plague the Outer Rim," Palpatine said in a world-weary voice. "Violations notwithstanding, the Republic would gladly trade with the Senex, if the Senex had something of value to offer. If that wasn't the case, the Trade Federation would have been disbanded long ago. But, in fact, the Neimoidians and the rest have set themselves up as irreplaceable, because of what they transport to the Core."

Gracus appeared flustered. "Nevertheless," he sputtered, "the Outer Rim worlds are now in turmoil. Even those who don't openly support the Nebula Front are decrying the fact that the Republic took it upon itself to intercede at Asmeru."

Palpatine summoned an ambiguous smile. "I'm certain that the Supreme Chancellor will ease everyone's concerns when he addresses the delegates."

"And we'll all be eager to hear what he has to say," Gracus replied contemptuously, "since with one hand he seeks to punish the Trade Federation with taxation, while with the other he strokes them by eradicating the Federation's most dangerous antagonist."

Palpatine's seeming good humor didn't falter. "One must make adjustments as necessary. Despite assiduous planning, not everything can be foreseen."

A faraway look came into his eyes. "The landscape we inhabit is an everchanging one, Senator. One moment we are in the light; the next we are in the dark, left to find our own way through. If events could truly be divined— if one were to be granted such awesome power—then perhaps the future could be directed along one line or another. But until then, we stumble through, groping blindly for the truth."

Gracus snorted. "Perhaps you should consider placing your name in nomination for high office, Senator."

Palpatine brushed the remark aside. "I'm content to play my small part behind the scenes."

"For the moment, I suspect," Gracus said, as Palpatine hurried ahead of him in the line.

Nute Gunray's red eyes meandered over the line of delegates waiting to be scanned by Eriadu's primitive scanning devices. His gaze fell on two human senators—one rotund and plebeian; the other, straight-backed and refined— engaged in what appeared to be a spirited exchange. He looked down from his mechnochair at Senator Lott Dod.

"Who is the human in the blue cloak—there, speaking with the pudgy one?"

Dod followed the viceroy's raised forefinger. "Senator Palpatine of Naboo."

"A friend of ours?"

Dod shook his head dubiously. "He gives all indication of holding to a middle course, Viceroy. Although I heard that he encouraged Valorum to send judicials to the Senex sector."

"A potential friend, then," Gunray said.

"Soon enough, we will know where everyone stands."

Behind them, squatting on the duracrete, was the shuttle that had carried them to the surface, an organic-looking ship, with a quartet of clawed and segmented landing gear, a pair of generator vents that resembled eyespots, and a rear deflector shield assembly that rose from the ship's flat body like a raised tail.

Gunray and Dod wore robes, mantles, and headdresses—crimson and cordovan for the viceroy; deep purple and lavender for the senator. Fore and aft and to both sides of them marched security droids, their blaster rifles mounted behind their right shoulders. The droids constituted the Neimoidians' reply to Eriadu's offer to provide protection. In addition, the Trade Federation Directorate had insisted that a small shield generator be installed in that section of the summit hall assigned to them.

A mere glance at the protestors who stood five-deep along the perimeter of the spaceport facilities told Gunray that the members of the directorate had made a prudent decision—despite the ridicule to which they had been subjected by their peers in the Galactic Senate.

The directorate's other six, shielded by Eriadu security agents, led the Trade Federation cortege as they neared the terminal. At the head of the line walked the Federation's four human directors—two from Kuat, one from

Balmorra, and the other from Filve. And behind them came the directorate's Gran and Sullustan members, all wearing costly tunics and caplets, though a far cry from the extravagant ones affected by Gunray and Dod.

"Can we take this Asmeru business as a sign that Valorum is secretly in our camp?" the Sullustan was asking the Gran.

"Not unless Valorum surprises everyone here by withdrawing his taxation proposal," the Gran replied.

"My attorneys assure me that the Republic has no legal right to tax the free trade zones," Gunray said in Basic, from atop his ambulatory throne.

One of the humans from Kuat looked over his shoulder at the Neimoidian and laughed. "The Republic will do as it wishes, Viceroy. You're a fool to believe otherwise. Valorum is as much our adversary as ever."

Gunray suffered the humiliation in silence. What, he wondered, would the Kuati have made of Darth Sidious's assertion that Valorum was the Trade Federation's strongest ally in the senate? Would the Kuati have been so quick to taunt and scoff?

Gunray doubted it.

The arrogant human and the others knew nothing of the covert deal Gunray had struck with the Sith Lord. They viewed the Neimoidians' continuing purchases of upgraded droid weaponry as wasteful, and symptomatic of the Neimoidians' increasing sense of paranoia. But they rarely contested the expenditures, since the weapons afforded the fleet an added measure of protection. Similarly, they knew nothing of Sidious's plan for the Trade Federation to extend its reach beyond the outlying systems to the galactic rim itself.

And yet, Gunray was anxious.

The Sith Lord had communicated with him only once since arranging the meeting between the Neimoidians and the Baktoid and Haor Chall arms merchants. The communication had been brief and one-sided, with Sidious stressing the importance of Gunray's attending the trade summit, and assuring him, as ever, that everything was going according to plan.

"The way to defeat Valorum," the other Kuati was saying, "is to persuade our signatory members that they gain nothing by decamping and seeking individual representation in the senate."

"Even if that requires offering them lucrative trade incentives," the Sullustan added.

"But our profits," Gunray blurted, despite his best efforts to control himself.

"The Republic taxes will have to be absorbed by the outlying systems," the directorate officer from Balmorra said. "There is simply no other way."

"And if the taxes are too exorbitant for the outlying systems to absorb?" the Gran asked. "Our share of the market will be lost. This could very well cripple us."

This time Gunray managed to stifle himself.

It is all a charade, Sidious had said. *Taxation is but a minor obstacle in our path to greater glory. Allow your counterparts in the directorate to say and do as they wish. But refrain from offering any response—especially at the summit itself.*

Our path, Gunray thought.

But had he entered into a true partnership, or one in which Sidious would emerge as the Neimoidians' overlord? How long could a Sith Lord content himself with mere economic power? And what was likely to become of Viceroy Nute Gunray once Darth Sidious set his sights on a target more worthy of his dark expertise?

Already Deputy Viceroy Hath Monchar and Commander Dofine had aired their separate misgivings about the alliance—scarcely realizing that the partnership had as much been *forced* on Gunray as offered to him.

The Sith Lord had promised that he would communicate with Gunray once more before the summit began. Perhaps, the viceroy hoped, all would then be revealed.

Havac and his cohort returned to the main room of the customs warehouse, and the distant rumble of spacecraft launches. The five mercenaries Cohl had assembled were sitting on the edges of the repulsorsleds that had borne them to the warehouse.

From the jittery way Havac moved, Lope knew that something unexpected had taken place. He jumped off the hovering sled to gaze down the corridor that led to the rear of the building.

"Where's Captain Cohl?" he asked Havac.

Above the scarf that swathed his face, Havac's eyes narrowed as he swung to face him. "Cohl went out the back way. But he sends his luck." Before anyone else could raise questions, he asked Lope, "What's your preferred weapon?"

Lope took a second look down the corridor, then returned to the sleds. "Blades—of any length."

Havac turned to one of the other humans. "Yours?" he asked, in an increasingly confident voice.

"Sniper rifles."

Havac glanced at the Gotal.

"I'm not a shooter. I'm a lookout."

Havac studied the remaining pair of humans—a brutish-looking man and an equally rough-cut woman.

"No preferences," the man grunted.

"The same," the woman said.

Havac took a portable holoprojector from his pocket and set it atop an alloy cargo crate. Everyone gathered round as an image of a Classic-era building with a domed roof took shape in the cone of light.

"The site of the trade summit," Havac said, as the image began to rotate, showing tall, slender towers at each corner, and four principal entrances. "The main hall is a rotunda, similar in design to the Galactic Senate, but on a much smaller scale and without the detachable balconies."

Havac called up a panoramic view of the interior.

"True to their exaggerated sense of self-importance, the Eriadu delegation has placed itself at the center of the hall. The Coruscant delegation will occupy east-side tiers of seats—here—with the members of the Trade Federation Directorate in west-side tiers. Delegations representing the Core Worlds, the Inner Rim, and the outlying systems will be dispersed throughout the rest of the hall.

"In the event of trouble, the Trade Federation Directorate will be able to activate a force field. But Valorum's delegation is deliberately unshielded, as a show of good faith."

The sniper scrutinized the image for a moment. "Valorum is going to be a difficult target—even from the highest tier in the rotunda."

"You'll be higher than that," Havac said. "The upper portion of the hall is a maze of maintenance walkways and gantries, along with booths designated for media personnel."

"We'd have a better chance of hitting Valorum before he enters the building," Lope said.

"Perhaps," Havac conceded. "But the plan hinges on our ability to infiltrate the summit and do the job there."

"Four entrances," the sniper said. "Which one is Valorum coming through?"

Havac shook his head. "Unknown. The route to the summit hall won't be revealed until the last possible instant, and we don't have anyone close enough to him to provide us with that data. That's why we need a spotter team on the outside."

Havac conjured another image from the holoprojector, showing the older quarter of the city, where the summits of innumerable buildings merged into an extensive range of rounded rooftops and elegant towers.

"Eriadu security is trying to keep the rooftops clear, but there aren't enough repulsorlift vehicles to provide steady surveillance, especially in areas like this, where the roofs are all interconnected. Instead, security is flying sweeps at regular intervals, concentrating their efforts on the buildings adjacent to the summit hall."

Havac indicated one of the domed rooftops. "From here, there's a decent view of the four boulevards that lead to the summit hall's separate entrances. The spotters—" He pointed to Lope, the Gotal, and the woman. "—will have just enough time to position yourselves on the roof between air sweeps. Access to the roof is through a safe house we maintain on Eriadu. The safe house will also serve as our rendezvous point after we're finished, or should something unforeseen occur beforehand. Valorum's hovercade will be easy to spot. As soon as you've ascertained the route, you'll communicate that information to the rest of us."

"Where will you be?" Lope demanded to know.

Havac turned to him. "The shooters will already be inside the hall, up in the walkways."

"That'll be the first place security will look," the sniper groused. "I want something extra if I'm expected to hang myself out to dry."

Havac shook his head. "You'll receive the same as everyone else. We all have important parts to play in this."

"Havac's right," Lope said. "If you don't like being the shooter, I'll take your place, and you take the rooftop surveillance. I don't like heights, anyway."

The sniper glared at Lope. "I didn't say I wouldn't do it. I'm only asking how I'm supposed to get to the walkways."

Havac motioned one of his alien confederates forward. The Nikto placed a suitcase atop the same crate that supported the holoprojector and opened it. Havac lifted a jacket from the suitcase and handed it to the sniper.

"This will identify you as Eriadu security," he explained. "I'll provide you with the necessary documentation later. The point is, you'll be in the summit hall before any of the delegations arrive. Once we've learned which entrance Valorum is coming through, you'll get into whatever position you deem best."

The sniper folded the uniform jacket over his arm. "When do I take the shot?"

"The proceedings will commence with a series of three prolonged trumpet fanfares," Havac went on. "Plan to fire at the start of the third fanfare."

"Valorum will already be in his seat?"

Havac nodded, as he brought back the image of the interior of the hall. "He will. But you're going to place your first bolt here."

The sniper stared at the spot on the summit hall floor

Havac had indicated, then gazed in puzzlement at Havac. "I don't get it. Who's going to be there?"

"No one."

"No one," the sniper repeated, then began to shake his head. "I don't know where you're going with this, but I've got a reputation to uphold, and when I'm hired to shoot, I don't miss."

Havac grumbled beneath his scarf. "All right, so choose a target. Wound someone."

Lope stepped forward. "I thought we had a target— Valorum."

Havac confirmed it with a nod and glanced at everyone. "But I don't want any of you doing the actual shooting."

While Lope and the rest were trading looks, Havac deactivated the holoprojector and set it aside. At the same time, a pair of Bith began to open the alloy crate the device had been sitting on, and slid from it a boxlike tangle of alloy limbs and a long cylinder of head.

"Meet the most important member of our team," Havac said. "Built specially for us by the same company that supplies the Trade Federation with its security droids."

Taking a small remote control from his pocket, he entered a code into the touchpad, and a battle droid unfolded into an upright posture, its arms at its side and a blaster rifle mounted alongside its backpack. The Nikto pried a restraining bolt from the chest plastron of the almost-two-meter-tall droid and stepped to the side. The restraining bolt hit the floor and rolled beneath the closest repulsorsled.

Havac keyed in another code.

Instantly, the droid reached over its shoulder for the blaster rifle. With matching speed, the mercenaries reacted by adopting defensive positions and drawing their own weapons.

"Settle down," Havac said loudly, gesturing with his hands.

Again, he keyed the remote. When the battle droid had returned the rifle to its mounting, Havac began to circle it.

"It's harmless," he assured everyone, "unless I tell it to be otherwise."

The Gotal was the only one who hadn't reholstered his weapon. "I can't work with a droid," he said angrily. "Their energy waves overload my senses."

"You're not going to have to work with it," Havac said. "It's also going to be inside the hall."

Lope and the sniper swapped concerned glances. "Who's leading him in?" Lope asked.

"The Trade Federation."

The sniper worked his square jaw. "Are you telling me that the droid is the actual shooter?"

Havac nodded.

"Then why do you have me shooting at the floor?"

"Because your bolt is going to touch off a chain of events that will allow our alloy teammate here to execute his commands." Havac regarded the droid. "It doesn't need a control computer. But it does need to perceive a threat before it can be tasked."

Lope started shaking his head. "You want this to end up looking like it was the Trade Federation that killed Valorum."

The rest of the mercenaries stared at Havac.

"You object to that?"

"Captain Cohl said that this was going to be a straight-forward job," the sniper protested. "He didn't say anything about the Trade Federation."

"Captain Cohl wasn't briefed on the full extent of the plan," Havac replied coolly. "There was no point risking a leak."

Lope forced a short laugh. "I guess we can appreciate

that, Havac. But the fact is, if word gets out that we helped set up the Trade Federation . . ."

"They've got a longer reach than the Republic, Havac," the sniper took over. "They'll have every bounty hunter from Coruscant to Tatooine after us. And I, for one, don't want to have to spend the rest of my days hiding in a hole somewhere."

Havac showed everyone a stony look. "Let's be clear about this. We're going to have to outwit Eriadu security, Republic judicials, and Jedi Knights just to pull this off. And, sure, you might have to buy off some bounty hunters when we're done. But all that means is simply living up to your reputations. If any of you don't think you're up to that, now is the time to say so."

Lope glanced at the sniper, then at the Gotal, then at Havac's several human and alien confederates, and back at the sniper again.

"It's settled?" Havac asked, breaking the long silence.

Lope nodded. "Just one more question, Havac. Where will *you* be during all this?"

"Where I can watch over all of you," he said, and let it go at that.

From the tile mosaic floor of the summit hall, Qui-Gon peered up at the tiers of seats, the banks of ornate, arch-topped windows, and, high overhead, the media booths and maintenance walkways. He rotated through a full circle, his gaze taking in groups of droids inspecting the hall's several hundred video monitors, and teams of judicials and security personnel moving through the tiers with leashed beasts that sniffed, tasted, and probed the stale air.

In that quarter of the hall designated for the Coruscant delegation, Masters Tiin and Ki-Adi-Mundi were snaking among the seats, open to the slightest disturbances in the

Force. Elsewhere in the rotunda, Adi Gallia and Vergere were doing the same, stretching out with their feelings, in the hope of discovering some indication of what Havac and Cohl's assassins had planned for the summit.

Agape in four directions, and perforated by its many windows, the hall was a security nightmare. Worse, Eriadu had decreed the summit open not only to delegates, but also to HoloNet reporters, assorted dignitaries and veterans groups, musicians, corporate representatives, and just about anyone with a modicum of authority or influence. So many diverse species were expected to attend—each with their individual entourages of aides, attendants, translators, and security guards—that it was going to be near impossible to determine who was legitimate and who wasn't.

Qui-Gon turned through another circle. The Eriadu delegation had granted itself the center of the floor, with Supreme Chancellor Valorum to their left, and the Trade Federation Directorate to their right. The Commerce Guild and the Techno Union had an arc of seats between the two, buffered by delegations from the Core and the outlying systems.

Qui-Gon's eyes were drawn once more to the overhead walkways and gantries, many of which supported arrays of spotlights and acoustic devices.

Snipers could be placed almost at will, he told himself. Assassins without regard for their own lives could inflict incalculable injury.

"Do you sense anything, Master?" Obi-Wan asked from behind him.

"Only that we are fighting something unseen, Obi-Wan. Each time we draw close to identifying our adversary, it subverts and evades us."

"Then it isn't Captain Cohl?"

Qui-Gon shook his head. "There is an organizing

hand at work here—one that moves Cohl about as ef-
fortlessly as it moves us."

"Not this Havac."

Qui-Gon pondered it momentarily, then shook his head
again. "It has no name that I know, Padawan. Perhaps
the mystery owes to nothing more than my inability to
see beyond the moment. What do you feel?"

Obi-Wan's expression became serious. "I feel that
we're close to resolving this, Master."

Qui-Gon touched him on the shoulder. "That's comforting to hear."

Adi Gallia and Vergere stepped down to the first tier to
speak with them.

"Security assures us that the entry scanners are capable
of detecting explosives, along with weapons—regardless
of their composition," Adi said. "Guards will be stationed
on the floor of the hall, and circulating up top, along the
walkways. Security units and other droids will provide
continuous surveillance of the roof areas."

"That may hamper Cohl from initiating an attack
here," Qui-Gon replied, "but what about outside the
hall?"

"The Supreme Chancellor's route will be determined
by computer, at the last moment."

"I'd rather that the route be by skycar to the rooftop
pad."

Adi shook her head negatively. "I'm sorry, Qui-Gon.
He insists on arriving by ground-effect vehicle. We'll have
to trust in the same precautions that safeguarded him on
the route from the spaceport to Lieutenant Governor
Tarkin's compound."

"Qui-Gon!" Master Tiin called out suddenly.

Qui-Gon turned to find him and Ki-Adi-Mundi hurrying across the floor toward them.

"Captain Cohl's freighter has been found," Tiin continued. "The Corellian freighter. Ten customs agents were found tied up in the rear cabin."

Qui-Gon and Obi-Wan swapped brief looks. "How do they know it's the one Cohl piloted here?"

"The navicomputer indicates that the ship jumped to Eriadu from Karfeddion space," Ki-Adi-Mundi explained.

"Cohl must have piloted the customs agents' ship to the surface," Qui-Gon surmised.

Tiin nodded as he came to a halt in front of Qui-Gon. "The customs ship has been located at the spaceport."

"We should see for ourselves," Obi-Wan said in a rush. Then he stopped himself and regarded Tiin. "What prompted anyone to conduct a search of the freighter?"

Tiin appeared to have anticipated the question, along with Qui-Gon's look of wary concern.

"The authorities received an anonymous lead."

28

Cohl's eyelids fluttered, then snapped open. Boiny's blood-smeared face swam unfocused in his gaze. He felt nauseated and wired. He knew that he should be in great pain, but he was only vaguely aware of his body. Boiny had obviously dosed him with pain blockers. Cohl tasted blood in his mouth, and something else—the syrupy astringency of bacta.

Boiny's features began to sharpen and come into focus. A blaster bolt had burned a deep furrow in the left side of the Rodian's greenish skull. The wound glistened with freshly applied bacta, but Cohl doubted that the miracle substance would prevail.

His memory made a hurried return. He gave a start and tried to sit up.

"Wait, Captain," Boiny said. His voice was weak and raspy. "Rest for a moment."

Cohl paid him no mind. He pushed himself upright, and immediately fell face first to the hard floor. He heard the tip of his nose crack and felt a trickle of blood course down over his mustache and drip onto his lower lip.

He began to drag himself across the floor, to where Rella's body lay unmoving—unmoving and cold when he stretched out his hand and grazed her face with his fingertips.

Boiny was suddenly beside him again.

"She's dead, Captain," he said, anguished. "By the time I came to, there was nothing I could do."

Cohl crawled the final meter to Rella. He threw his right arm over her shoulders, tugging her to him and weeping quietly for a long moment.

"You had to come back," he said quietly, between sobs.

Then he rolled over and glared at Boiny.

"You should have let me die."

Boiny had clearly anticipated his rage.

"If you were close to dying, I might have been able to do that." He tugged Cohl's ragged shirt aside to expose the thick armorply garment beneath. "The vest absorbed most of the charge, but you have internal injuries." He glanced at Cohl's tattered left thigh, then leaned over to examine his forehead. "I did the best I could with your other wounds."

Cohl raised his hand to his head. The bolt from Rella's blaster had burned away all the hair on the right side of his head and left a wound every bit as deep and ragged as the one that trenched Boiny's skull.

"Where'd you find—"

"An emergency medkit in a cabinet by the door. The bacta patches are a couple of months expired, but they probably have enough potency to sustain us for a while."

Cohl passed the back of his hand under his nose, then took a stuttering breath. "Your head . . ."

"Fractured, as well as burned. But I gave myself a healthy measure of the pain blockers I fed you. I came close to overdosing myself. But at least I'm seeing only one of you now."

Cohl managed to sit up. Glancing around the room, he spied the man he had killed lying faceup on the floor, exactly where the blaster had dropped him. Otherwise, the room was empty. He looked back at Boiny.

"Why didn't they finish us?"

"This wasn't supposed to happen. I figure that Havac panicked."

Cohl thought about it for a moment. "No. The Jedi are on to us. He wants us to be found." He paused briefly, then added, "But he isn't fool enough to believe I'd keep quiet about this mission, out of some misguided sense of honor."

"I'll wager that he's counting on the fact that you won't betray Lope and the others."

Cohl nodded slowly. "Havac read me right. But he's going to regret not killing me when he had the chance." With visible effort, he raised himself up on his uninjured right knee. "Are any of them still in the warehouse?"

"Only the customs agents secured in the corridor. The cargo bay is deserted."

Cohl extended his arm to the Rodian. "Help me up."

He winced as Boiny tugged him to his feet. Gingerly, he planted his left foot on the floor and nearly collapsed.

"I'm going to need a crutch."

"I'll fix you up with something," Boiny said.

Cohl balanced on his good leg. He thought his heart might burst if he looked at Rella again, but he forced his gaze downward nevertheless.

"Some of us were born to be betrayed," he whispered. "I can't make it up to you, Rella. But I can try with everything I've got left to avenge you."

Supported on the crutch the Rodian had fashioned from a length of pipe and a cloth-padded brace of plasteel, Cohl followed Boiny out into the corridor. The bound and blindfolded customs agents were scarcely aware of them as they moved stealthily toward the warehouse's spaceport entrance. The female agent whose uniform Rella had taken remained unconscious from the shot Boiny had given her aboard the ship.

The front room was loud with the noise of launches and landings, despite the roll-away doors being closed. The repulsorsleds were still hovering a meter off the sawdust-strewn floor, and everything else was much as Cohl remembered it.

Boiny studied the room for a moment, then walked to the center of the floor, two meters from the lead sled.

"There was a cargo crate here."

Cohl eyed the telltale marks in the sawdust. "Too large for a weapon's crate."

Looking around, the two of them spotted the portable holoprojector at the same time. It was resting on the retracted landing strut of one of the sleds. Boiny reached it first. Setting it atop the sled, he activated it. Cohl limped over as the device was beginning to cycle through its stored images.

"The summit hall," he said, in response to the 3-D image of the majestic dome-roofed building, and the mount it crowned.

Boiny allowed the images to cycle again, pausing the device when it displayed a remote view of the wooded mount, and the four broad avenues that terminated at the hall.

"The vantage from the cluster of rooftops we saw earlier," Boiny said, already initiating a reverse scan through the images. "Havac could be planning to attack Valorum before he arrives at the summit."

Cohl tugged at what was left of his beard while he considered it. He gestured to the holoprojector. "He didn't forget to take this. He wanted it to be found—just the way he wanted us to be found."

Abruptly, Boiny ducked down beneath one of the repulsorsleds. "Here's something he probably doesn't expect to be found," he said as he was standing up.

Cohl narrowed his eyes at the stubby metallic cylinder Boiny showed him. "A restraining bolt?"

"But an uncommon variety." Boiny brought the bolt to eye level. "Similar to the ones we fired into the security droids aboard the *Revenue*, but altered to suit a more advanced droid. Maybe a combat model."

"Havac has a droid," Cohl said, mostly to himself. His eyes searched the floor. "Could that be what was in the crate? Or is this one restraining bolt of a bunch?"

Boiny adopted a skeptical look. "The Nebula Front employing droids? That can't be right." He regarded the bolt again. "One thing is certain, Captain. This bolt has already been in a droid. I can see the impressions left by whatever tool pried it out."

Cohl took the bolt and clenched his hand around it.

"I warned Havac that someone in the Nebula Front had informed the Judicial Department about our plans to attack the *Revenue*. Suppose he decided to take extra precautions when planning this operation." Cohl looked at Boiny. "Havac said that the Front had lured the Jedi to Asmeru. That could mean that the attempt on Valorum's life on Coruscant was a ruse, designed to divert attention from Eriadu."

"Right," Boiny said uncertainly.

Cohl glanced at the holoprojector. "Havac leaves us and the holoprojector to be discovered by the authorities . . ." He grinned wickedly. "I'm not sure how Havac plans to do it, Boiny. But I think I know what he's planning to do."

"Captain?" the Rodian said in confusion.

Cohl shoved the restraining bolt into his breast pocket and began to limp toward the corridor.

Boiny followed him, gesturing back to the holoprojector. "Shouldn't I at least delete this thing?"

Cohl shook his head. "Hide it in plain sight, just as Havac did. The only way we're going to get to him is by making sure that everyone else keeps chasing their own tails."

Outside the front entrance to Lieutenant Governor Tarkin's palatial residence, Valorum, Sei Taria, and the rest of the Coruscant delegation waited for their caravan of repulsorlift vehicles to arrive. Fashionable tunics and brocaded cloaks were once again the order of the day, except in the case of security personnel, who were nearly as numerous as the diplomats.

"I trust that your stay with us has been pleasant," Tarkin was saying to Valorum.

"Very pleasant," Valorum replied. "Permit me to extend the same courtesy to you, should you ever visit Coruscant."

Tarkin smiled without showing his teeth. "I hope, Supreme Chancellor, that Coruscant will one day be a second home to me. All the Core, in fact, from Coruscant to Alderaan."

"I'm certain it will."

The captain of the Senate Guard detail approached with a durasheet in hand. In place of the customary ceremonial rifle, a state-of-the-art blaster was slung over his shoulder.

"We have the hovercade route, Supreme Chancellor."

"May I have a look at it?" Tarkin asked.

The guard looked to Valorum for permission.

"Let him see it."

Tarkin perused the durasheet. "A bit circuitous—perhaps needlessly so. But we should have no problem arriving at the summit hall by the appointed time." He glanced down the long drive that led to the mansion. "The governor should be here momentarily. Then we can all depart."

Tarkin was about to add something, when a landspeeder leapt into view, making fast for where he and Valorum were standing.

"What now?" Tarkin asked as the two-seater pulled up to the house and came to a halt.

Absent their Jedi cloaks, Adi Gallia and Saesee Tiin climbed from the hovering vehicle and made straight for Valorum. Tiin did the talking.

"Supreme Chancellor, there is a problem. We have confirmation that assassins contracted by the Nebula Front have breached Eriadu security. Qui-Gon Jinn and several other Jedi have gone to the spaceport, in the hope of intercepting them."

"The danger is no longer conjectural, Supreme Chancellor," Adi said earnestly.

Valorum's forehead wrinkled in apprehension. "I want them found," he said at last. "I will not have the summit interrupted."

Tiin and Adi nodded. "Will you now consent to our accompanying you?" Tiin asked.

"No," Valorum said flatly. "Appearances must be maintained."

Adi looked hard at him. "Then will you at least agree to keeping your vehicle's force field enabled?"

"I absolutely insist on it," Tarkin interjected. "It is Eriadu's obligation to assure that no harm comes to you."

With obvious reluctance, Valorum nodded. "Until we've reached the grounds of the summit hall."

His face blushed with sudden anger, Tarkin swung to a group of Eriadu security guards, who were standing behind him. "See to it that the streets are cleared. Arrest anyone you have cause to suspect. Don't concern yourselves with legalities. Take whatever steps are necessary."

Eriadu security agents were already on the scene by the time Qui-Gon, Obi-Wan, Vergere, and Ki-Adi-Mundi reached the customs warehouse.

One human agent was aiming a scanning device at several repulsorsleds parked just inside the entrance, still supporting a dozen tall and narrow cargo containers, whose opened hatches revealed them to be empty. Elsewhere in the large space, a group of infuriated customs agents were being interrogated.

The uniformed human commander of the security detail entered from a dimly lighted corridor. Behind him moved two green-scaled and chitin-sheathed insectoid bipeds, with large black eyes, short ridged snouts, and toothless mouths.

Qui-Gon saw Obi-Wan's jaw go slack.

"Verpine," he explained. "Organs in the chest enable the species to communicate by means of radio waves. But they can also speak and understand Basic, with the assistance of translator devices. Their keen senses make them brilliant at detail work."

"Verpine," Obi-Wan said, shaking his head in wonder.

Seeing the four Jedi, the commander approached, while the pair of aliens set about scrutinizing the sawdust-covered floor.

Qui-Gon introduced himself and the others.

"We have two dead humans in the rear room," the commander said, after giving Vergere the same look Obi-Wan had given the Verpine trackers. "One male, one female, each dead of blaster bolts fired at close range, but from different weapons. Carbon scoring on the floor and walls indicate a full-scale blaster fight. Blood spots show

that at least one of the combatants who got away was a
Rodian. Bacta patches, synthflesh, and who knows what
else is missing from the room's medkit. We're waiting for
results on finger- and handprint analysis."

"Captain Cohl's partner is a Rodian," Qui-Gon said.

The commander made note of it on a datapad, then
pointed to the group of customs agents. "They were
taken by surprise by no less than eight heavily armed as-
sailants, most of them human, but at least four Nikto
and a couple of Bith.

"After the surprise raid, they were stashed in the corridor, so they can't provide much in the way of additional
information. But the woman, there, is chief officer of the
customs ship the terrorists commandeered. She identified
the dead female in the back room as captain of the Corellian freighter she boarded. She's still a bit dazed from a
knockout injection, but she says she also saw a Rodian,
and she thinks she remembers seeing a Gotal and a
couple of human males.

"Everyone appears to have left the warehouse through
a rear door that opens onto the spaceport service
road. We're assuming that they're piloting skimmers or
landspeeders."

The commander stepped toward the center of the room
and gestured broadly. "Everything here is just as we
found it, except that little piece of hardware, which we
discovered beneath one of the sleds."

Qui-Gon and the other Jedi followed his finger to a
portable holoprojector, sitting atop a cargo crate.

"Whatever else he is, Cohl is not careless," Qui-
Gon said.

"Deliberate is the way we're reading it, too. But even
professionals have been known to make mistakes."

The commander walked over to the holoprojector.

He was about to activate it, when one of his assistants intruded.

"Commander, the Verpine say that there are signs of well over a dozen men, several of whom arrived inside these tall containers. At some point, most of them gathered around what must have been a crate, just over here, perhaps to observe whatever images the holoprojector contains. Among them was a Gotal, who also arrived inside one of the containers. Bits of fur were found inside the second-to-last container, and also on the floor there, in large amounts."

"A tussle?" the commander asked.

"Could be, sir. Gotals have a tendency to shed when they're taken by surprise or frightened."

"What would have frightened him?"

"No telling, sir."

The commander glanced up from his datapad. "Anything else?"

"The prints leading down the corridor and back. One pair is certainly Rodian. The blood in the rear room explains why the Rodian was walking unsteadily when he returned to this room. The one who accompanied him back here wasn't doing very well either, judging by the fact that he was supporting the left side of himself on a crutch, improvised from a length of pipe. Footprints of the two walking wounded are all over this room. The Rodian retrieved something from underneath one of the hoversleds, but we can't be sure what that was—unless it was the holoprojector. Evidence suggests that the pair left by the rear door, same as the others, but they were on foot, at least until they reached the pubtrans booth on the corner."

The commander finished his note taking and looked at Qui-Gon. "All this give you any insights?"

"Captain Cohl, the Rodian, and the woman must have been ambushed in the rear room."

"Ambushed? By Havac?"

Qui-Gon nodded.

"Havac thought all three were dead?"

"No, he expected us to find Cohl and the Rodian alive."

"Why would he risk that?" the commander asked.

Qui-Gon looked at him. "Because he wants to throw us off the scent."

The commander scratched his head in thought.

Obi-Wan slid the holoprojector toward him. "Let's see what we find in here."

Lope peered through the small doorway that led to the roof of the Nebula Front's safe house in the southern part of the city. A security craft made a low pass from the south, continuing on in the direction of the summit hall.

"Right on schedule," he told the five human and alien terrorists crouching on the stairs below him. "We have ten minutes."

The Gotal squeezed by him and scampered out onto the roof, his ringed horns twitching as they monitored the hazy air for portents.

Five meters from the doorway, the Gotal flashed Lope an all-clear sign and disappeared behind the first of the many domed rooftops they would need to traverse before attaining a clear view of the summit hall.

Lope and the rest hurried outside, rounding the same dome that now concealed the Gotal. On his hip, Lope wore a sheathed vibroblade, and on his wrist, a rocket launcher. The others carried both in-close weapons and blasters.

Beyond the first dome, the expanse of interconnected

roofs was a terrain of spherical hills and steep peaks, cut through with shallow ravines and washes. Octagonal towers, slender steeples, and antenna arrays rose above the domes like isolated trees.

The diverse domes resembled the knobbed lids of giant cook pots. Some buildings were topped by long barrel vaults, and others with hip roofs, covered with tile or slate. Small houses with tiny windows graced the few level sections.

With the Gotal at point, they began to move at a steady clip, worming through tight meanders, negotiating precipitous ledges, and leaping to adjacent rooftops. Their mimetic suits allowed them to blend with the gray roof tiles, reddish bricks, and acid-rain-stained domes.

They scaled a tall roof and dropped down into a hollow formed by a quartet of contiguous domes. Then they edged around a massive cupola that gave them their first unobstructed view of the summit hall. East of the domed building was a range of high hills, shrouded in particle-laden haze. Far to the north, a broad river emptied itself into a slender projection of the sea.

A long stretch of flat roof ran all the way to the final dome, below which two streets joined to become a broad boulevard that arrived ultimately at the summit hall mount.

They were halfway across the flat roof when sounds of a commotion reached them from street level. Forging through his fear of heights, Lope crawled to the edge of the roof and looked down over the low retaining wall. Squads of riot-control security troops were rerouting ground traffic and dispersing bystanders who had gathered for a glimpse of whatever dignitaries might pass by.

In a building across the street, people drew curtains over their windows or pulled shutters closed. From slowly cruising landspeeders, announcements blared in half a dozen languages, threatening dire consequences for anyone caught on the rooftops or found loitering in restricted areas around the summit hall.

Lope saw a hovercade approaching from the south and waved for one of Havac's men to join him at the wall. The convoy of ten repulsorlift vehicles was being escorted by as many speeder bikes piloted by helmeted police.

Havac's man trained electrobinoculars on the fifth vehicle in line. "Valorum," he uttered in a hushed voice. "Eriadu's governor and lieutenant governor are with him."

Lope asked for the electrobinoculars.

"Your boss should have listened to reason and let us hit Valorum here." He patted the rocket launcher strapped to his right wrist. "One shot with this and the job would be done."

Havac's confederate took back the electrobinoculars. "For the moment, Havac's your boss, too. Besides, Valorum's riding under the protection of an energy shield. Now, get on the comlink and inform the team at the summit hall that the target will be arriving through the south gate."

Lope crawled back to where the others were waiting, and removed a small comlink from his pocket. "Valorum's right below us," he explained.

He activated the comlink and keyed in the number Havac had given him, but all he got for his efforts was an earful of static. "You need to get above some of these antenna arrays," the Gotal suggested. "Try from the top of the big dome."

Lope nodded. Jogging in a crouch to the base of the dome, he began his ascent. But he was just short of the ornamented summit when he heard engine noise behind him. Over his shoulder, he saw three airspeeders approaching rapidly from the direction of the summit hall.

He slid down the dome and hurried back to the others. "Hover patrol headed our way."

The woman Cohl had hired glanced at her wrist timer. "It's too soon for them to be making another sweep."

Everyone hunkered down as the blunt-nosed hovers sped overhead. But the trio of vehicles went only a short distance before coming about for a second pass.

"They spotted us," the Gotal said.

Lope armed the rocket launcher. "We can remedy that."

Raising his right forearm, he fixed his sights on the lead vehicle.

From the passenger seat of an airspeeder, all of Eriadu City looked the same. That, at least, was Qui-Gon's considered opinion after more than an hour of searching the city from above for the location of the roofscape image stored in Havac's holoprojector.

Bisected by a slow-moving, muddy river, the city was a confusion of domes, interior courtyards, and precarious towers, cleaved by narrow streets and a few broad avenues. Dwellings were built on top of one another in haphazard fashion, sprouting annexes here and additional levels there, extending from the bay clear to the barricade of hills at the city's back.

It was little wonder that none of the security officers had been able to identify the span of roofs Havac's holoprojector had singled out. When a quick study of 2-D maps had only complicated matters, copies of the stored image had been fed into the terrain-following computers of three airspeeders, in the hope that a series of overflights would allow the computers to match the image to an actual roofscape. But flights to the north and to the east of the summit hall had failed to yield even a possible match.

Qui-Gon continued to believe that Havac had wanted the holoprojector to be found, but he wasn't willing to take the chance that Havac's leaving the device behind hadn't constituted a genuine oversight.

Just now the trio of airspeeders was approximately two kilometers south of the summit hall. Qui-Gon and Obi-Wan were passengers in the lead vehicle, trailed by Ki-Adi-Mundi and Vergere in the second, and two judicials in the third.

Gazing down over the speeder's starboard gunwale, Qui-Gon thought he glimpsed movement on one of the rooftops. But when he shielded his eyes with the edge of his hand and looked again, all he saw was what might have been heat shimmer at the base of a slender brick tower.

He reached out through the Force.

At the same instant the speeder's terrain-following computer began to chirp repeatedly, indicating that it had matched the image. The computer's screen displayed the stored image superimposed on the roofscape directly below. Pivoting in his seat, Qui-Gon saw Ki-Adi-Mundi wave a sign of acknowledgment that the computer of the second airspeeder has also discovered the match.

The Eriadu security officer at the controls banked the airspeeder through a sweeping turn and was headed back toward the stretch of roofs when the craft's threat assessor suddenly added its voice to the steady chirping of the terrain-following computer.

"Missile lock!" the pilot said in astonishment.

Obi-Wan leaned over the side of the craft and pointed to something below. "There, Master!"

Qui-Gon caught sight of the small rocket and realized at once that it had been launched from the base of the tower, just where he had detected movement moments earlier.

The pilot dropped the airspeeder into an abrupt dive, prepared to execute another maneuver should the missile home in on them, but the rocket stayed true to its original course. Narrowly missing the rear of the craft, it exploded high overhead, raining shrapnel on the airspeeder, which came about and shot for the source of the fire.

"Movement below," the pilot said, glancing at one of the scanner displays. "I count six figures."

Obi-Wan raised himself out of his seat. "I don't see anyone."

"Mimetic suits," Qui-Gon said. He swung to the pilot. "Find a place to set us down."

Another rocket streaked into the sky, detonating between the second and third airspeeders.

"Targets are headed south," the pilot said.

Qui-Gon let his eyes roam over the varied domes and hip roofs. Emerging from a narrow cleft between two domes, three humans came briefly into view, only to disappear against a background of roof tiles.

The pilot steered the airspeeder for the top of a long barrel vault and let the craft settle down. Blaster bolts began to whiz past the fuselage and ricochet erratically from the vault's arched walls. Lightsabers ignited, Qui-Gon and Obi-Wan leapt over the gunwales. Hitting the vault, they somersaulted through the air for the flat area below. Some distance behind, Ki-Adi-Mundi, Vergere, and the two judicials hit the roof running.

In a blur of motion, Qui-Gon and Obi-Wan bolted to the end of the flat roof, wound between several domes, and covered a length of sheer ledge without a moment's hesitation. Side by side, and with blaster bolts darting beneath them, they hopped across an interior courtyard and continued the chase without breaking stride.

The terrorists were retreating deeper into the sinuous topography. Qui-Gon pursued a pair of fleetingly visible figures, ultimately bounding far ahead of them. With lightsaber raised, he waited for them to rush directly into his path.

His green blade hissed and thrummed as it sliced through the air, deflecting a dozen blaster bolts—along with a hurled blaster to top it off. Perceiving the direction of the pair's revised retreat, Qui-Gon dropped both of them with a Force push. The two judicials arrived in time to pounce on the terrorists, before their mimetic suits had a chance to reenergize.

Sensing something behind him, Qui-Gon whirled, but not quickly enough. A meter-long vibroblade secured to the fist of a nearly indiscernible assailant pierced the right side of his brown cloak, just missing his ribs. Qui-Gon spun through a full turn, slashing diagonally with his lightsaber and halving the vibroblade.

The terrorist scampered to the center of the roof, where the brick wall of a small dwelling afforded him better camouflage, and drew a blaster. Qui-Gon rushed forward, evading blaster bolts, then moving in to grapple hand to hand with a human of similar size.

A hail of bolts tore past Qui-Gon's left ear as he threw his quarry to the roof. Two more bolts singed his long hair in their passing. He leapt to the right and rolled for cover. Drawing on the Force, he coaxed a slate tile loose from the dwelling's peaked roof. The tile slipped from the grasp of its fasteners, shot spinning through space, and clipped the terrorist in the side of the head, felling him instantly.

Qui-Gon rushed in, grabbing a handful of the mimetic suit and tearing it from the man's prone body. Its circuitry interrupted, the suit failed and the wearer became visible.

Qui-Gon determined that the terrorist would be unconscious long enough for the judicials to find him. Off to his left, he spied Vergere leaping from dome to dome, as if she were wearing a rocket pack. Following after her, he saw that the Fosh and Ki-Adi-Mundi were closing on a Gotal, whose mimetic suit couldn't camouflage the trail of shed fur he was leaving.

He glanced around for Obi-Wan and found him standing at the base of a large dome, atop a wall that enclosed a deep courtyard. Qui-Gon was headed toward him, when he spied an indistinct shape sliding down the steep curve of the dome. The shape collided with Obi-Wan and sent him flailing over the edge of the building.

Qui-Gon dashed forward, holding his lightsaber at hip level, then flicking the blade upward when he reached the spot where he predicted the terrorist would land.

A pained cry rang out, and a right arm flashed into visibility and went sailing over the edge of the roof. Disabled, the mimetic suit phased out, revealing a howling human female, down on her knees, her left hand gripped on what remained of her severed right arm.

Qui-Gon rushed to the wall, hoping to find that Obi-Wan had found a soft spot to land. Instead, an airspeeder rose out of the courtyard, with Obi-Wan clinging by one hand to the craft's aft starboard stabilizer.

The airspeeder gently deposited Obi-Wan on the roof next to Qui-Gon. Nearby, Ki-Adi-Mundi, Vergere, the two judicials, and a couple of Eriadu security officers were securing the six terrorists that had been captured.

Neither Havac nor Cohl were among them.

"That was quite a stunt, Padawan," Qui-Gon said.

"I guess you would rather have found me dangling by my teeth, Master."

Qui-Gon showed him a perplexed look.

"The thought-puzzle Master Anoon Bondara put to his students on the day we spoke with Luminara,"

Obi-Wan explained. "About the man dangling by his teeth from the strut of a skimmer over a treacherous pit."

"I remember now," Qui-Gon said, with sudden interest.

Obi-Wan blew out his breath. "After much though, I decided that the skimmer is meant to be the Force, and that the pit represents the dangers that await any of us who stray from the path."

"And what of the lost travelers who asked for help?"

"Well, on the one hand, travelers—even when they've lost their way—should know better than to ask questions of a man dangling by his teeth over a treacherous pit. But, more important, the travelers were merely distractions that the man should ignore, if he is to remain in the Force."

"Distractions," Qui-Gon murmured.

He thought back to the attempt on Valorum's life, the events on Asmeru, and the evidence that had been discovered in the customs warehouse.

Qui-Gon clapped Obi-Wan on both shoulders. "You've helped me see something that has been eluding me." He glanced at the half-dozen terrorists. "There's little more we can do here. Hurry now, Padawan, Havac's scheme is afoot."

"Where are we going, Master?"

"Where we were meant to go from the beginning."

The scene outside the south entrance to the summit hall was chaotic, with mobs of onlookers and security personnel milling about, and media reporters jostling for close-ups with their holocams and recorders. Cordons of body-armored police fought to keep the masses from pressing too close, as vehicles ranging from the most primitive to the most luxurious conveyed delegates to the porte cochere that hooded the entrance. Judicials circulated through the crowd, trying not to be obvious, despite the communicator beads in their ears and the sophisticated comlinks on their wrists, while Jedi Knights, with their brown cloaks and belt-mounted lightsabers, made themselves all too obvious.

"I don't see a hope of getting inside," Boiny said to Cohl, at the leading edge of the crowd. "Even if we managed to reach the door, we'd never be able to slip any hardware past the weapons scanners."

The two of them were wearing loose-fitting robes, sandals, and turbans that concealed their head wounds. Cohl had found himself an actual crutch made of a lightweight alloy, but he was weaker than when he and the Rodian had made their hasty departure from the customs warehouse. Both were surviving on bacta patches and periodic injections of pain blockers.

Cohl gazed up at the summit hall. In addition to the security guards posted at the entrance, there were sharpshooters in the towers that stood at the corners of the enormous building.

"Let's have a look at some of the other entrances," he said, quietly and short of breath.

They began a circular zigzag around the grounds. The west and north entrances were no less crowded or confused, but the east entrance wasn't nearly as mobbed, or as well guarded.

Waiting to be admitted were administrative aides and freelance translators, protocol and service droids, an ensemble of drummers and trumpeters sporting tall helmets and garish uniforms, and mixed-species groups representing the Rights of Sentience League and the Association of Free Trade Worlds, among others.

"Strictly second-tier attendees," Boiny remarked.

"Our kind of folks." Cohl nodded with his chin, indicating that they should saunter down the long line.

Partway along, announcing themselves with a colorful banner, waited a hundred or so veterans of the Stark Hyperspace Conflict. A brief though bloody conflict that had erupted twelve years earlier, it had been fought largely on worlds where bacta was scarce or too expensive. Consequently, many of the veterans, human and alien alike, still showed gruesome scars, patches of horribly puckered or wrinkled flesh, and missing limbs or tails. Paralyzed as a result of disruptor fire or electromagnetic detonations, a few were confined to repulsorlift chairs and sleds.

It was the latter group that caught Cohl's attention.

"I think we've found our way inside," he told Boiny.

Centered in the 180-degree arc of tiered seats that separated the Coruscant delegation from the Trade Federation Directorate, Senator Palpatine sat with Sate Pestage, Kinman Doriana, and others, in the section designated for the Naboo system.

Palpatine had angled himself to the left, in order to watch the seven members of the directorate assume their seats. Flanking the four humans, the Sullustan, the Gran, and the Neimoidian, contingents of security droids stood with blaster rifles affixed to their squarish backpacks, like skeletal sentinels of death.

Palpatine was so engrossed that he failed to observe the approach of Senator Orn Free Taa, despite the fact that the bloated Rutian Twi'lek had arrived by means of a repulsorlift chair, with his retinue of attachés and aides trailing behind him like servants.

"An impressive showing," Taa said to Palpatine, glancing around the resplendent hall as he lowered his chair to the floor. "Delegates from Sullust, Clak'dor, the Senex sector, Malastare, Falleen, Bothawui . . . Why even some of the Hutt worlds are represented." Taa paused to track Palpatine's gaze to the Trade Federation section. "Ah, the objects of everyone's fascination."

"Assuredly," Palpatine said in a distracted way.

"How like the directorate to bring droids—though I suppose it makes little difference whether one chooses Jedi Knights or droids. I have heard, however, that the directorate also insisted on a shield projector."

"Yes, I heard the same."

Taa regarded Palpatine for a long moment. "Senator, permit me to say that you seem somewhat preoccupied."

Palpatine finally swiveled in his chair to face Taa. "In point of fact, I have just received some rather distressing news from my home system. It seems that Naboo's King Veruna has abdicated the throne."

Taa's massive head-tails twitched. "I . . . I must confess, Senator, that I don't know whether to feel sorry or glad for you. But where exactly does this leave you, in any case? Is there some danger of your being recalled?"

"That remains to be seen," Palpatine said. "Naboo will have an acting regent until elections are held."

"Who is in the running to replace Veruna?"

"That, too, remains to be seen."

"Dare I inquire as to your hope?"

Palpatine shrugged lightly. "Only for someone enthusiastic about opening Naboo to the galaxy. Someone less—how shall I put it?—*traditional* than Veruna."

A glint came into Taa's eyes. "Or more easily persuaded perhaps?"

Before Palpatine could respond, a swell of agitation began to sweep through the hall. To all sides, heads were turning toward the south entrance. Shortly, Supreme Chancellor Valorum and the rest of the Coruscant delegation appeared. The hall responded with extended if merely cordial applause.

"He arrives," Taa said, as Valorum was being escorted to his seat. "But who is that with him? I recognize the sector governor, but not the lean and hungry-looking one beside him."

"Lieutenant Governor Tarkin," Palpatine replied, while clapping his hands.

"Ah, yes—Tarkin. A bit of a throwback, isn't he? Very militant and authoritarian."

"Power can turn even the meekest of bureaucrats into a raging manka cat."

"Just so, just so. And speaking of that, Senator," Taa

added in a conspiratorial tone, "do you recall the information I brought to your attention a while back, regarding Valorum family holdings here on Eriadu?"

"Vaguely. Something about a shipping company, wasn't it?"

Taa nodded. "As you know, many small concerns are poised to see their market status considerably advanced as a result of Valorum's taxation proposal, and also as a consequence of investments from Core worlds, like Ralltiir and Kuat, who are ever on the alert for opportunities."

"What does all that have to do with Valorum's holdings?" Palpatine asked mildly.

"It appears that said shipping company has recently received a significant inflow of capital, and yet the Supreme Chancellor failed to inform appropriate parties in the senate. Naturally, I began to wonder if he was even aware that someone had invested so heavily in the family business, and just who it was that had invested."

"It wouldn't be like Supreme Chancellor Valorum to conceal something of that nature."

"Initially, I believed the same. My assumption was that if it could be determined that the funds had indeed come from investment speculators who had no direct ties to Valorum, then—despite all outward appearances—no breach of protocol or propriety had occurred. But when I endeavored to establish as much, I kept finding myself beset with obstacles, dead ends, and ambiguous leads. As you yourself suggested, I resorted to turning the matter over to Senator Antilles, who has the necessary leverage to pry into those areas to which I was denied."

"Has Senator Antilles made any progress?"

Taa lowered his voice another notch. "What I have to tell you is hardly equivalent to your revelation about King Veruna, but, in fact, I have just learned that Antilles was successful in tracing the origin of the funds to what he at first thought was a venture capital consortium, but which, in fact, appears to be a fraudulent bank account, set up expressly for channeling illicitly gained funds to areas of special interest."

Palpatine stared at him. "By special interests, I assume you refer to those senators who are receiving kickbacks from various organizations, criminal and otherwise."

"Precisely."

"But you have yet to learn where the funds originated."

"We are getting close, and the closer we get, the more potentially embarrassing this could be for the Supreme Chancellor."

"I'd appreciate being kept fully informed."

Taa smiled. "We'll make no announcement without consulting you."

Palpatine and Taa turned to watch Valorum waving to the crowd, which responded with a second round of gracious applause.

"This is the Supreme Chancellor's moment," Palpatine said. "We shouldn't spoil it with gossip."

Taa was chagrined. "Please accept my apologies, Senator. It was never my intention to spoil the moment." He glanced to his left. "I'll leave that to the Trade Federation."

Viceroy Nute Gunray felt as if everyone's eyes were on him, despite the fact that it was Valorum who had the hall's undivided attention. Gunray's own eyes, however, were on the battle droid that had been delivered into his care only moments before he and the members of the directorate had left their temporary quarters for the summit.

Indistinguishable from the dozen other droids providing protection for the directorate—save for a blush of yellow markings—the new addition stood just to Gunray's right, at the leading edge of the detachment on that side of the Trade Federation rostrum.

Gunray had barely had time to settle into his quarters on Eriadu when the Sith Lord, faithful to his word, had appeared, by means of the holoprojector Sidious had sent him months earlier. Although on this occasion the image was so distinct, so free of the usual noise and static, that Gunray might have almost believed that Sidious was on Eriadu or some neighboring world, rather than concealed in whatever manner of fathomless den from which he worked his dark magic.

Some strangers will be coming to give you an additional droid, Sidious had said, *a battle droid. You are not to question them, nor the purpose of the droid itself. You will simply instruct the droid to join the others you brought to Eriadu. It will respond to your commands.*

Gunray had been feverish with questions, but he had managed to restrain himself when the strangers arrived at his quarters with the boxed battle droid. He hadn't even informed Lott Dod of the communication, even when the senator—alone among the Trade Federation delegation—had casually remarked that he could have sworn that they had arrived on Eriadu with only twelve droids.

The shipping manifest would bear that out, of course. But considering that the Trade Federation enjoyed diplomatic status, it was improbable that Eriadu customs would raise a concern when the delegation returned to the spaceport with the extra droid in tow.

It was the second of the Sith Lord's directives that continued to prey on Gunray's thoughts, in any case, and was the cause of his present disquiet.

Even now he saw that the ensemble of musicians were assembling on the floor, in preparation of trumpeting the fanfares that would inaugurate the summit.

It was only a matter of minutes.

Gunray made note of where Lott Dod was seated.

Discreetly, he mopped away some of the perspiration that beaded his face, and he tried to calm himself. Mostly, however, he counted down the minutes in silence.

31

From the padded seat of a repulsorlift chair Boiny had helped him commandeer from an oblivious veteran of the Stark Hyperspace Conflict, Cohl gazed across the summit hall to where the Trade Federation delegation had an area to itself, opposite Supreme Chancellor Valorum and the Coruscant bunch. His vision was unfocused and narrowed to a tunnel, and his body was racked with pain, despite the injections Boiny had been administering with increasing frequency.

Cohl's seeming and actual nurse, the Rodian stood behind him, training a small pair of electrobinoculars on the Trade Federation's complement of thirteen droids.

"Only one of them is missing a restraining bolt," Boiny said, close to Cohl's left ear. "The droid with the yellow blazes on its head and midsection. Just to the Neimoidian's right, at the head of the line on that side of the rostrum."

Cohl put the electrobinoculars to his eyes. "I've got him," he said weakly. Then he began to scan the immense hall with the glasses. "Havac's somewhere in here, probably with a remote control in hand."

Boiny glanced around. "It's possible that the droid has been programmed to respond to a certain event, or at a specific time. But even if Havac has a remote, it won't necessarily have to operate by line of sight. He could be anywhere in the hall, or outside it."

Cohl shook his head. "Havac's the type who needs to watch this happen. He planned it. It's his show."

Boiny's gaze continued to wander over the tiers of seats. "He can't be in the delegate's section. And I doubt he plays the trumpet—"

Abruptly, Cohl looked over his shoulder at the Rodian. "What was Havac before he turned to terrorism, Boiny—before he joined the Nebula Front?"

Boiny thought about it. "Some kind of holomaker, right?"

"A documentary holomaker. A freelance media correspondent."

In concert they raised their eyes to the media booths high overhead.

Fresh from the rooftop chase, Qui-Gon and Obi-Wan joined Saesee Tiin and Adi Gallia on the floor of the hall, just inside the north entrance. Valorum was seated to the right and above them; the Trade Federation Directorate, to the left. In front of them, the members of the Eriadu delegation were taking their places in the stands that had been erected in the center of the hall. Below the stands, a group of drummers and trumpeters were tuning their instruments.

The air was charged with excitement.

"The six we captured maintain that they've never heard of Cohl or Havac," Qui-Gon explained to the other Jedi, "and that they don't know anything about an assassination attempt."

"Then what were they doing on the roof, armed and dangerous, and firing on you with a rocket launcher?"

"They claim to be a band of thieves, who thought they could take advantage of the disorder surrounding the summit by breaking into the Seswenna Sector Bank."

"Did you tell them about the roofscape image found in the holoprojector?" Tiin asked.

"There was no point. They might have been hoping to assault the Supreme Chancellor's hovercade from the roof, but I think they were simply there to distract us. That's what Cohl and Havac have been doing from the start, as far back as the incident at the Galactic Senate.

"Even if any of the six eventually admit to having been hired by Cohl, they could continue to claim that robbery was their intent. None were carrying documentation, so we don't even know who they are or what worlds they hail from. Eriadu security is running their likenesses and retinal prints, but, assuming Cohl gathered them from distant worlds, it could be weeks before any matches are discovered."

"Then we have nothing more to go on," Adi said.

"Only that the rest of Havac's assassins are somewhere in this hall."

"There have been no incidents at the entrances," Tiin said. "No one has been arrested."

"That means nothing," Qui-Gon said. "For experts like Cohl and Havac, this hall is as permeable as a Podrace finale. They would have no trouble getting inside."

Tiin compressed his thin lips. "The only thing we can do is be prepared to defend the Supreme Chancellor."

Qui-Gon glanced in Valorum's direction. "Will he permit us to get any closer to him?"

"No," Adi said. "He gave explicit orders that he doesn't want the proceedings disrupted—nor does he want us by

his side. He wants the Jedi to be seen as impartial in this
trade dispute."

"Nevertheless, we can't stand here, waiting for something to happen," Tiin growled. "We should divide and
look around; locate the trouble before the trouble finds
Valorum."

Obi-Wan, who had been standing quietly throughout
the exchange, noticed a familiar look come into Qui-
Gon's eye. It was as if Qui-Gon's gaze was fixed on some
invisible presence the living Force had highlighted.

"What is it, Master?" he asked quietly.

"I can feel him, Padawan."

"Havac?"

"Cohl."

The tiny, dingy booth assigned to the Eriadu Free
HoloDaily consisted of a couple of rigid chairs, a control
console of dust-covered flatscreen displays and holoprojector pads, and a large single-pane window that
looked out on the hall.

Havac stood by the window, staring down at the
mostly seated crowd while he mounted a holocam in its
stand. Behind him, and armed with blasters they had se-
creted in the summit hall weeks earlier, sat two of his human confederates. One of them wore a wrist comm.

When Havac had trained the holocam on the Trade
Federation's arc of seats, he attached a scanner to the
cam head. Then he aimed the device, which resembled a
directional microphone, toward the trumpeters on the
floor of the hall.

"Any word from the spotter team?" he asked over his
shoulder.

"Not a chirp," the man with the comlink replied.
"And Valorum has been here for over ten minutes. What
do you think happened?"

"The likely explanation is that they were discovered."

"Why do you say that?"

Havac turned to face the pair. "Because I notified the authorities about Cohl's freighter, and left the holoprojector behind to be found." He waited for smiles of revelation, but when none appeared, he added, "It was the only way to ensure that the authorities would be kept occupied while we went about our business here."

"Then Cohl has also been found—or his corpse, at any rate," the one with the comlink said.

The other man looked doubtful. "Suppose, as you say, the spotters have been found out, and they decide to cut a deal by telling what they know—credits or no credits."

Havac shrugged theatrically. "They know me as Havac, and no 'Havac' has been cleared by security to attend the summit. The credit transfers to Cohl's hired hands can't be traced directly to us. The safe house will be empty by the time they lead the authorities to it. We'll be long gone from Eriadu before anyone is able to assemble all the pieces of the puzzle."

Clearly meant to restore confidence, Havac's discourse failed to have the intended effect. If anything, the two men looked even more skeptical than before.

"Is our shooter in place?" Havac asked impatiently.

"Out on the walkway—just waiting for the music to begin."

"What do you want us to do with him afterward?" the one with the comlink asked.

Havac considered it. "He's a misfit with a counterfeit identity badge and a blaster, who has just fired at the delegates. You'll be a public hero if you kill him—or at least see to it that he falls from the walkway."

"No loose ends," the same one said.

"As few as possible."

*   *   *

Back on his alloy crutches, but still wearing a small flag fastened to the front of his robe that identified him as a veteran of the Stark Hyperspace Conflict, Cohl hobbled from the turbolift that had carried him and Boiny to the hall's main pedestrian level. From here it was possible to ascend to the perimeter walkways that accessed the media and security booths in the upper reaches of the domed building.

They were headed for the array of lifts when a voice called out behind them.

"Captain Cohl."

Cohl didn't stop until the stranger repeated the call, then he maneuvered himself through a resigned turn. Ten meters down the corridor stood a tall, long-haired, and bearded Jedi, displaying a green-bladed lightsaber.

"This just isn't our day," Boiny muttered.

Cohl heard the characteristic snap and hiss of another lightsaber and glanced over his shoulder. The second Jedi was a clean-shaven young man, wearing the thin braid of a Padawan.

"We've been looking forward to meeting you since Dorvalla," the older one said.

Cohl and Boiny swapped looks of surprised dismay.

"You were the ones in the diplomatic Lancet," Cohl said.

"You led us a merry chase, Captain."

Cohl snorted and shook his head. "Well, you found us now. And you can put your glow sticks away. We're unarmed."

Qui-Gon merely pointed the lightsaber toward the floor as he approached. "I congratulate you on surviving the destruction of the *Revenue*."

Cohl sagged on his crutches. "A lot of good it did me, Jedi. My partner and I are shot to pieces."

Qui-Gon and Obi-Wan regarded them through the

Force, and understood that Cohl wasn't lying. Both he and the Rodian were seriously injured.

"How did you find out about the Dorvalla operation, anyway?" Cohl asked.

"A member of the Nebula Front," Qui-Gon said. "Now dead."

"So there was an informant. I guess Havac was right to have been secretive about this one."

"We're eager to meet Havac, as well," Obi-Wan said.

Cohl looked at him. "You'd do better to destroy the droid Havac infiltrated into the summit."

"Droid?" the Jedi said in unison.

"A battle droid," Cohl elaborated. "It's right up there with the rest of the directorate's droids. We figure Havac plans to have the droid kill Valorum."

"That's impossible," Qui-Gon said. "Battle droids can't act without a cue from a central control computer."

"Havac's is one of Baktoid's new and improved models," Boiny said. "A commander. More of a freethinker. It only needs to be tasked, by voice command or remote signal, and it's capable of swaying the droids around it."

Obi-Wan's jaw dropped slightly. "Are you saying that instead of one assassin, there are a potential dozen?"

"Thirteen, actually," Boiny replied.

"It still can't initiate an act like that on its own," Qui-Gon insisted.

"That's where Havac comes in. He's the one with the remote."

Qui-Gon stepped toward Cohl. "Where is he?"

"I have some idea."

"Tell me what you know, and let me handle this. Obi-Wan will escort you and your partner to medical attention—and into custody."

Cohl shook his head. "If you want Havac, we go

together, Jedi, or not at all." He canted his head to Boiny. "Besides, we're the only ones who can identify him."

Qui-Gon didn't even have to think about it. He glanced at Obi-Wan. "Padawan, report back to Master Tiin and the others. Quickly."

"But, Master—"

"Go, Padawan. Now."

Obi-Wan showed him a tight-lipped nod and spun on his boot heels.

Qui-Gon watched his apprentice rush off, then he deactivated his lightsaber and put one arm under Cohl's trembling shoulder.

"Lean on me, Captain."

32

With ten drummers setting the tempo, twice as many horn players raised their long instruments to their mouths and trumpeted the first of the three prolonged fanfares.

By then Obi-Wan had reached Tiin and the other Jedi.

"It's the droids," he began in a sally of words.

Tiin had him slow down and repeat everything he and Qui-Gon had learned from Cohl. Then the Iktotchi turned to Adi, Ki-Adi-Mundi, Vergere, and the rest.

"Position yourselves as close to Valorum as possible," he instructed Adi and Vergere. "Obi-Wan, Ki, and I will be near the Trade Federation rostrum. The rest of you, disperse to deflect blasterfire. Be unassuming but prepared."

"Master Tiin, do you think the Trade Federation suspects what's in their midst?" Obi-Wan asked as they set out across the floor of the hall.

"They couldn't. They are aggressive only when it comes to commerce. However this Havac infiltrated the droid among the others, it had to have been done without the knowledge of the directorate members."

"Should we order the delegation to remove the droids, Master?"

Ki-Adi-Mundi replied. "Whoever is watching may decide to trigger the droids into action. If that happens, it could appear that we posed a threat, prompting the droids to respond with blasterfire. If there was time, we could get someone aboard the Trade Federation freighter to shut down the central control computer."

"Have you fought these droids before, Master Tiin?"

"I know only that they're not very accurate, Padawan."

Obi-Wan frowned as he ran. "With thirteen of them firing, that may not matter."

Not even a quarter of the way around the upper level corridor that accessed the media booths, Boiny spied Havac through a small transparisteel panel set high in the door.

Leaving Cohl to stand on his own, Qui-Gon pressed his back to the corridor wall. "How many of them are in there?" he asked the Rodian.

"Havac and maybe two other humans—seated to the right of the door."

Qui-Gon nodded to the door release lever. "Try it."

Gingerly, Boiny placed his hand on the lever. "Locked." He glanced at the touchpad mounted on the wall. "I can probably slice—"

"I have a quicker way," Qui-Gon interrupted.

Activating his lightsaber, he shoved the glowing blade through the lock mechanism. The metal glowed red and instantly began to slag, tainting the air with biting odors. With a grating sound, the door slid into its wall pocket.

By then, Havac and his two confederates were on their feet, weapons in hand. A flurry of blaster bolts glanced from Qui-Gon's blade, which he held upraised and threw left and right in precise parries. The deflected bolts blazed around the room, two of them wounding Havac's men and knocking them to the floor.

Undiluted terror fumbled the blaster from Havac's grip. As it fell, Qui-Gon called the weapon to him with a Force summons and tucked it into the wide belt that cinched his tunic.

Havac dropped back into his seat at the console, cowering in fear and raising his shaking hands above his head.

Boiny and Cohl followed Qui-Gon into the booth.

Cohl took stock of the situation and looked at Qui-Gon. "I'm glad I never had to go up against you people."

"Cohl," Havac said in genuine amazement.

Cohl made his eyes narrow. "Next time you'll know better, amateur."

"Where is the remote that controls the battle droid?" Qui-Gon asked Havac.

Havac adopted a look of innocent perplexity. "Remote? I don't know what you're talking about."

Qui-Gon towered over him. "You infiltrated a droid into those the Trade Federation Directorate brought with them." He reached down and picked Havac out of his chair, holding him up against the booth's fixed window. "Where is the remote?"

Havac clutched vainly at Qui-Gon's hand. "Enough! Put me down and I'll tell you!"

Qui-Gon lowered him to the chair.

"Our shooter has it," he said, biting out the words.

"I know the one he means," Cohl said. "A sniper."

Qui-Gon looked back at Havac. "Where is he?"

"Out on the walkways," Havac mumbled, averting his eyes.

Qui-Gon glanced at Cohl, making up his mind about something. "Are you well enough to remain with these three while your partner and I locate the shooter?"

Cohl lowered himself into one of the chairs. "I think I can find it in me."

Qui-Gon handed him Havac's blaster. He started to say something, but bit back his words and began again, gesturing to the two wounded men. "I'll send for medical attention."

"There's no hurry," Cohl said.

When Qui-Gon and Boiny had disappeared through the open doorway, Cohl stared balefully at Havac.

The trumpeters paused briefly, then began the second modulating fanfare.

The musicians were a stanza into the piece when a human page approached the Trade Federation rostrum and asked for Viceroy Gunray. The Kuati chair of the delegation directed the page to the far end of the directorate's curved table.

With palpable apprehension, Gunray watched the page advance.

"I'm sorry to intrude, Viceroy," the human began in Basic, loudly enough to be heard over the trumpets, "but apparently there is some problem with your shuttle. Eriadu Spaceport Control needs to speak with you at once."

Gunray made his face long and stuck out his already prominent lower jaw. "Can't this wait until after the summit concludes?"

The page shook his head. "I apologize, Viceroy, but this is a security matter. I assure you, it will require only a moment of your time."

The Kuati chair, who had been monitoring the conversation, swung to face Gunray. "Go attend to the matter. If luck is with you, you won't have to endure Supreme Chancellor Valorum's opening remarks."

Lott Dod came to his feet as Gunray was preparing to leave. "Should I remain in your absence, Viceroy?"

Gunray thought about it for a moment, then shook his head. "Come with me. You are better at dealing with procedures and legalities than I am. But let us be quick about it, Senator, I don't wish to miss any more of the summit than I have to."

One hundred meters above the floor of the summit hall, Qui-Gon and Boiny hurried through the network of walkways, gantries, and trusses that spanned the upper reaches of the building from wall to wall. The martial bellowing of the trumpets resounded off the curved walls, playing tricks with the sound. Sunlight, colored by the enormous ocular window in the center of the dome, poured in.

Suspended by brackets from the ceiling, or cantilevered from the walls, the walkways had openwork floors and tubular handrails and were just wide enough for a human of normal size to pass through. At regular intervals, especially where walkways intersected, were balconies that permitted maintenance to be performed on speaker arrays or banks of spotlights.

There were innumerable places where a lone shooter, armed with a remote or a blaster, might conceal himself.

Qui-Gon and Boiny hadn't gone far before they encountered the first security agent, who raised a hand weapon as they approached and demanded to know what business they had there.

Qui-Gon explained in as few words as possible, at the same time regarding the agent through the Force to determine if his demeanor of righteous authority was genuine.

Disconcerted by Qui-Gon's revelations, the agent activated his comlink and notified every agent in the vicinity to recheck the documents of anyone in the walkways, whether their badges identified them as fellow agents or technicians. In the same breath, he ordered that all exits leading to the periphery corridor behind the media booths be sealed off.

Within moments, Qui-Gon, Boiny, and the agent were joined by additional security personnel. Forming up into three groups, they fanned out into the walkways.

Qui-Gon and Boiny angled away from the perimeter and out over the floor of the hall. Directly below them stood the two lines of trumpeters and drummers.

They reached another intersection and split up.

Stretching out with his feelings, Qui-Gon moved warily toward the next balcony.

A security agent rushed into view, a blaster rifle cradled in his arms.

"I received word over the comlink," he said. "There are two technicians on the next balcony. I suggest we start with them."

The agent stepped aside to let Qui-Gon pass. Qui-Gon sprinted forward. But the Force drew him up short.

He began to turn.

Someone shouted, "Jedi!"

Qui-Gon spun and saw Boiny running full-out toward him. The security agent was between them, the blaster rifle still angled across his chest.

Boiny pointed to the agent. "That's—"

The agent glanced at Qui-Gon.

"He's with me," Qui-Gon started to say.

The agent crouched and fired, hitting Boiny square in the chest and hurling him backwards on the walkway. Then he whirled on Qui-Gon, firing steadily.

Qui-Gon unleashed his lightsaber. But the blaster bolts were delivered with such speed and precision that he was hard-pressed to deflect all of them. Two whizzed past his blade, grazing his left arm and right leg.

He stumbled slightly.

Drawn by the sounds of the blasterfire, a trio of agents raced into view from the same direction Boiny had come. Havac's shooter drew a second weapon from a shoulder holster and unloaded on the agents, wounding two of them.

Qui-Gon changed the cant of his blade to deflect bolts off to each side, rather than back at the shooter, for fear of hitting any of the reinforcements. By now the agents were returning fire, but showing little concern for Qui-Gon's predicament.

The shooter was dazzlingly fast with his hands and body, dodging bolts and throwing himself from one side of the narrow walkway to the other, concealed body armor absorbing the few shots that did manage to find him.

Qui-Gon leapt forward. Slashing horizontally with his blade, he severed two of the walkway's tubular vertical supports.

Then he slashed downward to rend the struts that braced the platform.

Abruptly both sections of the cleaved walkway tilted, sending Qui-Gon and Havac's shooter staggering toward each other and the increasing gap between the now dangling ends of the platform.

A crazed yell tore from the shooter's throat. He slipped to the floor and began to slide along the grating, firing both weapons at Qui-Gon as he fell.

*   *   *

Into the brief silence the musicians inserted between the second and final fanfares, came a rush of voices raised in panic.

Seated stiffly at the center of the Coruscant delegation's rostrum, Valorum wasn't sure what had provoked the screams until he saw Sei Taria, with one hand pressed to her mouth, pointing toward the hall's ceiling.

In the maze of walkways below the dome's oculus window, blaster bolts darted and crisscrossed in the tinted light. Others glanced from a lightsaber's green blade. Sparks showered down on the drummers and trumpeters like a benediction.

Sei screamed.

Jedi Masters Adi Gallia and Vergere rushed forward, their swords ignited.

Then a figure plummeted from one of the walkways.

From the Trade Federation's side of the hall, the chair of the directorate watched open-mouthed as a blaster fight erupted in the overhead trusses and gantries. On the floor, at the same time, three Jedi and several judicials were moving quickly if surreptitiously toward the directorate rostrum.

The Kuati glanced between the ceiling and floor. Had the summit been engineered to trap the directorate? he asked himself. Would the Republic be so bold as to attack them in public?

The security droids had gone from standing at attention to postures of readiness, crouching slightly, with arms crooked and left legs extended behind. They were programmed to answer to any or all of the directorate members—or at least relay a directorate member's commands to the central control computer on board the

Trade Federation vessel—but the droids responded best to the Neimoidians.

The Kuati chair looked around for Viceroy Gunray and realized that he hadn't returned. At a loss for what to do, he swung to one of his aides.

"Activate the force field!" he ordered.

The sounds of blasters and panic on the floor infiltrated the media booth Havac had secured. Seated in a chair with a hand weapon leveled at Havac, Cohl heard the holocam click on and saw Havac glance at it.

"Am I correct in assuming that you intend to kill me?" Havac asked. "Killing is what you are good at, after all."

"You're doing pretty good for an beginner, Havac."

Havac snorted in disdain. "I'm prepared to die for the cause, Captain."

"Maybe you are," Cohl said. "But I'm not going to give you that privilege. You're going to die for killing Rella. Besides, your cause is lost."

Havac glanced at the cam again. "You think so?"

Cohl gestured toward the transparisteel window. "You hear those blaster bolts? The Jedi found your shooter— the one controlling the droid. Valorum is out of danger. I never thought much of the plan anyway, seeing how Valorum is trying to dismantle the Trade Federation, the same as you are."

Havac laughed shortly. "You failed to see the truth, Cohl. You really are too old for the game. What makes you think that we were ever after Valorum?"

Cohl's grin straightened.

Grimacing in pain, he pushed himself out of the chair and limped to the window. The blaster fight had thrown the hall into utter chaos. The members of the Trade Federation Directorate were standing behind their curved table, surrounded by their security droids, everyone safe inside a shimmering force field.

Off to one side, a group of Jedi and judicials were closing on the Federation's rostrum.

Cohl swung to Havac, his eyes blazing.

"You're after the Trade Federation!"

Havac couldn't restrain a triumphant smile. "It was just a matter of getting them to activate the force field." He indicated the devices that were aimed down at the hall. "The scanner detected the activation. The holocam is going to do the rest."

"The remote," Cohl said, as if in a daze.

He lunged for the cam, meeting Havac halfway. They slammed into each other and fell grappling to the floor of the booth. They rolled toward the door, each man fighting for superiority, the blaster between them, in the clutch of four hands.

Cohl swung his elbow into Havac's face, knocking him sideways, then used Havac's momentum to pitch himself on top of Havac, pinning him to the floor with his knees.

Havac squirmed, but held tightly to the blaster, triggering a bolt into Cohl's abdomen. Cohl fell partially back, then slumped forward, bringing all his weight to bear on the weapon and forcing it down into Havac's chest.

With what little of his strength remained, Cohl squeezed out a final bolt.

Dangling by one hand from the swaying walkway, Qui-Gon looked down at the floor of the hall.

The trumpeters had stopped midfanfare and were scattering for cover, abandoning their horns as they ran. Everywhere else delegates were fleeing their seats, literally climbing over one another in a desperate attempt to escape.

Valorum was on his feet, but completely encircled by Senate Guards and Jedi Knights.

Saesee Tiin, Ki-Adi-Mundi, and Obi-Wan had taken up positions in front of the Trade Federation rostrum, their lightsabers lifted to deflect fire from the droids.

But the directorate members had raised their force field, which meant that no bolts could enter or leave the translucent energy shield.

The thirteen droids reached over their right shoulders for the blaster rifles secured to their backpacks.

The judicials loosed a storm of blaster bolts, which the force field simply consumed.

Then, all at once, the droids pivoted through an about-face.

The members of the directorate mouthed commands and curses and began to back away from the curved table.

The droids fired.

As the Jedi and judicials watched helplessly, bolts tore into the table and chairs and into the flesh of the members, shaking them about and hurling them to all sides of the rostrum.

The firing ceased as abruptly as it had started.

For a moment, the droids stood with their cooling blasters, then they put them back over their shoulders and turned to face the hall.

Stunned by what he had witnessed, Qui-Gon clambered onto the shaky walkway and dropped cross-legged to the slanted floor, staring off into space.

THE INNER CIRCLE

34

"The Nebula Front has largely disbanded," the judicial officer explained to Qui-Gon. "The few we've been able to track down contend that they knew nothing about Havac's plans for Eriadu. Some of them had never even met Havac, and assert that the name was applied routinely to almost everyone in the Front's militant faction. The Eriadu operation was conceived in great secrecy, in any case, since the militants were convinced that there was an informant among them."

"The informant was one of the moderates," Qui-Gon amended. "It was through him that I learned about Cohl's designs to raid the Trade Federation freighter at Dorvalla, and, on Asmeru, about a clandestine operation Cohl was executing for Havac."

The judicial, a thin, brown-haired woman with a personable manner, made note of Qui-Gon's remarks on a desktop datapad. It was just the two of them in a small cubicle in the Justice Department's cavernous headquarters on Coruscant. Almost a standard month had gone by since the assassinations.

Deactivating the shield the members of the Trade Federation Directorate had thrown about themselves—unknowingly ushering in their own demise—had required a team of technicians, using a pair of field disruptors. The two Neimoidians who had survived the massacre, Viceroy Nute Gunray and Senator Lott Dod, had not protested when the same disruptors had been employed to dazzle the thirteen droids into states of guaranteed submission. Diplomatic privilege had permitted the Neimoidians to depart Eriadu without answering any questions.

Supreme Chancellor Valorum had ordered the Justice Department to commence an immediate investigation, but the chief investigators had soon found themselves thwarted by Lieutenant Governor Tarkin. Tarkin insisted that, since Eriadu had failed to provide adequate security, the case should be handled by Eriaduan investigators. There was some concern that Tarkin, fearing retaliation by the Trade Federation, would seek to shift the blame to other parties. But, instead, he had simply impeded the investigation by allowing evidence and eyewitnesses to vanish. Ignored, the judicials Valorum had asked to remain behind on Eriadu had finally decamped.

Qui-Gon had tried to stay abreast of developments in the case, but the chief investigator who served as liaison with the Eriaduan team had only just returned to Coruscant.

"Havac turns out to have been Eriaduan," the judicial officer continued. "His real name was Eru Matalis, a media correspondent and holodocumentarian, with a long-standing grudge against the Trade Federation. At some point he became the leader of the Nebula Front's cell on Eriadu, and rose through the ranks to a command position in the organization.

"A search of the safe house the Nebula Front maintained in Eriadu City revealed that the Front had contacts in all quarters of government and law enforcement, and presumably knew as much as anyone about security for the trade summit. Evidently, Havac—Matalis—used his contacts to obtain security badges, uniforms, and documentation for the assassins Cohl had hired, and perhaps arranged to have weapons concealed inside the hall, prior to the summit itself."

"The operation must have been planned as soon as the trade summit was announced," Qui-Gon said. "Or soon after the attack on the Supreme Chancellor, here on Coruscant. I don't suppose we'll ever know whether that attack was genuine, or designed from the start to sidetrack us from what was being set in motion on Eriadu."

"Not unless Cohl or Havac learn to speak from beyond the grave," the judicial said.

"What of the assassins who were captured?"

"Everyone in custody upholds that Valorum was the target—even the two who you discovered with Havac in the media booth. As they tell it, Havac's goal was to make it appear that the Trade Federation's droids had killed Valorum, at the behest of the directorate. That would have led to the dismantlement of the Federation, which is what the Nebula Front wanted all along.

"We considered the possibility that something went wrong with the droids' programming, and that the attack on the directorate was a mistake. But Baktoid provided ample proof that that could not have happened."

"Could Baktoid have been involved in abetting Havac?"

"They vehemently deny any involvement. In fact, their technicians helped us analyze the battle droid—the so-called commander—which was found to contain a mechanism that allowed it to be controlled independently of the central control computer, but only for a brief period. Havac's holocam prompted the commander to act, and the twelve other droids followed the commander's lead. As

soon as the central control computer realized what was occurring in the summit hall, it shut down all of them."

Qui-Gon considered it for a moment. "Havac must
have had help getting the droid into Trade Federation
hands."

"Absolutely," the judicial said, nodding. "But diplomatic privilege has prevented us from learning all that we
wish to know. For example, Eriadu Spaceport records
show that the directorate arrived with only twelve droids.
So the thirteenth—the assassin—had to have been acquired while the delegation was on the surface.

"Gunray, the new commanding viceroy of the entire
Trade Federation, alleges—through his lawyers, at any
rate—that someone on the directorate must have accepted or introduced the droid. Senator Lott Dod claims
that when he drew Gunray's attention to the extra droid,
the viceroy appeared to be every bit as puzzled as Dod
was."

"What about the message that took Gunray and Dod
from the summit hall?"

"Legitimate—as far as can be determined. A plasma
leak was detected in the engines of the Neimoidians'
shuttle. The leak touched off scanners at the spaceport,
and someone at the spaceport contacted security at the
summit hall. The problem is, we haven't been able to
learn the identity of whoever it was that contacted security. Viceroy Gunray insists that the comlink the page led
him to was inactive when he reached it. The page has
verified this. By the time Gunray and Dod were headed
back to their seats, the violence had already broken out,
and security agents restrained them from reentering the
hall."

The judicial shook her head in exasperation. "It all
comes down to Havac."

Qui-Gon folded his arms across his chest and nodded, though not convincingly. "So it would appear."

"It's a pleasure to see you again, Senator Palpatine," the exquisite figure in the holoprojector field said. "I look forward to the day when we can meet again in person."

"I do, as well, Your Majesty," Palpatine said, bowing his head in a gesture of respect.

The figure sat in a round-backed throne, with a towering arch-topped window at her back, and, to either side, massive columns of native stone. Her low voice was as composed as her posture; the words emerged from her painted lips with scant inflection. She had a slight figure and a lovely, feminine face. She was remarkably solemn for one so young. It was clear that she took her responsibilities with the utmost seriousness.

Her birth name was Padmé Naberrie. But she would henceforth be known as Queen Amidala, the newly elected ruler of Naboo.

Palpatine was receiving the communication in his apartment, high in the craglike tower that was 500 Republica, in one of Coruscant's oldest and most prestigious precincts. The walls and floor were as red as Amidala's throne, with objects of art adorning every niche and corner.

He could imagine his own ghostly likeness hovering above the composite holoprojector in the floor of the Advisory Council chambers in Naboo's Theed Palace.

"Senator, I wanted to advise you about something, which has only now been revealed to me. King Veruna is dead."

"Dead, Your Majesty?" Palpatine frowned in apparent disquiet. "Of course, I was aware that he had gone into hiding following his abdication. But I understood that he was in good health."

"He was in good health, Senator," Amidala said in a

low monotone. "His death has been ruled 'accidental,' but much mystery surrounds it."

Even at fourteen years of age, she was not the youngest monarch ever elected to the throne, but she was certainly one of the most conventional, in dress and bearing.

She was sheathed head to foot in a wide-shouldered red gown, whose ample cuffs were trimmed with potolli fur. The gown's narrow bib was embroidered in priceless thread. Painted white, her face sat in the notch of a deep collar that not only bracketed her fine features, but also became part of an elaborate jeweled headpiece that flared behind her head. Her thumbnails were accented with white polish, and each cheekbone with a red, stylized beauty mark. A traditional "scar of remembrance" bisected her lower lip, which, unlike its red mate, was also painted white. Five handmaidens stood behind her, dressed in hooded burgundy gowns.

"I wish you to meet our new chief of security, Senator," Amidala said, gesturing to someone out of view. "Captain Panaka."

A clean-shaven man with light-brown skin moved into the holofield. Humorless-looking, he was dressed in a leather jerkin and matching command cap. Panaka may have been recently appointed, but he was not new to the court, since Panaka had served for a time under his predecessor, Captain Magneta.

"Because King Veruna died under suspicious circumstances," Amidala said, "Captain Panaka feels that additional security is required for all of us, including you, Senator."

Palpatine looked surprised, even entertained by the notion. "I hardly think that's necessary on Coruscant, Your Majesty. The only danger here comes from having to fraternize with other senators, and somehow remain immune to the greed that plagues the Galactic Senate."

The queen returned to the holofield. "What about the recent troubles between the Trade Federation and the Nebula Front terrorists, Senator?"

Palpatine shook his head in disapproval. "That sorry incident only pointed out how ineffectual the Republic has become at mediating such conflicts. Too many in the Senate place their own needs above the needs of the Republic."

"What will become of Chancellor Valorum's proposal to tax the free trade zones?"

"I feel certain that the Supreme Chancellor will pursue the matter."

"How will you vote, Senator, should the matter reach a vote?"

"How would you have me vote, Your Majesty?"

Amidala thought before replying. "My responsibility is to the people of Naboo. I would very much like to establish good relations with Chancellor Valorum, but Naboo can scarcely afford to become embroiled in a dispute that pits the Republic against the Trade Federation. I will abide by your decision on the matter, Senator."

Palpatine inclined his head. "Then I will weigh the matter carefully, and vote according to what is ultimately best for Naboo and the Republic."

Valorum stood at the tall windows, gazing out on the cityscape.

"The last time we met here, it was to discuss the Trade Federation's request for protection from terrorists," he said, "and in the months since, the situation has only intensified. When I reflect on the sequence of events that have brought us to this dark place, I find myself at a loss. If someone had tried to tell me months ago that we were headed here, I wouldn't have heeded the warning, because I wouldn't have considered it possible."

Senator Palpatine said nothing. He waited for Valorum to turn from the view.

"Out of respect for what occurred at the summit, I have deferred bringing the motion for taxation before the senate. But I am under pressure to resolve the matter once and for all—from those who support it, as well as those who oppose it."

Valorum pivoted to face Palpatine. "You, perhaps more than anyone, know the climate of the senate. Did the assassinations create sympathy for the Trade Federation, to the point where we won't be able to gather sufficient support for taxation?"

"On the contrary," Palpatine said. "What happened on Eriadu only reinforced everyone's fears that we are entering violent times, and that the conflict between the Trade Federation and the Nebula Front could be a sign of greater tragedies to come.

"What's more, with the profit-driven Neimoidians now helming the Trade Federation, tension is likely to increase in the outlying systems. Your plan to redirect revenue to the Outer Rim is praiseworthy, and is something that should be put into effect. Many worlds and struggling concerns stand to profit from such a move. Market competition will eventually temper the reach of the Trade Federation, without need for the Republic to intervene, beyond taxation."

Valorum nodded. "And what of the Trade Federation's request for additional defenses? Even with the Nebula Front eliminated as a threat, the Neimoidians will want permission to augment their army."

"That's true," Palpatine said slowly. "As an accommodation, if nothing else, we should at least consider allowing the Trade Federation to take whatever steps are necessary to safeguard their vessels. The breakup of the Nebula Front does not preclude the possibility of further acts of terrorism, launched by whatever groups rise up next."

Valorum regarded Palpatine. "Will we have Naboo's vote?"

Palpatine sighed with purpose. "Unfortunately, Queen Amidala is not prepared to support taxation, as Naboo still relies on the Trade Federation for many essential imports. She is young and inexperienced in such matters, but eager to learn." He fixed his gaze on Valorum. "However, I will continue to do all in my power to work behind the scenes. I feel certain that we will be able to rally the votes needed."

Valorum smiled in gratitude. "For all the support you have shown me, my friend, I trust that you will take on faith that, should need ever arise, I would do all within my power to render aid to Naboo."

"Thank you, Supreme Chancellor. As you say, I will take you at your word."

35

The public corridors of the Galactic Senate overflowed with HoloNet correspondents, well-wishers, and the more civic-minded of Coruscant's citizens.

Flanked by Senate Guards, a rejuvenated Valorum moved slowly through the principal corridor, trading dignified nods with senators and ignoring questions hurled by the media reporters.

"Supreme Chancellor, did you ever for a moment doubt that the taxation proposal would be ratified?" a Twi'lek correspondent asked.

Sei Taria answered for him.

"The issue has been controversial from the start. But everyone involved remained confident that the proposal would pass, once all parties had an opportunity to be heard."

An attractive human female shouldered her way to the front of the crowd. "Considering what happened at the trade summit, do you still feel that all parties were heard?"

Again Sei Taria intervened.

"While tragedy compelled us to abbreviate the summit, much was accomplished on Eriadu. Those who were denied an opportunity to speak were given ample time to voice their opinions here, when the discussions continued."

"Discussions or debates, Supreme Chancellor?"

Valorum waved his hand in dismissal.

"Do you feel that taxation strikes a blow for the rights of the outlying systems?"

"The outlying systems will surely benefit," Taria replied. "But all worlds stand to gain as a result of this historic action. Contrary to the claims of many a would-be political pundit, the passage of this bill demonstrates clearly that the senate has not grown too unwieldy or apathetic to act for the common good."

Another human correspondent shoved his way forward. "Would you consider this to be the high point of your administration?"

Taria held up her hands. "Later today, the office of the Supreme Chancellor will issue a statement. Until that time, there will be no further questions."

The correspondents grumbled, but ultimately fell silent and stepped aside, as Valorum's contingent of advisers and guards steered him toward the turbolift that accessed his private chambers. Once there, he removed his outer cloak, sat heavily into his chair, and loosed a prolonged exhale.

"Thank you for running interference," he told Taria when the two of them were alone in the office.

She smiled and took a seat opposite him. "We should issue a statement as quickly as possible. Do you want to compose something now?"

Valorum frowned, then got to his feet and walked to the center of the room, his hands clasped behind his back. Taria activated the record function of her wrist comlink.

"For too long a time the senate has been bogged down by policies and procedures," Valorum began after a moment. "But today we managed to sidestep that bureaucratic morass. We have succeeded in overcoming our inertia, by setting aside petty squabbles and self-interest, and by banding together to strike a blow for the Republic itself. In this, we have reaffirmed our mandate, and refound our way.

"While we are honored to have introduced this historic proposal, victory would not have been possible without the tireless efforts of several good and proper delegates. We shall refrain from going into the matter of how the vote was carried. But we do want to say that we owe much gratitude to delegates like—"

Valorum cut short his remarks when a tone issued from the office door. When Sei Taria opened the door, two Senate Guards conducted Alderaanian Senator Bail Antilles into the room. In his right hand, the chair of the Internal Activities Committee held a legal-looking piece of durasheet.

"Supreme Chancellor, I'm sorry to have to be the bearer of raw tidings on a day that should be devoted to celebration," Antilles said, extending the durasheet to Valorum. "But this document constitutes official notification that you are hereby requested to appear before the Supreme Court to answer allegations of corruption and illegal enrichment."

Valorum blinked in stupefaction. He couldn't make sense of what he had just heard. This had to be a mistake, or a joke in very poor taste. His heart thudded against his breastbone, and he grew short of breath. He stared at the durasheet he had accepted, then glared at Antilles.

"I demand to know the meaning of this."

Antilles compressed his lips. "Again, I apologize, Supreme Chancellor. But that is all I am permitted to say about the matter at this time."

Valorum was surrounded not by Senate Guards but by lawyers when he finally appeared before the Supreme Court almost two weeks later. During that time his legal team had managed to discover that the basis for the allegations was an investment made in Valorum Shipping, on Eriadu.

Beyond that, Valorum was in the dark.

The Supreme Court convened in closed session in the Galactic Courts of Justice Building, an enormous edifice of pointed arches, tall decorative spires, and elaborate statuary, located in the so-called Plains of Coruscant, not far from the Jedi Temple.

Valorum and his lawyers were seated at a long table opposite the twelve robed figures who comprised the judiciary council. Bail Antilles and the members of the Internal Activities Committee sat perpendicular to the bench.

The chief justice spoke, addressing Valorum.

"Supreme Chancellor, we appreciate that you elected to appear before us, without being subpoenaed by writ."

"We are given to understand that this is an informal inquest," one of the lawyers said in Valorum's stead.

"Your presumption is correct."

The judge looked to Antilles, who stood and spoke from his place at the committee's table.

"Your Honors, Supreme Chancellor Valorum," he began. "Just two weeks ago the senate met in special session to vote on a motion introduced by Supreme Chancellor Valorum, calling for a tax to be levied on all shipping and other mercantile activities in what were formerly known as the free trade zones of the outlying systems.

"An amendment to the original proposal directed that a percentage of all revenues collected by the Republic would be redistributed among the outlying systems, for purposes of social welfare and technological advancement. Many business concerns located in those systems have already begun to reap the benefits of the amendment, in the form of venture capital bestowed by investors, here in the Core. One of those concerns is Valorum Shipping and Transport, of Eriadu, which has received an enormous sum, for a company that has shown only marginal profits over the past several standard years."

Valorum's lawyer interrupted.

"With all due respect, Senator Antilles, Supreme Chancellor Valorum was not made aware of the investment in Valorum Shipping until last week. Regardless, while it's true that the company bears the Valorum name, and that the Supreme Chancellor is a member of the board of directors, he does not participate in company operations, or involve himself with each and every commonplace business transaction.

"More important, Your Honors, since when does it violate Republic law for a company to profit, based on merit alone? In the case of Valorum Shipping, it strikes me as good business sense for investors to be drawn to concerns owned by prominent public figures. It's not as if the Supreme Chancellor actively solicited investments. Furthermore, the Supreme Chancellor, as required by law, has made full disclosure of all his holdings, and his record, with regard to earnings and taxes, is spotless."

The twelve judges looked at Antilles, who was still frowning when the lawyer finished speaking.

"If I may be allowed to continue. The Internal Activities Committee does not take issue with any of the statements made by the Supreme Chancellor's legal representative. In fact, when this matter was first brought to our attention, we proceeded under the assumption that no infringement of protocol had occurred. However . . ."

Antilles let the word dangle for a long moment before continuing.

"Subsequent investigation has shown that the contribution to Valorum Shipping did not originate with a consortium or venture capital group. Rather, the revenue was drawn from a blind account, and moved to Eriadu through a Coruscant bank of dubious reputation. I use the term *moved* advisedly, Your Honors, since the investment was tendered in the form of hard assets."

Valorum's lawyers regarded one another in puzzlement. "Of what sort?" the spokesman asked Antilles.

"Aurodium ingots."

Blood drained from Valorum's face, and a stir went through the room. Valorum and his lawyers conferred for a moment, before the spokesman replied.

"Your Honors, we acknowledge that the investment begins to sound, shall we say, less than forthright. Nevertheless, Senator Antilles has yet to demonstrate exactly how this matter relates to the Supreme Chancellor."

Antilles's expression made clear that he had been waiting for just this moment. He gazed at Valorum while he delivered his finishing stroke.

"What the Internal Activities Committee finds most interesting, and questionable, is that the value of the aurodium—and indeed the quantity—corresponds exactly to a cache of ingots reported missing by the Trade Federation, following an attack on one of their vessels, the *Revenue*, in the Dorvalla system, several months ago."

Hushed conversations erupted throughout the room, as Antilles stepped out from behind the table and approached the bench.

"Your Honors, this is not an indictment. The committee merely wishes to be reassured that the Supreme Chancellor did not have a hidden agenda in supporting taxation, as part of a scheme to enrich his own holdings in the outlying systems. The committee also wishes to be reassured that the aurodium in question did, in fact, disappear from the *Revenue*, and was not simply transferred to Valorum Shipping, to seal a clandestine partnership existing between the Supreme Chancellor and the Trade Federation."

Senator Palpatine was one of a hundred or more senators who had been invited to Orn Free Taa's lavish penthouse for an evening of exceptional food and extravagant drink. What had been touted as an occasion, however, had all the undercurrents of a conclave; and where outsiders assumed that its purpose was to celebrate Valorum's seeming victory in the Senate, it was instead intended to cheer his recent reversal of fortune.

On the largest of the penthouse's many terraces, the blue-skinned Twi'lek host was holding forth for an audience of senators, who hung on his every word.

"Of course we knew about the alleged improprieties. But it was necessary to delay mention of the scandal to ensure that the tax proposal would be ratified, which wouldn't have been the case had Valorum been weakened beforehand."

Taa shook his head and fat lekku. "No, by waiting to reveal the allegations, and by supporting Valorum, we managed to turn what might have been perceived as an instance of ordinary corruption into what hints at a nefarious plot that threatens the stability of the very Republic."

"But is there actually anything to the accusations?" Quarren Senator Tikkes asked, his facial tentacles quivering in prospect.

Taa's enormous shoulders heaved in a shrug of indifference. "There is the aurodium, and there is the *appearance* of deceit. What else matters?"

"If it is true, then Valorum has become a danger to the general good," Mot Not Rab remarked.

Tikkes affirmed that with an enthusiastic nod. "I say we shake him, before worse days endure."

Others nodded in agreement, muttering among themselves.

"Patience, patience," Taa advised in a soothing voice. "Baseless or not, the allegations have essentially crippled Valorum. We need only to rid ourselves of those senators who have buoyed him in the past, enabling him to remain afloat despite our best attempts to sink him. Besides, there may yet be some advantage to keeping him high and dry."

"What advantage?" the senator from Rodia asked.

"With his influence further eroded, and the Justice Department stripped of some of its former authority, commissions will have to be appointed to render judgments and decisions he would ordinarily make. The power of the courts will increase. But cases will invariably take longer than ever to resolve. And yet Valorum will continue to suffer the blame."

"Unless a strong vice chancellor is appointed," the Rodian thought to point out.

"We must not let that happen," Taa said firmly. "We need a consummate bureaucrat to serve as vice chancellor." He leaned toward his circle of conspirators. "Senator Palpatine has suggested that we do our best to install the Chagrian—Mas Amedda."

"But Amedda is rumored to be well disposed to the Trade Federation," Tikkes said in disbelief.

"All the better, all the better." Taa was gleeful. "What matters is that the more fanatical he is about procedure, the more he stifles Valorum's ability to act."

"To what final end?" Mot Not Rab asked.

"Why, to Valorum's final end," Taa said. "And when that time comes, we will elect a leader with fire in his veins."

"Bail Antilles is already campaigning," the Rodian said.

"As is Ainlee Teem of Malastare," Tikkes added.

Taa noticed Palpatine standing by the terrace doors, engaged in deep conversation with the senators from Fondor and Eriadu.

"I propose that we consider nominating Palpatine," he said, gesturing discreetly.

Tikkes and the rest glanced at the tall senator from Naboo.

"Palpatine would never accept the nomination," the Quarren said. "He considers himself a supporting player."

Taa narrowed his eyes. "Then we must convince him. Think what it would mean to the outlying systems if someone from other than a Core world was elected Supreme Chancellor. There might finally be equality for all species. He can restore order, if anyone can. He has the right combination of selflessness and quiet power. And don't let yourselves be fooled: there is a strong hand concealed within those loose sleeves. He cares deeply about the integrity of the Republic, and he will do whatever is needed to enforce the laws."

Tikkes was dubious. "Then we will not be able to play him as we have Valorum."

"That's the beauty of it," Taa said. "We won't have to, because he thinks like one of us."

37

In all the years she had known him, Adi Gallia had never seen Valorum so despondent. He could be moody at times, and unjustly hard on himself, but the allegations of corruption had tipped him into a dark place from which he could not surface. In the month since she had seen him last, he appeared to have aged a year.

"The aurodium was the Nebula Front's final stab at me," he was telling her. "The terrorists were determined to take me down, along with the Trade Federation Directorate. That has to be the explanation. And do you know why my family members on Eriadu said nothing of the aurodium? Because they felt slighted that I had chosen to accept the hospitality of Lieutenant Governor Tarkin, who, it seems, has been something of a nemesis for them. I did so only as a courtesy to Senator Palpatine, who now feels that he played a guilty part in this whole wretched affair."

Adi was about to reply, but Valorum didn't give her the chance.

"Although I ask myself if certain senators weren't involved. Those who would sooner see me disgraced than simply disempowered."

Adi had come to his office in the senate, which had become a place of purposeful whisperings and innuendo. The entire climate of the senate had changed—and Valorum felt responsible.

"It will only be a matter of time before you are exonerated," Adi tried to reassure him.

He shook his head. "Few are interested in seeing me exonerated—the media, least of all. And with the terrorist Havac dead, there is no one to say with certainty that the Trade Federation wasn't trying to buy my influence."

"If that was the case, why would you have pushed so hard to tax the trade routes? The tax alone is proof of your honesty."

Valorum's weak smile belied his sense of hopelessness. "My critics have an explanation. To offset the tax, revenue that goes to the outlying systems will simply find its way back into the deep pockets of the Neimoidians' robes."

"It's all conjectural," Adi said. "It will disappear."

Valorum scarcely heard her.

"I don't care what they say about me personally. But now, all that I have accomplished in the senate is in question. I am made to answer to Mas Amedda, who is so consumed with procedure that no new legislation will pass. Yet more commissions and committees will come into being, and with them, expanded opportunities for graft and corruption."

Valorum fell quiet for a long moment, shaking his head back and forth.

"The assassinations on Eriadu, and now this scandal, will have wide-ranging consequences. It has already been made clear to me that the Jedi are not to become involved in trade disputes, without the express consent of the senate.

"But worst of all, is the disservice I have done the Republic. The citizenry take its cue from the head of state—even when that one has become little more than an ineffectual figurehead.

"I looked for the causes of corruption and found myself to blame. Did I conveniently forget all the deals I struck with malicious beings? Did I conveniently forget that I, too, had been corrupted?"

He put his elbows on the desk and pressed his fingertips to his temples, keeping his gaze downward.

"I had a terrible dream last night, that seemed as much a reflection of my present circumstance as a vision of the future. In it, I felt myself besieged by nebulous forces, by wraiths of one sort or another. Something was reaching for me out of the blackness, to crush me in its grip."

"Terrible, but only a dream," Adi said. "Not a vision."

Valorum managed to summon the same weak smile when he looked up at her.

"If only I had more supporters like you and Senator Palpatine."

"Better a few faithful supporters, than a wealth of false friends," Adi said. "Perhaps you can find some solace in that."

In the High Council tower of the Jedi Temple, the eleven Masters listened to Adi recount her meeting with Valorum. As ever, Yoda was in motion, walking about with his gimer stick cane, and, because of the part they had played in the events, Qui-Gon and Obi-Wan were present.

"The Supreme Chancellor is correct about one thing," Mace Windu said. "The aurodium could only have come from Havac. Cohl delivered the stolen ingots to him, then Havac set up the blind account and saw to it that the aurodium was invested in Valorum Shipping."

"But why?" Yarael Poof asked.

"By suggesting collusion, Havac hoped to bring down both the Supreme Chancellor and the Trade Federation."

"Valorum, perhaps," Depa Billaba said. "But the Neimoidians have much of the senate on their payroll. The Trade Federation hasn't been touched by the scandal."

"Indeed they haven't," Oppo Rancisis agreed.

"Too little thought we gave these events," Yoda said. "All of us."

Yaddle turned to face Qui-Gon and Obi-Wan, who were standing outside the Masters' circle. "You two: flying here, flying there, chasing clues . . . If stopped for a moment to listen to the unifying Force, see what was coming you might have."

"I did what I had to do, Masters," Qui-Gon said, without apology.

Yoda loosed a prolonged sigh. "Blame you, we don't, Qui-Gon. But exasperate us, you do."

Qui-Gon inclined his head in a bow.

"This scandal wasn't the sole work of the Nebula Front," Adi said. "The Supreme Chancellor has other enemies—hidden enemies, plotting against him. Trying to maneuver him into a position where he will err gravely, and be voted out of office or be forced to resign."

"To be replaced by the likes of Bail Antilles or Ainlee Teem," Saesee Tiin muttered.

Windu nodded. "He has been too trusting."

"Too naive," Even Piell remarked harshly.

Yoda paced, then stopped. "Help him, we must—in secret, if need be."

"We must heed the will of the Force in this matter," Windu said. "We must be open to ways to counter the treacherous vortex into which the Republic has been drawn. Perhaps we can help Valorum get wind of events before his enemies have an opportunity to stack those events against him."

"He senses perilous times ahead," Adi said. "As if some darkness has been awakened, intent on spreading itself across the galaxy."

Yaddle broke the long silence.

"Tipping the balance is."

Yoda looked at her. "Tipping, yes. But from troubled times to untroubled, or from bad times to worse?"

Windu steepled his fingers in front of his face. "And what unknown hand is doing the tipping?"

38

Darth Sidious visited Nute Gunray and his advisers by hologram, on the bridge of the Trade Federation freighter *Saak'ak*, known, in Basic, as the *Profiteer*.

"Congratulations on your promotion, Viceroy," the Sith Lord rasped, in a manner that made derision sound like a compliment.

"Thank you, my Lord," Gunray was quick to respond. "We did not imagine, when you said you would convince our competitors in the directorate, that you would . . ."

"That I would what, Viceroy? Perhaps you imagined that I would act with greater subtlety, is that it? Now there is no one to stand in your way of acquiring an army or directing the future course of the Trade Federation."

Hath Monchar, Rune Haako, and Commander Daultay Dofine looked at Gunray in stark apprehension.

"I meant no offense, my Lord," he stammered.

Sidious was briefly quiet. If only they could see his eyes, they might have had a hint of what he was thinking.

"Soon I will be taking steps to eliminate some of your

other competitors," he intoned a moment later. "But that does not concern you. Instead, I want you to devote your energies to becoming familiar with the capabilities of your newly acquired toys—your battle droids, and starfighters, and landing craft. Have Baktoid and Haor Chall Engineering been filling your orders on schedule?"

"They have, my Lord," Gunray said. "Though at exorbitant cost."

"Don't try my patience with talk of credits, Viceroy," Sidious warned. "There is more at stake than the health of your financial accounts."

Gunray was close to trembling. "What would you have us do, my Lord?"

"We are going to put your new army to the test."

Gunray and Hath Monchar exchanged fearful glances. "A test?" Monchar said.

Sidious seemed to gaze at him for an uncomfortably long time. "I suspect that you are hardly thrilled by the senate's sanction of taxation of the trade routes," he said at last.

Gunray nodded. "The senate has no right."

"Of course not. And what better way to demonstrate your displeasure than through a trade blockade."

"Of Eriadu," Gunray said eagerly. "Because of what happened—"

"Eriadu would respond with force, Viceroy. We don't want a war. We want an embargo."

"Which world shall it be?" Monchar said.

"I suggest we strike at the homeworld of the senator who was most responsible for championing the taxation bill: Naboo."

"Naboo?" Haako said in genuine bewilderment.

Sidious nodded. "Senator Palpatine is adept at dissembling his real nature. You scarcely realize how much damage he has already caused."

"But would such a blockade be legal?" Gunray asked. "Valorum will never sit still for it."

"I have a surprise in store for feeble-tempered Valorum," Sidious promised. "What's more, the scandal surrounding the Supreme Chancellor has led many senators to rethink the taxation legislation. Few will grumble about a trade embargo of a world so distant from the Core."

Monchar stepped forward. "And what of the Jedi?"

"They are already constrained from interfering."

"But if they do, my Lord?" Gunray said.

"We will not be subtle in dealing with them."

Gunray bowed his head. "Once again, we place ourselves in your hands."

Sidious smiled faintly. "As I told you once before, Viceroy, you serve yourselves best when you serve me."

STAR WARS:
THE NEW JEDI ORDER

The epic tale of invasion and adventure
with Han, Luke, and Leia
which began with VECTOR PRIME
by R.A. Salvatore, continues:

STAR WARS
The New Jedi Order
Enemy Lines I: Rebel Dream
By Aaron Allston

For a taste of Rebel Dream,
Please read on . . .

One Month Ago, Pyria System:
Borleias Occupation, Day 1

"A god cannot die," Charat Kraal said. "Therefore it
can have no fear of death. So who is braver, a god or a
mortal?"

Charat Kraal was a pilot of the Yuuzhan Vong—
humanoid, a little over two meters in height. His skin,
where it was not covered by geometric tattoos, was pale,
marked everywhere by the white, slightly reflective lines
of old scars. Some years-ago mishap had eaten away the
center of his face, eliminating even the diminutive nose
common to the Yuuzhan Vong, leaving behind brown-
crusted cartilage and horizontal holes into his sinus pas-
sages. His forehead angled back less dramatically than
many of the Yuuzhan Vong and looked a trifle more like
the forehead of a human, for which two warriors had
taunted him, for which he had killed them. He disguised
the trait as much as he could by yanking out the last
of the hair on his head and adding skulltop tattoos that

drew the eye up and back, away from the offending forehead. One day he would earn an implant that would further mask his deformity and end his problem.

He wore an ooglith cloaker, the transparent environment suit of Yuuzhan Vong pilots, over a simple warrior's loincloth. Both garments were living creatures, engineered and bred to perform only the tasks demanded of them, to aid the Yuuzhan Vong in their pursuit of glory.

He sat in the cockpit of his coralskipper, the irregular rocklike space fighter of his kind, but he did not wear his cognition hood at the moment; the masklike creature that kept him in mental contact with his craft, that allowed him to sense with its senses and pilot it with the agility of thought rather than muscle and reaction, was set to the side while his coralskipper cruised on routine patrol.

He and his mission partner, Penzak Kraal, were in distant orbit above the world Borleias. The planet had been recently seized from the infidels native to this galaxy so that it could be used as a staging area for the Yuuzhan Vong assault on the galactic throneworld of Coruscant. Borleias was an agreeably green world, not overgrown with the dead, crusty dwellings of the infidels, not strewn with their unnatural implements of technology; only a military base, now smashed, had affronted the Yuuzhan Vong with evidence of infidel occupation.

The voice of Penzak Kraal emerged from the small, head-shaped villip mounted on the cockpit wall just beneath the canopy. Though most coralskippers were not equipped with villips, relying instead on the telepathic signals of yammosk war coordinators for all their communications, long-distance patrol craft did call for a means for direct communications. "Don't be an idiot. If a god is the god of bravery, then by definition he must be braver than any Yuuzhan Vong, than anything living."

"I wonder. Let us say then that you could become immortal as the gods, and never die, but remain one of the Yuuzhan Vong. You would never face death. Could you then be as brave as the Yuuzhan Vong? You could kill forever but never truly risk death, defy death, choose your time and place of death. Which is better, to be brave for a lifetime or to kill forever?"

"Who cares? The choice is not ours. But if I were to choose, I think I would choose immortality. Live long enough, and you might learn how to be brave as a Yuuz-han Vong again. Kill long enough, and you could perhaps learn to kill a star."

Charat Kraal sobered. "I have heard . . ."

"What?"

"That the infidels did that. Learned to kill a star."

He heard Penzak Kraal hiss in irritation; in the villip he saw his partner's lopsided features go even more off center as his mouth pulled down in an expression of contempt. "So what if they did? They killed it the wrong way, with their wrong minds and their wrong devices. And, like idiots, they must have lost the secret. Or they'd be destroying the worldships one by one."

"I have also heard . . ." Charat Kraal lowered his voice, a foolish instinct, since no one but Penzak Kraal could be listening to him. "That gods may smile upon them, too. On the infidels."

"Ridiculous."

"Can you know the minds of the gods?"

"I can no more know the minds of the gods than summon one of the enemy battleships to destroy for my personal glory."

In the distance, away from Borleias, many kilometers from them, an enemy battleship winked into existence, its bow pointed toward them. The ship was already up to speed; it grew rapidly as it neared them, as it approached Borleias.

"Penzak, you *fool*."

"My words did not summon it, you idiot." The villip's face blurred and adjusted, reflecting a change to Penzak's features; Penzak had pulled on his cognition hood. Charat did likewise. His surroundings, the cockpit interior, seemed to become transparent, giving him a view in all directions through the senses of the coralskipper, showing him in breathtaking detail the onrushing enemy ship.

No, now it was *ships*. More and more of the loathsome things of metal were dropping out of hyperspace, all aimed at Borleias. At Charat and Penzak.

A moment later, Charat could feel a buzz through the cognition hood, a telltale sign that Penzak was sending a warning to the Domain Kraal commander on Borleias.

The foremost New Republic ship, a sharply angled triangle in white, passed over the two coralskippers, blotting out the sun, casting them into shadow. Nowhere near so large as a Yuuzhan Vong worldship, it was still of impressive size, and so near that Charat felt he could reach out and drag his finger along its hull as it passed.

Penzak Kraal sent his coralskipper into a dive and turned to match the larger craft's course. Charat paced him. Above, he saw thruster gouts from the ship's belly herald the launching of the hated infidel starfighters.

"How do we hurt them worst?" Charat asked.

"Follow me in," Penzak said. "While they're launching. Don't engage the fighters; bait them so they follow us. The ship won't fire on us with the fighters in close proximity. We'll enter their launching bays and destroy the facilities there, then gut the ship from within." He looped around, rising and angling in toward the ship's belly. Charat followed.

Mon Mothma, one of the newest cruisers in the New Republic's fleet, a Star Destroyer refitted with gravity-well generators capable of interfering with the short jumps made by Yuuzhan Vong craft, cruised straight toward Borleias from the point where it had dropped out of hyperspace. This hadn't been a timed drop—they'd plotted a course straight for the planet Borleias, and the planet's gravity well had dragged them into realspace when they'd come close enough. And now before them was the blue-green world they had come to recapure.

"No sign of a Yuuzhan Vong worldship in orbit," reported the sensor officer, a Mon Calamari male with deep blue skin. "The two coralskippers are turning to engage."

General Wedge Antilles, a lean man with a care-worn face and military posture, commander of the fleet group for which *Mon Mothma* was the flagship, nodded. "Gunnery, stay on them, vape them if they come against us. Fighter control, continue launching starfighter squadrons."

"Yes, sir."

"Yes, sir."

Data screens lit up with colored blips as New Republic starfighters—X-wings, A-9s, B-wings, E-wings, and more—streamed out of the docking bays and turned toward the planet. Wedge, standing at the captain's station toward the rear of the spacious bridge, ignored the screens. He concentrated instead on the live view of Borleias, which filled the main viewport at the bow end of the bridge.

I hope the Vong here have come to love this world, he told himself. *Because I'm going to take it from them. They're going to learn what it is to lose the things they love.*

Luke Skywalker hit his thrusters. His X-wing roared out of the main docking bay, losing altitude relative to the *Mon Mothma*. Behind him, eleven pilots of Twin Suns Squadron, the temporary X-wing squad that was his command, formed up on him. "Twin Suns away," he said.

"Twin Suns, copy." That would be the controller on *Mon Mothma*'s bridge. "Be advised, two coralskippers are maneuvering into your flight path."

Luke glanced at his sensor board. Two red blips were indeed turning from below to head toward them. "Squadron, follow me out, let's give these two the gauntlet treatment."

He heard a chorus of acknowledgments. There was tension in some of the voices, but not alarm. All his pilots were veterans, survivors of the Sabers, the Shocks, and other squadrons that had been reduced to shield trios, wing pairs, and solo pilots during the Yuuzhan Vong attack on Coruscant mere days earlier. Two of them, forming with him a shield trio, were his wife, Mara made Skywalker, and the Corellian-Security-officer-turned-pilot-turned-Jedi named Corran Horn. All his pilots were disciplined and competent. Many wanted revenge.

Luke understood how they felt. The Vong, aided by their human agent Viqi Shesh, had almost managed to kidnap his and Mara's infant son, Ben, just days ago. They had killed his nephew Anakin, and his nephew Jacen was missing. The losses, especially that of his apprentice Anakin, created an ache within him that he could not soothe.

In his youth, Luke would have been anxious for payback, but today he set that portion of himself aside. That was dark side thinking, immature thinking. It had been a long time since he had been a smooth-faced innocent; the scars of combat and lines of age had accumulated on his face, matching the weight of experience and calm that had accumulated on his spirit.

He extended his perceptions and sought Mara with them. He found her and almost flinched away from the contact; she was now an icy presence, concentrated totally on their mission.

He shrugged. Iciness was better than one alternative. Mara, despite her cool and controlled manner, was as anguished as he by the near loss of Ben and the loss of their nephews, and it would be no surprise to find her lit like a lightsaber with a desire for revenge. The fact that she wasn't meant that she was in control.

"S-foils to attack position," Luke said, and suited action to words by flipping the switch that split the X-wings' flight surfaces into their familiar X-shaped attack profile. "First and third trios, take the leader, the rest on the wingmate. Fire at will." He linked his lasers to quad fire, so that all four would fire with a single press of the trigger, and opened up on the lead coralskipper. Four red streams of destructive laser energy lanced out against the coralskipper—

No, it was *eight* streams. Luke's burst, aimed at the starboard side of the skip, never reached its target; a blackness appeared before it, distorting space around it like a gigantic magnifying lens, drawing the laserfire into it. Those four red lances of energy simply bent and disappeared. But Mara's burst, aimed at the port side, hit the coralskipper an instant after Luke's vanished. He grinned; she must have been using her own Force abilities to monitor him, as well. She couldn't have timed it so expertly otherwise. Her lasers raked across the enemy starfighter's hull until the distortion flicked over to interpose itself, then Luke fired again, chipping away at the coralskipper's stern. His blasts were joined by Corran's. The coral-like material of the skip's hull superheated and the lasers tore red-hot gouges along the surface.

Luke sent his X-wing into evasive maneuvers, moving back and forth, up and down with the randomness of a flying insect. He saw his target's counterattack, a glowing missile from the coralskipper's plasma cannon, flash by to port, far enough away to be no danger to himself, Mara, or Corran. In fact, there were no cries of alarm from his squadmates, no sudden and tragic disappearances of New Republic blips from his sensors.

"They're not engaging." That was Twin Suns Eleven, a Commenorian woman named Tilath Keer. "Turning to pursue." Luke saw the blips of Twin Suns Four through Six and Ten through Twelve turning back, following the coralskippers straight in toward *Mon Mothma*.

Luke felt a little tingle, but whether a warning from the Force or from his own years of combat experience he could not tell. "Negative, break off," he said. "Do not engage. Twin Suns, turn to original course and form up on *Record Time*. *Mon Mothma*, these skips are yours."

"Copy, Twins One."

Luke turned back toward Borleias, saw his pilots breaking off from pursuit of the coralskippers and maneuvering to form up with the squadron. The moment his fighters were clear of the coralskippers, *Mon Mothma*'s laser cannons opened up. One of the coralskippers was destroyed instantly, its dovin basal unable to absorb all the incoming damage with its void; the craft was reduced in a flash to glowing, molten particles no larger than a fingernail. The other, apparently more skillful at soaking up damage with its void, still sustained a grazing impact and spun away from *Mon Mothma*, out of control, no danger to the Star Destroyer.

Luke shook his head at the Yuuzhan Vong's pointless sacrifice, at the sad waste of life, and formed his fighters up in an assault wedge in front of *Record Time*.

Record Time was an armed troop transport. At nearly 170 meters, with two bulbous main portions—the larger stern housed the bridge and personnel bays, the smaller stern the engines—connected by a narrow access tube, the vessel looked impossibly vulnerable, impossibly fragile. But its captain-owner, a private trader—a smuggler, Luke believed—had volunteered its use to General Antilles during the fall of Coruscant, claiming it was the fastest, toughest vessel of its type. Now its bay was clear of trade goods and was filled with soldiers instead.

Luke's comm unit hissed with a moment of static, then a woman's voice: "*Record Time* to Twin Suns Leader, all set."

"Twin Suns to *Record Time*, you set the pace. We won't have any trouble staying where we need to be."

The transport surged forward, not fast by starfighter standards, but quickly enough for a freighter. Luke calculated its rate of acceleration and brought his X-wing up in front of the freighter's bridge. Mara and Corran settled in with him. Another shield trio dropped back to the port side of *Record Time*, a third to the starboard side, and the last astern of the transport.

All around Twin Suns Squadron, starfighter squadrons, frigates, destroyers, transports, and shuttles began accelerating to battle speed.

Luke heard Colonel Gavin Darklighter's voice over the operation channel: "Rogue Squadron to Borleias. We're back. We kicked your butt twenty years ago. Now we're here to do it again."

Luke grinned.

Squadrons of coralskippers were already climbing to their altitude by the time Twin Suns Squadron began its descent into atmosphere. Slightly longer than X-wings and comparable spacecraft, the coralskippers were far more massive. They were dense constructions of yorik coral, tapering toward the bow, broadening and deepening toward the stern, with rough exteriors reflecting their organic origins.

They could be quite beautiful, Luke had decided. The ones rising against them and the two they'd seen after leaving the *Mon Mothma* shared a color scheme, a pastel red and a pearlescent silver swirled together in a mottled pattern. At the bow, tucked into a sort of niche grown into the coral surface, was the round reddish shape of the dovin basal, the creature whose gravitic powers dragged the coralskipper from point to point in space and also brought up defensive voids that drank in damage like a Tatooine bantha drank water. On the top surface, just ahead of the point where the ship's body swelled to its greatest width, was the canopy over the cockpit; this one was tinted blue.

Their beauty was irrelevant. As soon as they came within range, they opened up with their plasma cannons, life-forms that spewed superheated materials that could eat through a starfighter's hull. "Break and engage, cover the transport," Luke commanded, and suited action to words; he spun out in a rapid descent relative to the planet below and opened fire, trusting his wingmates to stay with him, to fire out of phase with him and at different portions of his target to overload and baffle the dovin basal. This time the creature defending his target skip intercepted Mara's shot, fired from slightly below the skip's centerline, but couldn't whip the void around fast enough to counter Luke's and Corran's shots, which scoured the yorik coral all around the pilot's canopy.

Superheated blobs from his target's wingmate flashed toward Luke's X-wing. Luke heard a squeal of alarm from R2-D2, who was tucked into the astromech bay behind his canopy, but ignored it as an irrelevant detail. He continued his rolling descent, varying the speed of his roll and distance covered each half a standard second, and saw the plasma flash between his snubfighter and Mara's.

Then the three of them were well below their targets and rising again behind the coralskippers' sterns. The skips' voids swung around, hovering at the sterns, ready to soak up infinite amounts of weapon energy.

The first engagements between coralskippers and New Republic starfighters had been terrible for the New Republic. Even seasoned pilots had been thrown off balance by the skips' incredible durability, by the failure of proton torpedoes and laser blasts sucked into the voids to do any harm to the vehicles, by the tenacity of the damage done by plasma cannons, which kept on eating away at vehicle surfaces well after they'd hit.

Now things were different. The surviving pilots had adjusted their tactics and passed their information along to their fellows. The rules of the game were to overload the dovin basals, striking them from several directions at once to ensure that some damage got through to hit the coralskippers' surfaces. Starfighter pilots had to avoid taking any hits at all from skip weaponry; any hit could eat through shields and prove fatal.

And there were new tactics all the time, in every battle. Mara surged ahead of Luke and Corran, flying in a pattern that was oddly predictable, and drew fire from both coralskippers. She became suddenly erratic in her flight, as random as only Force skills could make a pilot, and flashed ahead until she was just behind the skips. She sideslipped to port, and as both streams of plasma cannon fire followed her, the fire from the starboard skip crossed the body of the port-side skip; two balls of fire thudded into the skip's belly before the starboard pilot compensated.

The port skip's void whipped around to shield the skip's belly. In that instant, Mara drop-fired a quad-linked burst of laserfire.

The skip detonated, hiding Mara's X-wing from sight for a moment, and Luke fired a laser stutter-burst at the starboard skip's underside. He hoped that the pilot's confusion at having hurt his own wingmate, along with the dovin basal's effort to shield this skip from the damage from Mara's attack, would leave it momentarily vulnerable.

He was right. His lasers hit the skip's underside and chewed through. That skip vectored away, trailing fluids that instantly froze at this near-vacuum altitude.

He checked his sensors. Two skips down. Mara was coming around to rejoin him and Corran. Diagnostics said his X-wing was undamaged.

Farther out, two of his Twin Suns snubfighters were gone. The pilot of one of them was extravehicular; Luke hoped that the flight suit would keep the pilot alive until a rescue shuttle could arrive. "Good tactics, Mara," he said.

"You always know the sweet thing to say."

Luke grinned and came around toward a new set of opponents.

Starfighter squadrons held the Yuuzhan Vong response to three points of conflict in orbit. The Twin Suns group took advantage of the opportunity and roared down through the atmosphere in an undefended zone, then banked toward the coralskippers' launch point, which had been detected on gravitic sensors. It was, not coincidentally, the same map coordinate as Borleias's New Republic military base. Luke didn't relish seeing what had become of the base during the Yuuzhan Vong occupation.

As they dropped low over the jungle canopy, Luke could make out the target zone ahead. It didn't have the same profile as the holocube he'd studied. The main building seemed to be lower, broader.

Small chips of yorik coral were rising above it, angling toward them. His sensors said there were six of them. "Twin Suns, up front," Luke said. "Engage all those skips. *Record Time,* it's your call whether you want to hang back with us or move on to the target without us."

"Twin Suns One, this is *Record Time.* We're here to fight. We'll see you at the landing zone."

"Copy."

Lando Calrissian, in *Record Time*'s troop bay, stood next to the ramp access and tried not to look concerned.

He was sweating. He didn't like sweating. It suggested hard work, something he wasn't fond of, and just didn't give the impression of someone who was infinitely cool, infinitely in control.

He looked over the units of men and women in the bay. Most were seated in rows of high-backed troop couches, strapped in against the turbulence that was likely to come. Their commanders walked up and down those rows, issuing last-minute instructions, advice, encouragements, jokes, insults.

He looked over his own troops. They stood in a circle, each with a hand on the metal post at the circle's center, and stared at him. They were impassive, fearless. "Ready?" he asked.

In unison, they answered, "Ready, sir!"

He knew that once they left the bay he'd never see some of them again. Unlike the other commanders present, he was content with that knowledge. His troops would serve their purpose.

The bay shuddered as enemy fire finally began to strike *Record Time.* Lando saw fear, even nausea, on the faces of some of the other troops.

Not his. They continued to stare at him, waiting.

* * *

Luke, with Mara and Corran tucked in beside him, roared along in *Record Time*'s wake. He grimaced. He had lost his top starboard laser cannon and engine to plasma fire. His power, maneuverability, and fighting strength were reduced.

Ahead, *Record Time* was settling down into the jungle canopy, or perhaps into the open field just before the base; from here, it looked the same. Little flashes of light were pouring up from the ground and hammering into the transport's hull, blackening it. Though he was situated directly astern of the transport, Luke thought he could see the edges of *Record Time*'s bow distorting as combat damage ate away at it. Then the transport turned to port and Luke saw that he was right; the bow had sustained terrific damage from plasma cannons. He'd be astonished if the transport was spaceworthy now.

After the last lurch and vibration, Lando knew the transport was down. He could barely hear over the systems alarms. He took a last deep breath and nodded at his troops, then slapped the button on the hull panel beside him.

The top portion of the entry slid instantly up out of sight. The bottom portion lowered, becoming a ramp. Warm, humid air flooded into the troop bay. Beyond the entryway was field, its stringy grasses calf-high, and beyond that was some sort of reddish Yuuzhan Vong construction, a large cylindrical building with arms radiating outward at regular intervals.

"Go, go, go!" Lando shouted, and his troops released the bar they'd been holding. Shouting an inarticulate battle cry, they surged for the ramp, readying blaster rifles.

As they reached the top of the ramp, incoming fire began to rain in. Lando heard the rear wall of the bay ring as ammunition pocked it. No, it wasn't ammunition, he reminded himself, but creatures hurled by the Yuuzhan Vong—thud bugs, the hard-hitting insect projectiles, and razor bugs, which sliced whatever they hit and came around again to attack whatever they missed.

One of his troops took a concentration of thud bugs, several of them hitting the man in the throat. The force of the impacts was enough to shear through. That soldier's body collapsed and his head clanked to the bay floor, rolling unerringly toward Lando.

Lando stopped it with his foot like a player trapping a ball and looked dispassionately at it. His first casualty of the day. The combat droid's features stared up at him with no more expression than they'd shown a moment ago. The damage didn't look too bad, he decided. This one would be easily repaired.

The unhurt nineteen droid troops charged down the ramp and into the field, turning to head toward the right flank of the big red building. Their war cry changed from a simple roar to words that Lando didn't understand.

But he knew what they meant. He'd arranged for the war cry to be installed in his droid troops. It was in the language of the Yuuzhan Vong, and it meant, "We are machines! We are greater than the Yuuzhan Vong!"

On the bridge of the *Record Time*, the communications officer, a Rodian, his green scaly hide immaculately clean and the mouth at the tip of his pointed chin puckering, said, "Captain, it's working. They're breaking cover, showing themselves."

The captain, a tall human woman with copper-colored hair tucked up under an officer's cap, extracted herself from her chair and stood. This put her head squarely in the smoke accumulating against the bridge's ceiling. She coughed, ducked, and moved to stand over the Rodian's shoulder.

On the screen was a panoramic view collated from the holocams situated on the transport's hull. It showed the ground all around the *Record Time*, jungle to port and open field to starboard.

Lando Calrissian's droid troops were off the ramp and

charging across the field, firing in a defensive screen all around them. And Yuuzhan Vong warriors were popping up all over the field, emerging from the jungle at a dead run, heading toward them, ignoring the transport—lunging like maddened animals toward the droids that insulted them by words and mere presence.

"Transmit this visual to all vehicles and vessels in our engagement zone," the captain said. "Transmit to *Mon Mothma* that the tactic does work. Then tell—oh, blast."

On the screen, something huge was approaching from the far side of the building with the radiating arms, moving around it. This was a living creature, vaguely reptilian, itself the size of a large building. Its skin was a blue-green, but patches of red and silver yorik coral grew over its head and along its spine. From the spine grew huge sail-like plates, and plasma cannons protruded by the dozens from the yorik coral.

The captain's voice rose into a commander's bellow. "Get the troops off this ship now. Nonessential personnel, follow the troops off. All weapons come to bear on that target. Fire at will. And vent the smoke here. We've got to breathe to fight."

This had to be one of those creatures that had fought in the Dantooine engagement. The captain had an ugly presentiment that *Record Time* would not survive to lift off again.